STUCK *in* MANISTIQUE

—— A NOVEL ——

DENNIS CUESTA

celestial eyes press

CELESTIAL EYES PRESS

Published by Celestial Eyes Press, San Jose, California

www.celestialeyespress.com

Library of Congress Control Number: 2018949790
LC record available at https://lccn.loc.gov/2018949790

Stuck in Manistique/ Dennis Cuesta – 1st ed.

ISBN 978-1-73241-090-9

For Jamie and Noah

STUCK *in* MANISTIQUE

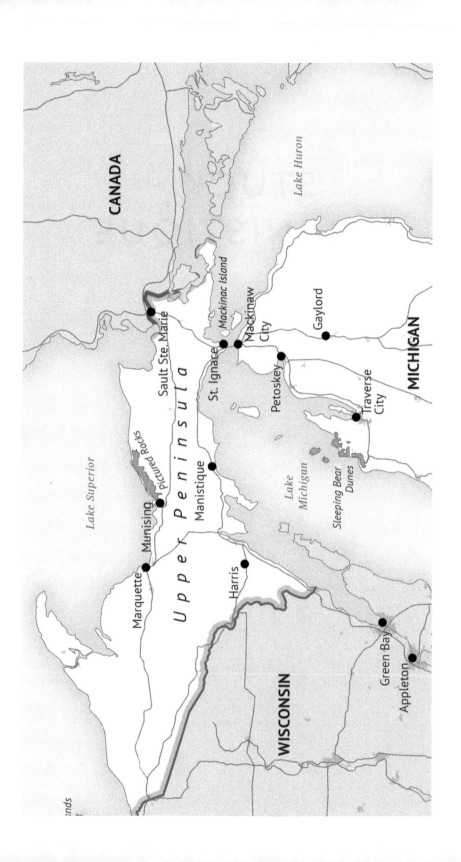

STUCK IN MANISTIQUE

Mark flinched at the ring of the doorbell. He felt more like a burglar than the sole beneficiary of his aunt's estate. Whoever was at the door, he thought, was there to offer condolences. Or, worse yet, didn't even know Vivian had died. Not interested in handling either case, he remained in the basement.

Another ring. Two knocks. He scratched his chin and reconsidered. Perhaps this person—a neighbor or a friend—could explain why Vivian, who lived most of her life in war zones as an international aid doctor, had settled way up here in Manistique. Three more knocks. Slow and hard. Each thud breaking down his reluctance.

By the time Mark had climbed the basement stairs, trekked through the house, and opened the door, a dark-haired woman had reached the bottom of the porch steps.

"Hello," Mark said warily. From behind she seemed too young to be one of Vivian's friends.

She finished the last step before turning around. A white bandage covered one of her eyes, distracting him from any swift assessment. The variegated blue sweater draped over her fell flat, far past her waist to her thin gray leggings. Nothing stirred in him, nothing except the downward contour of her lips, which made him suspicious, if not faintly afraid of her.

"I almost gave up on you," she said.

"Looks like you actually did," he replied. Her chestnut-brown hair, shiny with long curls and lightly streaked with copper highlights, landed on her shoulders. Fair-skinned with full, pink cheeks, she was in her early twenties, he figured. "You're not selling something, are you?"

"Huh?" Her head listed slightly to one side. "No. I was wondering if you had room, just for one night."

"Room for what?"

The girl smiled, a bit gravely, and then said, "To stay the night— what else?"

Mark wondered if this was some sort of quaint custom in the Upper Peninsula. Open your house to any stranger who needs a place. "Do you think this is some kind of hotel?" He crossed his arms.

The girl's cheeks burst with crimson. "Ummm . . ." She scanned the neighborhood before turning back. "Sorry, someone told me this was a bed and breakfast." She pointed to the two posts on the parkstrip. "And I thought—"

Mark swallowed his laugh and gasped. He ran past the girl, past the bushes lining the sidewalk, and stopped at the front of the property where two short 4x4 posts stood.

He pushed on the posts. They didn't budge. They were planted too firmly into the ground to be part of a real estate sign, as he had originally suspected. It struck him that the board leaning against the side of the garage, *Manistique Victorian*, would fit right there. And then there were the typed cards with the Wi-Fi name and password. Living quarters in the basement. Vivian had been running a bed and breakfast. No, no, she couldn't possibly—

"Is everything all right?" the girl called out.

It took him a couple more seconds to grasp this revelation and to fully compose himself. He nodded and waved back affably. "Everything is just fine," he answered, sauntering back toward her. "It's all good. Yep."

"Why did you . . ."

"Oh that? That was my John Cleese impression. Ever see that British show, *Fawlty Towers*?" His voice had risen higher.

She shook her head, leaning back slightly away from him. "No, I don't think so. But I'm sure it was a very good impression."

"You should see my silly walk."

"Maybe later." Her mouth flattened. "Is this a bed and breakfast or not?"

"*Indeed* it is." He pressed his lips together, tamping a chuckle. "Yes it is."

Her eyes narrowed. "So . . ."

"Yes, the Manistique Victorian."

She held out her palm. "So is there a room available?"

Mark shook his head, and unable to truthfully explain the absurd circumstances to a stranger—that he'd had no idea his dead aunt was running a bed and breakfast—he gave the simplest answer. "No, sorry, it's just we're not open for the season yet." He pointed back toward the posts. "That's what I was checking out down there. I thought the sign was up—you know, a prank by one of the neighborhood kids or something."

She sighed. "I see."

"I'm very sorry. There are hotels off the highway," Mark said confidently, only because he'd seen them on his way into town.

She frowned, shaking her head. "There's nothing available."

"Really?"

"One hotel is closed for renovations and the other is apparently taken up by a large group."

"Right!" Mark remembered. "A bunch of old folks touring the Indian casinos in the UP."

"Is that what they're doing?"

Mark nodded. "But there's hope. Maybe one of them will croak and a room will open up."

The girl stifled her laugh with a cough. "That's an awful thing to say."

He grinned, shrugged. "Only kidding, of course."

"Of course." She grinned back.

Mark pointed to his eye. "So what happened?"

"Nothing, really. A shard of glass got in my eye, made a slight cut on the sclera. But it's fine."

"'Sclera'? You a doctor or something?"

"As a matter of fact, yes."

"You are?"

She nodded. "You seem surprised."

"No, no, it's just—" She did look awfully young to be a doctor. But being in his mid-thirties, he realized it was him getting older not *them* looking younger.

"Actually, I just finished medical school. I start residency in July and then my plan . . ." Her voice thinned and her eyes wandered toward the street. "I really need to find a place." She pointed down Lake Street. "If I go down this street and turn right will I reach the car dealership?"

Mark didn't answer her. Partly because he wasn't sure and partly because he was considering the young doctor. She intrigued him. His mother and father had both been doctors—Vivian, too—and he felt an affinity with doctors.

"So how did you get glass in your eye?"

"Deer-car. Shattered the windshield."

"A what-car?"

"Deer-car. I thought everyone up here called it that. It must happen so frequently."

"Ah, you hit a deer."

"No," she returned sternly. "The deer hit me."

"What's the difference?"

"The difference is"— she shook her head—"Never mind."

"Where did you—I mean, where did this deer come out and assault your car?"

Her good eye narrowed on him. She pointed up north. "A few miles east of here. It's been towed to the dealership."

"I see." He felt a certain degree of concern for her, and a crazy thought thrust itself into his mind. Before considering it sufficiently, he asked, "How many nights do you need a room?"

"Just tonight. My car will be ready tomorrow. Why?"

He shrugged. Her plight yanked on him, but now he ruminated. Could he get away with it? She needed a place. He had a place. A bed and breakfast, after all. He briefly glanced up at the house that he'd been in one time. It was only for one night. He looked back at her.

"Well, if you're all right with things not being not being up to our normal standards . . ."

She shook her head. "What do you mean?"

"You can spend the night with me." He spoke the words before realizing how they sounded, and he laughed nervously. "What I mean is, I can set you up with a room for tonight."

She turned and eyed the house. "Do you run this place with your wife?"

Mark withheld his *If you only knew* response. The lost relationships—good, long relationships—that he had abandoned to avoid marriage. "No, no, not married," he answered, stepping past her, stopping at the base of the porch stairs. "No, this place belongs to my aunt."

She nodded feebly. "So is she here now?"

Mark picked up her apprehension, and *She's dead* sounded too harsh, so he shook his head. "She's away. I'm sort of filling in for her. Helping out, getting things in order and such."

"Ah." She turned her head momentarily toward the quiet street.

New leaves fluttered on the aspens across the road, the breeze pushing against the strands of her hair. "You sure it'd be all right with your aunt? I'd hate to—"

"Positive."

"I don't want to impose."

"Not at all."

She briefly sucked in her lips. "So what's the rate?"

"The rate?" He hadn't thought of that. "For a deer-car?. . . How about twenty-five bucks." He chuckled. "No pun intended."

She didn't crack a smile. "Twenty-five? Really?"

"You think it's too much?"

"No, not at all. Makes getting hit by a deer almost worthwhile."

"But the downside is you're stuck in Manistique."

She spurted out a laugh. "I'm not sure your aunt would approve if she heard you."

He grinned. "Believe me, she won't hear it from me."

"I hate to impose even more, but could I ask for one more favor?"

"Sure."

"Is there any way you can drive me to the dealership? My suitcase and bag are in my car."

Mark checked his watch. Ten minutes to five o'clock. "We can go now if you'd like. I just need to grab my keys."

She nodded. "Yeah, that would be great. I really appreciate it."

Mark held out his hand. "I'm Mark, by the way."

"Emily."

He shook her warm, firm hand.

"It's a pleasure to meet you, Emily."

Chapter One

Rising out of Midway, the plane ascended over Chicago and flew north, straddling the shoreline for twenty minutes before veering east over the waters of America's Great Lake. Mark studied the boats on the lake, mostly sailboats, wondering about their passengers. The white caps mesmerized him. A freshwater sea. Surveying the marvel, he became annoyed with himself at how easily he had taken it for granted. Living so close to the lakeshore, he rarely considered its awe, its magnificence.

Mark had considered driving the five hours from Chicago to the small town of Petoskey, far north near the tip of Michigan's Lower Peninsula. But he'd eventually chosen the one-hour flight to Traverse City followed by an hour's drive north to Petoskey.

On the plane he went over the tasks to be completed with Vivian's estate. Though he barely knew Aunt Vivian, he felt confident about settling her life's account. He had done this a few years earlier with his mother's estate, and having spoken to Vivian's attorney the day before, Mark knew she owned a house and had a couple of bank accounts. He expected it to take him no more than three days to handle her affairs.

When the streaking tan line of sand separating water from northern Michigan forest came into view, the plane began its descent. They flew over another lake, miles wide, barely contained by the mainland, a mere pond juxtaposed with Lake Michigan, the result of glacial recessions thousands of years earlier. Lakes formed and filled, sediments were left behind, and forests spread. Taking all this in from bird's-eye had an effect on Mark. The water and land and verdant seclusion moved him into deep wistfulness, like recovering a long-lost toy at the soft edge of adolescence. Whether it was only a reaction to his normal surroundings—the isolation of smooth concrete and pot-holed blacktop, skyscrapers and caged forest preserves—he didn't know. By the time the pilot notified the crew for landing, a subdued disappointment had crept into Mark. A hastily planned trip with a singular purpose and quick exit. He had never before been up here, and seeing it from the air called him to explore it. He'd heard about trips recounted by friends and clients, trips to Sleeping Bear Dunes and regattas to Mackinac Island. And he knew that historically many well-to-do's from Chicago in decades past had spent their summers here *Up North*. So as the plane taxied to the gate, with no one waiting for him back in Chicago, he decided to delay his return flight and stay through the long Memorial Day weekend.

Outside Cherry Capital Airport, a bright blue sky and light breeze from the southwest greeted him. Suitcase in tow, he felt his nerves catch up to him in the rental parking lot. A mixture of guilt and angst pulled on him. He had barely known his aunt and didn't quite know what to expect when he entered her house for the first time. He tipped his head skyward, briefly closing his eyes and letting the warm sun recharge him. After a deep breath, he felt ready to dispense with the duties ahead.

Mark drove through Traverse City, a lakeside town in a region known for its cherries and its annual Cherry Festival. But it was the week before Memorial Day, too early for tourists and too early for cherries, so traffic was light. He headed north on Highway 31, regularly turning his head toward the bay, leaving the city behind. Lake views soon gave way to inland pines and maples and the irregular whiteness of birches and aspens whose trunks appeared to have been painted by vandals rather than by nature. As the scenery did not change, Mark's thoughts drifted to his tattered memory of Vivian.

A humanitarian doctor in war-torn countries, Vivian had measured mythically to a young Mark. He met her only once that he could remember, when he was seven or eight. That encounter, replayed over and over again, was now burnished vague in his head. The shaded memory shifted obscurely and unreliably, no more real than a saint appearing to him in a dream. But he distinctly remembered the letters she had sent; he had read them over and over. Letters from Angola, Sierra Leone, Sudan, Sri Lanka, Bosnia. They always arrived a week or two before or after his birthday. Each time she was assigned to a new country, he would heave the dusty atlas onto the dining room table and turn its giant pages until he located the country.

The letter for his thirteenth birthday stood out. It had a peculiar vibe. Usually the letters started the same way. *Dear Mark, Greetings from [war-torn country du jour]*, but this one read:

Dear Mark,

It is very strange here in Sarajevo. Bosnia is the first country I've had to sneak into. It's also the first time that I'm a target—well not really me personally, although as Yossarian liked to say, What's the difference? (Ever read Catch-22? *Maybe you're too young for that yet.) Anyway, civilians here are targeted by snipers and subjected to random shellings . . .*

It became the first year Mark took an interest in a country beyond its shape and color in the atlas. Partly because he was older and more aware of the outside world, but also because there was no Bosnia in the atlas, only Yugoslavia. It unsettled him a bit that borders were not fixed. So he read accounts in newspapers and magazines of the breakup of Yugoslavia into several pieces and the ongoing siege in Sarajevo.

He admired Vivian, forsaking first-world comforts and risking her life to help others. Inspired by her work, Mark found a program in which he could join a humanitarian mission of his own, after his junior year of high school. It was in Belize, nowhere near a war, either in time or distance. Yet his mother quashed his idea with vitriol. It was one of the few times he remembered her struggling with such an emotional strain.

When she regained her composure, Margaret revealed by way of explanation that Vivian had been adopted. Vivian's childhood trauma, followed by feelings of abandonment when their father died, formed an early identity crisis. Though she considered Vivian well-meaning, Margaret judged her sister as restless and reckless. In Margaret's strictly professional opinion, Vivian sought danger to quell an underlying disturbance.

When Mark asked why he had never been told about Vivian's adoption, his mother said it was an irrelevant fact. Vivian was her sister.

Irrelevant? It hadn't been irrelevant to Mark. It struck him hard. He had thought he and his aunt shared an adventurous gene, quite apart from his mother's exacting steadfastness.

On his next birthday, no letter came from Bosnia nor anywhere else. Mark worried, but Margaret reassured him that Vivian was fine, still in Sarajevo. Soon humanitarian projects and letters from unstable countries receded to the back of Mark's mind before becoming mostly forgotten, replaced by the ever-present distractions of all young adults. He never heard from his aunt again.

Mark did attempt to contact Vivian when his mother died. He tried *Médecins Sans Frontières* in Belgium, which Vivian had referenced in some of her letters, but she was no longer there. He tried Doctors Without Borders's headquarter in New York, but they had no record of her. He eventually found her, working for a small international aid organization out of Washington, DC. Vivian was serving in Syria and the director of the organization promised to forward the message, but Mark never heard back. Figuring there was nothing more he could do, whether or not she got the message, he let it go.

Miles passed without Mark absorbing any of his surroundings. He was now driving by lines of trees, an orchard of cherries, he assumed. The highway to Petoskey ran through several small lakeside towns. Then he arrived to Charlevoix, nestled between Lake Michigan and

Lake Charlevoix. He particularly remembered this town on the map, and it was as he had imagined it. Picturesque with views of the lakes and a pleasant harbor, delightful shops and bakeries, all neat and well-kept and mid-upscale. It was the kind of town he would have liked to visit with Laura. Strolling through the shops. Taking boat rides on the lake. Dining on the waterfront. Enjoying the sunset together as it dipped under the gentle ripples of the lake. Though Charlevoix enthralled him, seeing this town without the ability to enjoy its charm with someone else magnified his loneliness. A self-inflicted wound, he knew, and a deep regret sunk in. He couldn't think of a single reason not to have married Laura, except that he wasn't completely certain about her.

Near the edge of downtown he waited in front of an open draw-bridge. It unsettled him a bit, the road flung up in the air like that. But he tried not to ponder it and instead watched a sailboat heading out to the lake. He envied those aboard as it smoothly maneuvered through the narrow channel connecting the two lakes. Once the bridge came down, he dashed over it and soon left the town and lake views behind, scratching Charlevoix off the list of places he might check out later. It was a place meant to be shared, not taken in alone.

A short time later, after a long bend in the road, Lake Michigan came back into full view. Past a resort-like lakeside development, the grade incrementally steepened before commercial buildings and retail businesses took hold. Petoskey city limits—population 5,671.

Mark pulled into a parking lot to use his phone, to look up the exact location of Frank Walters's office. The office wasn't far, and soon he found himself driving down an isolated road where industrial buildings were mixed with woods and meadows. When he saw a split-rail fence with reflectors marking the end of the road, he stopped, unsure of where he had made a wrong turn. He doubled back, and as he passed by one of the warehouses, he spotted the attorney's name on totem pole of signs. Engraved in yellow-painted letters: *Frank Walters, Attorney-at-Law*. The name was below *Arnot's Body Shop* and above *Mike's Mufflers*.

Mark pulled into the lot and drove by the truck rental facility and the tile store, until he reached Suite 8B, nearly all the way down the row. The glass door was scripted with a fancifully curved "Frank Walters" over "Attorney-at-Law" in straight block letters.

The small reception area held six wood chairs and a water dispenser. Mark stood in front of a short wall and desk with no receptionist, only stacked boxes behind the counter.

"I'll be right out," called a voice through a partially open door. It was the newly familiar voice of Frank Walters.

Mark caught a whiff, a musty odor, and he wondered what this place had been before it was a law office. Rust-colored water stains randomly spotted the ceiling tiles, and the carpet was hard and burgundy, as if it'd been repurposed from a church. One wall showed round, dirty spots as if someone had thrown a rubber ball against it.

A man appeared through the doorway. "Sorry, just wrapping something up," he said. Frank Walters was taller and brawnier than his voice and Mark's imagination had suggested. He was in his mid-fifties with a sturdy gray-and-brown beard and a genuine smile, and he wore a sport coat over a white button-up shirt and jeans.

They introduced themselves to each other, and as they grasped hands, Walters's smile retreated and his lips thinned. He preserved his grip. "I'm very sorry for your loss. Vivian was a remarkable woman."

Mark grimaced and nodded, pointedly ignoring his own shame. He thanked Walters and ended the long handshake before it became awkwardly sentimental.

"Come on in." Walters waved him back, and Mark followed into the office. This space was more befitting a lawyer: the furniture was dark and elegant, the carpet full, and there were two large bookcases. A window gave a view of the forest outside.

The bookcases were half-full, and several open boxes sat filled with books. "Are you moving?" Mark asked.

"Yes, but not far. Just down the row here, to the building closest to the road." He smiled brightly. "Better location."

Mark nodded. They headed for the desk, and Mark sat across from the attorney. "Did you know my aunt very well?" he asked.

Walters shook his head in a quick burst. "I'm afraid not. I met her last year when I helped her with her will. I learned a few things about her as I wrote it up. I really hadn't spoken to her in a while, not until last week when she called me from the hospital to inform me that she wasn't doing so well."

Mark nodded solemnly.

Placing his elbow on the desk, Walters joined his hands as if he were about to engage in deliberate prayer. "As I explained to you over the phone, your aunt left you her entire estate. There is the house, a couple bank accounts, and a brokerage account. The accounts combined are worth somewhere around fifty thousand and the house, as far as I know, is paid off. There isn't anyone else in her will except you. Did Vivian have any other relatives?"

Mark shook his head. "No. I'm the only one left." Then he remembered that Vivian was adopted. Perhaps she did have blood relatives somewhere. "Why do you ask?"

"No reason really, though it's good to know just in case. Occasionally you'll see a relative, usually a close one, contest the will. Not that there's an issue here, seeing as you're the sole beneficiary."

"All right, so what next?"

Walters recited a list of things to go through while Mark made mental notes. "Was she working recently?" Walters asked.

"She worked as a humanitarian doctor for many years, a couple different organizations." It was the best he could come up with. He didn't really know.

"Yes, she told me about that. Anything more recent?"

"No," he answered evenly, afraid Walters would think badly of him if the truth came out. That he barely knew Vivian at all. That he couldn't explain why he had stopped trying to reach her. That he felt like a fraud, a stranger absconding with her estate. Was his explanation that he was planning to contact her again someday a good enough excuse? That he hadn't expected Vivian to die so soon?

Mark turned his head away and looked out the window. Outside, a deer crept through the shallow woods where sunlight slipped between the evergreens. About to announce, *Hey, a deer!*, he stopped himself, fearing Walters would tag him as a pathetic city-dweller. And rightfully so.

The doe turned her head and stared at Mark curiously. They held each other's gaze for a few moments. When another distraction got her attention, the doe dashed off. Turning back to Walters, who was sifting through paperwork, Mark fired, "To be perfectly honest, Vivian and I weren't really that close." It came out strong-willed, defensive. "I mean, I haven't seen or heard from her in a very long time. I barely know her at all, really." He surprised himself a bit with the unforced admission; he generally wasn't forthcoming with anything personal, especially not to a stranger. And especially not about something he was ashamed of. And then he added tenderly, "I never imagined . . ."

No judgment came from Walters, neither by words nor expression. Only a single nod of understanding. The lawyer grabbed some papers on his right and handed them over. "You need to read and initial and sign these so that I can start the process of transferring the house to your name."

Mark cleared the lump in his throat. Barely reading past the first sentence, he initialed, went to the next page, initialed, and signed the final page.

"I have copies of her death certificate, which you'll need for banks, et cetera. About the house—"

"Oh, sorry," Mark interrupted. "Would you mind writing down her address for me?"

"Sure. Actually, hold on." Walters went to his computer and typed with two fingers. He rolled his chair over to the printer and grabbed the page that came out. He handed it over with a satisfied smile. "Here are the directions."

Mark scanned the page. 545 Lake Street, Manistique, Michigan. "Manistique? Where's that?"

"It's a small town north of here."

"Canada is north of here," Mark replied dryly.

Walters chuckled. "It's not that far north. More northwest."

"But I thought she lived here in Petoskey." He read the full directions. North forty miles. West eighty-seven miles. Two hours, seventeen minutes. His eyes traced the line on the map confirming what he already knew. "I've got to cross a bridge to get there," he blurted out.

"Well, sure. Manistique is in the Upper Peninsula."

Mark's eyes stayed fixated on the dark line that crossed over the water. "What the heck was she doing living way up there?"

"I don't really know. I've never spent any real time there myself. It's a lakeside town with a few thousand people. There's a casino. And there's your usual up there—hunting, fishing, boating. Yoopers aren't very fond of trolls, so I don't go up there too often."

He knew *Yooper*, a UP-er. "Trolls?"

A wry grin appeared on Walters's face. "Those of us who live *under* the bridge."

Mark cracked a smile, thinking he'd rather accede to the Yoopers' wishes and remain on his side of the bridge.

"I'm only exaggerating. You'll find people there to be friendly enough. They're naturally suspicious of strangers—people going there and snatching up their real estate because it's so cheap, that sort of thing."

"Then they'll be glad to hear that I plan to give some of it back."

"So you'll be selling the house?"

"Can't imagine keeping it. I don't gamble, hunt, fish, or go boating."

"Since it's in a trust, you can go ahead and start the selling process. There's just a couple of administrative things I need to take care of before the actual sale."

Walters turned back to the filing cabinet and pulled out a folder. He handed it to Mark. "Death certificates," he said as Mark flipped the folder open. "Vivian Jane Peregrine. Date of Death: May 20, 2014. Date of Birth: May 15, 1953." She had just had a birthday, he thought. He had never known her birthdate. All the years that he had received a letter from Vivian for his birthday, and he didn't once think of hers.

"The funeral home handling the cremation is off Highway 31. It's called Woodland Hills Funeral Home."

"Woodland Hills."

Walters nodded. "And remember, she wanted to be scattered over the lake."

Ten minutes later, Mark shook hands with Walters and left. He sat in his car and rolled down the windows, letting the trapped heat escape and the cool air blow on his face. His scattered mind worked on resetting his schedule. At least he had already postponed the return flight, but those plans to explore the area were dashed.

As Mark pulled away, Walters came rushing out of the building. "Hold on!" He stooped, sticking his head through the passenger window. "You're not heading for Manistique tonight, are you? I doubt the funeral home will have everything ready before tomorrow."

"No, I'm not leaving tonight," Mark answered, although the funeral home only counted as the second reason. "Why?"

"Are you by chance a Blackhawks fan?"

Mark smiled. "I had a ticket for the game tonight."

"Seriously? Well if it's any consolation, there's a bar in town where a few of us watch games together."

"You're a Blackhawks fan?"

Walters held a finger to his lips and nodded. "Don't tell anyone around here. Yeah. I'll be there tonight if you're interested."

With Walters's directions to the downtown bar and a double-pat on the roof, Mark left for the hotel.

The Mackinac Bridge connects the Lower Peninsula of Michigan to the Upper Peninsula. The "Mighty Mac" spans five miles over the Straits of Mackinac where Lake Michigan and Lake Huron exchange waters. Barely settled into his hotel room, Mark searched for other ways across the water.

Though he admitted it to no one, Mark feared bridges, or more precisely, he feared his reaction—the queasiness and panic-stricken jitters—when he crossed a bridge. There was even a name for it:

gephyrophobia. It comforted him only slightly that there were others like him. He nevertheless considered it a silly, unfounded fear, especially since flying didn't give him more than a brief pitter-patter of the heart during takeoff. He couldn't rationally explain the fear, he could only rationally avoid bridges. And he had successfully done that for most of his life, all while keeping it a secret.

A car ferry service across the straits had closed shortly after the bridge opened in 1957. But he found another way across, unconventional for sure. It was via Mackinac Island, a popular tourist attraction that had passenger ferries from both peninsulas. Take a boat from Mackinaw City in the Lower Peninsula and to St. Ignace in the Upper and rent a car. Except he couldn't find a car rental service in St. Ignace.

He really wanted to know the history behind the different-spelling, same-sounding, *Mackinac* and *Mackinaw*. But he checked his curiosity for the moment and continued searching for another way across. He found no other way except driving back down to Traverse City, catching a flight to Green Bay, and driving up the Wisconsin coastline to the UP. But this struck him as an untenable waste of time and money.

Given no good alternative, he turned his attention to Mackinac. The origin of the name, he found, came from the local Indians. The French spelled it with -ac and the British with -aw. The wayward tendencies of the internet and Mark's love of history drew him into a series of articles about the area's past. The Ojibwe/Chippewa Indians. The struggle between French and British, British and Americans. The Siege of Fort Mackinac. The War of 1812. The Battle of Mackinac Island . . . The Toledo War between Michigan and Ohio and Michigan statehood and the Upper Peninsula . . . Henry Schoolcraft . . . Longfellow's *Song of Hiawatha* . . . copper and iron ore mining . . .

Hours passed. It was nearing the time for the face-off when Mark noticed the hour. His mind churning with historical facts, he left for the bar.

Mark found parking a couple blocks away from The Tell-Tale, a corner bar in Petoskey's Gaslight District. As he walked to the bar, he took in the perfectly quaint and charming downtown. Though most shops appeared to be closed for the day, more than a few couples strolled hand in hand, checking out the storefronts. Through the window of one restaurant, he caught a woman shaking off a laugh from the gesticulating man sitting across from her. It reminded him of Laura reacting to some of his antics.

Unable to dismiss a restless ache, Mark walked passed the bar, wandering down the street until he reached a set of stairs that went down toward the lake. The excursion took him to a park and then a marina. Down the pier, he stopped to watch the fading sun, thinking about all that is true at last light. His pain over Laura, he recognized, was not an ache for her, but for himself. His loneliness. Then he thought of Vivian. Did she die with no one thinking of her? He deeply regretted not contacting her again.

Retracing his steps, Mark landed in front of the bar, and this time he went inside. An upbeat din filled the crowded Tell-Tale. A few more men than women took up the twenty-foot bar and half-dozen tables, everyone wearing Blackhawks jerseys and caps and shirts. Mark waded further in, searching for Walters when he felt a hand patting him on the back. Walters in a team jersey carried a plate of appetizers.

"You made it!" he yelled.

"Yeah. This is a good crowd."

Walters nodded. "I told you! I saved us a space at a table over there."

Mark followed Walters to a table they shared with three others, strangers to Walters. Everyone was in a festive mood.

The crowd cheered their way to a one-nothing lead in the first period. During intermission, the lawyer asked Mark what he did with his ticket to the game. "Gave it back," Mark answered. "It was my friend Brad's ticket. He and his sister have season tickets."

"He couldn't make it?"

"That's what he claimed, but I'll bet you he's there. I think he's trying to set me up with his sister."

"He must think highly of you, then."

Mark shook his head. "No, he knows my track record. He's just a romantic optimist."

"Or maybe he doesn't like his sister."

Mark laughed. "Thing is, he adores his sister." He envied Brad for that. Mark wanted a close sister like Annie that he could talk to, connect with, share good and bad times. And all of it without the burdens of living with someone for the rest of his life.

"You don't like her?" Walters asked.

"I like her plenty, but Brad and I have been friends since high school."

"So why not try it?"

"Like I said, I have a track record. I'm liable to lose Brad as a friend if it doesn't work out. Besides, I just got out of a pretty long-term relationship."

"How long?"

"Fourteen years."

"What?!" Walters exclaimed.

Mark chuckled. "Not really. It was actually two years. My friends measure my relationships in dog years—but two years was a personal best."

"What happened with her?"

Mark shook his head. "Intermission isn't long enough." There really wasn't much of an explanation at all. He might have continued in a static relationship with Laura, perpetually enduring the subtle talk of something more. But one night she threw down the ultimatum: "If we're not progressing toward marriage soon, then . . ." She never finished the sentence. Mark simply told her that he wasn't ready. As Mark reached the front door that night, her ten-year old son, Shane, ran out from his room and hugged him. He messed up the boy's hair and told him to always listen to his mother.

Mark didn't want to think about Laura or Shane. Especially Shane. He was having too good of a time. "So do you do anything besides estate planning?" he asked, reaching for the pitcher of beer.

"Not anymore. Believe it or not, I was originally in criminal defense. But I didn't care for it much, so I became an estate attorney."

"That's a switch. I had a similar experience, though not as big as that. I started out in corporate finance and then became a personal financial planner."

The camaraderie in the bar extended into the second period with more high-fives in the early going, but by the middle of the third period, the ruckus had died down and people started to leave. Having gotten another pitcher while times were good, Walters stayed. And Mark, not one for ditching even a bad game, stayed too.

"I have a question for you," Mark said. "Curiosity, really."

"Yeah, what is it?"

"Why did Vivian pick you as her lawyer? Not that you're not a fine attorney. But aren't there any good lawyers in this Manistique town?"

He nodded, slowly setting down his beer. "She came down here for cancer treatments, and from what I gathered, she wanted a bit of privacy."

Vivian had cancer? "Oh."

Chapter Two

Emily tended wistfully to her white coat, folding it in thirds before setting it in the box. She ran her fingers over the scripted Emily Davis embroidery. The letters weren't as black as they once had been, faded after so many washings—no, faded after that one washing with extra bleach. She thought back to when she had received the coat, to the sense of accomplishment and the fervor and anxiousness she'd felt.

She closed the box and taped it shut. Except for some clothes in a small suitcase, all of her belongings fit in five small boxes—mostly books and notes from medical school. Lauren, her roommate, helped her load them into her old Saab.

Emily gave her roommate a long hug—they exchanged goodbyes and good-lucks and promises to reunite someday soon.

"Wait! I almost forgot." Lauren turned back toward the house.

Emily leaned against the car, a sadness catching in her chest. The two had shared the Hillcrest bungalow for the past two-and-a-half years. Lauren, a third-year resident at a nearby hospital, was the closest friend Emily had had during her medical school years. A big sister of sorts, Lauren was ten years older and almost done with her residency. Yet Emily had never confided in her about her relationship with Dr. John Bulcher. Lauren would have certainly disapproved. And of her recent crisis at the hospital, Emily only vaguely discussed it. Had Lauren known the full story, she would have likely given Emily some disquieting advice. Even so, Emily deeply regretted never sharing these burdens with her.

Emily considered spilling it all out now. There was no one else in the world she could imagine telling. Not her parents. Not any of her medical school classmates. Not any of her high school friends back home.

Lauren returned with a book in her hand. "I know, I know, it's all you need, another book." She handed it over. "But it has stories from Médecins Sans Frontières."

Emily read the cover. Doctors Without Borders: Helping the Helpless. "You just can't say Doctors Without Borders, can you?"

Lauren grinned impishly and shrugged. "It's the French in me."

"You're not French."

"All Canadians have some French in them," she protested.

Emily rolled her eyes. "Are you still trying to recruit me?"

"Yes!" Lauren had done a one-year mission as a nurse in Mali before enrolling in medical school. "You said you'd think about it. Remember?"

"I was probably drunk."

"You know what they say about drunk confessions . . ."

Emily folded her arms. "No, what do they say?"

Lauren shrugged. "I don't know. But one of my psych professors—no wait, it was a boyfriend—"

"Or both."

Lauren chuckled. "You know I've done stupid things, Em, but even I know better than to do that."

Emily put up a quick smile, hoping to hide the awkwardness she felt.

"Anyway, whoever it was said that alcohol doesn't make you say something you don't mean, it only makes you care less about what you say."

"Careless? Yes, I agree."

"No. Care. Less. But probably careless, too."

Emily grinned. "I have to finish residency first, so I have a good couple years to think about it, right?"

"Sure, of course."

She lifted her hand to make an oath. "I promise to read this before then."

"That's all I ask. A mission will change your life and your perspective on everything in life, not just medicine."

Emily nodded absentmindedly, thinking about her life right now. She turned away for a moment, reaching deep inside. When she turned back ready to tell Lauren everything, her throat seized up. With Lauren's hair pulled back, exposing her makeup-free face and wrinkled brow, Emily caught a glimpse of a different woman. A familiar woman from long ago.

"Are you all right?"

Just then Emily saw her: her second-grade teacher, Mrs. Schubert, the strictest teacher in her whole elementary school. Even after she'd finished second grade, Emily tensed up each time she heard Mrs. Schubert's voice crackle through the hallways or outside on the playground. And throughout high school, Mrs. Schubert had continued to haunt Emily in bad dreams. She hadn't thought of that nasty woman in many years.

"Em?"

Emily lost the little fortitude she'd mustered, suddenly convinced that Lauren would upbraid her. After all, what med student in her right mind got romantically involved with an attending, her mentor, a man twenty years her senior?

Emily gave a terse nod and pulled Lauren in to hug her again, to escape the teacher's face. And after a few seconds Emily got in her car, and without saying another word, drove away.

It was a little after nine in the morning when Emily left East Lansing. She had a three-hour drive ahead of her, north to the tip of the Lower Peninsula and then a short ferry ride to Mackinac Island where John would be waiting.

In the beginning, Emily quickly fell in love with Dr. Bulcher, the way someone becomes enchanted by a movie star and their distant facade. But this movie star gave her attention, shared his personal life, put his arm around her, held her, kissed her. She couldn't help but feel special, even privileged, that Dr. John Bulcher had selected and trusted her.

None of it should have ever happened. A renowned pediatric surgeon with extraordinarily precise hands had acted carelessly with his career. It was a serious violation of Dr. Bulcher's position as an attending and teaching physician. As it stood, he could probably unravel it as a brief lapse of judgment and receive only a minor reprimand from the hospital.

His wife might not be so forgiving. Emily had seen her picture on his desk—the housewife-model, the gorgeous blonde who married a doctor. They weren't a match, Emily had concluded, and his wife was only interested in riding his prestige and wealth. The wife was described as cold and shallow, and Emily didn't care much about the disruption she might cause their marriage. But the two standing next to their mother in the photo, little Joey and Cory, caused her to sweat guilt—but only until she shielded herself with contempt. His wife was the reason for the dissatisfaction in his marriage.

She was generally pragmatic about it all, figuring it would end once school ended. She would leave for residency and he would remain, teaching another group of med students, eventually replacing her with another insecure, awe-struck girl. And with time and distance—especially distance—that part of her life would wither and fade into the past. That all changed when John asked her to join him on Mackinac. After he finished with a medical conference there, they would meet up at a secluded inn on the northwest side of the island. He had planned this rendezvous, and she had agreed to it without protest or glee. Now she felt terrified and alone.

She felt something for John, she was sure, but she wasn't sure what it was. Admiration, yes. He was a gifted surgeon and her med-school mentor. Maybe she could get over their age difference and the breaking-up of his family. Maybe they could make it work over the long distance during her Chicago residency. But she still hadn't worked out the death of Nicholas, a boy who had died under their care. It bothered her that John had so deftly put the whole episode behind him, even making the boy's name unmentionable between them. He had never apologized for putting her through that.

An hour into her journey north, the landscape around her grew constant, the ground covered in hues of browns and greens, deciduous trees with new leaves and evergreens running together. Only the sky changed, a typical Midwestern sky shifting between white and dark clouds, then long stretches of blue.

When the highway cut through denser forests, it reminded her of northern Wisconsin, of long-weekend camping trips to the North Woods, where birches mingle with pines and maples and summer barely arrives. She figured she was near or even passed the same latitude as her hometown, Appleton.

Since high school, she had wanted out of Appleton, and now all she wanted was for it to be the cozy center of her world again. And at least for a short while, that's exactly where she would be. Five weeks at her parent's house before starting residency at the region's best pediatric hospital, Lincoln Presbyterian.

Settling comfortably in Wisconsin for a month was a dreamy notion, she knew. Home had lost its comfort ever since her brother Kyle had died. Her parents, a gregarious pair, folded into themselves. Her mother fell into a deep solitude, and her father, after a couple more years of work, retired early from a job he loved. Emily dealt with her brother's death differently. Kyle had just started his medical residency when he died, so his pursuit became hers. A sophomore in high school at the time, Emily immediately volunteered at the local hospital.

An approaching billboard unsettled her. A picture of the Grand Hotel with its familiar expansive white porch, the landmark of Mackinac Island, conjured up the phone message John had left her earlier that morning while she was in the shower. Now she imagined John, standing stately on the balcony watching the world as if it were his ward, as she replayed the message in her head: "Hello from the Grand Hotel," he had said. He finished the message with "And Emily, I have some big news to share with you when you get here. Drive safely. See you soon."

Big news? The thought that he was divorcing his wife had immediately popped into her head. No, that'd be too reckless for him. But nothing else ever came to mind except that, so now she feared that's exactly what he was going to tell her. A hot sensation poured over her.

Emily missed the exit for the Mackinaw City docks and only realized it when she saw the sign for Exit 339. Jamet Street. LAST EXIT BEFORE FARE. She pulled off the highway and turned into the first gas station.

She walked inside the convenience store to ask for directions. The clerk joked that she hadn't actually missed the exit for the docks; there were boats leaving from the other side of the bridge in St. Ignace.

She thought for a moment. She'd have to cross the bridge on her way to Wisconsin anyway. This way she and John would part on the island and avoid the awkward ride back on the ferry. She drove off, taking the northbound highway entrance toward the bridge.

Chapter Three

It was at the age of thirteen that Mark confirmed and internalized his fear. On a visit to San Francisco—accompanying his mother to a psychiatry conference—Mark faced the Golden Gate Bridge. Before they'd even reached the tollbooth, the looming rust-orange towers caused his heart to beat spasmodically. He quickly became nauseated and dizzy. Crumpling into himself and blaming his illness on lunch, he leaned against the car door and shut his eyes. On the return crossing, he feigned falling asleep.

The fear afflicted Mark as a driver, too. He avoided overpasses by taking alternate routes or even getting off the highway, detouring through side streets, and getting back on the nearest onramp. Small bridges were mostly manageable, but only if crossed straightaway. Once, when he was in Galena for a 5K race, cars were backed up over a five-hundred-foot bridge leading into town. He wouldn't risk it. He parked near the steel-arched pedestrian walkway and sprinted across.

In the early morning, Mark drove up the lakeside highway and, as directed by the front desk clerk, he stopped at a park on the north end of Petoskey. There he jumped on a trail parallel to the bay and ran south, swallowing the cool gusts coming off the lake. Running hard under a gray sky, he hoped to sweat out his anxiety and enervate his fear. The longer and harder he ran, the more determined he became to conquer the bridge. After six miles he stopped and turned back; the trail had no end in sight. He was not a long-distance runner, neither by love nor by training, so by the time he reached his car, he had exhausted himself entirely.

At ten o'clock he checked out of the hotel and drove to Woodland Hills Funeral Home, a converted Victorian house on a busy street. After perfunctory condolences, the funeral director asked Mark whether he'd like his aunt's *cremains* placed in an urn, presumptively waving him to a nearby room. Thinking it would come across as obscene if he told the solemn man that Vivian's "cremains" were to be dumped in Lake Michigan and that a plastic baggie would do, Mark nodded.

Feeling compelled and idiotic at the same time, Mark chose from the display, an urn made of cerulean glass and waited ten minutes while Vivian's ashes were *settled*. When everything was done, the man set the urn on a desk, and as Mark paid, chagrin gripped him as he noticed that the suction lid had a white flower, a lily perhaps, painted on it. It was much too ornate and delicate for intrepid Aunt Vivian.

He said nothing about it and grabbed the one-foot urn with two hands and held it like a baby that wasn't his. Mark cradled the urn under his left arm and steadied it with the caring touch of his right hand, thanked the man, and left.

Mistrustful of the suction seal, Mark strapped the urn upright in the front passenger seat. As he drove away, he kept glancing to his right, in turns mesmerized by its color and annoyed by the flower on top. "Sorry, Aunt Vivian," he muttered.

Driving north on Highway 31, leaving Little Traverse Bay behind and heading toward the tip of the Lower Peninsula, Mark forcibly reinvigorated himself. He was determined to cross the bridge. "I can do this!" he yelled. He looked over at the urn and laughed out loud—Vivian had dealt with wars and diseases, and he feared a perfectly solid bridge.

A burst of rain fell. The shoddy wipers left a smear across his view of the road before him, and he gripped the steering wheel tightly with both hands. He certainly hoped the weather would clear before he reached the bridge. "What the heck are you doing living way up here, anyway?!" he erupted. He shook his head, feeling foolish for yelling at Vivian's ashes.

As he reached the lakeside town of Conway, the rain settled to a light sprinkle. The highway turned east, following the curve of Crooked Lake on his right, the banks at times stretching to the road. Ducks rested in the calm waters near reeds that barely poked above the surface. He went through another town with pleasant lakeside homes. The lake then vanished from view, replaced by tall trees and stands of birches, and not long after, the road turned north and the sky ahead cleared.

He thought of his mother. Had she ever known about his fear of bridges? She would have tortured him through some kind of therapy session, he concluded. "Tell me why you're afraid of bridges, Mark," he said, mimicking the haughtily soothing tone his mother used with patients.

"Are you afraid that they will collapse?"

No, I know they won't, though maybe deep down . . .

"Are you afraid of being trapped?"

I don't know, maybe, yes.

"So what you're really afraid of is being trapped, of not being able to get off the bridge if you wanted to."

OK. How does that help me?

"You have the power to overcome this fear."

How?

"Don't think of it as being on a bridge. Force your mind to think of it as any other road, that's all."

Mark patted the lid of the urn. "Of course, she'd say, 'Don't take my professional opinion as a psychiatrist as relevant here.' She had the answers to everyone's problems, right? If only they'd listen to her."

Mark watched the scenery as intently as he could, and as he passed each small town, he envisioned living there. *What would it be like?* he wondered, wishing he could experience living in different places. This peripatetic vision of his life ran counter to his real life, in which he'd resided almost exclusively in the genteel village of Oak Park, just outside Chicago. He was born there and left only briefly for college. When he returned, he found a job in Chicago and rented an apartment in

Oak Park, three blocks from the Green Line, four blocks from his parish, and half a mile from his mother's house.

As he reached the overpass where Highway 31 merged with 75, a queasy pang struck Mark. Not because of the overpass per se, but because he had diligently studied the map and knew the bridge was a few minutes away. After a long bend in the road, the first tower of the Mackinac Bridge came into view. It stood out like the work of a giant with his Erector set. Memories of the Golden Gate Bridge cascaded vividly through Mark's mind. He did the math. Five mile bridge at forty miles per hour . . . seven and a half minutes. The accelerator got stiffer, harder to press.

A sign announced: LAST EXIT BEFORE FARE. "Hah! As if paying a few bucks is the big deal here." With the blinker on for the last three hundred feet, he exited the highway with forged equanimity. He turned left on the first street, a road that traveled parallel to the highway, the two roads separated only by a metal fence.

"So close!" He banged the steering wheel as he watched cars go toward the bridge with perfect indifference. "I can't do it, Vivian. Sorry. I just can't."

He took the road as far as it would go and entered the parking lot for Colonial Michilimackinac, a historical village and fort from the 1700s at the tip of the Lower Peninsula. Mark had read about this place during his alternative-way-across search.

He parked and got out of the car. Tourists walked in and out and around the visitor center, which was housed beneath the base of the bridge. Next to the building, across a sidewalk and a patchy lawn, was the ragged edge of a beach and the splashes of Lake Huron.

Mark got back in the car. "This is it, Vivian. Sorry for not returning you home, but this is the end of the line for me." He reached over and slipped the blue urn out from under the seatbelt. As he stepped outside, a powerful gust barreled in from the northwest. He waited a moment, but the wind pushed on. Clinging to the Chicago adage *If you don't like the weather, wait fifteen minutes,* Mark set the urn back on the seat. He sauntered through the parking lot toward the lake. Up above, cars entered the first part of the bridge, the green trussed metal on piers, heading toward the two white towers that lifted the suspended road over the middle of the straits. The sight of the bridge on terra firma didn't scare him so much as it angered him that he couldn't drive over it.

He crossed the lawn and stepped onto the beach, a mix of sand and pebbles and islands of grass. The waves lapped onto the shore. Able to make out the green contours on the opposite side, he was tired of himself. He picked up a rock and hurled it as far as he could into the lake.

The wind diminished to a subdued breeze. Thinking that he might be able to spread the ashes soon, he walked along the Lake Huron shoreline, toward a lighthouse looking for the right spot. The brown brick structure sat some hundred yards from the water, and a few tourists ambled about the lighthouse grounds while others sat at benches on the lawn; a few others stood along the beach looking at the lake and taking pictures. Mark retraced his steps, finding an indent near a marshy bit of the shoreline where he could angle away from the breeze.

He stepped closer to the water, reached over, and dipped his hand. Chilly.

Back at the car, Mark unbuckled the urn. "Ready?" As he got back out, a lacerating wind came at him again.

"Seriously?" He waited, but after half a minute of the same, he ducked inside.

Restraining the urn once again in the seatbelt, he decided to have lunch and wait out the wind. He'd noticed a pleasantly inauspicious diner called Artie's on his way up the street, so he walked there.

At Artie's he was seated at a table with a crosshatched view of the highway. For the first time he noticed a small building about the size of a garden shed between the highway and the road. The top half of the structure was glass, and it seemed an odd location for whatever it was used for. When the waitress came by, he asked her about it.

"Oh that's a phone booth," she said matter-of-factly. The woman's dull brown hair was fixed tightly in a bun. "Can I start you off with something to drink?"

"That's a strange place for a phone booth, isn't it, way out there next to the highway?"

"It's not that kind of phone booth. It's for people who don't want to drive themselves across the bridge."

"What do you mean?"

"You call and a bridge worker drives you across."

"Really?"

She nodded. "So what can I get you to drink?"

After eating Artie's Special Turkey Melt, fries, and a local craft beer, Mark left a large tip and stepped outside. With the wind now a soft breeze—of course!—he stopped in the middle of the road for a second and stared at the bridge. The sun shone brightly. White cumulus clouds traipsed across the northern sky.

He retrieved his car, parked near the booth, and walked inside. Cars rushed by on the highway less than twenty feet away. He picked up the receiver and after several quick rings, someone answered. "Hello."

"Hi, yes, I'm over here in Mackinaw City, and I need some help crossing the bridge."

"What's the make and model of your car?"

Mark turned to look at the rental as if it had been switched out. "It's a green Chrysler."

"Someone will be there in about ten minutes. Wait on the shoulder. Stay inside the car."

"On the highway?"

"That's right, on the shoulder. Someone will be there soon."

Less than a football field away, it was a quick right turn onto the highway. Once on, there was no way off except to go over the bridge. Mark anxiously started the car, pulled out slowly, and drove toward the entrance. As he made the full right turn, he gripped the wheel tightly.

The first tower stood massively, taunting him for his failure. Yet there it was, a simple way of beating it. Driving right under it. He fixated on that opening.

Mark floored the accelerator. The engine revved as angry as he felt, angry about this eviscerating phobia. Then as if he'd been struck in the chest, he felt his heart give a hard thump. He immediately let off the accelerator and pulled to the side.

He breathed heavily. His heart beat strangely again, fast and erratic, and he worried that it was a heart attack. But he didn't feel a heavy weight on his chest, nor did he have any pain in his left arm. Even though nothing tickled his throat, he coughed a couple of times. He took a bottle of water from the cup holder and drank, and after a half minute, his heartbeat fell back to normal.

The whole episode left him exhausted—and about ten yards short of the booth. He rolled down the windows and gathered in the cool air. He removed his brown crew neck sweater, leaving a dark blue T-shirt with *Dekalb Dash 2013*. His gaze shifted to his right, onto the diner where he'd just had lunch. A car with an Indiana license plate pulled into the diner, and he watched through the chain-link fence as a family of four got out. Pleasantly on vacation Up North.

"Maybe I'm crazy Vivian. Afraid of bridges. Talking to an urn."

He realized that someone would be there shortly and unbuckled the urn. He checked the lid. It was on firmly, and he set it down on the floor of the back seat. He threw his sweater over it.

A large white pickup truck with two passengers pulled up behind Mark. A mustached man in a dark blue cap and jacket got out of the passenger side and approached the car from the right side.

"You called for a driver?" the man asked bending down.

Feeling small, childlike, Mark nodded. "Yes, sir, that would be me."

Chapter Four

To Emily a bridge was more than just a span over water or chasm. Her father, a structural engineer and bridge inspector, had taught her about bridge design, loads, and construction—intricacies that most driver's mindlessly disregard. As she crossed, Emily took in the Mackinac Bridge in its entirety, marvelous and inspiring, an epic tale of engineering discipline and construction perils, and a work of art.

She glanced over at the blue water on each side, Lake Michigan to the left, Lake Huron to the right, the waves rolling gently in the straits, the grand bridge carrying her across like a magic carpet. The magnificence of the bridge lifted her spirits.

She spotted a ferry leaving a wake on its way to Mackinac Island. She'd be on a ferry like that soon, on her way to see John. Angst tugged at her. She stared at the boat for several seconds and imagined herself on it. She pretended she changed her mind midway, plunging into the frigid lake. She could never swim back to shore—hypothermia would set in too quickly. Syncope, asphyxia . . . a fairly painless death.

The humming tires switched to a lower octave as the road changed from pavement to lighter grates. She passed under the first tower, and, approaching midspan, Emily became resolute: after crossing the bridge, she would simply continue on toward Wisconsin, leaving

Mackinac and John behind. He'd be disappointed and angry, but it would be much better to end it now.

Passing under the second tower, she wished the bridge went on forever. The decision to leave John behind triggered a sharp pain that cut through her abdomen, like a scalpel had pushed through her navel. She reached for her phone.

"You wanted to tell me something earlier, didn't you?" Lauren said without a "hello."

"Hi. Yes." After a long sigh she confessed: "I'm meeting John Bulcher on Mackinac Island."

"Dr. Bulcher?"

"Yes."

"You've been seeing Dr. Bulcher?"

"I'm sorry for not telling you about this earlier."

"He should know better," Lauren declared. "Isn't he married?"

"Yes. And he has kids. And he's twenty years older than me. And I'm moving to Chicago. And—"

She stopped herself. She couldn't talk to Lauren about Nicholas. Too much too fast. She might hyperventilate. She took in slow breaths.

"Emily, are you okay?"

"Yeah. Give me a second."

"Sure."

Emily steadied herself. "I've never asked him to leave his family."

"Good. So why not break it off now?"

"I know I should."

"Em, I've been in a few relationships, and what I can tell you is that being away from him, away from school and on your own, is the best thing for you right now. You'll realize then how much he really means to you."

"I know you're right. It's just hard, you know?"

"I know."

She was approaching the end of the bridge and the toll booths. "Thanks for listening. I'll call you later."

After she paid the toll, the signs appeared almost immediately—the first one east to St. Ignace and the Mackinac ferries, the next exit west for Highway 2 toward Manistique/Escanaba. She kept to her lane, but as the exit-only lane shortened, her determination faltered, her unresolved ambivalence for John laid bare by the proverbial fork in the road. Then, convincing herself that she could still make up her mind at the docks, she got in the lane for St. Ignace.

She was immediately annoyed at her inability to keep to her clear-headed decision of five minutes earlier. She acknowledged the slippery slope: by taking that exit she'd be getting on a ferry to the island. Lauren would certainly be disappointed in her.

Emily swerved back, erratically crossing the diverging white lines, narrowly missing a swath of off-road sandy soil and a not-too-distant pine tree. A car horn's retribution rattled her. She looked back and raised a shaky hand in apology. Gripping the steering wheel tightly, she took the curved on-ramp that went west into the Upper Peninsula toward Wisconsin.

Her heart beating rapidly, breathing heavily, Emily felt the adrenaline easing after a few minutes. Then she resisted a spate of grief—the realization that she and John were done.

She knew her emotions couldn't be fended off forever, like blood from a gash held closed by hand pressure. Her arms began to quaver uncontrollably. She drove through a traveler's strip of food, fuel, and lodgings and pulled into a gas station, parking off to the side near the restrooms.

Her sight blurred. Though theirs hadn't been much of a relationship, they'd had a life together in her regular reveries where complications were easily dismissed. Instead of letting tears flow, she clamped down on her heartache. John had not allowed her to cry for Nicholas, so she wasn't about to cry for John now.

When she had gotten teary-eyed that awful morning, after her shock and disbelief had subsided, as they stood in the surgical room where a sheet barely covered Nicholas's head, John lashed out: "Get a hold of yourself, Emily. This is going to happen. You work in a field that deals with death. If you can't handle it, find another occupation." That day she swallowed an immense grief and later recognized a change in herself, a hardening she did not care for.

These feelings of unresolved sorrow and anger now spun inside her as in a centrifuge, and a physical illness emerged, an empty sickness with her stomach retreating. It overwhelmed her body, and she felt herself losing control. She burst from the car and toward the restroom. *Be unlocked! Be unlocked!*

She pushed the door and it opened. Disregarding her genuine fear of germs, she dove straight for the toilet and heaved. Barely anything came out since she had skipped breakfast. Her stomach contracted twice more but she produced nothing but thick spittle.

She stood and leaned against the wall. Exhausted. Embarrassed. But alone.

After a minute she regained her equilibrium and walked over to the sink and rinsed her mouth violently. Seeing herself in the murky mirror, she nearly cried. She wiped her face with a rough paper towel.

Outside in the midday sun, she stopped and inhaled deeply, expecting a dose of exhaling forest. But instead she gathered in a noxious breath of gasoline fumes. So she walked over to the edge of the property, against the gentle southern breeze, and stepped over a curb into the midst of cedar trees. She took in a slow, sweet breath.

Walk into the woods and continue on . . .

Back at the car, Emily brushed off the small cedar bits clinging to her sweater. She concentrated on the positive in her life—her upcoming residency at Lincoln Presbyterian Hospital in Chicago, the finest children's hospital in the Midwest. *Work hard and do good there*, she kept telling herself.

Feeling better, though exhausted, she got back on the highway toward Wisconsin, leaving John and Mackinac Island behind. Lake Michigan soon disappeared behind a forest that lined both sides of the road. Not long after, a clearing in the road and a sign appeared. Lynnie's Pasties. A red banner below read: The Best Pasties East of 94. A native of northern Wisconsin, Emily knew about the baked pastry crusts filled with meat and vegetables, and how to pronounce the word properly (with a short "a"). But unlike in Wisconsin where pasties were a novelty item, here they were a staple, a part of the UP's identity. It was the name, "Lynnie," her favorite aunt's name, that grabbed her attention. And, feeling a bit peckish, she pulled into the empty parking lot.

After she ate half a pasty, her appetite stalled. John kept circling in her mind. Nothing had changed in his world yet, and she contemplated it all over again. Instead of letting the thought metastasize, she pulled out her phone and found the number for the inn on Mackinac. She spoke with the innkeeper and asked him to pass a message to John: "Please tell him that Emily won't be able to make it." *There. Done. No going back.* She got in her car and drove off, through the split in the forest, five hours away from Appleton.

But John's reaction to that message—and her imaginary dialogue with him—played continuously in her head, so she turned to the radio for a distraction. Searching for a clear station, she encountered two old women gabbing. She wondered what they could possibly be discussing worthy of a radio slot.

"I'm not snobby. Anyway, this is sort of a perfect segue for 'Knitting Time.'"

"You forgot to press the button," the other whispered.

"Oh dear."

Music came on.

"Now let's talk about knitting."

They sang: "It's knitting time, it's knitting time. Knit, purl, ravel, unravel. It takes time, but it will be fine. It's knitting time."

The music stopped.

"Okay, Doris, we received a question from a listener in Naubinway. An email."

"Oh, I love getting email!"

"Oh yes, me too!"

"Though I hope people don't stop handwriting letters. Those are nice to receive too."

"Yes, I completely agree. You know, Doris, it's becoming a lost art."

"Yes, yes, I do know. In fact, my grandson—"

"Which one?"

"Ronnie."

"Okay. Ronnie is twelve."

"Yes, that's right. Thank you. Would you believe he can barely write in cursive?"

"Oh dear."

"But he can certainly type fast. Faster than me. And I used to be a secretary!"

"It is a changing world."

"Yes, ma'am, that it is."

"Though I'm glad for email because I don't think I'd ever hear from my grandson in college if there weren't email."

"Yes. So what's the question from Naubinway, Evelyn?"

Emily sorted out which was which. Doris had the uneven, slow voice. Evelyn had the slightly raspy voice.

"Oh, right, I almost forgot." Evelyn giggled. "Here it is—oh, gosh, my screen just went blank. Let me—"

"Move the black thingy."

"The mouse—yes, I'm moving it."

"And press the buttons."

"All right, here we go. It's back."

"Oh good. Computers can be such confounding things."

"Yes. Okay, let me read this before the screen disappears again: 'Dear Doris and Evelyn, do you ever use bamboo needles? What are the pros and cons?'"

"Okay, yes, I do use bamboo needles, and I like them."

"Yes, I love them."

"But I don't like them when I first buy them because they have a kind of dry friction. You know what I mean?"

"Yes, I do."

"They'll slow you down like wood. Now over time as they get use, they become smooth, slick."

"We're still talking about knitting, right?"

"Oh my gosh, Evelyn, you are so wicked."

Amused and distracted, Emily listened to the two chatty old ladies as she drove.

Chapter Five

Mark emerged sheepishly from under his jacket. The car was parked on the shoulder, less than a hundred yards from the toll booth. He muttered a groveling apology.

"No problem. You're not the only one."

"How many times do you do this every month? Five? Ten?"

"In a month? We get two, three *a day*. More if the weather's bad."

"Really?" His shame eased, but only slightly.

"Yep," the man said, handing over the keys and getting out.

Mark stepped out of the car. Beyond a wide lawn sat two buildings, the closest with a stately brownstone exterior and expansive windows. With the toll station and the official-looking buildings and the two state troopers parked beyond the booths, Mark felt more like he was entering another country than the other half of the same state.

"There's this truck driver who comes every few weeks," the man commented. "Can't drive over. He jumps into the sleeper and ducks under a blanket."

"Really? Wow." He raised his hand to wave goodbye. "Thanks again."

Back in the car, Mark reached behind his seat and grabbed the urn, then buckled it in the passenger seat again.

Having happily paid the $4 toll, he felt his shame quickly dissipated. The release of his fear and anxiety launched him into rapture. Passing the Welcome to Michigan's Upper Peninsula sign, Mark exclaimed, "We're across!" and pounded the steering wheel, giddy. "Yes, with some help," he admitted out loud, "but the point is, we're on our way to Manistique." He drove onto the ramp, a 270-degree turn that took him west on Highway 2.

What were you doing way up here, Vivian? Trying to get away from it all? If that's what you were going for, you succeeded.

Approaching a house with a sign reading, The Best Pasties East of 94, Mark wondered what a pasty was and how far it was to 94. Laura came to mind. If she were with him she would have forced him to stop there. She loved trying new foods, and as much as he resisted, he often found himself in front of some new or unusual cuisine. A Ukrainian/French-Canadian fusion restaurant was the last place they'd eaten together. It wasn't so bad.

Soon the buildings grew sparse. White-painted houses emerged here and there in clearings at the edge the forest lining the road. Businesses were separated by miles, and some were open, some abandoned. A motel. A bar. A gift shop. A restaurant. Lake Michigan appeared again, disappeared, and then continued to come and go between the pines and cedars.

"Why didn't you answer my letter in high school?" Mark glanced over at the urn as if he expected a response. "I really wanted to go on an aid trip. Mom said I couldn't, but I wrote hoping you'd give me some advice or encourage me to do it anyway. Maybe suggest a place near you."

He was silent for a minute and then went on. "I tried contacting you after Mom died. Belgian MSF said you no longer worked there. Doctors Without Borders didn't have any record of you. I tried all the offices. Finally I found you at—what was it called? Christian World Care? I can't remember. They said they would get the message out to you. But I'm thinking you never got it."

He stopped talking, wondering if Vivian did get his message and just didn't care. It was certainly possible. Vivian and his mother had never gotten along, that he did know. But he didn't know why, and whenever he queried his mother about anything to do with her sister, she was reticent at best, hostile at worst.

The silence in the car felt odd, so Mark reached for the radio. A clear AM station immediately came through, and at first he tuned out, thinking he was hearing a commercial for a denture adhesive or arthritis cream or some such thing. But the same two voices went on too long and then shifted to a different topic entirely. Two old women chatting on the radio. He'd expected a fishing report or hunting talk but not this. He was intrigued.

"Her migraines are triggered by strong scents, so I stopped using Pine-Sol."

"I love the smell of Pine-Sol. If I don't smell the pine I don't think it's clean. Plain and simple."

"So you want my friend to have a migraine."

"No, of course not."

"Well then you have to stop using it."

"Who is she? Maybe she never comes over to my house."

"Hold on. Let me find the mute button thing. Okay. Hold on."

It was silent for several seconds.

"No, she never comes over. So I'm fine."

"But what if she did come over, or someone else with the same problem? More and more people are having migraines."

"Evelyn, you want me to stop using Pine-Sol because Su—I mean, someone who gets migraines *might* come over to my house?"

"Yes."

"I think that's crazy."

They squabbled about it for another minute. Then they changed topics but soon enough they were politely bickering again. Another topic, another quarrel, including a conflict over the opening of a new Mexican restaurant in town. Neither had gone yet, though each claimed to have better credentials for judging its authenticity. One said she was qualified because her son lived in California, and every time she visited him, she ate at a Mexican restaurant. The other asserted her superiority because she'd taken a Caribbean cruise in 1998 that included a stop in Mexico.

Mark found Doris and Evelyn to be entertaining, despite not caring about any of the topics they discussed.

"Did I tell you? I ordered my new spinning wheel," Doris said.

"Oh, Doris, tell me you didn't."

"Yes, I did, and I'm not ashamed."

"You bought the Babe Bulky wheel?"

"Yes, ma'am. And I like it."

"The wheel is plastic!"

"It was within my budget, and it really does the job. And I'm not limited to small bobbins."

"Some people think it's ugly."

"Well I'm going to decorate it."

"You are?"

"Yes, and it will look fabulous and personal when I'm done."

"Let's talk about it when you've finished."

"Sure, but you don't always have to be so snobby."

"I'm not snobby. Anyway, this is sort of a perfect segue for Knitting Time."

A few seconds into a song about knitting, Mark found his limit with them and turned off the radio. A half hour later, after a long run through forests filled with evergreens and the occasional stand of white trunks, past more buildings off the highway, then a clearing, Lake Michigan appeared once again. Mark passed by several motels and a grocery store before seeing a large sign: Manistique.

"Here we are, Vivian. Back home."

He turned right at the corner of a car dealership and made his way into downtown. He turned again when he reached Cedar Street and decided to check out the town before going to Vivian's house. Manistique was the largest town he had encountered on his drive through the UP.

He parked on the street and got out to stretch his legs, taking a good look around this downtown area and considering the economics of the place. He always wondered how people survived this far away from a large city or industry. Tourism?

Several older people roamed the sidewalks, some with walkers and canes, and even one lady on a scooter. Mark wondered if this was some kind of retirement community, but who would retire up here willingly? This wasn't a warm place like Arizona or Florida. Wanting to get a better feel for the town his aunt had led him to, he walked around, weaving past the other pedestrians, eventually landing in Jake's Bar, which had a Green Bay Packers banner hanging outside.

"Packer fans, huh?" Mark said to the bartender after sitting down.

"What else?"

"I would have figured Lions."

The bartender snickered. "The trolls cheer for the cats . . . Where are you from buddy?"

"Chicago—well, Oak Park really, just outside."

"Sorry, but I hate the Bears."

"Will you still serve me a beer?"

The bartender laughed. "Sure, but only during off-season."

Mark laughed. "Lucky for me, then. What do you have on tap?"

The bartender told him, and Mark asked for the Canadian brew.

"Visiting or just passing through?"

Mark sighed. "Sort of both—my aunt lived here. She just passed away."

"Oh I'm sorry to hear that. What's your aunt's name?"

"Vivian Peregrine."

The bartender looked away for a moment and thought. "No, I don't think I knew her. Did she live here full time?"

Mark nodded, "Yeah, mostly." He lowered his voice. "So I noticed a lot of older people walking around. Is this some kind of retirement community?"

The bartender laughed and shook his head. "No, they're part of a tour group. They visit every Indian casino in the UP. There's one a couple miles east of here."

Mark had seen it. The bartender wiped the counter, walked over to the other side of the bar, and returned promptly with Mark's beer.

"Thanks." He took a drink. "So is there a real estate office around here you can recommend?"

"Well there's only one in town." He pointed. "It's one street over. Block Properties. My cousin Ron is an agent there. Tell him I sent you."

"Okay, I will."

"You thinking of selling your aunt's place?"

Mark nodded. "Don't know what else I'd do with it."

"You should consider keeping it. This is a nice getaway in the summer. Lots of people vacation up here. They come up from Wisconsin or downstate."

"I thought you guys hated people from downstate."

The bartender smiled. "They're not all bad. The ones who've had places up here a while are all right."

Mark asked more about the town, and the bartender told him about the paper mill, the largest employer. Mark remembered reading about the mill, originally built in 1920 to produce newsprint. There were rumors about the plant closing, the bartender said.

Mark finished his beer. Before leaving he asked, "You guys serve food here?"

"Yeah, grilled chicken, burgers, fries, salad, and coleslaw. We do a boiled hamburger with cole slaw dressing. It's our specialty."

"Boiled?"

"Yeah."

"Never heard of a boiled burger."

"It's juicy. It's good if you're in the mood for something different."

"Sounds intriguing. I'll be back later." He finished his last bit of beer, thanked the man, and left.

Back in his car, Mark looked at a map on his phone. Vivian's house was not far. 545 Lake Street. A right on Walnut, a left on Maple, a right on Main, and right on Lake.

He drove off unsure what awaited him.

Mark came to a stop when he reached 545 Lake Street. The house was a light blue Victorian on a corner lot. Two wooden signposts on the park strip made him wonder if Vivian had already planned to sell the house before she went to the hospital. He wrapped the corner onto Cherry Street, parking in front of the detached garage.

When he got out, he noticed a board leaning against the side of the garage. It looked like a sign, and he thought it might be the real estate sign. But it wasn't. Manistique Victorian. It meant nothing to him, except perhaps that this was a historic home.

Mark retrieved the urn from the car and strolled down the sidewalk toward the corner of the property. He absorbed the neighborhood with a sweeping glance. The other houses were white or washed-out hues and sat on one-third-acre lots with scraggly pines and wind-swept oaks scattered about patchy lawns. The houses floated amid fenceless properties, drifting toward and away from the steepled church at the northern end of Lake Street.

Vivian's house stood out with its manicured row of bushes and wide, welcoming lawn next to the house where a balsam fir stood tall in perfect Christmas tree form.

On his phone, Mark looked up the real estate office in Manistique and called. He had already forgotten the name of the bartender's cousin and said to the woman who answered the phone, "Sorry, I forgot the agent's name, but his cousin bartends at Jake's."

"Ron."

"Ron. That's it."

"Did you meet Mikey at the bar?"

"Yeah, that's right. He recommended Ron."

"Isn't he great?"

"Who—Ron?" Mark asked, perplexed. "I haven't met him."

"No, Mikey."

"Oh. Sure, I suppose so."

"Best bartender in all Manistique."

"What about Jake?"

"Who's Jake?"

"Isn't that the name of the bar?"

She giggled. "You're funny. I'll get Ron for you."

He told Ron his story, including the part about Vivian's possibly having a real estate agent already. They agreed to meet at Jake's for lunch the next day. He felt suddenly better, now that things—something at least, after his rotten start in Petoskey—had started to move.

After taking in a deep breath of cool, fresh air and exhaling, Mark marched up the front path to the house and climbed the steps to the wooden porch. When he reached the door he inserted the key. A thought struck him before he turned it. What if Vivian had a someone living with her? He rang the doorbell. There was no answer. He knocked loudly. Still no answer, so he turned the key and opened the door. The house exhaled scents of cinnamon and orange. Not at all what he had expected, and he felt uneasy at once—in a stranger's house in a strange place.

He stepped into an open space with rich brown, wood flooring. Straight ahead, a staircase made a left quarter-turn up to the second floor. To the left, a cozy living room with a fireplace. Two overstuffed couches on a soft rug faced each other with a tufted leather otto-man/coffee table in between. Next to the living room was a dining table, and to the right of the front door was a carpeted sitting room. It was a bit more formal, wallpapered, furnished with two wingback chairs, a leather sofa, and a console table with a phone and what looked to be business cards in an upright tray. He grabbed a card.

WiFi name: MVBB

Password: Monistique

He wondered how often people came to Vivian's house that she'd prepared instructions for the WiFi. He put the card in his back pocket.

Passing through the living room and to the fireplace, he set the urn and the front door key on the mantel. On the walls hung photographs of gentle scenes: an autumn grove of birch trees, a stream, the face of a cliff. Beautiful and serene. He shook his head. He had expected a stale-smelling, disheveled house with photographs of children with missing limbs or of a gap-toothed, smiling old man standing next to his hut.

Next to the base of the stairs was a glass-paneled door, closed. He walked over and peeked through the window before going inside. He still felt uneasy, as if this might be the wrong house, and he had to keep reminding himself that the key had fit the lock. The room was a small den, a library with the stale odor of books. Two large bookshelves and a couch with a book flared open on, its cover displayed: *History of the Ottawa and Chippewa Indians of Michigan*. He picked it up and started reading, unconsciously sinking down to sit on the couch.

Forty pages later, Mark stood and stretched his legs. He continued his exploration of the house. Past the dining room table, through a stiff swinging door, he entered a small kitchen with oak cabinets, a light gray countertop, and an old gas stove. Against the far wall was a half-windowed back door, and through the sheer curtain, he could see the detached garage. A couple of steps away, perpendicular to the back door was another door. He opened it, pulling toward him, revealing stairs down to a dark basement.

He flipped the light switch and found downstairs a laundry room, and then, past a short wall, a large open space, mostly empty. Besides a few boxes stacked along the side, the room had only a couch, coffee table, and a stand with a small television. He walked into another room, a fully furnished bedroom with its own bathroom. When he opened a closet door, dread struck him. The closet was full of clothes. *Vivian does have someone living with her.*

But then a thought crossed his mind, and he headed to the bathroom. Inside the medicine cabinet, among the bottles of over-the-counter pain reliever and eyedrops, he grabbed an amber pill bottle. He turned the bottle to read the label: Vivian Peregrine.

Chapter Six

Emily's body tensed. She couldn't make sense of it. As if puzzle pieces had been thrown at her, a scattered grotesque scene. She heard a scream. From the radio? She comprehended that she was still driving, but she'd entered a liminal state, between dreamlike catatonia and real life. She knew that she was being assaulted somehow, everything moving in a thousand still frames progressing to . . . How did the windshield burst? Why was a deer galloping alongside the car?

She stopped screaming and slowed the car as the deer stumbled off to the opposite side of the road. She pulled over, breathing heavily. Comprehension streamed back into her.

When Emily loosened her tight grip on the steering wheel, her hands shook. She noticed her rapid heartbeat. As the adrenaline slowly subsided, she stepped out of the car to survey the damage. The windshield on the driver's side was shattered. The side mirror hung loosely, held only by a spiral cable. Then she looked back across the road to where the deer was lying about fifty yards away. She turned around, covering her face with her hands.

When she looked back up, she saw a car heading west, an old, cream-colored sedan. It slowed. The driver, a scraggly fortysomething, seemed to take in Emily's lost stare, then looked ahead at the deer, passed it, and sped away.

Inside the car, pieces of glass were scattered all over the dashboard and seat. She used a book to brush the glass off the old leather before sitting down. She quickly determined it would be impossible to drive the car to the nearest town.

She wasn't sure who to call. Her dad? Two hundred miles away. She looked at the time. A quarter past two. John would have gotten her message. She wasn't going to call him unless it was absolutely necessary. It didn't matter. Her phone read *No Service*.

An SUV heading in the opposite direction slowed, then turned around, pulling in just behind Emily's car. A man got out. A woman sat in the passenger seat.

"Are you all right, miss?" He had a gray beard and soft eyes.

Emily nodded, "I think so." She felt a sting in her eye. Moving her eye around slowly, she noticed the deer twitching. Emily turned away and screamed, "It's still alive!"

She heard the man's shoes digging into the gravel as he spun around. "I'll take care of it," he said. "I'll be right back."

The man got back in his SUV, made a U-turn, and headed toward the deer.

What is he going to do? Shoot it? Oh God this is awful.

Emily covered her face. She wanted to crouch down and disappear. Death, again.

"You work in a field that deals with death. If you can't handle it, find another occupation."

With angry determination, Emily pushed herself to look, but the SUV blocked her view of the scene.

An old pickup truck approached slowly, crossed the lane, and stopped in front of the SUV. A few minutes later, the bearded man drove back to Emily.

Before he got out of the SUV, the man said something to the woman. She opened her door but stayed inside.

"All right," he said. "Taken care of."

Emily's voice crackled a "Thank you," which did not convey her true gratitude, only the horror.

He cleared his throat. "Do you want the deer?"

"What?!" she exclaimed.

"Harold!" the woman yelled out.

He turned back to her, and stuck out his hands, helpless. "It's her deer by law!" Turning back to Emily, he calmly said, "That fella over there wants to take it if you don't want it."

She looked *over there* and saw an old man smoking a cigarette, standing a few feet from the lifeless deer. Emily raised her hand to her forehead. The question tipped her over the edge of any normal world. Dazed, she leaned against the car. "No, of course I don't want it."

Harold whipped around and waved at the man, who turned toward the deer with a hop and pattered around as if dancing a short jig.

"You made his day."

She grimaced. "I'm glad," she answered sarcastically.

"Are you all right, miss? You look a little pale."

Emily gathered a deep breath and nodded. "How far is the nearest town?"

"A few miles. We'll give you a ride to the dealership. They'll tow your car back."

"Oh, thank you." She realized that she knew nothing about this man, but she felt comforted by the woman's presence. Emily's eye still stung, and she felt around again with her fingertips.

"You sure you're okay?"

"Maybe a shard of glass got in my eye? I'm not sure."

"You should probably have that checked out."

Emily nodded.

Another car approached the deer and stopped behind the old pickup.

The bearded man shook his head. "Someone must have gone to the local bar and announced the deer-car."

"Why so much interest in one deer?"

"Lots of people in these parts live off the deer . . . and social security."

Emily nodded. "Let me get my purse," She considered grabbing her medical bag, too, but she left it. She locked the door and got into the back of the SUV.

Emily thanked the man and woman and told them her name. The bearded man introduced himself as Harold, and the woman, his wife, as Gail.

"Do you live around here?" Emily asked.

The man shook his head. "No, we're from the Detroit area, but we have a cottage up here on Indian Lake."

"Where are you from, dear?" the woman asked.

"Don't you think it's too early for deer jokes, Gail?"

Emily laughed politely, to show her easygoing side, but deep down she was still horrified.

"Now stop it, Harold."

"I'm originally from Appleton. I just finished medical school in East Lansing."

"A doctor. Wow. Good for you," Gail said.

"So what is the nearest town?"

"Manistique," Gail added. "It's a big town for these parts."

Emily repeated it, mostly to herself: "Manistique." Sounded intriguing . . . like *mystique*.

Having dispatched a tow truck, the car dealership on the corner of Maple and Oak refused to rent a car to Emily, as she was only twenty-four years and three hundred fifty-eight days old. "Twenty-five is the minimum age, dear," the service administrator repeated in an affectionately unyielding way. Emily, too enervated now to argue with a stranger, left the pleading to Harold. He first tried with a good-natured, "Barbara, that's only seven days. I won't tell if you won't," and then attempted to sway her with guilt: "I was telling Emily how kind people are here in Manistique." But Barbara wouldn't budge—a kind and friendly town, but one that followed the rules. Barbara did promptly offer to give her a ride to the hospital once Emily was finished reporting the accident at the state trooper's post.

And that's where Emily's benefactors dropped her off before heading off. "Stop by if you get a chance," Gail said, leaving verbal directions and an address, which Emily typed into her phone.

Emily nodded, profusely thanking the two. "I don't know what I would have done without your help."

"Plenty of people would have stopped and picked you up," Harold replied modestly.

That's exactly what Emily was afraid of.

The state trooper, "C. Bryst," was stocky and short with receding sandy brown hair. He had the aura of a high school football coach. "A deer hit my car," Emily said, but no words of sympathy came in return. He simply licked his index finger, reached under the counter, and pulled out a form.

"It must happen a lot around here," she said

"We get our share. See your driver's license please?"

Emily got her license out.

He filled in the form. "Is this your current address?"

Emily shook her head. "No, I'm in the middle of moving."

"To Manistique?" he asked. His eyes reflected the light blue of his polyester tie.

"Of course not," she said, before quickly adding, "Just driving through."

He turned the page around. "Put down your new address."

Emily wrote down her parents' address. There was no other address yet. She answered a series of other questions related to the car. Make, model, license plate number. He turned the page toward Emily.

"Okay. Mark the part of the car where you hit the deer," he said matter-of-factly.

"You mean where the deer hit me."

The trooper laughed. "Sure, whatever you say, miss."

She frowned at him and then drew the X on the side of the car before pushing the paper back sharply. "See? Who hit whom?"

He smiled, looking at the page. "How am I supposed to know? The other witness is dead."

She glowered at him.

"Did the airbag go off?"

"Airbag? No. Why?"

He marked something. "I'll be right back."

When he returned several minutes later, Emily said, "Is this going to take much longer? I need to go to the hospital."

As she spoke, the radio came on, a garbled voice. The trooper put a finger up to Emily. He pressed the little walkie-talkie on his chest. "No. You can go ahead, Marv."

He looked back at Emily. "Did you get hurt in the accident?"

It didn't hurt much, but she leveraged the minor sting. "I think a piece of glass got into my eye."

"Okay, I'll note that here, and then we'll be done." He wrote on the page, then signed the document and handed a copy of it to her. "Your insurance will need that."

Emily had started the trek back to the dealership, a couple of blocks away, when her phone rang. She looked to see who it was. She sighed, debating whether to answer, then pressed *Answer* without fully deciding.

"Emily?"

"Yeah, hi, John."

"Why aren't you here? What happened?" His tone was more tender than she'd expected.

"I got into an accident."

"What?! Are you okay?"

"Yes, I'm fine. But my car isn't. A deer shattered the windshield." This was how it would end. She'd continue on to Appleton, move to Chicago, talk to John once or twice more, and their physical separation would force their relationship to fade quickly into the past, just as Lauren had said. No animosity. No hurt feelings. An accident caused things to end. A dead deer.

"So can they replace it today?"

"I don't know. I don't know how long these things take. I'll have to call you back when I know more."

"I can come and get you. How far away are you?"

"No, no. Let me get more information first."

"But—"

"I have to go. I'll call you back. Bye." She ended the call.

Arriving at the dealership, Emily scanned the parking lot for her car. She went inside the building and found Barbara. Barbara was in her late fifties, ash colored hair in a tousled bob. She had a kind face that resonated warmly with Emily, even after not being allowed to rent a car. Barbara reminded her of a friend's mom. "I didn't see my car out there."

"No dear, it's not here yet. He left about fifteen minutes ago. He should be back soon. Would you like me to drive you to the hospital?"

"How far is it?"

"Not too far. I'll drive you. I'll just get my purse."

Emily waited outside, wondering how long it would take to replace a windshield. Could it be done today? Then she thought of John again. She'd have to call him back at some point. But she wasn't sure what to tell him.

"Ready?" Barbara said when she came outside.

It took Emily a second to respond. "Yes. I'm ready."

In the car, Emily inquired about the windshield repair.

"It should be ready tomorrow," Barbara said.

"Tomorrow morning?"

"Maybe. It depends on when we get the windshield."

"Okay."

"Do you have a place to stay the night?" Barbara asked.

"No, not yet. I came straight from the police station."

"Hmm."

"What's the matter?"

"You might have trouble finding a place."

"Why?"

"Well, there's this senior group that's here right now. They're pretty much taking up the entire hotel."

"Isn't there another hotel in town?"

"There is, but it's not open yet. They had a fire a couple months back, and they're still renovating."

"Are you sure the hotel is full?"

Barbara nodded, "Yes. My cousin, Marilou, works there."

"There has to be something else?"

"There are some motels further east on 2."

"How far?"

"Well, far if you're walking—oh, there's a bed and breakfast on Lake Street. You can try that. It's actually pretty close to the hospital."

"Bed and breakfast?" Emily laughed uneasily. "Okay." *Bed and breakfast* conjured up a romantic getaway.

"It's nice, only been open a year or two."

Barbara made small talk about the town and the sights to see. The boardwalk. The lighthouse. Indian Lake. The Big Spring. "Too bad you're not with your boyfriend . . . do you have a boyfriend?"

Emily took an unusual amount of time to answer that question. She finally shook her head. "No, not at the moment." It was true.

They arrived at Schoolcraft Memorial Hospital. "This is it," Barbara said.

"So how do I get to that bed and breakfast?"

"It's very close. Just a couple blocks. You go down this street here, make a left at Church Street, and then make a right on Lake. It's on the corner of Lake and Cherry. I can't remember the number, but you can't miss it."

"Lake and Cherry. Okay. Thank you very much. I'll stop there first and then come by to get my stuff from my car."

"Oh yes. Your car should be at the lot by then."

Emily thanked Barbara and headed inside the hospital. Her phone rang as she entered. John again. She pressed *Ignore*.

A wind had picked up from the north and though the sun still shone brightly, the wind made the late-May day almost chilly. A patch covered Emily's left eye—a scratch on her sclera. The examination revealed no residual debris. The patch was unnecessary, palliative perhaps for someone who didn't know any better. She hadn't let on to the ER doctor that she, too, was a physician.

Emily went in the direction that Barbara had told her and entered a residential neighborhood of cracked sidewalks and simple homes.

Nearing the end of the street, she walked by an Episcopal church badly needing a new coat of white paint. As directed, she turned right onto Lake Street and scanned the street for a bed and breakfast. Her hope that she'd find fancier homes was dashed. Lake Street was another residential street—nothing awful, just nothing charming—and she didn't want to stay at some random split-level home. She had an idea of what a bed and breakfast should look like, and none of these fit the bill. Then a little farther away, she spotted it, a two-story house behind manicured bushes and large trees. Getting closer, she confirmed that it was "on the corner," along a perpendicular road that terminated on Lake Street. *That's got to be it,* she thought.

She felt some relief. She'd treated multiple patients for bedbug bites, so staying at any hotel disquieted Emily a little bit. This house, a Victorian, was painted a pleasant cornflower blue. It appeared well kept from the outside, and she expected that would extend to the interior, too.

She crossed the street and crossed her fingers, hoping for one vacant room. *Please, please, please. Just one!* But no sign hung between the double posts on the parkstrip, and suddenly she worried that perhaps it was no longer in business. It was, after all, an unusual location for an inn.

Emily rang the doorbell. It echoed inside, and she stepped back, straightening her hair a bit with her hand as she waited for someone to answer.

No one did, so she knocked on the glass. She turned an ear toward the house and listened. Nothing stirred. Desperate and frustrated, she pounded hard on the wood, but then reality abruptly set in, and she started for the steps. The best alternative, she decided, was to return to the car dealership and seek Barbara's help. Beg one more time for a car. Perhaps the patch and the fact she had no place to stay would yield some sympathy.

The door opened, and Emily nearly tripped on the last step.

"Hello." A man's voice.

She regained her footing and twisted around, immediately taken aback by the proprietor. She had expected a woman wearing an apron or an older man, a grandfather figure, retired and running a bed and breakfast with his wife. But this man was fit and tall, not unattractive, and not that old.

"I almost gave up on you," she said.

Chapter Seven

When he went inside to retrieve the house key, Mark's stomach churned. He'd agreed to let a strange girl stay with him under false pretenses. He wondered what had possessed him. Compassion? Embarrassment? An unknown force? To make a decision with such ease and careless consideration was completely contrary to his usual cautious ways. But it was only for one night.

Since he hadn't seen any of the rooms, he ran up the stairs to check on their condition. The first room was mostly taken up by a queen-size bed and antique dresser. There was an adjoining bathroom, and seeing that everything was in perfect order, he ran back down.

Grabbing the house key from the mantel, he paused. With the knowledge that Vivian ran an inn, he suddenly had a new perspective about the house. The console table in the front room now became the check-in desk, the TV-less living room transformed into a sitting area where guests could enjoy a glass of wine in front of a warm late-afternoon fire, the intimate dining table was the place morning risers gathered for an elaborate breakfast after spending the night upstairs, and the library was a quiet hideout to read a book or newspaper.

The mystery surrounding Vivian grew. The "Why Manistique?" question became secondary. Why a bed and breakfast? Why would Vivian, adventurous and gritty as she was, open her house to complete strangers and keep the rigid schedule of an innkeeper? *Perhaps someone told her she couldn't do it,* was his trite answer. He knew barely anything about her. His image of her was entirely shaped by postcards and his mother. His mother's descriptions. Her stories. Her opinions. His mother, the older, wiser, steadier sister who finished medical school before her adopted sister graduated from high school.

As Mark headed for the door, he noticed the left drawer of the console table was slightly ajar. He pulled it open and found some stationery with a *Manistique Victorian* letterhead and a set of keys. He opened the right drawer and found a calendar. He quickly flipped to May.

It struck Mark when he saw the writing on the calendar. Vivian's handwriting. The familiar hand from the letters he had received each year.

May 23—Peter Hinton
May 24 & 25 & 26—Ellen Terrence
May 30—Mathieu

It was May 22, and his head instantly filled with minor apologies. He anxiously picked up the phone and dialed the number next to Peter Hinton's name. He needed to get hold of him right away.

There was a knock on the open door. "Mark?"

He hung up the phone. "Yes?"

"There's someone out here for you," Emily said.

Feeling a bit heady now, Mark rushed to the front door. At the bottom of the porch stairs, an imposing man with black hair, tired dark eyes, and a faint frown stood with his arms crossed.

Mark smiled. "Hello, can I help you?"

"Where's Vivian?" the man asked coldly in his deep voice.

"Oh, Vivian, well, um—she's not here. I'm her nephew. Can I help you with something?"

The man's eyes remained cool and fixed on Mark, and he stayed silent for a long second. "She called me the other day about some work she needed done. When will she be back?"

Mark gestured to the man. "Come inside." He lifted his finger to Emily. "Can you give me one minute?"

"Sure," she replied.

The man came inside, and Mark gently pushed the door so that it remained only slightly ajar. "Did you know my aunt Vivian well?" he asked quietly.

The man nodded. "Yes. I do her lawn and small jobs around the house. Stuff like that. Clear the snow in the winter. Watch the house when she's not here. She's also a friend." His dark eyebrows came together. "Where is she?"

Mark looked down and then back up. "She passed away a couple days ago," he said softly.

"No!" He covered his face with his hands. "Not Vivian."

A compelling sadness that had been absent when he was first told of his aunt's death now tore at Mark.

Tears fell down the man's cheeks. Mark placed his hand on the man's shoulder and pulled him further into the house. "It's okay, it's okay." He wasn't sure how to console him except to pat him on the back. Mark grabbed a couple of tissues and handed them to the man.

"I can't believe it," the man said. "Vivian was a thundering spirit. There's no one else like her. She encouraged me—What happened to her?"

"She had cancer. She was down in Petoskey and fell ill," Mark answered.

The man gasped. "I remember now."

"Remember what?"

"Vivian. I heard her calling my name two days ago."

"Huh? She died two days ago in Petoskey."

"But when the spirit leaves the body, it wanders for a short time."

Mark stifled a laugh, cleared his throat, and nodded agreeably. "I see. Do you know—"

"I should have known," the man blurted. "But I thought maybe it was because I was so sick."

"What do you mean?"

He snapped his finger. "She also came to me in a dream, but what did she say to me?" His voice trailed off and he mumbled something.

"Do you know how long Vivian's been running this bed and break-fast?"

The man sniffed and shrugged. "A couple years now." He wiped his eyes. "Didn't you know?"

Mark shook his head. "No, we weren't very close."

The man eyes narrowed on him, almost a glower. "That's too bad."

"Do you think we can talk later? I could use your help."

The man took in a deep breath, then nodded slowly. "Yes."

"Good. If you can, can you come back tomorrow, say noon?"

"Okay."

"I'm Mark, by the way. What's your name?"

"Bear Foot Hemenway."

"Barefoot?"

"No," he said. "Bear"—he lifted his arms over his head and growled—"and Foot," he said, pointing to his leather workboots

"Oh, I see . . . .Hemingway, like the writer?"

He shook his head. "Hem-en-way."

"Got it. All right then, I'll see you tomorrow."

They started for the door. "Did Vivian get that electrical problem fixed?" Bear Foot asked.

Mark shrugged and shook his head. "What problem?"

"I don't know. I barely talked to her the other day. And then I was so sick—don't order the fish at Diner 37."

"Okay."

"But they make the best pies. Definitely have that."

"Sure, thanks for the tip . . . if I see something with the electricity . . ."

"I can check around if you'd like."

"How about tomorrow when you come back?"

"Okay."

Mark accompanied him to the door.

"The grass—she wanted it cut before this weekend, and she wanted the posts painted," Bear Foot said, a bit exasperated.

"It's okay, it's okay. Don't worry about it right now."

"I didn't know she was—" He started to get teary-eyed again.

"We can talk some more tomorrow."

Bear Foot nodded somberly. "Okay. Tomorrow." He left.

Mark locked the front door behind him. "You ready?" he asked Emily from the top of the stairs. She was turned toward Bear Foot, who was getting into his truck.

She nodded. "So what's the matter with him?"

"Who? Bear Foot?"

"What? He wasn't barefoot, was he?" She turned back.

Mark laughed. "No, that's his name, Bear, like the animal, and Foot." He pointed at his feet.

"Oh. Well what's wrong with him?"

"What do you mean?"

"He looked distressed, like he was about to cry."

He shook his head. "Just pollen in the air or something. Let's go. The car is parked in front of the garage, at the side there," he said pointing.

They got into the car, and when it was started, the contralto voice of Doris came through the staticky radio.

"How did the radio turn on?" Mark said reaching to shut it off.

"Wait! It's Doris and Evelyn."

"You know them?"

Emily nodded. "I was listening to them when the deer ran into me. I can't believe they're still on."

"Thanks for tuning in today," Doris said.

"We'll quote-unquote see you again tomorrow," said Evelyn.

He reached and turned off the radio. "I could swear it was one-something when I started listening to them. That's four hours. At least."

"Maybe they replay the show."

"Maybe. Where did you say your car was?"

"It's supposed to be at the dealership. Buick or GM, just off the highway."

"Yeah . . .okay." Mark remembered seeing it earlier when he entered the town. They drove off. "Did you hear the part where they were arguing over using Pine-Sol?"

"No, I missed that."

"They sure are entertaining, like watching two old ladies play tug-of-war."

Emily laughed. "I wonder if it's all an act."

"I don't think so. But if it is, they're really good at it."

It was quiet for a few seconds and then she asked, "So your B&B opens next week?"

"Actually, Saturday."

"I thought you said next week."

"What I really meant was that we weren't open this week, meaning through Friday."

"So I'm really not so early."

Mark shook his head. "No, not really. So where are you from?"

"Appleton."

Mark made a turn toward downtown and spotted the dealership.

"Do you live nearby?" she asked.

Mark laughed. "No, no. I live in Oak Park, outside of Chicago."

"Really?" she said excitedly. "I'm moving to Chicago at the end of June."

"Oh yeah?" He pulled into a parking spot.

"Yeah. I'm doing my residency at Lincoln Presbyterian."

"That's a great hospital."

Her lips trembled slightly, trying, it seemed, to tame a prying smile. "Maybe you can help me figure out which area to live in. I don't have a place yet."

He nodded. "Sure, I can give you some ideas."

"Great."

They got out of the car, and Mark followed Emily into the lobby where she asked a man for Barbara.

"She went home," the man said. "She wasn't feeling well."

"Did she have the fish at Diner 37?" Mark threw out.

"What? Diner 37? No, not that I know about. Why?"

Emily looked at Mark askance.

"A joke. Never mind," he answered.

"Great pies dere," the man said excitedly.

Mark nodded.

"My car was being towed here," she said a bit abruptly.

"Deer-car?"

"Yes."

"Yah, over here."

Mark couldn't help smiling as he followed Emily, who followed the man out to the lot. The man's strong Yooper accent, a mix of linguistic influences, particularly Finnish, had been missing from the people he had spoken to until now. Mark had expected everyone in the UP to speak in *yahs*, *das*, and *ehs*. The few people he'd encountered so far sounded more like other Midwesterners, if with slight Canadian-like accents.

"You sure were lucky, eh?" the man said. "Way you hit dat deer."

"The deer ran into me!"

The man turned to Emily with a confused look. He glanced at Mark, who simply shrugged.

"Whadya do wi' da deer?"

"What do you mean?" Mark asked with a chuckle. "Was she supposed to tie it onto the hood?"

"Apparently you hit it, you get to keep it," she explained.

"And you didn't keep it?" Mark asked, amused.

"Not funny," she replied. "Some man took it."

"Ah, okay." The man pointed to a Saab parked against a chain-link fence. "Dere's your car over dere." The side mirror dangled loosely like a broken limb.

"Wow," Mark said as they reached the car. He inspected the little pieces of glass. "I never thought a windshield could break into little pieces like that."

"Neither did I," she said, pointing to her eye.

"Got a piece of glass in your eye, eh?" asked the man.

"Yes, but it's fine. So when can you fix the windshield?"

The man shrugged. "On dis car, not so sure. We need ta find a whole new windshield."

"You sure you can't repair this one?" Mark interjected.

The man laughed. "No, no. You see da problem here is da car."

"What's wrong with the car?" Emily fired, tense lines appearing on her brow.

"No, no, nothin' like dat. You see, dis ain't no regular car. Dis here's a different breed."

"A different breed?"

"Yah."

"It's a Saab," she cried.

The man raised his hands defensively. "Yah, dat's just it, not popular in these parts. But don't worry, we'll find it. Barbara's already made some calls. Come back tomorrow morning, and we should have it. An hour or two to install it and, snap, you're on your way!"

Emily opened the car door.

Mark looked through the hatchback window. "What are all of these boxes?"

She heaved her suitcase out from the backseat and sighed. "Huh? Oh, that's all my stuff. I told you, I'm in the middle of moving."

"Were you planning to stop somewhere besides here?"

"What?" She reached back into the car and grabbed her smooth brown leather doctor's bag, which was about the size of a large purse.

Mark pointed. "You packed a suitcase."

She didn't answer immediately. She moved the suitcase out of the way and then gently shut the door. "Well I needed to bring it home, right? It's just packed with clothes."

He nodded. "That makes sense."

She looked through the back and loudly exhaled. "I don't know if I should leave all this stuff here."

"Anything valuable?" Mark asked.

"No, not really. I guess it's all right. It's mostly medical books and clothes."

"At least they won't have to smash through another window to break in," Mark joked.

The man laughed.

"You're not funny."

"Don't worry miss, dere's always somebody around, all hours."

Mark bent down to grab the suitcase.

"I got it," Emily told him, reaching for it herself.

Gone was the upbeat girl ready to start residency at Lincoln Presbyterian.

Heading back to the car, Mark spotted a car rental sign. "Look, they have car rentals here."

Emily frowned. "I know. But they won't let me rent one."

"Why not? They're afraid another deer will jump out at you?"

"Ha, ha. No, it's because I'm not twenty-five—which I'll be in a few days."

"Seriously?"

"Can you believe it?"

"You're only twenty-four?"

She rolled her eye—the one he could see. She left the suitcase next to the trunk and headed to the passenger door with her leather bag.

Mark opened the trunk and set the suitcase inside.

Once they were in the car, Mark said, "Why not test-drive a car . . . and don't bring it back for a few days?"

"Don't tempt me."

He started the car. "Are you hungry?"

"Wait!"

Emily unbuckled her seatbelt and jumped out of the car. Mark looked over his right shoulder and watched her walk briskly toward her car.

She came back a minute later. "I almost forgot this." A brown paper bag.

"What is it?"

"A pasty."

"Where did you get it?"

"Some place back near the bridge."

He nodded. "I know it's a little early, but I was thinking of going to Jake's just down the street here for a bite. Would you like to go or would you like me to drop you off at the house with your pasty?"

She thought for a moment. "Do they serve wine?"

"It's a bar—though I can't vouch for how good their wine is."

"Sure, count me in."

Chapter Eight

Mark parked across the street from Jake's. Only a few other cars lined the main street, now desolate, void of the casino tourists who'd been roaming downtown an hour earlier. "Here we are," Mark said.

"I hope you don't expect good company right now. I'm not in a particularly good mood."

"That's fine. I'm just hungry."

As they got out, a faint ring sounded. Emily dug into her jeans and pulled out her phone. "Hello." She turned and faced the opposite direction.

Mark crossed the street toward the front of Jake's. He barely made out, "I told you, the deer ran into me! No, it'll be too late by the time you get out here." By her curt tone, he figured she was talking to a man, her boyfriend.

Standing there, he contemplated the economics of the town. The slow-paced downtown, barely quaint with its flat-roofed brick buildings and scripted signage from generations ago. Could this whole town—the knickknack store, the antiques shop, the electronics repair store, the bars and restaurants, the small department store—could it really all be sustained if the paper mill did close?

Emily was still on the phone, mostly out of earshot now. Mark shook off his worry for the town and went inside.

"Hey, you're back," Mikey said.

"Yeah, and I'm bringing some business your way."

"Great, we could use it. The bus rolled through and rounded up the seniors."

"Yeah, I noticed the street's pretty quiet."

"The casino has free appetizers at five."

"Pick up your cane and run!" Mark gestured with his arm.

"Sounds about right."

Mark approached the bar. "By the way, I spoke to your cousin. I'm meeting up with him tomorrow."

"Good. Ron will take care of you."

"Thanks." Mark smiled and then landed a fist lightly on the bar. "So it turns out that my aunt was running a bed and breakfast."

"Where's the house?"

"On Lake and Cherry."

"Lake and Cherry," he repeated to himself. "Hmm."

"Hey, do me a favor, though, and don't mention anything about my aunt to this girl who's about to come inside. She's staying at the house as a guest and doesn't know my aunt passed away."

Mike nodded and winked, and as he did, Emily pulled open the door and walked into the vestibule.

"No, no, it's nothing like that," he rushed to say.

Emily came inside. "Sorry about that."

"No problem. Everything all right?"

She shook her head. "No, not really, but—where are we sitting?"

"Wherever you want. Booth or bar?"

"How about the booth?" she said and headed for the nearest one.

The waitress came out a moment later. "Can I get you something to drink?"

"What kind of white wines do you have?"

She enumerated the list of two, and Emily chose the chardonnay. Mark asked for a beer.

"So you're a doctor," Mark said, looking to start a conversation.

"Yes." She ran her fingers through her hair, in long, slow strokes, all the way down to her shoulders.

"My mother was a doctor, too."

"Oh yeah?" she said with a raised eyebrow.

"A psychiatrist."

"Did she have her own practice or . . ."

Mark shook his head. "No, she worked at the county hospital, and she had patients at a mental facility in the city."

"I did a psych rotation. I hated it. I'm not equipped to deal with people's hang-ups."

"Me neither. I heard plenty of horror stories from my mom to ever want to be a psychiatrist."

"Does she still practice?"

He shook his head. "She died a few years ago."

"I'm sorry."

"She was very good at it." Staring off into the bar, he sighed. "Too good really."

"What do you mean by that?"

"You know, give the power of subtle persuasion and manipulation to a mother . . ."

Mark had received the usual parental advice, but his mother had doled it out in unusually effective ways. When Mark's teenage interests shifted to motorcycles, his mother warned, "Don't get a motorcycle until you learn to write with your toes." To impress her point, she guided him through a ward full of accident victims at the county hospital. It was many years later when it dawned on him that the amputees and wrapped heads and ghastly moans that had haunted him since that day had nothing to do with riding motorcycles. But by that time, its profound effect was complete.

"I can imagine."

"She used to say that a magician didn't change the world, only how you looked at it, and that her job was the same."

"So what do you do back in Chicago?"

"I'm a certified financial planner. I'm independent. It's nothing too exciting."

The waitress came out with the drinks and asked if they wanted to order food.

"I'm not eating, just him." Emily pointed at Mark.

Mark scurried to open the menu. "I heard about the boiled hamburger . . ."

"Boiled?" Emily said.

The waitress nodded unenthusiastically. "It's juicy. We put extra seasoning in it. They're small, so I usually recommend you get two."

"Two boiled hamburgers it is, then." He shut the menu and held it out for the waitress to take.

Emily put up a finger, her head suddenly in the menu. "You know what, I do want something."

"I thought you weren't eating," Mark said archly.

"A girl can change her mind," the waitress declared.

Emily peeked above her menu. "Yeah."

The waitress hit him lightly on the shoulder with the menu.

He held up his hands in surrender. "Okay. Okay."

"Anything you recommend?"

"Turkey open-faced is my favorite," the waitress replied without hesitation. "Good ol' comfort food."

"That's exactly what I need right now. I'll take it."

"Okay. Anything else?"

"And can I have the fried pickles appetizer?" Emily added.

"Of course."

That's a lot of food for someone who wasn't planning on eating a minute ago, Mark wanted to say. But he didn't. Besides, she was thin and could use it.

After the waitress left, Emily grinned. "So do you help your aunt out a lot with the inn?"

Mark shook his head. "No. Actually, this is my first time with guests."

"So I'm your first?"

He twisted his lips, trying not to smile. "You could say that."

"I'll try to be easy, then."

Mark chuckled. "Okay. Thanks."

"What's so funny?"

"Nothing, nothing—so where were you heading when the deer rudely interrupted?"

"I'm heading to Appleton. Didn't I tell you that already?"

"Sorry, I did hear you say that you were from Appleton. I didn't realize that's where you were going now."

"Yes." She sat back and sighed. "Sorry, I'm not usually so punchy. It's been a long day."

"I get it. No need to apologize."

She folded her arms and leaned on the table. "I'm going to my parents' house."

"Where are you driving from?"

"From school in East Lansing."

"East Lansing?" Mark asked, thinking about the bridge—avoiding the bridge. "Is this way shorter or something?"

Emily shook her head. "No, not exactly. But this way is more scenic. Now I wish I had gone through Illinois."

Mark opened his arms wide. "And miss all this? Dinner with a stranger in a strange town."

She looked down before meeting his eyes with a smile. "I guess it could be worse."

"Yeah you could be living here," he said softly, seeing the waitress returning.

Emily burst out laughing.

The waitress dropped off the appetizer and two plates. Emily pushed the plate of pickles toward Mark.

"Didn't *you* order these?"

"Yes, but you have some too."

Mark grabbed one of the fried pickles and took a bite.

He dropped it. "Hot!" He gulped down his beer.

"What are you, six? Do you want me to blow on it for you?" She grabbed a pickle and blew on it, and then took a bite. "Mmm, these are good."

Eyeing her with mock disdain, Mark blew with exaggerated force and took another bite.

"That's better." She laughed.

He shook his head at her and then thought of his first date with Laura. He remembered it as a conversation of starts and stops, generic questions whose answers ended with *How about you?*

"So now that you have your MD—"

"DO," she corrected.

"Huh?"

"I have a DO not an MD"

"Oh, okay. That's osteopathic medicine, right?"

"Yeah, that's right. Good."

"What exactly is the difference between the two? I never quite understood it."

"Not a lot. Both have to go through four-year medical programs, do a residency, and pass a board exam. As part of the DO program, there are some extra courses in pain management and total-person health."

"What does that mean? I mean, if I saw Emily MD versus Emily DO, what would be the difference?"

"Depends. What are you coming in for?"

"I don't know. Let's say it burns when I pee."

A smile flickered at the corners of her mouth. She shook her head a little and kept her gaze on him. "Okay. So both are going to ask about your sexual history."

"None. How about you?"

Emily's gaze fell for a brief second, her cheeks turning slightly red, but she recovered quickly. "I'm the doctor. I ask the questions," she said firmly.

"All right. Then what would you do differently than an MD?"

"So both kinds of doctors are going to order a urine test. But as DO's, we're taught to garner more information about the types of activities you do and the food you eat to try and prevent the problem from occurring again, assuming it's not something serious, like cancer."

"I see . . . DO's *do* more than MD's."

"I'm not saying that."

"That's what you just implied."

"No, I mean each one has a different point of emphasis, that's all."

Mark smiled. "All right."

"The funny thing is, my nickname in high school was Em D, for my name Emily Davis."

"And you're a DO Funny."

The waitress came out with the food. She set down Mark's boiled hamburgers and Emily's open-face sandwich. "Do you want another beer?"

He shook his head, remembering it would be number three for the afternoon. "I better not. Thanks."

She left.

"Let me know how your burger tastes," Emily said.

"Have one," he insisted.

"No, no."

He paid no attention to her and held one out to her. "Here."

She shook her head.

"Just take a bite then. I know where you've been."

"I doubt that." She took it, and they both took bites of their burgers at the same time.

"It's different," Mark said. "Nothing to write home about, but it is juicy, like they said."

She handed her burger back to Mark. "I prefer grilled."

They ate quietly for a while.

"I haven't had an open-face sandwich in forever," she said. "In fact, I haven't eaten like this in a long time."

"You mean dinner?"

"No, I mean—" She stopped herself.

"Maybe it was that hospital cafeteria food?"

Emily smiled. "Probably, though it's not as bad as it used to be."

"You feeling better? You seemed a little stressed out earlier."

She sighed and shrugged. She took a bite and hid her mouth behind her hand. "My whole life has been stressful lately. Interviewing for residency, waiting to get matched, and now finding a place to live." She looked down at her plate. "This *deer-car* is like the cherry on top of it all." She dug out a bite of mashed potatoes and gravy.

Despite wanting to probe further, Mark sensed a wall. He brought up Chicago and places to live, and this topic seemed to pick her up a bit. Since Emily's residency was on the west side of the city, Mark verbally guided her through Chicagoland, from Lincoln Park neighborhood up north through Lakeview (too many fresh graduates) to Evanston (maybe) and some of the northwest suburbs, Forest Park and Oak Park north of the Green Line (too expensive), and as far west as Clarendon Hills (decidedly too far). They were talking about Evanston when Emily ordered a second glass of wine.

When they headed back to the house, it was nearly six o'clock. As they turned the corner onto Lake Street, Emily said, "Is that smoke coming from your house?"

A steady stream of white smoke billowed over the trees.

"Electrical fire!" Mark yelled.

Chapter Nine

Mark slammed on the brakes, abruptly stopping the car several feet from the curb. He jumped out and sprinted by the bushes toward the front door. The smoke appeared to be coming from the back of the house, so he ran around, keeping his eyes fixed on the second floor. He hadn't yet seen this side of the house, and he took note of the spigot and garden hose. When he rounded the corner, he stopped in his tracks.

Between the detached garage and the house, in a small dirt hole, a campfire was burning.

"Is that the fire?" Emily asked, gasping as she ran up beside him.

"Yeah."

"Who started that?"

"I don't know."

"Maybe it's one of those prankster kids from the neighborhood."

Mark shot her a sidelong glance.

"What?" she protested.

"I'm going to get the hose," he replied, and slogged back around the corner.

Emily followed.

"So strange. Do you need any help?"

"No I've got it. Thanks."

"I'll get my suitcase out of the car."

Mark attached the nozzle sprayer onto the hose and twisted the spigot on. *Might be better off if the house burned down,* he thought as he dragged the hose. *Easier to collect insurance money than sell it.* He chuckled, not seriously considering this option. As he reached the corner, the hose gave some resistance. Mark saw that it was tangled, so he yanked hard to free it. It loosened easily, and he stumbled as he rounded the corner. In a single move, he caught himself and lifted the sprayer, ready to play fireman. Except instead of the fire, he encountered a large figure in front of him and reflexively triggered the sprayer—

"Whoa!" exclaimed Bear Foot, arms raised as if surrendering.

"Ah!" Mark stopped spraying. "You surprised me. Sorry."

Bear Foot looked down at his gray sweatshirt, now with a dark stain from the chest down to the stomach.

"I'm so sorry," Mark repeated. "What are you doing here?"

"What are you doing with the hose?"

"Putting out that fire, of course!"

"No, you can't," Bear Foot insisted. "It's for Vivian."

"What?"

"It's a ritual, to keep her warm during her journey."

"What journey? She's dead!"

Bear Foot craned his neck toward the sky. "The journey we all have to take some day."

"You mean, you started that fire?"

Bear Foot nodded. "Yes, of course."

Mark pointed the nozzle toward the ground. "You freaked me out. Driving up, I thought the house was on fire."

"I should have mentioned it."

Mark nodded, then gestured at Bear Foot's wet sweatshirt. "Let me go get you a towel."

"I'll be okay."

"You sure?"

Bear Foot nodded.

Back near the spigot, Mark turned off the water, and coiled the hose.

Emily burst from around the corner, an excited expression on her face. "Hey! There's a truck parked on the other side of the house. I think it's that Bear Claw guy."

Mark snorted a laugh and put his finger to his lips. When Emily got close enough, he said softly, "A bear claw is a pastry. You think he's named after a pastry?"

"That's what you called him."

"No. Bear *Foot*."

She pursed her lips and shook her head. "It should be Bear Paw then, not Foot. People have feet. Animals have paws."

"Well he *is* a person."

"Whatever," she sighed. "So did he know anything about the fire?"

"He's the one who started it."

"Seriously? Why?"

"For Vivian." It had slipped out, and he blamed his careless lips on a waning buzz.

"Who?"

"Oh, my aunt. She asked Bear Foot to do it. Apparently an old Native American tradition. Wards off evil spirits or some such nonsense. Who knows what she was thinking?"

"You did warn me you weren't quite ready for guests."

Mark laughed. "That's right. You're taking your chances staying here."

"I already knew that." She smiled.

He started toward the front of the house. At the porch, he hesitantly picked up Emily's suitcase. But this time, she didn't deter him.

"Smells wonderful in here," Emily said as they walked inside.

Mark nodded, though he didn't really care for it. In fact, he kind of detested it. "It's all my aunt."

"It's nice. I like the parlor," she said looking to her right.

"There's a library here if you'd like some place quiet to read," he said when they reached the stairs.

"Nice."

When they reached the top, Mark said, "You can have the first room here."

"Thanks again for letting me stay here tonight," she said.

He briefly turned back toward her and gave her a quick smile. "Not a problem."

"I don't think I would have much liked the motels down the highway. I doubt they do anything to ward off evil spirits."

He laughed. "No, probably not."

Mark set the suitcase next to the antique dresser. When he saw the key inserted in the knob, he realized how bad he was at being an innkeeper. He hadn't even thought of a key. Luckily Vivian had. He pulled it out and held it out for Emily. "Here you go."

Taking it, she smiled. "Thanks."

Mark smiled back and they stared at each other, and before it became too awkward, he pointed downstairs and said, "I should really get Bear Foot a towel."

"Why, is he going to make smoke signals?" She laughed.

"No," he replied with a feeble smile. "I accidentally sprayed him with the hose."

"*Accidentally?*"

"Well when I turned the corner, he caught me by surprise."

"So you hosed him down?" Her smile broadened into a flabbergasted grin.

"No, not like that." He laughed defensively. "I barely got him, really." He gestured in a tight circle around his chest. "I thought he was something else."

"Like what? A big bear?" Emily laughed hysterically.

Mark shook his head at her. "Come downstairs whenever you like."

"Only if you promise not to hose me down."

"I don't promise any such thing." He shot a reflexive wink at her, and swiftly left the room, closing the door behind him.

Mark quickly checked out the other bedrooms on the second floor. Four in total, each with its own bathroom. He took a towel from one of the bathrooms and rushed downstairs. Outside, he searched around, walking the perimeter of the house, but he couldn't find Bear Foot. The truck was still parked on the street, just past the garage.

He went back inside and, in the *parlor*, he set the towel down on the console table. He grabbed the reservation calendar and flipped to May. As he went through the months, he saw boxes were filled in sporadically until the end of September. He considered leaving a note on the door rather than calling each one. But he couldn't leave things that way, disappointing guests with a For Sale sign, leaving them to fend for themselves and find vacancies off the highway.

So he picked up the house phone and marked the number under Peter Hinton's name. Staring out the window as it rang, he saw Bear Foot passing by.

He hung up the phone, grabbed the towel, and hurried out of the house, down the steps, and around the corner.

Bear Foot had already disappeared.

When Mark reached the back of the house, he was mesmerized by the plume of pure white smoke, whiter than he had ever seen. He inched closer. Something was vaporizing, drifting up and off, slowly dissipating in the sky. Bear Foot stood close to the fire, his eyes closed, his lips moving as if he were reading to himself.

Mark stood there with a towel in his hand, waiting for Bear Foot to open his eyes.

"Was that the finale?" Mark asked.

"Finale? No, of course not. Her journey is three days long."

"Three days," he repeated, a little annoyed.

Bear Foot nodded. "We must keep this fire going. Will you take care of it while I'm away? I've stacked some wood at the side there."

No way! "There must be some kind of ordinance against this."

"Ordinance against what?"

"Fires—doesn't the city have rules about having open fires like this?"

Bear Foot shrugged. "Never heard of anything like that. That would be a strange law."

Mark thought for a moment. "Oh!" he exclaimed, much too excitedly. After a long pause and a solemn grimace, he said, "Vivian died on Tuesday morning, so this is the third day."

Lines appeared on Bear Foot's forehead. "Then we'll keep it going through the night. At least she'll have one night of comfort during her journey."

A chill wind suddenly enveloped Mark. He flinched. Sitting in front of a fire actually sounded pleasant. "Hey, do you think we can use the fireplace instead? I have a guest inside, and I'm not sure she appreciates smoke outside her window." He pointed up, where there was, in fact, a window, but he wasn't sure it was to Emily's room. "Besides that, Vivian's remains are in an urn on the mantel."

Bear Foot looked away, frowning in thought, as if reviewing some manual on rituals. "Yes, that should be fine," he finally said.

He followed Mark to the front of the house. Mark turned back slightly as they reached the door. "I'm sure Vivian would have appreciated this," he said as sincerely as possible.

"It's the way of her people."

Mark snapped around. "What people?"

"Chippewa."

"What do you mean? Was Vivian somehow Native American?"

"Yes, of course. You didn't know?"

"No," he got out softly. His gaze fell to the ground. "She was adopted," he muttered as explanation. "And we were never really that close."

Inside the house, in front of the fireplace, they stood in silence, the blue urn stationed on the mantel. Mark watched Bear Foot solemnly stare at the urn. He softly laid his thick fingers on it and shut his eyes.

A stirring noise came from upstairs, a gentle creaking as Emily moved about. Mark reached for some wood on the rack at the left side of the hearth.

"I'll take care of the fire outside," Bear Foot said and left.

After piling wood on top of the fireplace grate, Mark poked around the kitchen, looking for matches. He found some in a drawer, then grabbed two small brown paper bags to use as tinder. Back in the living room, he crumpled the paper bags and shoved them under the grate.

He struck a match and lit the bags. Shoving the matchbox into his pocket, he stood back and folded his arms, watching the bag flash into a quick burn, hoping that the logs would catch.

There was a single knock on the door before it opened. Bear Foot came inside and said, "Everything is taken care of out there."

"Thanks."

"What's this?" Bear Foot said pointing at the fireplace.

"Trying to get the fire going," Mark replied, abashed by the listless flame.

"That's too much wood in there to start."

"Oh." Mark leaned over and grabbed two of the logs.

"Don't burn yourself," he said, laughing.

Mark smiled and nodded, even more embarrassed. He placed the logs back on the rack.

"I'll go out and find some twigs." He left.

Mark couldn't remember the last time he had made a fire. Maybe never. His mother always bought artificial logs. And he had lived in an apartment since. Bear Foot was getting a big laugh out of this, he thought. City Boy couldn't even start a fire.

He bent down and watched the bags dissolve into thin black wisps, still hoping that the logs would spontaneously ignite and vindicate him. Alas, there was hardly a scar on the wood when Bear Foot returned holding a bundle of twigs in the crook of his arm. Mark stepped aside as Bear Foot set the twigs down and moved the remaining logs to the side. He stuck his head all the way inside the fireplace. "Good thing you didn't get this fire going," Bear Foot said.

"Why's that?"

"This is closed." He pulled on a lever; which made a low scraping sound.

"Do you have any newspaper or whatever you used here?"

"Paper bags."

"That will do."

Mark went back into the kitchen and found larger brown bags from the grocery store. He grabbed a couple and jogged back to the living room.

Bear Foot ripped the bags into strips, covering the grate with it. Then he layered the twigs, and set the two logs on top.

Mark dug into his pocket. "You need a match? Or do you do have a couple of rocks?" He laughed.

Bear Foot pulled out a lighter. "I'm good." He flicked it and lit the bags.

Mark shoved the matchbox back into this pocket and watched the fire easily move to the kindling.

"Keep this fire going until tomorrow morning."

Mark nodded. He thought about buying some artificial logs. "Tomorrow, I'll scatter her ashes on the lake."

"Which lake?"

"Lake Michigan. Where else?"

"There's Indian Lake," Bear Foot said.

"Is that on some sort of reservation?"

"No. Although lots of Indians did live there at one point. I mention it because she used to talk about her father taking her fishing there."

Mark nodded slowly. He liked the idea, the historical tie to Vivian's heritage and the familial tie to his grandfather. "How far away is it?"

"Only a couple miles."

"Do you know if I can rent a boat there?"

Bear Foot shook his head. "That lake is shallow—can be a little tricky. You need to know your way around. I can borrow a boat and take you. We can go tomorrow if want."

"Yeah, that would be great. Thanks. What time works for you?"

Bear Foot thought for a moment. "How about in the morning? Ten o'clock?"

Mark nodded. Bear Foot gave him directions: north on 94, left at the community center. "Then turn left on . . ." He grimaced and stared at the ceiling for a moment. "I can't remember the name of the street. Just turn when you see the sign for the golf course, but go the other way. Go left. All the way down you'll run into a boat slip next to the old Arrowhead Inn."

They walked to the door. Mark extended his hand, and they shook. "See you tomorrow then."

Bear Foot nodded and left.

Mark closed the front door and headed back into the parlor. All right, Peter Hinton. He dialed the number again. No answer. Nothing. No way to leave a message, either. Damn.

Mark walked out of the parlor when he heard steps coming down the stairs. "Finding everything okay?" he asked.

Emily nodded. "Yes, everything is fine. It's a nice room."

"Good. I need to run to the grocery store. Do you want anything?"

Emily shook her head and yawned. "No. Thanks."

"Okay. I'll be back. Make yourself at home." He started to turn to leave.

"Oh wait! Actually, I do need something."

"What?"

"Tampons."

"Seriously?"

"No. Just getting you back from earlier."

"What did I do earlier?"

"Really?"

Mark shrugged and went into the kitchen. He hastily checked the cupboards and the refrigerator and left.

Chapter Ten

The long day whirled and banged around inside Emily's head. The deer. Ditching John. The long drive. The deer. The damaged car. Deer-car. Mark. John. Mark. Deer. Mark . . .

His aunt had really picked him to be in charge? He seemed wholly unprepared for running a B&B. Too blunt. Too abrupt. Not . . . not congenial enough. Irreverent. Weird. John Cleese? What was that all about? Maybe he was the only one available. Not creepy, though—that was a plus. Tried hard to be charming. Too hard, really. Maybe that usually worked for him. Older. Reminded her a bit of Kyle, but only a bit. Still . . .

Emily walked upstairs. To find what? She didn't really know. She walked by her own room, the door closed. The Mighty Mac, said a small plaque on the door that she hadn't noticed before. The next room had a name too: Indian Lake. The door was open and she walked in. It was similar to her room except the walls were painted a soothing gray-blue. Like her room, this one had two windows. She opened the drawers to a tall, narrow dresser. Empty. The nightstand drawer had a Gideon Bible and a thin phonebook. The next room, the Breakwater Lighthouse, was narrower and longer with one large window that faced the front of the house. Three walls in this room were painted beige and one a wagon red. An elegant cream-colored coverlet whose bottom quarter was the same red as the wall was spread over the bed. Nothing unusual there, either. She continued to the last room, Lake

Michigan. This was the largest of the rooms, with the same beige on three walls and one dark blue wall. But again nothing. No personal items to be found. *Where's Mark's stuff? Where does his aunt sleep?*

Emily headed downstairs to search for another room. But there was only the library. She knew there was a basement. She had seen a window outside a couple feet off the ground. She opened a door. Closet. She laughed at herself and moved on. In the kitchen she found the door that led to the basement. Flicking the light switch, she gingerly stepped down. Her imagination ran vividly, a horror movie playing in her mind where she was about to make some weird, *Psycho*-esque discovery . . . Mark's dead aunt in a rocking chair.

"Hello," she said loudly, though she didn't really expect a reply.

The basement was cool with a faint smell of bleach. She walked by a laundry room, and then a large, carpeted area with a television and then a bedroom with a full bathroom. Emily opened the closet and found women's clothing. She closed it immediately, feeling silly for being so paranoid and ashamed for snooping around.

She scanned the stack of books on the nightstand (other people snooped in medicine cabinets, but Emily was always curious about their books). *Under the Volcano* was the top book, but it was the second book that she immediately grabbed: *Doctors on the Borderline*. She turned to the back. A book about doctors in MSF who struggled. *A sign?* she wondered. *The counterargument to Lauren's book?* Too astounded by the coincidence, she flipped it open.

Six stories in the table of contents. One stood out. "Still in Sarajevo," by Vivian Peregrine. Emily had been born in Sarajevo and came to the United States during the siege in 1992. She immediately flipped to page 132.

THE MISSION

"There is an urgent need in Sarajevo," Marie told me over the phone. (Marie was my contact at the MSF office in Belgium.) Do you know anyone? she asked. Her tone gave her away, but I played along, asking her casually to tell me about the situation there. It wasn't a gesture. I really didn't know. Despite

living and working in places that regularly made the news, I never kept up
with the affairs of the rest of the world. It depressed me too much to know about
all of the places in dire need—and you couldn't accuse me of being selfishly
insensitive.

"The Mission" was about a three-week assignment in the city of Sarajevo, early on during the siege of the city in 1992. The doctor had recently returned from Sri Lanka, and restlessly annoyed with civilian life in London, accepted the new assignment.

With her finger marking her place, Emily dropped to the floor. She rested her back against the wall and continued reading.

It was ten or fifteen minutes later when she heard a car door slam. Though she had devised an excuse in case she was caught in the basement ("I was looking for some tape"), it was flimsy. So she rushed to finish reading the section called "Welcome to Hell," in which a man named Ratko was driving Vivian to Sarajevo at dusk.

"We are going through an area with snipers, so go down. I will be driving
fast, but no worry."

I obeyed him and saw nothing more. The last bit of the ride was turbulent,
with uneven roads and sharp turns. When I popped back up, we were parked
near a yellow building vanishing in the darkening landscape. "This is it," he
said. It was the back entrance of the hotel.

The Holiday Inn was home to most foreign journalists. Marie had told me
that local MSF volunteers could either put me up or find me a place, but I de-
cided on the Holiday Inn since I wouldn't be staying very long and someone
had recommended it, especially as a place to get information.

"You go through there," he said, pointing to a door riddled with bullet holes.
"Will I get shot at?"

"Not likely, but you should run. I run behind you with your things."

It did cross my mind that he might take off in his car with my suitcase. But
there was nothing of value to him in there. Plus I still had the other half of the
fare to pay him.

My experience with the siege was starting. A run to the back door of a hotel, perhaps in the sights of a sniper. I laughed nervously before counting to three, taking a deep breath, and making a run for it.

Emily hastily set the book back in place and scurried up the stairs.

Chapter Eleven

Rushing through and out of the kitchen and around the dining table, Emily grabbed the top magazine on the coffee table in the living room and landed on the couch. She turned to a random page waiting for the front door to open. A gentle fire in the fireplace and Emily casually reading a magazine—she blew out a laugh at the ridiculous contrast, that doctor dodging snipers and her dodging Mark so she wouldn't be caught snooping around.

A scuffling came from the kitchen. "I'm back."

"Need any help?" she asked as a throwaway gesture.

His head popped out of the kitchen. "Sure. You can help unload the stuff from the bags. I've got more bags in the car."

"Oh, okay." She chuckled under her breath. He sure lacked the fawning sensibilities of an innkeeper. For $25 a night, though, she couldn't complain. She did admire his casualness with her. She'd been a complete stranger only a few hours earlier.

Emily tossed aside the magazine and got up. In the kitchen, she started unloading the plastic bags.

Flour, sugar, two loaves of bread, vanilla, bacon, sausages, eggs, fruit, milk, orange juice.

Mark returned with two more bags. "All right, we have enough for breakfast now."

"How many people are you expecting?" she asked incredulously.

Mark smiled. "I know, I know. I got a bit carried away, but I didn't know what you liked. Plus, there wasn't much food in the house."

"I didn't realize my special rate came with breakfast."

"Of course, this is a bed *and* breakfast, after all."

He opened a cabinet, closed it, opened the next, and stuck the cereal inside.

The doorbell rang.

Mark kept putting things away.

"Did you hear the doorbell?" she asked.

"I'm not expecting anyone. Are you?"

A broken laugh came out of Emily. "Seriously? You don't answer the door if you're not expecting them?"

"Pretty much. Yeah."

"You're kidding, right?"

He put the eggs in the refrigerator. "No. Usually unexpected people at the door are just soliciting."

There was a knock.

"But this is a bed and breakfast."

"It's my *aunt's* bed and breakfast."

"Well wouldn't your *aunt* want you to open the door?"

"She's not here, and I'm not taking any other guests. It's not open for business."

"Is that why you took so long to answer when I was at the door?"

Mark stopped, his eyes flitting over her. He shrugged.

Emily frowned. "You weren't planning on answering the door, were you? That's what took you so long to answer."

"But I did, and look at the trouble you're putting me through."

"I'm not any trouble. Maybe that friend of yours who starts fires."

"You mean Bear Claw?" He smiled.

She shook her head. "It's not funny anymore."

"I guess not." Then he laughed. "No, it's still a little funny." He dramatically pulled out a package from the bag and held it up. "Didn't you ask for these?"

Bear claws. She answered him with a wry laugh.

He grinned and grabbed a gym bag that was on the floor next to the door. "I'll be back in a minute." He headed down the basement steps, his laughter reverberating.

Emily stood in the kitchen, wondering how to get back to *Doctors on the Borderline*. She wanted to read more about Vivian and Sarajevo.

There was another knock, and then she heard the door creak open. "Hello?" someone said.

Emily rushed out of the kitchen. A man in his seventies stood in the entry, the door still open behind him. He was wearing black sneakers and dark slacks. He would have probably measured around five-eleven, but his hunched posture stole an inch or two.

"Oh, hello," he said. "Is this the Manistique . . ." He fidgeted his fingers in the air. "Darn it! I've forgotten. Is this a hotel?"

"Um, yes it is, but—"

The man turned around and waved good-naturedly. He shut the door. Through the window, Emily watched a car drive away.

"Phew," he said, turning back to Emily, wiping imaginary perspiration off his forehead. "I didn't just barge into someone's house. That would have been embarrassing." He pointed behind him. "I rang the doorbell several times." He said it a bit testily.

"I'm not the owner."

"You're not Vivian?"

"Vivian?" Emily echoed, stunned by the name. "What Vivian?" The image flashed in her head of a doctor running toward a hotel pockmarked with bullet holes.

"The owner. Isn't her name Vivian?"

Mark's aunt's name was Vivian, too, she remembered. Emily let out a little nervous laugh. "No, I'm only a guest here."

The man's eyebrows lifted. "My suitcase. I left it outside," he said, turning towards the door.

Emily tilted her head towards the kitchen, hoping to hear Mark coming. *Where is he?* She started that way when the man said, "I sure hope there's a vacancy." She stopped and watched as the man stepped gingerly into the house carrying a leather-trimmed fabric suitcase. "Do you know?"

"Ummm . . ."

He set down his suitcase and closed the door. "Uh oh."

Emily turned and called out for Mark.

"Who's Mark?"

"The owner."

He sneezed.

"Bless you."

"It's allergies. The antihistamine must be wearing off."

Emily nodded. *Mark's not going to like this.*

"Is he Vivian's husband?"

Emily shook her head. "No. I only meant that Mark is in charge right now. The actual owner isn't here right now."

"I only need a room for tonight."

Emily smiled and nodded absentmindedly.

"That was my ride that just left," the old man said, pointing back with his thumb. "Not that I have anywhere else to go," he muttered.

She turned around and yelled, "Mark!"

Mark heard his name being called as he climbed the stairs from the basement. He caught a tinge of tension in Emily's voice. *She probably doesn't like pulp in her orange juice,* he thought. He walked briskly into the kitchen without finding her then went into the dining room and abruptly stopped.

"Who are you?" he asked brusquely. He strode toward an old man with a suitcase by his side.

"I need a room for tonight."

Mark took a halting step toward the man with a forced smile.

"You really need to work on your hospitality etiquette," Emily whispered.

He turned his head, just enough to give her a slanted glare. Arm extended, gesturing for the man to turn and leave, Mark said, "I'm so sorry for the misunderstanding, but we're not open for the season yet."

The old man's brow furrowed. He pointed at Emily. "Isn't she a guest?"

Mark turned to glower at Emily.

She demurred. "I didn't let him in."

Back to the old man. "Cyclops here is a special case."

"Hey!" she protested.

"We're just not open yet for regular guests," Mark finished.

"I'll pay extra," he pleaded with dismal eyes. "I have nowhere to go. The hotel I was staying in is completely full."

Mark couldn't let go of his curiosity. "What do you mean the hotel you were staying in? What happened to your room?"

"My wife is staying in it."

Mark laughed heartily. "That's funny." He looked over at Emily, who wasn't laughing at all, and then back at the old man. He took in a deep breath and then exhaled. "I don't know." He looked back at Emily. "Do you mind if he stays?"

"Why are you asking me? I'm only a guest here."

"Right. Okay. You can stay," he said to the man, "but only tonight. Tomorrow, I'm afraid you'll need to come up with another arrangement or make up with your wife."

The old man nodded eagerly. "I'm making up with her right now."

"What do you mean?" Emily asked.

"Where there is a reconciliation, there must first have been a sundering."

"Huh?" Mark said.

"I'm getting away from my wife," he said. "A sundering, a separation . . . .*Ulysses*? No? Just a play on a famous—well, maybe not. Sorry, I get to read more now that I'm retired. My wife never laughs at my jokes either. Highbrow humor."

Mark pointed at Emily. "As you can see, we only do *half*-brow humor here."

The old man chuckled.

Emily glared at Mark with her visible eye. "Yes, that's right, only lowbrow humor here." A smile crept onto her face. "Mark can demonstrate his goofy-walk if you're interested."

"You don't mean silly walk, do you?" the old man said.

Her grin wilted.

"Yes!" Mark affirmed.

"Is this place *Fawlty Towers*?"

"Ugh," groaned Emily.

"Ha!" Mark nodded gleefully. "She's never seen it. Can you believe it?"

The old man shook his head pityingly.

Mark approached and extended his hand. "I'm Mark."

"George."

"Pleasure to meet you, George."

Weakly raising her hand, Emily said, "I'm Emily."

"I'm glad to meet both of you."

Mark grabbed the suitcase.

"Where's Manuel?" George asked, smiling.

Mark chuckled. "He's done for the day."

"Who?" Emily asked.

Mark shook his head. "No one."

"Well this is a fun hotel," George said. "I like you two better than the curmudgeons I'm traveling with."

Mark paced himself up the stairs, letting George keep up. He didn't exactly know what had gotten into him, letting the man stay. But what was one more guest for one night? "Are you part of that casino tour?" Mark asked.

"Yes, that's right. Bunch of grumps," George replied, slightly out of breath.

Mark laughed. When they reached the top, he asked, "How many days are you folks staying in Manistique?"

"Just two nights. We leave tomorrow morning for St. Ignace."

"Where are you all from?"

"Milwaukee area."

Mark entered the room next to Emily's and set the suitcase on the bed.

"Nice room," George said.

Mark nodded agreeably as he surveyed the room. He slipped the key from the knob and handed it to George.

"Thank you. I never asked you about a rate. How much is it here per night?"

"It's twenty-five dollars. I hear it's a good rate."

"Twenty-five? I would have stayed here last night if I had known that."

"It's a special rate. I'm charging Emily the same. Actually, you have similar situations."

"She got into an argument, too?"

Mark smirked. "No, only that you're both stranded with nowhere to go. She got into an accident a couple miles from here."

"Oh really? That's too bad. What happened?"

"Deer-car."

"She ran into a deer?"

Mark chuckled. "Sort of."

"What do you mean?"

"She's adamant that the deer ran into her. Apparently it was the deer's fault."

"Isn't Michigan a no-fault state?"

Mark laughed. "Anyway, she's touchy about it. So whatever you do, don't bring it up."

George shook his head. "No, I won't mention it at all." He groaned as he sat down on the bed.

"Do you need a ride back to the hotel in the morning?"

George nodded. "If you could. The bus leaves at ten thirty sharp."

"I can give you a lift, but it'll have to be a little early. I've got to be somewhere by ten o'clock. Gives you plenty of time to finish making up with your better half."

George smiled. "That works for me. I'm very grateful to you."

"Sure. No problem." He checked his watch. It was eight o'clock. "I'm going to open up a bottle of wine downstairs, if you're interested."

George yawned and shook his head. "No, but thanks for the offer. Doctor says I should avoid alcohol. I think I'll just read for a bit and turn in."

"Just as well. I have a feeling the wine I got isn't that great. Well, have a good night, then." Mark started to leave.

"By the way, is Vivian your wife?"

Mark shook his head. "No, my aunt. This is her place. I'm only helping out for a short bit."

"Where did she go?"

Mark turned, preparing to tell him that she was simply "away," but he paused. The old man reminded him of a venerable actor whose name he couldn't remember. Mostly black-and-white movies. Always played forthright roles. Mark couldn't lie. "Yes, about that . . ." He lowered his voice: "Can you keep a secret?"

George nodded. "Sure."

Mark pushed the door mostly closed. "She passed away a couple days ago."

The folds in George's skin recessed into deep grooves, and his lips fell flat, colorless. "I'm very sorry to hear that." His sorrow seemed genuine. "But why is it a secret?"

"Emily doesn't know."

"Who's Emily?"

"The one-eyed girl downstairs."

"Oh, right. Emily." George scratched his head. "Why can't Emily know?"

"Because I don't run this bed and breakfast. I'm only here because my aunt died."

"Then why are you letting guests stay?"

Mark smiled. "I had no intention of letting anyone stay, but Emily had nowhere to go and I felt sorry for her. As for you . . ."

George grimaced a tacit apology. "So Emily doesn't know you're not the owner."

"I *am* the owner."

"You know what I mean."

He briefly glanced down. "She thinks my aunt left me in charge—in a sense, that's exactly true. I am in charge. She just doesn't know the rest, and she doesn't need to know. She's the type who'd get all uptight about it. She'll be gone tomorrow, anyway. No harm, no foul, right?"

"Take it from me, son. Be careful. I know all about getting in trouble with women."

"Like I said, she's leaving tomorrow. She'll be no worse for the wear."

"So we're spending the night at a stranger's house."

Mark gave him a wry smile. "All three of us, really. But how's that different from any other hotel?"

George shrugged and nodded. "I suppose you're right. And I appreciate you taking me in. I had nowhere else to go."

"We all have the same goal: to leave Manistique. You'll be heading for the next casino in the morning. Emily will get her car fixed and be on her way. And I'll meet with a real estate agent tomorrow and be on my way soon too."

"You're not thinking about keeping it?"

Mark smiled. "What would I do with it? I live in Chicago."

"Run it."

He laughed. "That's funny. I don't know the first thing—"

"That's clearly not true. You have two guests."

Mark shook his head. "Ask Emily what kind of host I am."

"What's your occupation? When you're not pretending to be running hotels, that is."

"I'm an independent financial planner."

"Sounds interesting."

Mark chuckled. "It's not. It's mostly dull. How about you? What are you retired from?"

"High school shop and PE teacher."

"If I could do it all over again, I'd be a high school history teacher."

"Why didn't you?"

Mark shrugged. "I don't know."

"Kind of ironic though, isn't it?"

"What is?"

"You wanted to teach history but instead you plan for people's futures."

"Hmm. Never thought of it that way. You're right," Mark said. "Well, have a good night. Breakfast will be ready by eight."

"Breakfast? See, you *are* good at running this place."

"Wait until after you've had breakfast before you rate me."

"Okay. Good night."

"Good night." Mark closed the door behind him.

Chapter Twelve

The magazine lay open on Emily's lap, though she stared dazedly into the dim fire. She tried to remember something—anything—about Sarajevo, but nothing came to her quickly. She was so young when she left there.

Her phone vibrated in her pocket. She leaned to one side, wriggling her hand into her jeans to dig out the phone. John. She was wrecked again—she supposed she could still go to Mackinac, one day late, but the image of the dead deer kept popping into her head. An accident or a sign? The road ahead was empty and lonely. The road back was full of angst and insecurity. The phone stopped.

She soothed herself with controlled breathing. The phone went off again. She exhaled and answered.

"Hey, it's me."

"Hi, John. How are you?"

"I won't lie," John started, in a vulnerable tone he only ever used over the phone. "I'm a little lonely."

"Sorry."

"How about you?" he asked. "Where are you?"

"I'm at a hotel for the night."

"What town are you in?"

"Oh, some small town, an hour or so away."

"So you still think they'll have your car fixed in the morning?"

"First thing, is what they told me."

"So you should be on the island before noon."

Emily's stomach twirled. "I suppose."

"I can't wait to see you. You'll be so excited with my news. But it has to be in person."

She heard steps and said, "Okay. Listen, I've got to run. Bye."

"Miss you," was the last thing Emily heard as she removed the phone from her ear and ended the call. She buried the phone back in her pocket.

Emily lifted the magazine and watched over the top of it as Mark slowly came down the steps. His feet, legs, torso, then head.

"Hey, your patch is off!" Mark exclaimed at the bottom of the stairs. "Are you upset because I called you Cyclops?"

"No, but thanks for that. To tell you the truth, I didn't really ever need it."

"I don't understand." He glanced over at the fireplace. "I should add a log," he said to no one. "So why were you wearing it in the first place?"

Emily shrugged. "Because it makes the doctor feel good if he thinks he's made the patient feel better."

He picked up a log and threw it on the fire. "You didn't tell the doctor that you're a doctor?"

Emily shook her head. "When you stay at an inn, do you say, 'Hey, I run a bed and breakfast in Manistique?'"

Mark laughed. He picked up the poker and shoved the logs. The fire briefly erupted. "No, because I don't run a bed and breakfast."

"You could have fooled me."

"All I can say is that it's a good thing you had the patch on when you showed up. Otherwise I wouldn't have felt so bad for you."

"What do you mean by that?"

"I mean I probably wouldn't have let you stay if you didn't look so . . ."

"So *what?*"

He shrugged. "So pitiful."

"Gee, thanks."

"Don't take it personally."

"No, I'll take it as a compliment."

"You know what I mean," he said, then pressed his lips together. "You let George stay, and he's not wearing a patch."

"I didn't have much of a choice."

"Why not?" she asked.

"Because you told him you were a guest here. I couldn't refuse him after that."

Her eyes shot back up to him. "So it's my fault? He let himself in!"

"You're right," he admitted. "It's my fault. I should have locked the door. In fact . . ." He rushed to the front door and locked it. "There. That should keep guests out."

Emily laughed incredulously. "You are the strangest hotel manager I've ever met. You're supposed to want guests."

"I told you, my aunt runs this place. I'm only babysitting. Would you like a glass of wine?"

Emily shook her head at him.

"No?"

"No, I do want wine. I was just shaking my head at you."

"Because I don't want more guests?"

"Yes!"

He waved her off. "Do you want white again? I got a Chardonnay."

Emily put up her best endearing smile. "Yes, please."

"I'll be right back."

Emily pulled up the magazine, *UP Traveler*, and began reading an article about Pictured Rocks National Lakeshore on Lake Superior. When Mark returned, he carried two empty wine glasses in one hand and an opened bottle in the other. He set the glasses on a tray on the coffee table and filled her glass two-thirds of the way.

"Wow, thank you," she said.

He poured a smaller portion into his glass.

"Is George in his room?" She knew the answer but wanted to make conversation.

Mark nodded and sat down across from Emily. "I asked him if he wanted some wine, but he said he was done for the night." He looked at his watch. "It's not even eight. Arguing with your wife must be exhausting."

"Wonder what they argued about."

He shrugged. "I don't know." Then he smirked. "Maybe she let a stranger into their room."

"It wasn't my fault!"

"I know, I know." Looking away, he added, "Nothing ever seems to be your fault."

"What do you mean by that?"

"Nothing—just kidding."

Emily shifted her body slightly toward the fire and watched it. She downed a large amount of wine. "I make mistakes," she blurted.

"We all make mistakes."

She gazed at Mark, who looked away. "But have your mistakes ever caused a death?"

His eyes seized back on her. "What?!"

"Of course not," she said evenly. "You manage people's money. No one dies if you make a mistake."

Mark stayed silent. She drank more wine, and then stared at the fire once again.

They sat in silence, the incomplete confession lingering in the room. She drank in small sips and only saw Mark out of the corner of her eye, imagining what he thought of her. Crazy. Unstable. Fraudulent.

Emily slipped off her shoes and tucked her feet under her—gauche or not, she only barely considered it. "It happened a few months ago," she said without looking at him. "On New Year's Eve."

After performing hernia surgery on a ten-year old boy, Dr. John Bulcher gave Emily some instructions. This disappointed Emily bitterly. She believed he had planned the surgery in order to surprise her—that he would relieve the resident on duty that night so they could watch the ball drop together. Though it would have been unusual for John to stay, the surgery's timing was unusual too, and it would have provided sufficient cover. Instead, before leaving, Dr. Bulcher asked Emily to keep an eye on the doctor running the floor that night, Dr. Greg Olsen, known to the medical staff as an unconfident resident, regularly second-guessing himself and frequently paging the attending for advice. Dr. Bulcher planned to be at a party that evening and wanted to have a couple of drinks without worrying about Olsen calling him. Emily complained that she was just an intern and couldn't be expected to babysit Dr. Olsen, but Dr. Bulcher simply reiterated his trust in her.

It was later that night when the boy, Nicholas, started complaining about pain. Dr. Olsen quickly increased the prescribed pain medication to the maximum dosage. Emily relaxed. Perhaps Olsen had finally matured into his role.

Not long after Emily shared a glass of sparkling apple cider with the nurses, Nicholas's mother came out of his room. The boy's intense pain had returned. Emily followed Olsen back to the room and watched him intently as he wrung his hands. He couldn't increase the dosage again, so Emily spurred him on, enumerating the pertinent clinical questions, the ones Dr. Bulcher surely would have asked him. How was his blood pressure? Normal. Temperature? Normal. How did the incision look? Everything checked out fine. Emily suggested a different pain medication. Olsen agreed.

Two hours later Nicholas's mother came out to the nurses station, worried that something was really wrong. Nicholas's intense pain was back, and it was worse. Dr. Olsen and Emily conferred. He discussed paging Dr. Bulcher, but Emily—imagining him inebriated—asked what they could do without disturbing the attending. Olsen suggested an increase in the second pain medication, but he still felt that Dr. Bulcher should be consulted. Emily steered him to wait, and he agreed that if this medication didn't work, they would immediately page Dr. Bulcher.

At seven in the morning, with no other disturbances in the night, Emily and Olsen met at the nurses' station ready to begin the morning rounds. They shared a smile and headed for the first room when an alarm went off. Alarms went off regularly. But Emily sensed that something was wrong. She looked at the monitors. Nicholas's blood pressure was low.

When Emily arrived at the room, the boy was unconscious. She tried waking him up, but nothing. Olsen put the cuff around the Nicholas's thin arm and did a manual reading, then yelled out, "Code Blue!" By the time the emergency crew arrived, Nicholas had flatlined. Emily, who was performing CPR, was pushed out of the way as the emergency crew attempted to resuscitate the boy. They carted him to surgery, but Emily knew. It was all too late.

Emily told Mark this story, except the part about her relationship with Dr. Bulcher. "He was my close mentor," was her full description. Mark had remained silent throughout, but now he said, "That Dr. Butcher shouldn't have forced you into such an awkward situation."

She turned to him with tight lips. "It's Bulcher, and he—"

Mark's cell phone rang. He glanced at it and said, "Sorry, do you mind if I get this?" He got up before Emily could answer. He dashed toward the door, pulled on it, sighed, and unlocked the bolt. As soon he opened the door, he answered, "Hey," and shut the door behind him.

This was the first time she had told the story to anyone—to a man she barely knew, who briskly abandoned her at the ring of his phone. The heaviness of the storytelling caused an ache in Emily's chest. And now that morning played over and over in her head again. . . . She hid in the stairwell, in shock, trapped in an unreal world hoping that a series of *Why didn't I?* questions might result in time travel if tried enough. She was eventually found and summoned to the surgery room. There, she was left alone for several minutes. It was impossible to reconcile the lifeless body under a thin sheet with the boy who'd had his whole future in front of him just a couple of hours earlier. All of it gone in an instant. Something fell over her like hot goo from her head all the way down to her feet. Nauseated, punch drunk, she summoned all of her strength to hold herself together, to stop herself from wishing that she were gone, too.

Emily quickly downed the rest of her wine. Edging toward a precipice of depression, her mind jumped to Sarajevo. . . . Sarajevo and Vivian, and the driver, Ratko, who had just dropped Vivian off at a bullet-hole-riddled door.

Feeling sufficiently reckless, Emily got up, determined to retrieve *Doctors on the Borderline* from the basement. The getaway magazine in her hand, she strode to the front door and peeked between the panels of sheer curtain. Mark was at the bottom of the stairs talking. She softly locked the door and walked briskly to and through the kitchen. At the basement stairs, she eased up, her head whirling enough that she needed to cling to the railing on the way down. In the bedroom she grabbed the book and hid it, pinched inside the magazine. It wasn't until she was climbing the basement stairs that she heard knocking on the front door.

As she approached the door, the knocks grew louder with shouts of "Emily!" When she finally opened it, Mark gave her a probing look. "Did you lock the door?"

Emily nodded, the book and magazine tucked tightly against her body. "I didn't want to be blamed for any other guests staying here."

He shook his head. "Nice."

Emily shrugged and forced a smile. She turned, a bit too quickly, and wobbled.

"Are you okay?"

"Yes," she returned, dashing toward the stairs. She felt as if she were keeping her balance on an angled plank.

"Wait. Where are you going? Sorry, I had to take that call."

She continued without looking back at him. "Don't worry about it. I'm tired, that's all."

"Oh. Good night then." His tone was softer.

"Good night."

Emily reached the top of the steps, and after entering her room, she locked the door and eagerly fell into the bed, searching for where she had left off . . ."The Gang."

My lucky flashlight illuminated the way through the dark hall to the front lobby. There was a close-knit confluence of people talking/smoking in dim light, and automatically I felt out of place. A few eyes fell my way . . .

Chapter Thirteen

Mark woke up a little after six, the cold glow from the narrow basement window prodding him. Sitting up on the couch, he rubbed the slight ache in his neck. He yawned twice and eagerly yearned for a bed—his own bed and his own perfectly stuffed pillow back home. Sleeping in Vivian's bed wasn't an option he'd considered and sleeping in one of the guest rooms upstairs had struck him as odd. He got up and dressed for a run. A run, a shower, a shave. Make breakfast for the guests. And then get rid of them. He grunted a laugh, groggily wondering how he had gotten to this point, where he was sleeping on the basement couch and had two guests upstairs.

The stairs creaked as he climbed to the kitchen. He felt uneasy moving through the quiet house, whose walls and reverberations were still foreign to him. About to walk out the back door, Mark caught the faint smell of coffee. He noticed a soft blue glow from the coffee machine. Emily or George?

In the dining room, he found George sitting at the table with a small flashlight in his hand and a book and a mug in front of him.

"Why are you sitting in the dark?"

"I have a flashlight," he answered defiantly. He flung the light in Mark's eyes.

Blocking the beam with his hand, Mark said, "I mean, why don't you turn on a light? Or better yet, there's a den over there with a comfortable chair. It's full of old books."

The old man pointed the flashlight at the ceiling. He shook his head adamantly, with a slightly pouty grimace—at least that's how he appeared in the dim light.

"Why not?"

"The smell of old books makes me want to go."

"Go where?" Mark asked before he got it. "Oh. Really?"

He nodded. "If I walk into a library, I head straight for the restroom."

Mark didn't understand this, but it was much too early for this topic, so he let it go. "What are you reading?"

Flipping the book to the cover, he shined the light on it. *Speak, Memory.*

Mark nodded. Nabokov. "You like Russian authors?"

"Sure, but what's that got to do with Nabokov?"

"I thought he was Russian, no? *Nyet?*"

"Dostoyevsky. Tolstoy. Chekov. Pushkin. Those are Russian authors. Nabokov wrote most of his novels, at least his famous ones, in English."

"I see."

George lifted the mug. "I hope you don't mind. I used the coffee machine and made myself a cup. I have one just like that at home."

"Great. Later you can show me how it works."

At the sound of a crackle, Mark surged toward the fireplace. "I totally forgot."

"Forgot what?"

"The fire." There were a few embers left, mostly buried by a pile of ashes. He stuck his hands out. *It's still warm,* he thought. *That's all it needs to be. A little warm.* He threw on another log. "I was supposed to get up in the middle of the night—it doesn't matter."

"I was perfectly warm all night," George said.

Mark smiled. "Good, good," he said, breezing by George into the kitchen to fetch paper bags.

When he returned, the log had already started burning. He didn't think the embers had been hot enough to get it going again. He tossed the bags into the fireplace anyway and watched them smoke, flash, and burn rapidly.

"I like that vase," George said pointing his flashlight at the mantel.

Mark nodded. "So you ready to leave Manistique?"

George shrugged. "I don't know. It's kind of nice here. I could stay."

Mark laughed. "Are you serious?"

"I guess I should wait to see what breakfast is like."

"Oh you mean stay here. I thought you meant stay in Manistique."

"Couldn't really say. I haven't seen much besides the casino and the little downtown. But it seems like a quiet community. Lakeside. I heard there's a new hospital being built. What else does a man my age need?"

A cemetery . . ."If you really want to stay in this house, you can just buy it. I'll give you a great price."

"Are you selling it?"

"Yes."

"I'm fairly certain I'm not up for running a hotel."

"You don't have to run it as a hotel. You can just live here."

He craned his neck and stared up at the ceiling. "You know, I don't really remember how it all started with her."

"What? Oh, your disagreement?"

He answered with a slow, steady, pensive nod. "I mean how am I supposed to apologize? For what?"

"Maybe she doesn't remember either."

George grinned. "You're right."

Mark shrugged. "I guess you'll know soon enough."

"Yes. By the way," he said, pointing up, "that bed is very comfortable. More comfortable than the bed at the hotel. You should mention that in your promotional materials."

Mark laughed. "Sure, I'll do that. Do you want the light on?"

George shook his head. "I kind of like the quiet of the dark."

"All right. I better go for my run so I can be back in time to make breakfast. It is a bed and breakfast after all. I've got to play the part, right?"

"Maybe I'll go for a walk myself."

Mark returned to a quiet house, too hot after his hard run. He had run east until he reached the lake, then along the lakeshore trail to the Manistique River. He pushed himself on the way back. Almost four miles, most of it along the lake, all of it under a gray sky. For about two miles, he obsessed over Emily. He had no physical attraction to her, yet he yearned to be with her, to talk to her, to fill the hole from the night before—the quick ending between them had disquieted him. She'd revealed something quite personal and had certainly expected some kind of sympathetic embrace. The implication was clear: Emily felt at fault for the death of the boy. He regretted taking that call from Frank Walters. But how to revive last night's conversation with Emily now? Before she left for good. It'd be nauseatingly difficult. Like serving cold pop and cereal for breakfast.

George was not in the dining room, and Mark figured the old man had gone for a walk after all. With the fire burning gently around the log, he headed down to the cooler basement to get ready for the day.

It was a little after eight when Mark returned to the main floor of the house. There was still no one around, though he heard floorboards creaking up above. After tinkering with the single-serve coffee maker for a minute, he brewed a cup. At the sound of a series of quick, soft steps down the stairs, Mark walked out of the kitchen to greet Emily, who was wearing a robe and socks. Her hair was tamed, and her cheeks glowed crimson on an otherwise blanched face.

"Good morning," he said.

"Good morning," she said, yawning. "Excuse me."

"Did you sleep all right?"

She nodded. "Yeah, really well. I don't usually get up this late. That bed is awfully comfortable."

"I've heard."

Emily pulled a chair from the table and picked up a book on the seat. "Is this yours?"

Mark shook his head. "No, George's."

"Why is it on the chair?"

Mark shrugged. "Maybe he's saving a spot for breakfast."

She tossed it on the table. "I hate Russian writers." She moved to the chair at the head of the table.

"I don't think Nabokov is really considered to be a Russian writer."

"Isn't he Russian?"

"Yes, but—"

"So he's a Russian writer," she snapped.

"You always this cranky in the morning?"

She glared at him. "Only before I've had my coffee."

"In that case . . ." He stepped into the kitchen, grabbed the mug, and came back out. "I got a fresh cup for you right here."

She took it, eyeing him a little suspiciously before sitting down.

"I just made it a minute ago—do you want cream or sugar or something?"

"No." She closed her eyes and angled her face toward the cup. She took a sip, then hummed an ecstatic sigh. "I guess I'm the last one up."

"Yep. George has been up since—I don't know—before six."

Mark stood there in silence for a moment, Emily drinking her coffee. He clammed up, desperately wanting to make amends for the previous night, but he didn't want to bring it up, either.

"What time is checkout?" she asked.

"Checkout?"

"Yeah, you know, when people have to leave their rooms."

"Yes, I know what checkout is. It's just that I'm leaving here around nine thirty—I'm dropping George off at his hotel, and then I have an appointment."

"What time is it now?"

"Eight fifteen."

"I better go get ready then."

"Don't rush on my account. You can leave whenever you want."

"Really?"

"Sure."

She thought for a second. "Yeah, that would be great, actually. Thanks."

"No problem." *Just don't let any other guests in*, he wanted to say jokingly, but he withheld it.

"Where is George, by the way?"

"On a walk, I think. I haven't seen him since I went for a run. He's been gone for a while—tell you the truth, I'm a little concerned."

"Why?"

He shrugged. "I don't know. Small things, I guess."

"Like what?"

Senility. But he couldn't say that to Dr. Emily. She'd retort with some kind of medical jargon. "Like, he can't remember what he and his wife were arguing about?"

"People forget why they started arguments all the time."

"An argument where you left the hotel you were staying in?"

A thin frown emerged. "I suppose you're right."

"Maybe he's in his room." He started for the stairs. Emily followed him up, stopping in front of her room as Mark continued down the hall. He knocked on the partially open door to George's room. "Hello?" he said, reluctantly entering. "George?"

He wasn't there. Mark did find the old man's clothes hanging neatly in the closet.

"Not there?" Emily asked when he stepped out into the hallway.

Mark shook his head, "No, but . . ."

"But what?"

"He unpacked all his things. Should I be worried now?"

"Maybe he likes it here so much he wants to stay," she said with a grin.

He frowned. "Not funny. The tour bus is leaving this morning."

Emily pointed behind her. "Well, I'm going to go get ready. I'll be down in half an hour."

"I'll go make breakfast."

But breakfast was not on Mark's mind as he rushed down the stairs and out the front door. He worried that George had wandered off and wouldn't be back in time to catch the bus. Under the morning sky, still gray with clouds that gave no sign of retreat, he looked about the street, end to end. Where had the old man gone?

Emily finished packing her toiletries and closed her suitcase. From the nightstand, she grabbed *Doctors on the Borderline*, hidden beneath the *UP Traveler* magazine as if it were a banned book. She flipped through to find her place, skimming until she got to the point she had left off, mid-chapter, and quickly read:

I kept busy the rest of the day, gathering information on the other clinics in the city. My sources were mainly hotel employees and locals, like Rijad, who came and went either assisting journalists or trying to sell something. Eventually I made my way to the second floor to see the journalists. I wanted to hear their opinion of how safe they thought it would be for medical staff. ("A good doctor is one who is breathing," my boss at MSF headquarters always liked to remind me.)

Overall I had a fairly complete rough sketch of the medical situation and safety issues. Both were bad and getting worse. But I wanted to work in the hospital for a few days before reporting anything back to MSF. The next morning I'd be starting a twenty-four-hour shift at the hospital—hell inside hell, as Rijad called it.

I awoke the next morning thinking for the first time about the siege and the Serbs inflicting pain. The night had been filled with rumbles, just intermittent enough to startle and frighten and terrorize people all night. The insanity of this place was taking hold as reality. It's strange how the hyperawareness doesn't allow for reflecting—only surviving and being more hyperaware, as if there is only so much a mind can take and reflecting takes a backseat. Like watching a movie, then reflecting on it later. I was able to think about it now as I lay in bed: The Serbs lobbing mortars into a city of civilians, sniping at people trying to get food and water, destroying thousand-year-old libraries and landmarks.

Emily shut the book for now, figuring she could read freely after Mark left for his appointment. It was nearly nine o'clock when she headed downstairs and found no one about. The book from that Russian writer was exactly where she had left it. There was no breakfast out. She called for Mark before entering the kitchen. She went to the edge of the basement stairs and called again. No reply.

Back at her room, she found a Post-it note stuck on her door. "Went looking for George. If he comes back, call me." And he'd left a number underneath.

"That's a stupid place for a note," she said aloud, yanking the note off the door.

She got out her cell phone and dialed his number.

"Is George with you?" Mark asked anxiously.

"No, I—"

"I've been driving around for half an hour, and I can't find him."

"Where are you?"

"I don't know. Not far. I'm going in and out of streets here—Uh-oh."

"What?"

"I'm being pulled over."

"Seriously?"

"Yeah. Gotta go."

Emily hung up and stared at the phone for a second. Then she went to George's room and stood in front of the closed door. The Indian Lake room. *Violation of privacy*, she thought. But if he was really lost, her prohibited entry was for good reason. She opened the door and crept in. She checked the bathroom. Nothing on the counter. She pulled on the mirrored medicine cabinet. Inside she found two pill bottles. The first one was a statin. High cholesterol. The other was a memantine. Emily immediately got out her phone and dialed Mark.

Emily heard laughter over the phone. "Hello?" she said.

"Sorry. Hold on."

"What's going on? Hello?"

"Found George."

"You did?"

Mark cleared his throat. "Yeah, yeah. The trooper had picked him up."

"Oh good." There was a commotion in the background. "What's going on?"

"The trooper knows you. We were just talking about your—" His voice was cut off.

"Huh?"

"Nothing. Never mind. Connection's not good. We'll be back in a few."

"Are you guys talking about me?"

The call ended.

Emily forcefully shut the medicine cabinet and left George's room with an indignant edge. "They're making fun of me," she huffed, then went back to her room and made up her mind. She stuffed the few remaining items into her suitcase. As she lifted it off the bed, she saw the book on the nightstand. She grabbed it, thinking about stuffing it into her suitcase.

A car door thudded closed, and she set the book back on the nightstand. Mark or his aunt might wonder how the book got into her room, but she didn't care. She stomped down the stairs, setting the suitcase near the door.

The front door opened a minute later. Mark stepped inside and held the door as George followed.

"Good morning there," George said sprightly to Emily.

"Everything okay with you?"

"Just fine," he answered, his eyes glittering with youthful ignorance.

Mark closed the door and looked at his watch. "We need to get going soon," he said to George.

George nodded. "Yes, indeed." But he didn't budge.

"When you have your suitcase ready, call me. I'll bring it down."

"Thank you, sir," he said and started for the stairs at his slow pace.

Emily stared at Mark watching George go up the stairs. Her ire at him had subsided to annoyance. When George reached the top of the stairs and disappeared completely, Mark turned toward Emily. "So it turns out the trooper picked up George walking east on Highway 2 and was looking to bring him back to the house when he pulled me over."

"Why did he pull you over?"

"For barely running a stop sign."

"He give you a ticket?"

Mark shook his head. "No. I apologized and told him I was frantically looking for an elderly man. He immediately pointed to his car and asked if his passenger was the guy. Imagine my surprise . . . So why did you call me? The second time."

Emily's head fell. She wanted to tell him about the Alzheimer's medication she'd found, but some sort of twisted doctor-patient confidentiality ethic prevailed. She glanced back up and shook her head. "Why were you guys laughing at me?"

"At you?" He waved his hand erratically, grinning. "No, nothing, just the whole situation. I'm just glad we found him." He looked at his watch. "I've got to get going soon—which reminds me. I'm so sorry about breakfast. There's cereal and milk—and bear claws!"

She pursed her lips. "Thanks. I'll be fine."

Mark headed toward the stairs. "Is that your suitcase? Looks like you're rarin' to get the heck out of Manistique."

"Sort of. Actually, do you think you can drop me off at the car dealership on your way?"

"Sure."

"I should be there, make sure they're actually working on the car."

Mark nodded. "That's not a bad idea. Leave your suitcase here, though. I'll give you a key. Hopefully, you're gone by the time I get back."

"Gee, thanks."

"No, no," Mark said, his face flushing. "I mean I hope—you know what I mean."

Mark set the urn in the trunk of the car, positioning it snugly up against George's suitcase and the wall of the trunk.

"I really like that vase," George remarked.

Mark smiled and closed the trunk. "Ready to go?"

George nodded. Emily was already in the back seat.

"We're going to drop Emily off at the car dealership," Mark said as they got going.

"You buying a new car?" George asked her.

Emily snorted, "No."

Mark wasn't sure of George's game, whether he was playing along as if he hadn't heard about her car or if this was something else.

"A deer hit my car," she continued.

"What do you mean a deer hit your car? Were you driving?"

Mark shuddered. Now the old man was simply being provocative.

"Of course," she exclaimed. "Deer don't just run into parked cars, do they?"

George shrugged. "I suppose not. You just have an unusual way of describing it. So what kind of damage did the deer do?"

"The windshield is shattered, and the side mirror broke off. They had to get the windshield from another town."

Mark slammed the brakes. A loud thud came from the back of the car. "Sorry. It's the same stop sign I missed earlier."

"It's in an awful spot behind that tree," Emily said.

"And his bad memory," George quipped.

Emily laughed. "What's in the trunk, anyway? A dead body?"

Mark shook his head at both of them. "It's the suitcase. I should have secured it better," he said. Flashes of a cracked urn horrified him—George's suitcase dusted with *cremains*!

He made a gentle right turn toward town.

"Where do you live, young lady?" continued George.

"Actually, I'm in between places. I'm heading to my parents' house, but I'll only be there for about a month."

"Do your parents live in the UP?"

"No, they're in Appleton."

"Appleton is a nice town. Where are you going after that?"

"Chicago."

"She's a doctor," Mark added. He pulled into the dealer's parking lot. "She's starting her residency."

"Good for you. Congratulations."

"Thank you. It's been a long journey," she said, suddenly sounding exhausted. She opened the car door. "Thanks for the lift."

"Sure thing."

She got out but held the door open. "Where should I leave the key if you're not back?"

"Under the doormat is fine."

"Oh! I never paid you. How should I pay you?"

Mark shook his head. "Don't worry about it."

"Really? But—"

"Let's just call it a graduation gift. Good luck with your car. Maybe we can catch up in Chicago."

"I'd like that. I'll leave my number on the table." She kept the door open for an extra second. They held each other's gaze, as if more needed to be said before they parted for good. When she shut the door, the thud felt too permanent. He saw the future. Holding a piece of paper with her number but never calling her. Too awkward after so long. *Hey, it's me, Mark, the guy you stayed with in Manistique two months ago. Remember? I really should confess something . . .*

Mark watched Emily head into the dealership.

"I didn't pay you, either."

"Well I'm not really running a hotel, so it's not a problem."

"I still feel like I owe you something."

"It's okay. Really." Getting everybody out of the house was a gift in itself, Mark wanted to say. He drove slowly out of the dealership and made a long left onto Highway 2.

"That friend of yours is quite the catch," George remarked.

"Emily? No, no, she's not my friend. She was just a guest at the house."

"I didn't mean it that way. I only meant that she's impressive, being a doctor and all that. Kind of cute too. She's bubbly."

"Sure, you can call it that."

"It's not a bad thing in moderation. You're not married, are you?"

"No. And the fact that you spent the night at the house and not at the hotel makes me think I've made the right decision so far."

"What are you talking about?"

"Nothing."

"You should really consider things with her."

"Emily?"

"Yes. Why not?"

"She's not really my type."

"And what is your type?"

Mark shook his head. "Look, there are certain things I can't do in the morning, like drink pop or watch a movie, or talk about my likes and dislikes in women."

"Or gamble!"

"Sure, that either," he agreed, even though he'd never gambled. But if he did, he couldn't possibly do it in the morning.

"Well, I suggest you ponder it this afternoon, then."

"Sure," he answered dismissively. "Here we are." He slowed to turn left.

"The bus isn't even here yet," George said.

"Gives you time to smooth things over."

Mark parked in front of the lobby. He hurried to open the trunk before George got out. Relieved the urn was still intact, he pulled out George's suitcase.

"Thanks for everything."

"Sure thing. Good luck," Mark said. Before he left, he secured the urn in the passenger seat.

Chapter Fourteen

Mark, following the directions on his phone, drove a mile parallel to Lake Michigan, and then away from it as he headed north on a county road. The town quickly dissipated, giving way to farmland and forest on either side. A couple of miles from town, at a T-junction with a school-like building plopped on the corner, Mark turned west toward a forested area. Eventually homes appeared, at first between wooded lots, then more regularly, modest homes with spacious yards, a lakeside community, permanent homes for some, perhaps. A plywood sign in one of the empty lots was spray-painted: TRESPASSERS WILL BE VIOLATED.

When he turned left onto Birch Street, still laughing about the sign, he caught a glimpse of the lake. Not far down the narrow road, the street met the water of Indian Lake at the boat ramp where Bear Foot had said to meet him.

Mark parked on the shoulder, a few yards from where the road sharply curved left onto a lakeshore drive that cut in front of the homes there. He got out and looked about him; Indian Lake didn't seem very large.

"Well, here we are, Vivian," he said aloud, tapping the urn. "Indian Lake. You're Native American, huh? That sure was news to me."

To the right was a park, and where the grass stopped and a wooded area started, a series of old structures stood: wigwams of bark and logs, a small building, and a bell hanging from an open teepee-like structure. Atop the small building was a cross—a chapel. What was this place?

Mark got out, unbuckled the urn from the passenger seat, and carried it with him. He walked along the road to a nearby sign that stood at front of the park. The sign had a long inscription:

Near this site, on May 15, 1832, the Rt. Rev. Frederic Baraga, then a young Catholic missionary to the Indians, established and blessed his first church. A small building of logs and bark, it was built with the willing help of the Indians and dedicated "to the honor of God under the name and patronage of His Virginal Mother Mary." Until his death in 1868 Father Baraga labored selflessly in an area from Minnesota to Sault Ste. Marie, from Grand Rapids to Eagle Harbor. World famous as a missionary, he became upper Michigan's first Roman Catholic Bishop in 1853.

With the urn securely tucked under his arm, Mark perused the dwellings and an exhibit of food and tools. At the small chapel, he pressed his head against the window and was enthralled by the colors inside produced by the stained glass window. He barely noticed a gap in the bushes where an arrowhead pointed innocuously to the Indian Cemetery. He stepped a bit cautiously into a small clearing surrounded by maples where a dozen rectangular boxes sat like wooden crypts. A few of them were small—children. He stayed back, fearing some curse on White Man Who Traipses over Native Burial Grounds, though he wasn't really certain anyone was buried there.

Back at the chapel he made his way across the large lawn. The view of the lake mostly obstructed by birch and oak trees. When he saw that the lawn extended into another clearing on the opposite side of the park, he walked there. The view opened up to the lake in front of a shrine to the Virgin Mary. From there it was a different lake, a much larger lake, miles and miles of water.

Mark heard a truck engine echoing through the still morning and hurried back. The truck came from the other road, and sure enough, it was Bear Foot, towing a boat.

Mark waved. Bear Foot acknowledged him with a quick nod, turned right on to Birch Street, and stopped when truck and trailer were in line with the ramp.

"Good morning," Mark called out.

"Mornin'," he said and started backing the boat down the ramp. Mark wasn't afraid of water, but this was an aluminum skiff with an oversized outboard motor. It looked like a kid wearing grownup shoes.

Across the street on the corner a slightly unkempt white house on a large lot caught his eye—or rather an arrowhead-shaped sign caught his eye. The Arrowhead Inn, obviously shuttered. Mark's vigorous imagination revitalized and reopened this inn, returning it to the glory of summers past.

He laughed at himself. He didn't need a second inn—he didn't even want the first one. But he suddenly felt wistful, and a yearning to open and run an inn like that captured, prodded, and yanked on him.

Bear Foot got out and started untying the boat. Mark asked, "Can I help?"

"Yep. You can back up the truck in a couple minutes."

"Sure."

"The keys are on the seat."

Mark got into the old truck with the urn, setting it down on the bench seat, then waited for Bear Foot to signal him.

"Okay," Bear Foot said, walking toward the dock holding a rope. "Nice and slow."

He backed up the truck slowly, Bear Foot in the sideview mirror directing him with a raised thumb. A few seconds later, his whole hand went up. "Stop," he said.

Mark put it in Park and got out. The back truck tires were just touching the water, the trailer submerged, the boat afloat. With the rope, Bear Foot guided the skiff, which tilted slightly backwards. He tied the boat to the dock and hopped out.

"Should I pull the truck up?"

"Hang on," he said. He tugged on the starter.

There were several tries, but nothing. Bear Foot turned around.

"Darn. Motor's not turning. It started earlier."

Mark leaned on the truck with his elbow. Bear Foot fidgeted around for a few minutes, tugging on the starter a few more times before putting up his hands.

"It's not starting," he said in a disgusted tone. He pulled the boat back toward the trailer. "Pull the trailer out a few feet."

Mark got back into the truck and moved it up. "Is that good?"

"Yep."

Bear Foot jumped into the water and muttered something.

"Okay, pull it out onto the street," he said a moment later.

Mark drove it into the street and stopped. He grabbed the urn and got out, then approached Bear Foot, who was leaning down securing the boat to the trailer.

"I'm very sorry," Bear Foot said plaintively.

"It's not your fault. These things happen."

"It's my friend's boat, and he's had some trouble with the motor lately. But I started it this morning, so I thought it would be fine."

"Maybe it's a sign," Mark said.

"A sign? Of what?" he asked skeptically.

Mark was taken aback, thinking Bear Foot would have been all over that. "I don't know, just thought . . . it'll be fine. I'll just scatter the ashes from this dock here."

"No, that's not far enough, the waves will bring her all to shore." He stood up.

There's no her, Mark wanted to say. *Just ashes . . .*

"Look over there," Bear Foot pointed. "Providence."

Mark looked in the direction Bear Foot was pointing.

"Three houses down."

Mark spotted a hull, upside down, sitting on the shore like a beached animal. "What is it?"

"A paddleboat."

Mark wasn't convinced that it was actually *providence.* Paddleboating with Bear Foot struck him as treacherous. He was a large man, and Mark himself was six feet. "You really think we'll fit?"

"It will be okay. You'll see."

That's what Mark was afraid of—finding out in the middle of Indian Lake that the boat didn't support the two of them. Even if it was shallow, it looked cold.

Bear Foot finished with the trailer and pulled the truck up near the Arrowhead Inn sign.

Mark met him in the street. "Hey, is that cemetery over there real?"

Bear Foot nodded. "The buildings are reproductions."

"Interesting."

They started down the street. When they got to the house, Bear Foot headed toward the water.

"Wait. Shouldn't we ask first?"

"They won't mind."

"You know them?"

"No, but it's okay. You can go up to the door and knock if you'd like."

With Chicago sensibilities in mind, Mark walked up to the house, a charming cottage—white with blue trim, a hipped roof, and a pleasant front porch. He knocked on the door, holding the urn in his arm, ready to explain his situation. But Bear Foot had already started overturning the capsized paddleboat. Luckily, no one answered.

By the time Mark reached the lake, Bear Foot had already dragged the boat into the water and was gingerly stepping in. The front of the boat listed, planted on the small rocks near shore. Mark handed Bear Foot the urn, who laid it down in the back where there were seats for two more passengers. Then Mark stretched, setting one foot in, but he lost his balance and his other foot landed in the water.

"Whoa!" Bear Foot exclaimed.

"Dang it!" Mark quickly pulled his leg out and fell into the boat. He laughed. "I'm a klutz."

"Water's cold, huh?" Bear Foot said.

"Yeah."

The boat had mostly evened out, but now it was really planted into the rocky shore.

"Let's see if we can go," Bear Foot said. He began pedaling in reverse. Mark helped.

They started moving, but barely, the paddle blade scraping against the bottom. Finally they cleared the shore and reached deeper water, turned around and headed into the lake.

Two grown men in this tiny boat must look ridiculous, Mark thought.

"I haven't done this in a long time," Bear Foot said, beaming. "Since I was a kid."

The boat's edge barely topped the waterline. The lake was not entirely calm, but they paddled with the current and made quick progress.

"Do you ever fish here?"

Bear Foot shook his head. "No, there are better lakes. But there *are* fish here. Walleye and pike. But I like trout fishing, myself. This lake's too shallow."

Mark looked over the side, but he couldn't see the bottom. "If I were staying longer, I wouldn't mind fishing."

"Aren't you coming back?"

Mark shrugged, shook his head. "I don't think so."

"What about the house?"

"I'm going to sell it."

"That's a shame. Been in the family for so long."

"What do you mean?"

"The house—it belonged to Vivian's father."

This was news to Mark. His mother had never mentioned anything about living in the UP. Perhaps it had been a summer home.

Bear Foot steered. He had first kept them parallel to the shore for about a hundred yards, and now they were heading toward the dead middle of the lake, or at least what looked like the middle.

"How far are we going?"

Bear Foot pointed ahead. "Just up there."

Just up there was more water, and the other side of the shore was a long way off.

"How big is this lake?"

"Pretty big. Seven or eight miles by three miles or so."

They continued cruising slowly toward the center and, beyond it, the blue ridgeline of the opposite shore.

"Did you know Vivian well?" Mark asked.

"Yes." Bear Foot wiped his face with his hand. "I would keep an eye on the house when she was away. She'd be gone for long stretches."

"Do you know why she opened her house to guests?"

He shrugged. "She never told me exactly, but I always like to think of it as a return to her Chippewa roots."

"The Chippewa ran a chain of hotels?" Mark joked.

"No, only casinos." Bear Foot howled with laughter. Mark joined in, seeing Bear Foot get a kick out of his own joke. "I mean settling in one place," Bear Foot explained. "The Indians in this area moved south in the winter to the Lower Peninsula and never really called one place home."

Mark thought for a second, then replied. "I don't get it. What does that have to do with running an inn?"

"It's abstract, but think of the house like two places. In season it's a hotel and out of season it's her personal home. In season she moves her things downstairs, and then she moves back upstairs in the winter. Like living in two places. Besides, I think she got lonely."

Mark nodded. "I see," he said, but he didn't really understand it completely. His legs had started to tire, but more than that, his back hurt against the hard plastic. He mentioned none of this to Bear Foot.

"Okay, I think this is far enough," Bear Foot said and stopped pedaling.

They both just sat there for a long moment, swaying back and forth in the small current.

Mark reached back and for the urn. He pulled the lid off. He saw now that the ashes were contained inside of a plastic bag.

"One second," Bear Foot said and reached into his back pocket and fished out a folded piece of paper. "I'd like to read this first, a poem written by Jane Johnston Schoolcraft."

The lake was quiet. No one else was out on the water. Bear Foot read:

Awake my friend! the morning's fine,
Waste not in the sleep of the day divine;

Nature is clad in best array,
The woods, the fields, the flowers are gay;
The sun is up, and speeds his march,
O'er heaven's high aerial arch,
His gold beams with lustre fall
On lake and river, cot and hall;
The dews are sparkling on each spray,
The birds are chirping sweet and gay,
The violet shows its beauteous head,
Within its narrow, figured bed;
The air is pure, the earth bedight,
With trees and flowers, life and light,
All—all inspires a joyful gleam,
More pleasing than a fairy dream.
Awake! the sweet refreshing scene,
Invites us forth to tread the green,
With joyful hearts, and pious lays,
To join the glorious Maker's praise,
The wond'rous works—the paschal lamb,
The holy, high, and just I Am.

"Very nice," Mark said after a long moment of silence.

"Do you have any words for Vivian?"

Mark shrugged. "I don't know . . . no, not really."

Bear Foot thumped Mark twice in the chest with a fist. "From the heart. Just say anything."

"Um, okay." Mark felt awkward, and he wished he had added something extra to his coffee this morning, but it was only the two of them, so he looked at the urn.

"Dear Vivian, you were so inspiring. You did so much good for so many people. The world will miss you, very, very much." A solemn nod. "Very much."

"Yes, so true."

"Now?" Mark gestured toward the urn.

Bear Foot nodded. "Whenever you're ready."

Mark undid the tie on the plastic bag. If he had been alone, he would have simply turned the bag upside down and dumped the ashes into the lake. But for Bear Foot's sake, he wrapped the top of the bag over the urn's opening. He gently shook the urn, gradually coaxing the ashes into the water. Bear Foot pedaled forward slowly and turned the boat, keeping the wind to their backs.

When all the ashes were out of the urn, Mark looked back at the long line floating on the water. The ashes slowly dissipated underwater, creating a mesmerizing cloud beneath the surface. "It's done," he said. "We have returned her to nature. This is where Vivian wanted to be. She will stay here for a while, then flow through the river and into the Great Lakes."

"Yes," Mark said. A moment of solemn camaraderie passed between them.

"It's a shame Vivian's child couldn't be here with us," Bear Foot said.

Mark's head snapped in Bear Foot's direction. "What child?"

He shrugged. "Don't know. She once told me she had a kid. Put up for adoption."

"No one ever told me about that." He looked out over the water, shaking his head. That would be like Vivian. Got pregnant on some mission, dropped off the baby at the nearest adoption agency and ran off to another mission. . . . Frank Walters needed to know.

"Ready to head back?" Bear Foot asked.

Mark nodded, and they both started pedaling.

The current ran against them, and Mark noticed that they made very little progress. "Going back is much harder," Mark said. The houses on shore passed by very slowly.

"My legs are getting worn out," Bear Foot admitted.

A motor boat zipped by them in the opposite direction a hundred yards away. Mark felt silly. Bear Foot waved.

But they went on, taking a short breaks in turn, then making a burst of progress pedaling together. Nearly a half hour of cycling later, they were close, though the last hundred feet were the most difficult. The breeze felt good, a relief against the sweat of the workout.

Bear Foot was closest to shore, and he got out and pulled the boat closer to the rocky beach. Mark hopped out but slipped and landed in the lake again.

"You okay?"

"Fine. This is just not my day," he said, looking down at his pant leg, which was wet about halfway up his calf. They both pulled the boat across the rocks, and then Mark grabbed the urn. Bear Foot flipped the boat over.

"There's a towel in the truck if you want to dry off."

Mark nodded. "Thanks."

They headed for the truck. "Not exactly what we had in mind, but. . . ." Mark said.

"Yeah, that trip back was tough," Bear Foot said. "But we made it." He put up a high five. Mark slapped his hand.

"Yeah, we made it back," Mark agreed.

"My legs are rubber."

Bear Foot retrieved the towel out of the truck and tossed it to Mark, then got back on the boat and fidgeted with the motor.

"Where should I set this?" Mark asked after drying off as much as possible.

"Just throw it anywhere on the boat."

"Thanks again for your help," Mark said. "Couldn't have done it without you."

Bear Foot made a single nod. "Anything for Vivian."

Chapter Fifteen

On his way back to town to meet with the real estate agent, Mark called Frank Walters to let him know that Vivian had a child. There was no answer, so he left a message.

Ron was already at Jake's Bar when Mark arrived. Paunchy and middle-aged with dark brown hair in a bowl cut, Ron wore a long-sleeved blue shirt, khakis, and sneakers. His transition lenses kept a little tint inside the bar. Mark would have guessed Mikey's uncle rather than cousin, but perhaps they were second cousins or cousins once removed. Everyone around town seemed to be related in one way or another.

In his jolly manner, Ron described the slogging Manistique market, slinging out statistics—average days to sell, average selling price, average size house, acreage. Two hundred days to sell a $100,000 house didn't sound appealing, but Mark didn't blame Ron for that.

"He's got a guest staying there," Mikey said with a smirk as he dropped off beers.

Mark held up two fingers.

Mikey's eyes lit up. "Another girl?"

Mark shook his head. "One of the oldsters from the casino tour. Had a fight with the missus and ended up at the house."

"What?" Ron's eyebrows lifted.

"Don't worry. They're both gone now," Mark said. He glanced at his watch. It was a quarter past twelve. *Emily must have left by now.* A melancholy void opened up in him, like the contorted remorse he'd felt when a school year ended.

"Is this a house or a hotel?" Ron asked.

"It's a bed and breakfast. The Manistique Victorian."

"Really? You mean Vivian is your aunt?"

"Yeah. Did you know her?"

Ron nodded slowly and explained how he had met her a few times at commerce events in town. "I'm very sorry. I wish I had gotten to know her better."

Mark grimaced, nodding. He felt the same way.

"I remember the open house she had a couple years ago—seems like yesterday. She told me it was her dream to turn the house into a B&B."

"Grilled burgers and fries, guys?" Mikey called out.

Both said yes.

"Well I didn't realize you wanted to sell a business," Ron continued. "That's a little different."

"I don't, really, unless it helps."

"Depends on how it's doing."

Mark shrugged. "Beats me."

"You might get more for it if it's bringing in income, but it might take longer too."

Mark shrugged. "Not sure."

After lunch, they agreed to meet at the house.

"I need to make a quick stop at the office," Ron said.

"So you know where it is then, right?"

"Yep. I'll meet you there in ten minutes."

Mark thanked Mikey for lunch.

"Hey, if I get any customers who need a place to stay, I'll send them your way."

Mark laughed. "Don't you dare!"

The poem Bear Foot read reverberated in Mark's head as he drove back to the house. . . . *Awake my friend.* . . . As he approached, he spotted a parked car in front of the house. "Damn it!" Peter Hinton had arrived.

But then he recognized the red car as an all-electric Galvani and figured no traveler through this area would be in an electric car. Then again, who in this area could afford a $100,000 car?

Mark scanned the porch and yard. No one. And after turning the corner and seeing the side yard was empty, he felt relieved. Still, half expecting to be accosted by someone wanting to stay the night, he dashed to the back door.

When Mark entered the kitchen, he heard a voice, a man's voice. He slammed the door. What was it with people walking into someone's house? And he was upset with Emily for leaving the door unlocked.

Filled with determination to kick out whoever was there, he charged through the kitchen and into the dining room. Instead he became instantly tongue-tied. It took him a few seconds to process the entire scene and even longer to absorb it.

Sitting at the table, with a book in front of him: George. Standing in the living room: Emily. And sitting on the edge of the couch were two strangers, a man and a woman.

"What are you—" he started to say to George but then fired at Emily: "What's going on here?"

"These are your guests for tonight," Emily answered in a placating way, extending her palm toward the two strangers.

They stood up. "Sorry for being so early. I'm Peter Hinton," the man said.

A little shocked, Mark approached. "I'm Mark," he replied, then stumbled to add that Vivian was his aunt.

The man introduced the woman, Yvonne, before extending his hand. Mark didn't want to know people's names or shake hands. He wanted everyone to leave. But of course he was cordial and shook hands with the man.

"That's not your car out there, is it?" he asked.

He nodded. "It is. In fact, that's why we're here early. Vivian said I could charge the car here, in a 240 outlet," Peter said.

"She did?"

Yvonne added, "We don't need to check in yet. We just need to plug in the car in so that we can get to Munising."

"So you're not spending the night here," Mark said, hoping.

Peter nodded emphatically. "No, we are. We're just making a daytrip to Munising and then we'll be back later." He looked at his watch. "That is, if we plug in now. We only need to plug in for about half an hour right now." He checked his watch again. "So is the 240 outlet in the garage?"

"I suppose. I've never seen it." He tried to remain pleasant, but in his mind he was saying, *Vivian's dead. Everyone out!* "Bring your car around. I'll meet you out there."

Mark shot a glare at Emily.

"What?" she mouthed.

He gave her a brief, tight shake of his head.

Yvonne followed Peter out the front while Mark headed toward the kitchen. He darted through the back door and dashed across the yard to the garage.

Mark hadn't been in the garage—didn't even know if he could get inside. But of course the side door was unlocked. He flipped the nearby switch to light the windowless space. It was near pristine for a garage. Cabinets lined one wall. There were two bicycles and a lawnmower against another wall. And parked near the back of the garage, a motorcycle. He recognized it as a mid-sixties Triumph. He found the 240 near the motorcycle and pressed the button for the garage door. His car was a bit in the way, but there was enough room to pull in from the far side.

Mark pointed to the plug as the Hintons pulled in.

"Do you mind if I pull into the garage?" Peter yelled. Yvonne got out of the car.

Mark shook his head and stepped out of the way. He approached Yvonne, prepared to tell her that they could use all the electricity they wanted, but they couldn't stay.

"This is great of you," she said putting a hand out toward Mark before he could say anything. "If not for this place, we wouldn't have been able to make this trip."

"What do you mean?"

"Didn't you know? We're doing the circle tour around Lake Michigan in this car."

"The entire lake?"

She nodded enthusiastically. "The first all-electric car to do it."

"Wow. How far can you go on a charge?"

"Two hundred and some miles."

As he stepped out, Peter said, "A million thanks," and hurried to the trunk of the car, where he pulled out the charging cable.

Mark heard his name being called. It was Emily.

"Excuse me one second."

He met her on the path around the house. "There's someone at the door," she said.

"Shoot, that's right." Mark suddenly remembered. Ron, the real estate agent. "Is he in the house?"

"No, he's waiting on the porch."

"Well at least you've learned one thing," he said before hurrying toward the front of the house.

"What's that supposed to mean?!" she yelled out.

Mark ignored her. "Hey," he said to Ron.

Ron, standing on the porch, turned and started down the steps. "I sense a good story here," he said.

"And I don't even know the half of it yet," Mark said.

"More guests?"

"More and more of the same. The two that were supposed to be gone are back. Then these other people showed up."

"Maybe you should consider selling it as a business. Seems like a popular place."

Mark shook his head in disbelief. "These people that just arrived are driving around the entire lake in a Galvani."

"Electric car?"

"Yeah, apparently that's the point. To be the first ones to ever do it."

"Interesting," Ron said. "So you want to meet some other time?"

Mark nodded slowly. "Yeah, sorry, if you don't mind."

"Not at all. Just give me a call when you're ready. Good luck with your guests."

Mark inhaled deeply, fresh air filling his lungs, readying himself for George's story. But before he could walk inside the house, he heard someone call out, "Excuse me."

It was Peter Hinton. "The car isn't charging," he said.

Bear Foot immediately came to mind. Must be the electrical issue that Vivian had wanted him to look at. "I know exactly who to call."

Two suitcases sat in the entry. George was at the table reading his book, and Emily was nowhere in sight. "So what happened?" Mark asked, arms partially upright.

There was a confused look on his face. "With what?" He glanced down as if the question were about his book.

Mark laughed softly. Was he joking? "Why didn't you get on the bus? Did you have another argument with your wife?"

"My wife? Why would you say that? No, the bus left at nine."

"What? I thought it was at ten thirty."

"That's what I thought too!"

Mark shook his head. "And they left without you?"

He nodded. "Even worse, my wallet is missing, so I can't stay at the hotel. I had nowhere else to go, so I came back here."

Mark struggled between being touched and being annoyed. "Have you called her?"

"I did, but no one answered." He sneezed.

"Bless you."

"It's allergies." He pulled out a handkerchief and blew his nose. "I just took an antihistamine, so hopefully that'll help."

Mark pulled out his phone. "Let me try to call. What's her number?"

"You think she'll pick up if you call? She doesn't know you."

"Exactly. It's worth a try."

"I don't think she's mad at me."

"She left Manistique without you!" Mark instantly regretted his exasperated tone.

George glanced down at his phone and punched at it with his index finger. He read out the number.

Mark connected but only got a generic voicemail. He cancelled the call. "No answer. So what now?"

George shrugged. "I don't know. The bus went to St. Ignace."

"That's the town by the bridge, isn't it?"

He nodded. "Yes."

There was a noise in the kitchen, scuffling. "We'll figure something out," Mark assured him.

Emily stumbled through the kitchen doorway, struggling with two suitcases.

"What are you doing?" Mark asked.

"Oh, the Hintons wanted to leave their suitcases here."

Mark shook his head.

"Why are you looking at me like that?" she asked.

"Why are *you* carrying their luggage?"

Emily shrugged. "They feel like they're imposing for arriving so early. I offered to carry their stuff into the house while they went for a walk. They told me they'll be back in a half hour."

"Do they think you work here or something?"

"Um." Her eyes darted to the ceiling. "Maybe they thought that. I don't know. Maybe because I answered the door."

"You answered the door?"

"They had reservations! At least that's what they said. I thought I was helping you out."

"Yes! Right. Thanks." He forced a smile of gratitude. "What about your car? I thought you'd be long gone by now."

Emily sighed. "They haven't found the right windshield yet."

"Didn't they say they were getting one this morning?"

"They got the wrong one."

"Different species—that's not even funny anymore."

"No . . ." she admitted.

"I thought you'd be more upset."

"I was, believe me. I was livid at first, but what am I going to do?" She pointed her thumb behind her. "If those two get into a deer-car, they'll be here for a year. I mean, who drives that car through these parts?"

"Did they tell you what they're doing?"

Emily shook her head.

"They're trying to be the first people to drive an electric car around Lake Michigan."

"That's a thing?"

"Apparently. I take it you're spending the night again?"

Emily gave him a helpless frown. "If I can."

Mark nodded. "Stop it. Yes, it's fine. What's gotten into you?"

"What?"

"I don't know. I thought you'd be feistier about your car, and now you're carrying other people's luggage."

"I can be *feistier*," she fired back making air quotes, "if you want me to be."

"No, no, it's all right. Just checking that you're okay." He turned toward George. "As for you, how do we get you to St. Ignace?"

"You go east on Highway 2," Emily said, laughing.

"Very funny. Actually, since you're running things here now . . ."

"What do you mean by that?"

"Well, let's see, letting people in. Carrying their luggage," he said, gesturing to the door and suitcases.

"I thought I was being helpful."

"I know, I know. Thank you. Bear Foot is going to come by. Can you tell him the 240 in the garage isn't working?"

"Sure. Where are you going?" Emily asked.

"Driving him to St. Ignace, unless you have a better idea."

Emily shrugged, staring at George. She shook her head and sighed. "No."

He grabbed the Hintons' suitcases and set them next to the base of the stairs. He picked up George's suitcase. "All right, sir. Ready?"

Emily dashed over to Mark. "There's something I have to tell you," she said in a hard whisper.

"Yeah, okay."

She turned back toward George who was out of the chair and collecting his book.

"It's about . . ." she whispered, and gave a slight head jerk toward George.

"What is it?"

"I think he has a problem."

"Yeah, his wife abandoned him here—in Manistique of all places. Hopefully they'll work things out."

"No, I mean something else." She turned her head back and then sighed, looking up at Mark with worried eyes.

Mark set his hand on Emily's upper shoulder. "It'll all be fine once he's in St. Ignace. Worst case he can stay at the St. Ignace Victorian. My aunt runs a chain of these." He laughed.

Emily smiled, then asked, "Will your aunt be back before you return?"

"Where is Vivian?" George asked.

Mark gave George a sharp glance, and looked back at Emily. "She's not going to make it back this weekend." The formless ashes floating on Indian Lake flashed in his mind.

"Really?"

"Yeah, unfortunately."

Emily's phone rang. Her face soured when she saw the number. She turned and gave George a hug and kissed him on the cheek. "Good luck." She ran up the stairs, answering the phone.

What has gotten into her? Mark wondered. George was grinning. Someone cared. Mark wanted to be the one to give George the hug and let Emily drive him to St. Ignace.

Emily wondered if she had done the right thing, not telling Mark about the medication she had found in George's room. But what would he have done with the information? He was taking George back to the tour, and George's wife must have known about it—

"Emily?"

"Sorry. No. They got the wrong windshield, so it's not going to be ready today."

"Where are you? I'll come and get you."

Emily cringed. His voice had taken on that paternal tone. Dr. Bulcher was talking. *Dr. Butcher*, Mark had called him. "It's too far."

"Just let me come and get you. At least we can spend the rest of the day and tomorrow morning together."

Emily didn't respond.

"Where are you, Emily? What town?" He sounded exasperated. "There's only one more night here."

"Yes, I know."

"So where are you?"

Emily fell back into the bed and stared at the ceiling. "Manistique," she finally revealed.

"Okay. Where's that? How far away?"

Emily sighed. "It's over an hour away." She closed her eyes. "West of you." There, she had said it. It was over now.

"West? You mean south."

"*John*," Emily said softly.

There was a moment of silence, then, "Oh . . ."

"Yeah."

"But why didn't you tell me before?"

Emily took a deep breath. "I don't know. I was never sure. But the longer I'm away, the more I'm sure."

"You have to give me a reason."

Emily sat up. She couldn't enumerate the reasons out loud now. *Your wife and kids. Our age difference. A long-distance relationship. Nicholas. What about Nicholas?* "I can't do this right now." She ended the call.

He called back immediately.

Emily shut off the phone.

Chapter Sixteen

George flinched, then gasped. "I fell asleep." He straightened up and rubbed his face. "Sorry."

Mark turned off the radio and smiled. "I don't blame you. Those two were way too civil today. And that's a 'best of' show. You should've heard them yesterday."

George yawned. "Excuse me."

"We're almost there." Mark took a sip of lukewarm coffee. "We'll cross 75 here soon, then it's only another ten, fifteen minutes." He looked at the clock. Almost two thirty. An hour and a half back. Four o'clock.

"Thanks for driving me."

Mark briefly turned toward George, giving him a solitary nod. A few minutes later they passed over 75 and then headed south on a two-lane road surrounded by wildflowers on the shoulders and walls of evergreens beyond, their waxy needles dulled a bit by the perfect glare of the afternoon sky.

"How much do I owe you?"

"Let me check the meter . . ." Mark chuckled. "Forget about it. Just have a good time on the rest of your trip."

"I really don't know what I would have done without the two of you," George continued.

"Two? Who? Oh, you mean Emily." *What did she do?* He wanted to say, *She didn't drive an hour and a half each way so you could get to St. Ignace.*

"Yes, Emily," George said. "She's very sweet."

"At least she was this afternoon. Not sure why. I thought she'd be more up in arms about her car not being fixed."

"She's having car troubles?"

"No—well, yes. I mean, they didn't get the right windshield for her car."

"That's too bad."

After a curve in the road, a few houses appeared in a cut clearing, then a little further ahead was a gas station. George mumbled something.

"What?" Mark asked.

"Nothing."

"I don't see any hotels around here," Mark said. "Do you know where you're staying?"

George shook his head. "No, I don't."

The casino sign came into view a few hundred yards ahead. Mark turned left, onto a road that headed to a large parking lot. Off to the side was separate parking where several RVs and buses were stationed. He drove up to the front of the casino, a warehouse-like building made cozier by the gable of a protruding canopy and a stonework facade around the bottom.

"Déjà vu," muttered George.

"Yeah, another casino. Why don't you check inside and see if you can find anyone in your group? I'll park and meet you in the lobby."

George nodded. Slowly and stiffly, he disembarked. "Oh, and keep calling in case she's turned her phone back on. They might be at the hotel or in town," Mark said before George shut the door. In the second-to-last row, Mark found the nearest open spot. It was the Friday before Memorial Day weekend, after all, and it seemed that more than a few had gotten a jump on the holiday.

The lobby was magnificent, with high ceilings and exposed trusses and a shiny wood floor. Where the carpet began, several rows of slot machines rang and buzzed, and people sat pulling levers, jeering, cheering, but mostly sitting flat-faced. *It'll take George a while to find her here*, he thought. He went over to a small waiting area with red upholstered couches and chairs. A woman who looked to be in her seventies sat there knitting, with a large cloth bag next to her.

Mark looked at the map on his phone. The town of St. Ignace was few miles south. When he heard a merry jingle, Mark turned and watched the old woman fidget in her cloth bag. She pulled out a phone, looked at it for a second, and dropped it back in the bag.

The silver-and-gold-haired woman whisked the wisps of her bangs aside and went right back to knitting. Her small mouth kept a bit of a frown.

Mark got up, thinking she might be George's wife. He watched her hands, sunspotted and wrinkled, moving in perfect rhythm. He approached her, mesmerized by the movement and the soft scraping sound of the needles.

Her eyes shot up at him briefly.

"Are you by any chance—" Mark started to say.

"Are you a fan?"

Mark cleared his throat. "No. I don't know the first thing about knitting—actually, that's not true. I do know a little thanks to a show I listened to on the radio."

"Doris and Evelyn?"

"Yes! You listen to them too?"

"Sort of. I'm on the show. I'm Doris."

"Come on," he laughed. "You're pulling my leg." Her voice did sound similar, now that he thought about it.

"Correction. I *was* on the show."

"Was? What do you mean?"

"I quit yesterday. Station manager keeps calling me to come back, but I'm not going to."

"Why did you quit?"

She took in a deep breath. "I just got a little tired of the bickering."

Mark smiled. "I thought that was part of the shtick."

"Really?"

Mark wanted to say: *Do you think people want to listen to two old ladies in polite conversation?* Then, after staring at her for a second—she had an honest face, like George's, but more than that, she looked like she could handle the truth—he told her just that.

Doris smirked.

Mark's phone rang. "Excuse me." He recognized Emily's number.

"Hey, you're not going to believe—" he started, but she interrupted him.

"Bring George back."

"What? What are you talking about?"

"A woman from the Cozy Inn just dropped off his wallet and—"

"Forget it! I'm not driving George back just so he can get his wallet. I'll mail it to him."

"You're not listening. The bus just *came* from St. Ignace. They went west not east."

"What?" George's déjà vu. Of course. "I just drove all this way for nothing," Mark exclaimed. He headed toward the lobby. "The old coot."

"I was trying to explain this to you before you left."

"You knew?!"

"No, not exactly—only that he has some medical issues."

"What do you mean? What kind of issues?"

"Memory. Alzheimer's. Maybe other dementia, maybe even delirium."

"Delirium?"

"You've got to bring him back."

"But how do you know all this?" He had drifted into the lobby and his eyes scanned the area for George.

"I saw his meds this morning."

"And you didn't tell me?"

"I tried, but I . . ."

"But what?"

"There's doctor-patient confidentiality."

"He's a patient of yours?" he asked with sharp incredulity.

"No, not technically, but—"

"I need to find him." Mark scanned the crowd on the red-and-gold geometrically patterned carpet. "I don't see him."

"Be nice to him."

"Of course."

Mark waded through slot machines and video poker, dizzied by the bombardment of lights and sounds. After several minutes, he found George sitting at one of the blackjack tables toward the back of the casino. He was the only player.

"What are you doing?" Mark asked.

"Waiting for someone to turn up."

"While playing blackjack?"

"I only play blackjack. It's everyone against the dealer."

There was a stack of chips in front of him. "Where did you get money? I thought you didn't have your wallet."

"I have my wallet." George reached for his back pocket. "My wallet!" He stumbled getting off the chair. Mark grabbed him, then held him up. "Relax. You left your wallet back at the hotel."

"Vivian's hotel?"

"No—well, yes, it's there now. Where did you get the money to play?"

"I had a quarter in my pocket and I played a slot machine. I won twenty dollars and then sat down here."

Mark looked down at the chips—$5 chips. He figured twenty chips. "You've won here too?"

"Seems like it's my lucky day."

"We've got to go," Mark insisted.

"Where?"

"Back to Manistique."

"Why? I need to rejoin the tour."

"Your tour was already here, before Manistique."

George looked around for a second. "Yes, I thought so. But I wasn't sure. All these casinos look the same, don't they?" He collected his chips and thanked the dealer.

Mark and George drove west, the sky filled with tufts of high-up clouds as if cotton balls had been dropped to show the way back.

"I'm sorry," George said for the third or fourth time.

"No need to apologize." Mark was certainly frustrated but not angry. In his head he was already telling his friends the story over a beer and having a good laugh. Really, he felt sorry for the old man.

"I wasn't apologizing to you."

"Huh? Who then?"

"Trudy."

How could anyone leave their ill spouse in a strange town? *She's the one who should be apologizing to you*, he wanted to say, but perhaps she was just as senile as he was. "If she could only hear you."

George stared out of his window. "She can," he answered softly.

Mark didn't push to question him, and miles passed with Mark lost in reflection. He dwelled on the vibrancy of life as a fading memory.

The jarring ring of his phone brought him back around. He cleared his throat before answering.

It was Frank Walters returning his call. He explained there were no grounds to change heirs—unless Vivian had another will elsewhere. Mark still wanted to find out the truth. Did Vivian have a child out there? Walters could check, but chances favored a closed adoption. He agreed to call an old friend, a private investigator who might be willing to help, but beyond the state's borders, the search would be more complicated.

Chapter Seventeen

Emily had last left Vivian's story as she arrived at the scene of a mortar shell attack, where victims had been blown to pieces while standing in line for water: *Violence unfurled, the furious grotesquery of* Guernica *in sound and color.* Emily opened the book again.

I nudged Dr. Divjak, but I felt what he certainly must have felt: overwhelmed. We couldn't help everyone; about thirty bodies and body parts were strewn across an area about the size of a high school gym. We started triage, providing immediate care if it would help; otherwise, we moved on. I approached the closest person, a man lying on his back . . . in cases like this, the only thing to do is to stop the bleeding.

A paramedic yelled out for help. I heard his distinctive voice above the crying and screaming. Dr. Divjak was working on a woman whose arm was barely attached to her body. I finished applying two tourniquets on the man's legs, and I ran over to the paramedic. I realized why he had called me. The woman was pregnant. She was barely conscious, but she had no outward bleeding. I feared internal bleeding. "Take her back to the hospital," I told him. "Right now."

He called out for the other paramedic, and I moved a few feet over and treated a woman lying prone and crying in pain. She was grasping at a piece of metal lodged in her abdomen. Knowing that this was no place to remove anything, I moved her hand, but she became angry and pushed me away. I tried to explain that she needed to leave it alone, that she could bleed to death if she pulled it out. I checked her pulse, which was strong enough. I forcefully pushed her arms away once more and promised her that I'd be back.

Triage is a difficult prospect in any situation, and deciding who to help in a chaotic situation with a language barrier makes it even worse. There are no good answers. Another car arrived, and I could have told them to take this woman, but I pointed them to the woman Divjak was working on, if only to get him to move on to others.

Apprehensively, I left this woman and went over to a man a few feet away who was missing his right arm. His eyes were open, but he wasn't making any sound. I checked his pulse. Dead. Next to him, another man was groaning faintly.

Journalists arrived ten or fifteen minutes after us, Claude and Eva among them. One photojournalist was taking pictures of the scene, and the bloody mess would be reported in the news and in magazines in the days and weeks to come. I called Claude over. His eyes were glued to the massacre in disgust and shock. Again I called him over.

"Can you take a couple people in your van?"

He blinked several times and then nodded.

"Okay. Good," I said, and I had him take two of the ambulatory victims.

The ambulance returned, and I immediately thought of the woman with the metal in her abdomen. My stomach dropped when I saw her. She had pulled out the metal and had bled out profusely. Yelling for a paramedic, I dropped down and checked her pulse. It was very faint. "Take her now!" As the paramedic ran back for the stretcher, I got a blanket and put it over her. She said something, faintly, "Em-e-la." But I didn't understand what she meant; she was going into shock. We put her on the gurney and rushed her to the ambulance.

I looked over at the field of bodies, some dead, some dying, some living with concussions and missing limbs. I wanted to go with the ambulance, to see this woman through, but there were too many left here. "Go," I said, my voice cracking, thinking that I shouldn't have left her alone. I had asked too much of her.

The ambulance left, and I felt like screaming. But I dove back into the blood-guts-limbs-pain-death strewn out in front of me and took care of as many as I could.

When I returned to the hospital near the end of the day, I first checked on the woman with the metal shard injury. I didn't know her name, but when I described the wound to one of the nurses in the emergency room, she immediately shook her head.

In a room where fifteen bodies were lying, waiting to be taken to the makeshift morgue at an adjacent building, I found her. The nametag on her toe was blank. "I'm so sorry," I told her.

I got a bucket of cold water and added a drop of detergent. I dunked my head, holding my breath for as long as I could. After washing my hands and arms thoroughly, I went back to work.

The pregnant woman survived, and the pregnancy was fine too. Yes, some good. A miracle really—the man standing next to her in line had died. Still, stamped in my mind was the panicked face of the nameless woman I didn't save.

Emily shut the book and set it down on the bed. Commiserating with Vivian, she felt an ache weighing on her chest. She held onto it, strengthening the connection they had. Not only the shared experience of being doctors and losing patients, but of being in Sarajevo at the same time.

Chapter Eighteen

She was sitting under the balsam fir facing away from the street, her
back against the trunk, her legs outstretched, elongated over the tall
green grass. Barefoot. Emily had legs, Mark thought, staring for a long
second as George walked up the porch steps ahead of him. She didn't
seem to notice that the two were back. Deep in thought or lacking
thought, Mark couldn't tell.

After dropping off George's suitcase on the porch, Mark strolled
onto the lawn. Then he noticed the white wires leading to her ears, her
shut eyes. He slowed his pace, staring at her profile, her hair, her arms,
her legs. Her peach dress covered only half her thighs.

She opened her eyes and turned toward him.

Mark awkwardly jerked, jauntily raising his hand. "Hi!"

The corners of her mouth turned up slightly. "Hi," she said, pulling
out the earbuds. "I didn't hear you."

He pointed behind him. "We just got back."

"Is everything okay?"

"Not sure. George seems sad."

She gently shut her eyes and nodded. "So what do we do now?"

We. That was endearing. "Figure out where the tour went next, I
guess."

"I know where they went," she answered matter-of-factly. "Marilou
told me."

"Who's Marilou?"

"Your competition," she answered, smirking. "The lady who manages the Cozy Inn."

"Competition," he sneered. "Would Marilou have driven George to St. Ignace?"

"No. Because she knew that was the wrong direction."

He waved his hand dismissively at her. "So where did the tour go?"

"Harris. She said it's the next casino west of here, about an hour-and-a-half drive."

Mark sighed. "I don't know if I can do another three hours today."

"Why don't I just take him tomorrow? It's on my way."

"You'd do that?"

She nodded. "Of course."

Mark smiled. "That would be great. Can I repay you with dinner?"

She didn't answer. She held out her slender hand and bent her legs. "Help me up?"

Mark extended an arm and pulled her toward him. Her hand was warm, smooth. She was light.

"Thank you." Brushing off the back of her dress, she asked, "What time is it?"

Mark looked at his watch. "Almost four thirty. A little early for dinner, I guess."

"Actually I need to stop by the dealership. Do you mind if we go there now? I got a call that the windshield was on its way, but I'm a little more skeptical of things now."

"I don't blame you," he said. "So Bear Foot figured out the electrical problem . . ."

"Yeah, took him like ten minutes. He's versatile. He can ward off evil spirits and fix electrical problems."

"Yeah, quite the handyman. So the Hintons charged their car and left?" Mark asked.

Emily nodded. "I want to say hi to George. I'll let him know we're going out."

"See if he wants us to bring him something back."

When they got into the car, Mark snapped his fingers at Emily. "I forgot to tell you!" He recounted meeting Doris at the casino, mistaking her for George's wife, and finding out she had quit the show.

"Quit? Why?"

"She's tired of the bickering."

"But that's what makes it fun to listen to."

"That's exactly what I told her!"

"You did? You actually told her that?"

"Well—yeah, I guess I did. But that's when you called. When I went back to find her, she was gone."

"Maybe she felt insulted."

Mark shrugged. "I sure hope not."

At the dealership, Barbara led Emily and Mark into the shop and showed them the windshield on the floor. She confirmed that an installer would work on it first thing in the morning.

"I guess this means it's your last day in Manistique," Mark said.

Emily, with her arms folded and lips pressed together, nodded, though not convincingly, as if doubts about that lingered.

"Didn't you say Marilou was your cousin?" Emily asked Barbara as the three of them walked back to the lobby.

"Yes, that's right."

"I met her today."

"At the hotel?"

"No, she dropped off a wallet for a guest."

"Oh yes, she told me about that. The man who got left behind, right?"

"Yes," Emily answered.

"You're staying at that bed and breakfast I told you about?" Barbara asked.

Emily pointed at Mark. "His."

Barbara turned to Mark, eyeing him suspiciously. He smiled, gestured without words, then answered, "Well, um, not mine, my aunt's."

"Where's your aunt?"

Mark stumbled, then got out, "She's not around right now. I'm just filling in." He clasped his clammy hands together and said to Emily, "We should get going to dinner now."

"Where are you two going?" Barbara jumped in.

Mark had gotten used to the easy probing that went on in this small town. "Diner 37."

"Oooh, lucky you," she said, patting Emily on the back. "They have great pies."

Emily smiled.

Mark had driven by Diner 37 on his way to and from Indian Lake, so he knew exactly where it was. He'd started getting familiar with the town, knowing where things were and how streets met up. That encounter with Barbara was too close, and an idea nudged at Mark: tell Emily the truth about Vivian.

"You're quiet."

Mark smirked. "No—well, yes. I'm just thinking . . ."

"About what?"

"George," he said.

"You're worried about him?"

"I think it might be worse than we think."

They pulled into the parking lot of Diner 37.

"Why? What did he do?" she asked.

"Just something he said." Mark turned off the car. He faced her. "He apologized to his wife."

"So?"

"He said, 'Sorry, Trudy,' out loud in the car and then claimed she could hear him."

"Maybe he was pulling your leg."

He shook his head. "No, I don't think so."

As they walked from the parking lot into Diner 37, Bear Foot's warning rang in Mark's head: *Don't have the fish at Diner 37.* Warning aside, a couple of people other than Bear Foot had praised Diner 37's pie as the best in the whole UP, maybe all of Michigan. He wouldn't warn Emily about the fish unless she decided on it, and even then, at least the food poisoning came with visions—well, visions of dead people.

The decor inside was nicer than that of a typical diner, and once they got their menus, Mark saw the brief history of the restaurant written on the back. He read it as Emily paged through the offerings. "Diner 37 was originally a bakery, but interestingly, it doesn't say what the thirty-seven means."

"Strange."

The waitress arrived, slightly out of breath, drawing her long hair into a ponytail. "Hello, how are you today?" Her hair was dark with streaks of white. Her face wasn't smooth, but her lips had natural color. She was maybe in her late forties.

"Doing great," Mark said. "We were wondering what the thirty-seven stands for?"

She shook her head. "No one really knows. I've heard it's because the bakery opened in 1937, but I've also heard someone bought it from the original owner for thirty-seven hundred dollars. Other people think it's because there was once that number of different pie recipes."

"Wow, that's a lot of pies," Mark said.

"We don't have quite that many now, but we do have a good selection to choose from."

"I've heard the pies here are good," he said.

"All this pie talk. Pie sounds good for dinner," Emily said.

The waitress smiled, "Sure, dear. You could use a little pie."

Mark glanced at Emily. "You serious?"

"Yeah, why not? I'm not really craving food."

"All right. Let's just have pie then," Mark said.

"No, no, you eat something. I can wait."

"Nah, I'm with you. Pie sounds great. I'll run an extra mile tomorrow. Let's get a few different ones. What pies do you have?"

The waitress left Mark and Emily to peruse the menu of pies. After arguing and negotiating—Emily wanting to try the more unusual versions (apple-cheddar), and Mark steering her back—they finally chose four: apple crumb, pumpkin spice, peach, and pecan. When the waitress came, they asked about wild thimbleberry pie. "It's a berry that's native up here, kind of like a raspberry, but better."

"Add that one too," Mark exclaimed. "Why not?"

"Sure. Any pies warmed up?"

Emily and Mark both made sour faces and pronounced their hatred of hot pie, as if it violated some law of nature. After the waitress left with their order, they debated whether they could actually eat five slices of pie, working themselves up to the challenge.

Mark fidgeted with his knife and fork. He smiled at Emily. Somehow she had grown on him. He liked her, but there was a barrier, a reluctance on his part for anything more. Maybe it was her age. Maybe it was a reluctance to find out that there was actually nothing there between them. He did wonder if she had any interest in him.

"Maybe she's dead," Emily said.

Mark's head snapped to her. "Huh?"

"George's wife. That's why he said she can hear him. She's dead."

"What?"

She gave an annoyed laugh. "Why are you looking at me like that? I'm kidding, of course."

"No—"

"Why can you joke about people dying and I can't?"

"When did I ever joke about people dying?"

"Yesterday when you made a joke about a room opening up."

"Oh yeah," he chuckled before leaning in. "But what if she really is dead?"

"Seriously?"

"Think about it. That would explain a lot."

"You mean he came to the house after arguing with no one," she said in a skeptical voice.

"It's better than believing his wife abandoned him in a strange town."

"I suppose."

"How about this? His wife is dead but he has a lady friend, and he got into an argument with her."

Emily shrugged. "Maybe. So how do we find out? We can't just ask him."

"Why not?" he said sarcastically. "'Hey, George, are you demented? Is your wife actually dead?'"

She shook her head. "You're awful."

The waitress brought out Emily's milk and Mark's coffee. "Pie's coming right up," she said.

Mark took a sip of his coffee. "You seemed upset or, I don't know, skeptical at the dealership."

She sighed. "Barbara showed us a windshield, but how am I supposed to know if it's the right one until they put it on?"

"I thought maybe you were upset because you have no more excuses to stick around here."

Emily snorted a little. "The truth is, you're going to miss me when I'm gone."

Mark smiled. "I'm sure."

She turned her head away and gazed into the restaurant. "To tell you the truth, in some ways this has been a good break. Getting away, you know?"

"From medical school?"

Emily nodded indecisively. "Yeah, that, and . . ." But she said no more.

"Being a doctor is tough. I remember several doctors coming around to see my mom."

"Your mom?—Right, you said she was a psychiatrist."

He nodded. "They'd come to the house and see her. Off the books, so to speak."

"Off the books?"

"Yeah, they didn't want anyone to know. I'd occasionally overhear some of the conversations. Accidentally, of course."

"Of course. What did you *not* hear?"

He made a wry grin. "Mostly it was more like they just wanted someone to confess to."

"Confess what?"

"You know, the usual stuff. Admitting a medical error that was covered up. Or having affairs, multiple affairs. Even doctors who hated their practice but felt trapped. They'd want to quit but they couldn't, either because of their loans or because they felt unprepared for any other career."

Emily's face had blanched and her eyes intensified "Really?"

"You think every doctor has it all together like you do?"

"No—I mean, I get it. Doctors don't like to admit mistakes."

As if to prove some insider status, that he was a knower of secrets of the medical profession, he pressed on, even though he could see that she was slightly disturbed. "Some even talked about suicidal feelings. And, as my mom would always say: There's no such thing as *attempted* suicide when it comes to doctors."

"What do you mean by that? Oh, you mean doctors don't get it wrong."

Mark nodded. "And it's totally underreported."

"What makes you say that?"

"Well unless it's egregious, like someone shooting himself in the head, it's covered up by other doctors."

"I've never heard that."

"Exactly."

"Sounds a bit like a conspiracy."

Mark shrugged.

Just then, the waitress arrived with four slices of pie. Mark and Emily both groaned, shocked at the size of the slices, each blaming the other for ordering so many, then blaming the waitress for not telling them. The waitress smirked, "I'll bring your thimbleberry pie in a minute." They both groaned again, shaking their heads, capitulating before the first bite.

They decided which pie each would start with. Mark had a knife in his hand and asked if she wanted her slice cut now. She waved him off, and then pointed her fork like a weapon. "Just don't eat it all."

He pointed the knife back. "You either."

They dug in. "Wow this is good," he said.

"This is perfect," she agreed.

"I have to confess to something," Emily said after another bite.

"What? You're not going to share your pie?"

"Maybe not." She took another bite, then looked up at him with a nervous smile. "I hope you don't get mad at me."

"For what?"

"I sort of snooped around yesterday when you were at the grocery store."

"You snooped around the house?" It sounded too much like an accusation, and he immediately tried softening it with a broad smile.

"Nothing invasive. Just walked around the house, checked the basement. I was just a bit uneasy because I didn't know who you were. A stranger. Your aunt wasn't there." She laughed anxiously.

"I guess you didn't find anything too incriminating or you would have left," he said flatly.

"Actually, I did find something."

"What?"

"A book."

"Which book? The one about the history of local Native Americans?"

"No, a different book, about doctors—"

"Because the book I read," Mark interrupted, "had some interesting bits. I'm a bit of a history buff, did I tell you?"

She shook her head weakly as the waitress arrived with the last piece of pie. "Here's the thimbleberry."

They thanked her but she lingered. Mark looked up at her. She was biting her lip. "I have a confession," the waitress finally said.

"What, did you snoop around my house too?" Mark said.

Emily jabbed her fork in his direction, frowning hard.

"No," the waitress answered. "Why would I do that? I'm talking about this thimbleberry pie. The berries are from Minnesota, not from the UP. I just found out. When they're in season, we do get the berries fresh from Keweenaw."

Emily dramatically raised a hand to her chest. "Mud duck berries?"

"If you come back in a couple months, you can get the authentic UP version," the waitress said before leaving.

"I suppose you'll still be here," Mark said, poking at Emily.

"Ha, ha."

"What's a mud duck, anyway?"

"A person from Minnesota, of course."

He shook his head. "Never heard that."

She scrunched her nose. "Really? Maybe it's a Wisconsin thing. You know what we call people from Illinois, right?"

"That one I do know. And I can say it's well deserved."

Emily laughed. "So should we trade now?" she suggested.

He looked at her pie, which was *at least* half gone, and nodded. He nudged his plate toward her, but he kept his grip. "You push yours first."

"What's this, a prisoner exchange?" She laughed.

"I don't trust you."

They successfully swapped pies after counting to three. After she finished the last bite of apple pie, she started to reach for the peach, but stopped, sticking her tongue out as if exhausted. "I can't eat any more. Too much, and then the milk."

"It's fine. We can have it later."

Mark finished a quarter of the pecan, and they each took a bite of the thimbleberry. He ordered an entire apple pie to go. "It's for George," Mark said, responding to Emily's dubious frown.

The restaurant was now half full. It was five forty-five and every few minutes another group came in.

Mark paid, and as they waited for the change Emily said, "Thanks for helping me out. Letting me stay at your aunt's place. Paying for my pie."

"Sure," he replied.

They stared at each other at each other for a long second, neither disengaging. The moment endured, normally at first, then smiles swelled slowly on their faces, ready to burst into awkward laughter—

Screeeeech! came from one side of the restaurant. They turned to see someone moving a microphone stand in front of a tall chair.

"Live music?" Mark asked.

As they walked towards the parking lot, Mark told Emily that he, too, had a confession. "Bear Foot told me he got food poisoning here last week," he said.

Her head snapped toward him. "What!"

"But not with the pie!"

"What did he eat?"

"Fish."

Emily frowned and wagged her finger at him. "If I get sick . . ."

"You won't. If you had wanted to order fish, I would have stopped you."

"Gee, thanks." She gave him a sarcastically stern look.

In the adjacent empty parking lot, some young men were hanging out in front of a closed bank. Five of them Mark counted. All of them with floppy brown hair. Talking loudly, each seemingly wanting to outdo the other. Twenty-somethings—barely.

"Watch this," one of them yelled to the other. He took a beer bottle and attempted a handstand on the top, but he crashed on his side instead. He brushed himself off while the others mocked him for failing. He challenged the others. "Fine, I'll do it," one of them said.

He set the bottle back up.

"What idiots," Emily said.

Mark grunted, "Who, those guys?" pretending not to have noticed.

"Yeah."

Mark unlocked the car.

The guy put his thumb on the bottle, but this time the bottle fell and shattered.

There were screams of "Oh my God!" and profane scoldings.

Emily ran to the scene. Mark, frozen for a second, thinking whatever it was wasn't that bad, that there was no need to overreact, set the plastic bag with the pies in the car. When he heard Emily yelling for someone to give up his shirt, he ran over. He flinched when he saw the blood spewing.

She wrapped the injured young man's bloodied hand and had him raise his arm. "Mark, get your car. We have to get him to the hospital."

For a split second, Mark hesitated. The thought of returning a blood-soaked rental car and being charged for "excessive wear and tear" crossed his mind, and he lamented opting out of the extra insurance.

In the back seat, the failed stunt performer banged his head several times against the seat and called himself an idiot. Emily held his hand up, telling him to calm down.

As they raced out of the parking lot, Mark spotted Bear Foot walking down the street carrying a guitar case. He was about to point him out to Emily but stopped himself when he saw her in the rearview mirror. She was in a zone, and pointing out Bear Foot with a guitar sounded lame.

A few minutes later, following directions grunted by the young man, named Conrad, they arrived at the hospital. Emily directed Conrad out and rushed him inside. Mark parked the car and waited in the lobby. About five minutes later, Emily came out. "It's under control. He won't be doing much with that hand for a while. He sliced it down to the abductor pollicis brevis."

"I love it when you talk dirty."

She grinned and shook her head. "Shut up."

"Seriously, though. Good thing you were there," Mark said.

She blew out a long breath. "You don't have to wait around. I know my way back," she said with a smirk.

"You sure you don't want me to wait with you?"

She shook her head. "No, there's nothing for you to do here. Plus, aren't the electric car people due back any time?"

Mark nodded. "Oh right." *The Hinton's can't stay!* "I'll see you at the house in a bit then." He started walking away, then stopped. He yelled out, "Hey!" She turned around, her eyebrows lifted. "You did a great thing there. I'm really impressed."

She smiled modestly and gave a delicate wave.

As Mark pulled into the driveway, his phone rang. Emily, he thought, wanting him to go back to the hospital. But it wasn't. It was Frank Walters

"I've got some news for you," the lawyer said flatly. He told Mark that Vivian did have a child, though the adoption was closed. Nothing in the will had changed because of this, Walters reiterated.

Instead of walking into the house, Mark started down the sidewalk toward the lake as he asked Walters questions. But nothing was known—all the information was sealed in court documents. Mark asked how they could find out more, and Walters blew out a breath testily. The fact that his private investigator friend had found out as much as he had was extraordinary enough. Mark asked him to thank his friend, and after a few seconds, Walters explained that getting more information would involve paperwork, the court system, and the state bureaucracy. But even then he thought it unlikely to be successful. He also suggested that they keep Vivian's wishes in mind. She hadn't mentioned her biological child when she wrote her will, he said, and perhaps she wanted to keep it all in the past.

By the time they had finished talking, Mark was at the highway. He crossed it and strolled along the beach. He took in the air, the waves of the lake, its vastness, and he pondered the aunt he barely knew and the child she gave up for adoption. His cousin.

Chapter Nineteen

The doctor treating Conrad came out to talk to Emily. It was Dr. Currant, who had treated Emily the day before.

"How is he?" she asked.

"He'll be fine, thanks to you."

"Right place, right time, I guess. It was nothing, really."

"I'm Jim, by the way," he said, sticking out his hand.

"Emily." His shake was as gentle as a surgeon's, and his hand was warm.

"I didn't realize you were a doctor when I treated you yesterday."

"You didn't ask."

He laughed. "You're right. In fact, I've been told by our new patient advocate that I should interact more with the patients, get to know them better, as people."

Emily smiled. "I see."

"Where do you practice?" he asked.

"Actually, I'm starting residency next month."

"Oh yeah? Where?"

"Chicago. Lincoln Presbyterian."

"Great hospital."

She grinned, "I'm excited about it."

He pointed to his eye. "How's your eye? I see you've removed the patch."

"Yes." She smiled impishly. A tacit understanding passed between them. "I think it's all right now."

"Good," he said. Dr. Currant was maybe thirty but looked younger with his smooth face and reddish-brown hair, parted in the middle, if intentionally parted at all. He had no hint of a Yooper accent, so she figured he was from somewhere else, somewhere out west. "Are you from this area originally?"

IIe shook his head. "No. Overland Park, Kansas. But my grandfather was from here. He had a summer home on Indian Lake. We'd come up here every year."

"Neat."

"You're sure you don't want to do your residency here? In fact, we have a new, state-of-the-art hospital off Highway 2 opening up in a couple months. It's going to be a gem."

Emily laughed. "I appreciate it, but—"

"Nah, I'm only kidding—well, I'm not really. We're always looking for talented, young doctors, but Lincoln Presbyterian . . ."

She shut her eyes for a long second, and a life with Dr. Currant flashed in her mind. She smiled. "If I ever change my mind, I'll come and see you," she said.

It was more gesture than offer, but he smiled and his eyes lit up as if she meant it genuinely.

Emily strolled back to the house, taking the same path she had the day before. But now she didn't feel uneasy. She felt high on herself. Part of it was from helping the young man, but then she thought of Mark.

She couldn't believe the transformation he'd made in a single day, from oddball stranger to a friend—perhaps more than just a friend. He inexplicably filled a void, and she worried she'd have that emptiness all over again when she left. Then again, Chicago was a month away, and they'd be near each other, and hopefully they could reconnect. . . . She wondered what he thought of her.

As she approached the house, an amusing idea popped into her head. She'd knock on the door and ask if there was a room available.

She jauntily climbed up the steps and knocked three times before turning around, trying to contain her smile and energy. When she heard the door creak, she waited a long second before facing the house.

But it wasn't Mark who opened the door. As if she'd been punched in the stomach, she fell back a couple steps. For a few seconds, Emily couldn't breathe. She couldn't form any words, either. And when she could, she stuttered. "W-w-what are you doing here?" Darkness encroached on the edges of her vision. John towered over her.

"I came for you, of course," he said matter-of-factly. He smiled gently, the kind of smile a parent offers to their dismayed child.

She swayed a bit. "But . . ." She hastily reached out to John's arm and tugged him. He stepped outside onto the porch.

"Are you angry or something?" he asked.

She needed to move this conversation away, far away from the cavernous house where Mark might be listening, wondering, ready to ask questions. Was he confused? Upset? What did he know? Had he put it all together?

She reached around John and shut the door, scarcely looking inside. Without a word, she walked down the steps, her legs wobbly. She stepped onto the grass and stopped near the fir tree under which she had been chilling out a couple hours earlier. She turned around and folded her arms, thinking of what to say. "You shouldn't have come," she said breathlessly.

"Did you think I'd give up on you that easily?"

In fact, she had. Her eyes darted to the house—no sign of Mark—and then set back on John. "How did you find me, anyway?"

"I stopped at the hotel along the highway and asked the clerk if you were a guest. She told me you might be here. I wasn't expecting you to be at a bed and breakfast."

"It's a long story. Where's your car?"

He pointed across the street. "Over there—that rental. I drove by the house twice. It's hard to find. There's no sign. I mentioned it to the owner."

"He doesn't like guests. Besides, he's not the owner, his aunt is."

"His aunt? Really?"

"Yeah. I just can't believe you came all the way out here."

"Well I wanted an explanation."

She met his eyes briefly. "Don't you know why?" He was wearing a polo shirt with asymmetrical stripes of yellow, gray, blue, and white, untucked over dark, unscathed jeans. A strange casualness—ersatz as it was—that she'd never seen in him before. She knew him in button-down shirts and tan pants, a white overcoat.

"No," he said simply. "I need to know what's changed for you."

"Can't we just move on? It's better this way."

"I need to know. Can you just tell me?"

She went with the easiest. "Distance, for one."

"What if I took a job in Chicago?"

"You're going to move to Chicago?" she said doubtfully.

He nodded. "I have an offer. That's what I was going to surprise you with on Mackinac."

Emily turned around, tears welling in her eyes. It was then that she noticed a figure walking up the street. She rubbed her blurry eyes, and confirming who it was, she demanded that John leave.

"Emily, please—"

She pushed on his shoulder, but he didn't budge. "Let's go. I'll go with you," she said.

He moved. "Where?"

"Anywhere. Let's go."

With her hand on his arm, she guided him faster toward the car across the street. Mark shouted out, "Hey! Emily."

Emily stopped and looked back at Mark. "I'll meet you in the car," she said to John, forcefully nudging him once more before walking back toward Mark. They met at the edge of the street.

"What's going on?" Mark asked. He looked in John's direction. "That's not another guest, is it? Because if it is, I like how you got rid of him."

Emily shook her head. "No, just a friend."

"A friend? I didn't know you had friends here."

"I'll explain later."

He glanced over her shoulder and nodded. "Sure. I have something I want to tell you." His mouth curved into a frown.

She sensed a looming confession, and what flashed in her mind was that it had something to do with how he felt about her. She started stepping away, pointing back toward John. "I'm going out for a quick drink with my friend. Tell me when I get back. I won't be gone long."

"Okay, sure. See you later," he said, but his voice fell flat.

Emily couldn't handle whatever Mark was about to tell her, or give it the attention that it deserved. Not in front of John. But she also felt bad for cutting him off so abruptly. She got into the car. "Let's go," she said. She briefly checked over her shoulder and saw Mark staring curiously at the car—or rather, the driver of the car.

"Where are we going?" John asked.

"To a bar."

"A bar?" He started driving. "So who's that guy?"

"Oh, that's Mark, the owner's nephew."

"Huh? Then who's the one who let me into the house?"

"That must have been George. He's a guest."

John laughed. "I thought it was strange when you told me *his* aunt was the owner. His aunt would've had to have been a hundred."

Emily laughed. "Sorry. I thought you had spoken to Mark at the house."

They laughed a little more.

Emily got serious. "Actually, we think George might be having some cognitive issues."

"We who?"

"Mark and me."

"Why do you think that?"

She told him the story about George and his wife and the bus and St. Ignace and his possibly having no wife. Then she told him about the mishap with Conrad and the bottle.

"Sounds like you've had an interesting time here in Mystique," John said, sliding his hand onto the small of her back as they walked into Jake's.

"Manistique," she corrected him.

"Right, right."

They sat at a booth, and John went to the bar to get some wine.

Emily couldn't believe it. Half of her wanted to run out the door right then. The other half still felt something for John. She'd thought she had resolved to leave him for good, but he was slowly reeling her back in.

John brought back white wine. "Have you lost more weight since I last saw you? You look really thin, Emily."

She dismissed it with shake of her head. "Tell me about the job in Chicago."

"It's not exactly a job. I was nominated to be on the board of Lincoln Pres."

"What? Are you serious?"

"Yes. Now I have a reason to come out and see you on a somewhat regular basis."

"Then what?"

He glanced down, then looked up with that long face of his. She couldn't help but try to reconcile his face now with the stern one she'd seen when Nicholas was dead on the surgery room table. "Should I be completely honest, lay all the cards on the table?"

"Yes, of course," she said, though she wasn't altogether sure.

He looked down slowly spinning the stem of his glass. "You asked me what kind of man would leave his kids, be that selfish for any woman, right?"

Emily nodded.

"And you're right, I shouldn't leave them. I couldn't leave them. And if you're willing to wait . . ."

"Wait until when?"

"Well, Cory is thirteen. So I'll stay until he finishes high school, goes away to college."

"That's a long time."

"But you'll be busy with residency for the next three years anyway."

"True, but that's a long time to live a lie with Lisa." *Lisa* crackled. She had never uttered his wife's name.

"She already knows."

"You told her about me?"

"No, not like that. I mean, she's thinking the same thing I'm thinking. We're not going to last and once Cory finishes high school . . ."

"John, what can I say?"

"Why don't you say you'll try and make it work?"

Emily drank her wine. She still couldn't believe that someone wanted her this badly. She rubbed the bridge of her nose as she mentally reviewed the list of complications. Only two, maybe three, remained. But two of them were related, his age and her desire for children. Both were awkward to discuss now, so she brought up the last—

"What about Nicholas?"

"Who's Nicholas?"

She glared and pursed her lips.

"The boy—of course, of course." He looked down and shook his head. "Sorry. Look, I know that's eaten you up. I get it. I thought about the first time I lost a patient. Nicholas was Dr. Olsen's mistake—and me too, my fault too. Okay. I'm sorry."

Emily rested her face on her hand and closed her eyes for a second. When she opened them again, she stared off, her gaze passing over some young men entering the bar. She did a double-take.

Emily jumped out of the booth and accosted the group. "What are you doing?" she yelled at Conrad.

"They let me out of the hospital," he answered nervously.

"You should be at home with ice on that hand, not at a bar. Are you out of your mind?"

Conrad's face went pale, and his flabbergasted friends stayed still, their wide eyes on Conrad as he sputtered an answer. He finally got out, "I'm sorry. I'll go home now."

"You lost a lot of blood. And with your meds, you definitely should not be drinking."

"I didn't know," he said, stepping backwards. "I'm very sorry. Thank you." He and his friends scurried out of the bar.

When Emily turned around, she found John standing behind her, and a dozen patrons watching her. The din of bar, which had gone quiet, crept back.

"That's the guy who sliced his hand an hour ago. Can you believe it?"

John nodded. "Yes." He gripped her shoulder. "I do have some idea how stupid patients can be."

"Yeah, but come on." She stomped her foot on the wood floor. "It's crazy."

"Do you want another glass of wine?" he asked.

She shook her head. "No, let's go." They started for the door.

"Where to now?"

"Don't you have to get back soon?" Emily asked.

"To where?"

"Mackinac."

"I checked out."

"You did? Where are you staying?"

"Isn't there any more room at the bed and breakfast?"

"No," she said, laughing briskly. "It's full."

"Then I'll stay in your room," he said brashly.

"You can't! I have a special rate. The deer-car rate."

"I'll pay the difference."

"No, no. You'll have to go somewhere else. Mark knows I'm not married."

"So? Is he a priest or something?"

"Yes, something like that."

"You're joking."

She had pitched it as a joke, but . . ."Well not a priest. A pastor or some such thing."

"Seriously."

She stumbled. "Something, I don't know. Looks like one, doesn't he?"

He sighed. "All right. In that case . . ."

"That place off the highway should have room. The Cozy Inn."

He scratched his head. "Sure."

They got into the car. He started it and asked nonchalantly, "Why don't you just stay with me at the Cozy place?"

"I can't." But she didn't have a good reason. "Marilou runs it."

"Is she a nun?" He busted out laughing.

Emily rolled her eyes and shook her head at him. "It's just everyone around here knows everyone else, and they talk."

"Do you really care what they say? Nobody here knows us."

She shrugged. "No, not really, but still. I don't know . . ."

John shrugged. "Fine," he said and drove her back to the Manistique Victorian.

Chapter Twenty

Mark returned to the house, the blunt burden of a withheld confession weighing on him. He had been on the verge of telling Emily that Vivian was dead. But she'd easily dismissed him, showing more interest in that stranger, her friend—whoever it was. Mark really didn't want to deal with people at the moment, but when he saw George, he instantly ached for the old man. George sat at the dining room table reading his book, sounding the words quietly. "Can I get you anything?" Mark asked in a soft voice as if they were in a library.

George looked up, smiled, and shook his head. "No, I'm fine. Thank you."

"So tomorrow, Emily will drive you to Harris. Okay?"

"That's very kind of her."

Feeling slightly underappreciated, he added, "Luckily, she's going in that direction."

"Where is she now? Is she with that man?"

"Yeah. Do you know who he is?"

George shook his head. "He came looking for Emily. He asked if he could wait inside. Seemed like a nice fellow, so I let him in. I hope Vivian doesn't mind."

Mark was briefly bemused, then realized that poor George didn't remember Vivian was dead. "No, I'm sure she wouldn't."

"Good."

"He didn't give a name?"

George shook his head. "Why? Nervous about competition?"

"Huh? Over what?"

"The girl, of course."

"No, no," Mark protested with a weak laugh.

"That's how my wife and I ended up together. We were sort of on and off, together with a group of friends, and then one day, this friend of her cousin's came around and started making the hard play." George whisked a punch at the air. "And I took care of it right then."

"You fought the guy?"

"No, but I would've if I had to," he replied adamantly. "I asked her to marry me that day, and she said yes."

Mark nodded his head slowly. "Luckily Emily and I aren't even remotely like that, so I won't have to fight this guy—or any other guy."

"Well you should give it some thought before it's too late."

"Speaking of your wife . . ."

"Yes?"

Mark suddenly remembered the pies on the hood of the car. "Hang on a second. I'll be right back."

Outside, heading toward his car, Mark caught the pitched whine of an electric car. He turned and saw that the Hintons were back. *Sorry, but you can't stay. Sorry, but you can't stay. I'm so sorry, but you can't stay,* he practiced in his head.

The car pulled into the driveway and Mark went to open the garage door, then walked back to the front as the car entered.

The driver's side door swung open first and the woman got out. "We made it," she exclaimed and then stretched.

What's her name again? The man's named Peter. Peter and, er—

"Close one," Peter said, still inside the car. "I'll plug it in, Yvonne," he said.

Yvonne!

"Well hello, Mark," she said.

"Welcome back, Yvonne."

"Good to be back. We almost didn't make it." She winked at him, closed the car door and approached.

"Why? What happened?"

"It was a little farther than we expected. We were down to a single mile of battery. We're not exactly sure what happens when the battery completely runs out."

"Wouldn't it just stop?"

Yvonne smiled, casually set her hand on his arm and squeezed lightly. "It will continue to go on for a short while, but we don't really know for how long."

He glanced at her hand. Her fingernails were painted black. "I have some bad news," he said, slyly backing away from her. "My aunt Vivian got held up and won't be here this weekend. I wish I were capable of managing this place myself, but . . ."

"Oh," she said sadly.

"I'd be happy to drive you to another hotel—you can leave the car here to charge."

She called out, "Peter!"

Peter got out. "Yes?"

"Vivian won't be here this weekend, so I guess we need to move to another hotel."

"But you can leave the car charging here," Mark added. "That's no problem. I'll drive you over to the Cozy Inn. I'm happy to do it."

"That's a rotten bummer," he said. "What about that other fella? George. Is he still here?"

"Yes, he's still with us," Mark answered, deflating. "It's just—"

"And you still have Emily to help, right?" Yvonne asked.

"Well—"

"It's decided then, we'll stay," Peter asserted with a nod and a small smile. "We won't be any trouble." He opened the rear passenger door.

Mark scratched his head. *I'm so sorry, we made a mistake, all the rooms are taken!* But no, he couldn't quite fully muster his inner-Fawlty. Peter pulled out a guitar.

"This way," Mark said evenly, and they walked on the cement path along the side of the house.

Before they returned, the picture of the Hintons had been fuzzy. Yvonne: late forties with light brown hair, permed in loose spirals.

Neither pretty nor unattractive, her face reminded him of a woman he saw regularly at the gym. Peter: early fifties, wisps of gray in his dark head of hair, salt and pepper goatee, average height.

Now it was different. They were staying, and he worried about pulling the whole thing off. Four guests. Breezy Yvonne in particular made him nervous. There was almost a forced or medicated peppiness to her personality. And her big blue eyes, sort of alluring, sort of crazy. Peter gave off the listless mannerisms of a retired person, always prepared to laugh, his distended belly hidden somewhat by his loose Hawaiian shirt of yellow flowers and palm trees. Mark couldn't quite put Yvonne and Peter together. Only money could do that, he determined, and judging by the car, he had money.

"Hiya there," Yvonne said to George as they entered the house.

"Hey there, George," Peter announced as if they were all old friends. "How goes it?"

George looked up. "Fine, fine," he replied, his stare a bit lost.

Peter approached him. "How's the book?"

A genuine smile appeared on George's face. "Oh, it's interesting."

The stranded pies popped into Mark's mind again, so he steered for the backdoor. As he went into the kitchen, he pushed the stiff swinging door closed, happy to separate the guests from the kitchen. Then Yvonne called out, "Oh, Mark," a bit too expectantly, and he considered ignoring her. But he stopped and plodded back through the swinging door. "Yes?" he said, the kitchen door against his back.

She grinned at him. "Can you show us to our room please?"

Mark thought about telling her, *It's up the stairs, very last room*, but instead he nodded pleasantly and answered, "Of course, if you're ready."

"An idealist without firm ideals," George said to Peter.

"This way please," Mark said, a forced cordiality in his voice. Emily would have been proud of him.

"I'd love to chat more with you about it later," Peter said, finishing his conversation with George. "Something that I read about him not long ago that I'd like to discuss with you."

"Excellent," George replied.

Mark picked up the two suitcases and headed up the stairs. The two guests followed their reluctant host around two corners to the last room, the Lake Michigan room. He dropped off the suitcases at the foot of the bed.

"I'll see you later then," Mark said and proceeded to leave.

"We'll be down shortly," Yvonne replied.

Shortly was two minutes later while Mark was making a call in the library. He turned his back to the glass door when he saw Yvonne at the bottom of the stairs. He left a brief message: "Sorry, the Manistique Victorian will not be able to accommodate you tomorrow. Please arrange to stay at another hotel. I am very sorry." He hung up, and almost immediately there was a tap on the glass.

He turned to an overwrought grin and fingers waving at him. He begrudgingly opened the door. "That was fast," he said.

"What was?" Yvonne said, congenially barging her way into the room. She passed by Mark and settled herself in.

"Coming downstairs," Mark replied, turning around. He now noticed her chest—or more to the point, he hadn't noticed before how low her V-neck sweater dipped.

"Well Peter decided to take a short nap, and I decided not to," she said a bit sternly. "This is nice," she said, looking at the bookcases. "Are guests allowed in here?"

Mark gestured toward her. "Apparently."

She barely laughed, and then briefly glanced around, before saying, "Plus I wanted to tell you something."

He immediately dreaded whatever it was she wanted to tell him. She grabbed him by the elbow.

"It's about Peter," she said in a hushed voice.

"Can we talk about this later?" Mark threw out immediately. "I need to make a phone call."

"This will only take a second," she insisted.

She stared intently with those big eyes, but to him she seemed to look past him, not at him.

"Okay, what is it?"

"Peter is quite the yelper."

"What?!"

"Yelp. You know, the review website."

"Yes, yes. I know."

"He's reviewed every place we've gone to on this trip. So if you want a good review . . ."

"Isn't electricity enough?" he said sardonically.

"Sure that helps, but in the end he either loves a place or he hates it. There's rarely an in-between. I can give you some tips."

Mark raised his hand to stop her. "No." *I'd throw you out of here in a second if I had it in me,* he wanted to say. "I'd rather earn it. That's what Vivian would want."

"Of course," she replied. "I had pegged you as completely authentic." Then she gazed at him without a flinch or a blink. "I love that in a man."

Mark's winced smile came with a twitch. "Thanks for the heads up. I appreciate it." He moved slightly out of way, leaving an open path to the door.

She pointed to the living room. "I'll be sitting out there . . ." She fluttered her eyelashes and slightly brushed up against his arm as she walked by.

Mark closed the door and let out a long breath of relief. He hoped Peter's nap would be a short one. He made the rest of the calls—the immediate needs, the ones for this weekend and next. Not a single person answered their phone, and he left a similar message for each.

Fearing any interaction with Yvonne, Mark sequestered himself in the library—that is, until he heard a car door closing. He moved swiftly out of the library and into the front room and watched from the window as Emily strolled up the walk. She turned back momentarily toward the car but didn't gesture. Mark focused on the driver. He couldn't make out any more than what he'd seen earlier. A man, tall, older, but nothing else. Must have been the guy on the other end of the call yesterday, he figured. Boyfriend? Too old, too . . . The car disappeared down the street.

Mark went to the front door and opened it. Emily stopped in her tracks, there on the porch.

"Do you have room for the night?" she asked unevenly, her eyes drifting lower.

"We're not open for the season," he said, a bit mechanically like a bad actor reading a script.

"That was yesterday," she returned, smiling a little. "You need a new reason today."

"You're right." Mark gestured with his head. "Come on in."

She came inside.

"Everything okay?" he asked.

"Yeah, fine."

"So . . ." Mark said.

"So?"

Mark cocked his head toward the street. "Who was that guy? Your uncle?"

Emily choked back a laugh. "Uncle? No."

"Who then?"

"It's a long story." She turned toward Yvonne. "Hello."

"Oh, hi there," Yvonne replied, and waved at her.

Emily approached. "How was your trip?"

As Yvonne gave her a detailed account of their half-day trip to Lake Superior and their harrowing return, Mark noticed George, his lips no longer moving. His head sat like a deadweight on his hand. His eyes were shut.

It was just after seven o'clock. The light in the house was dimming quickly, so Mark turned on the living room light.

"Good, good," Emily was saying to Yvonne.

"I must say, I love your dress. You look so pretty."

"Thank you."

Yvonne pointed. "Oh dear, looks like you got something on the bottom there."

Emily looked down.

"Right over there, to your left, on the bottom."

She grabbed the bottom of the dress and groaned. "Oh, no."

Mark walked over to see. A dark semi-circle stain at the hem. He thought of pie. "Thimbleberry?"

"No," she answered sharply. "It's blood."

He felt stupid.

Yvonne sat up. "Blood? Are you okay?"

"It's from earlier, I was helping someone."

"'Help' is an understatement," Mark interjected. "She saved someone's hand."

"What happened?"

Emily grimaced and shook her head. "It's not as dramatic as that." Her eyes widened. "Oh!" She turned to Mark and grabbed his arm. "You won't believe this! Guess who was at Jake's just now."

"I don't know. Jake?"

"No, Conrad!"

"Are you kidding me?"

"No. But I'm afraid I made a bit of a scene."

"What do you mean?"

"I yelled at him to go home, in front of his friends."

"He deserved it, I'm sure."

She nodded then frowned as her eyes fell on her dress again.

"Can it be washed?" he asked. "There might be a stain remover down in the laundry room."

She nodded. "I'll give it a try," she said and headed up the stairs.

"Is she related to Vivian too?" Yvonne asked.

"Emily? No, she's a guest here," he said, and added, "And a friend."

"Oh, she let us in earlier, so I thought . . ."

"She was doing that as a favor to me."

"She's very kind. So how did this person hurt his hand?"

Mark explained, partially demonstrating with a rolled-up magazine.

Yvonne cringed. "Ouch! That's crazy."

"Bled all over the place. Lucky for him, Emily was right there—she's a doctor, by the way."

"Really? Is she here on vacation?"

"No, she's waiting for her car to get fixed. She hit a deer yesterday."

"Poor girl," Yvonne said, pouting in sympathy.

Remembering again the pie on top of the car, Mark excused himself. George gave a snort in his sleep. As Mark passed him by, the old man groaned for a second, then grumbled an apology to no one in particular.

Having retrieved the pies and set them in the refrigerator, Mark pushed through the swinging kitchen door and did a double take when he saw Emily at the base of the stairs. She had changed into old jeans and a gray, ribbed tank top. She carried her dress over an outstretched arm. It took Mark a second to realize that George was gone. "Do you know where George went?" he asked Yvonne, who was flipping through a magazine. Her bare feet were planted on the coffee table.

She set the magazine down. "George?" Her eyes briefly showed confusion. "Oh. No. I don't know." She lifted the magazine back up.

Mark and Emily locked eyes. He immediately went to the front door.

Down the steps, looking out to the street, was George.

"You going somewhere?" Mark asked.

George shook his head. "No, not yet." Patting his stomach, he said, "I am getting a bit hungry though."

"I'll take you to go get something. Come inside for a second."

Emily stared as Mark escorted George back to the dining room table. "Have a seat, and we'll go in a few minutes. Okay?"

George nodded. "Sure. Thank you."

Mark and Emily headed to the kitchen and then down to the basement.

"I'm worried about George," Emily said once they reached the bottom.

"Me too. But I'm more worried about Yvonne."

"Yvonne? Why?"

They turned into the laundry room, and Mark spoke softly, not certain how far voices carried in the house. "She keeps flirting with me."

Emily burst out laughing.

"I'm serious. Peter isn't around, he's napping. I just don't know what to do." He opened the cabinet above the washing machine.

"Maybe she's just friendly. She seems very friendly."

"It's more than that."

Emily shrugged. "Why don't you just shock the heck out of her and give her a big smooch?"

"Huh?"

"She'll stop flirting—or want more, who knows?"

"That's great advice, doc," he answered with a glower.

Emily laughed.

"Here. Spot cleaner. Might this do the trick?"

"Maybe."

"Mark?" Yvonne called.

"Oh no. See?"

"I can take care of this. Good luck," Emily said, pushing him on the shoulder.

"I need you to come up soon," he said.

"Mark?" Yvonne called out again.

Emily smiled. "Sure, I'll be right up." She winked at him.

"No, seriously. Don't leave me alone with her for too long."

Mark found Yvonne peering into the kitchen, as if the kitchen were a restricted area. *Trespassers will be violated!*

"Yes?" he said as pleasantly as possible, entering the dining room.

"Can you unlock the door to my room?"

"Didn't I give you the key?"

"You did, but Peter has it, and he accidentally locked the door."

Mark headed to the parlor. He had seen a set of keys in the drawer and assumed one would open the door.

"I love this house," Yvonne said as they headed up the stairs.

Mark turned back, giving her a perfunctory "Thanks," and jogged the last few steps to pull away. He stopped in front of the Lake Michigan room and inserted one of the keys. But it only went in part-way. He twisted the knob anyway, and it opened.

He didn't say anything about its being unlocked already. He simply opened the door slightly and stepped out of the way.

"Thank you so much." She brushed her hand across his lower back as she went past him.

Back down the stairs, Mark found George standing near the door. "What would you like to eat?" he asked him as he returned the keys to the drawer.

George shrugged. "I don't know."

"How about pizza?"

"Yes, that would be fine. Yes, pizza sounds good, if it's not too much trouble."

"Not at all. I'll be right back."

Mark walked into the kitchen as Emily emerged from the basement.

"Where's your girlfriend?" Emily asked.

"Funny. She's upstairs in her room. You doubt me, but . . ."

She laughed. "There is something odd about those two."

"Yes, especially her." He picked up his car keys from the counter. "I'm taking George to get pizza. Do you want anything? Or do you want to come?"

She shook her head. "No, thanks. I'll just hang out here."

"I hope the stain comes off."

She nodded. "Me too."

Figuring the dress had another twenty minutes or so in the wash, Emily went to her room, grabbed *Doctors on the Borderline* from her nightstand, and returned downstairs. For all the grief she'd given Mark, Emily didn't want to chance a chatty encounter with Yvonne. So she continued to the basement, and sat on the couch, thinking that Mark wouldn't mind if she waited there for the washing machine.

She scooted some mail out of the way in order to put her feet up on the coffee table. And then she saw it. "Can't be," she said aloud, looking at the mail. She turned to the beginning of *Doctors on the Borderline*, and confirmed it on the table of contents page. Vivian Peregrine. "No way!" She leaped off the couch, ready to pounce on Mark for not telling her.

But she knew he was gone. So she sat down, a bit heady at this revelation, and read on with new fervor . . ."The Orphanage."

Phil approached me one day about accompanying him to an orphanage. He was writing a regular piece about a nine-year-old girl named Sonja, an orphan there. But she was only one of dozens under the direction of the two women who ran the place. The facility had no medical care, and he thought some of the children might not be getting the medical attention they needed. I agreed, and we, along with an interpreter, left for this orphanage on the outskirts of town. It was safe out there, Phil reassured me, as the Serbs did not bomb such desolate places . . .

Chapter Twenty-One

Mark trailed behind George as he climbed the porch steps carrying a small flat box from Ace's. Entering the house, Mark half-expected coquettish Yvonne to be waiting in the entry with puckered lips. She wasn't in the room at all.

Peter was pacing near the dining table with a wayward expression. "Finally, you're back," he said, approaching Mark with long strides. "Where's Yvonne?"

"I have no idea," Mark replied, irked by the implication that he had gone off with her. "She was here when we left."

"She took my car!"

"Well she couldn't have gone too far, right?" Despite the growl this elicited from the man, Mark didn't cut short his jovial smile.

"I'm going to call the police!" His nose quavered.

Mark erupted with an anxious laugh. "You're joking, right?"

"This is embarrassing," he muttered. He turned and stomped up the stairs.

George set his pizza on the table. "Can I bother you for a plate?"

"Certainly. Any idea what's going on?"

George shook his head. "No, sir. I'm only a guest here."

Mark chuckled. "Maybe Emily knows." He left for the kitchen and grabbed a plate for George. As he returned to the dining room, the front door opened.

It was Yvonne, carrying a brown paper sack.

"I'm glad you're back," Mark called across the room.

"You're so sweet." She smiled genuinely.

Mark approached. "No, no. Your husband is desperately looking for you. He's about to call the police. At least that's what he said."

"Who?"

"Peter. He was upset about you taking the car. He wasn't serious about calling the police, was he?"

"He's not my husband," she said.

"Oh—sorry." He hadn't bothered checking her ring finger. "Your boyfriend."

She shook her head. "I better go fix this." She rushed up the stairs with the bag.

"This can't be good." Mark walked back toward George.

"What's the matter?"

"Yvonne and Peter, some kind of argument about the car. Did you know that they aren't married?"

"I figured as much."

A commotion erupted upstairs. "Uh-oh," Mark said. After a couple frustrated outbursts, he heard steps coming back down.

It was Yvonne, shiny lines down her face. She went straight for the front door. When she opened it, she turned at a slight angle and left the house.

Stepping over to close the door, Mark saw that Bear Foot was in the doorway. He was staring in the direction of Yvonne's wake.

"Hey, thanks so much for fixing the outlet this afternoon. Come on in," Mark said with a long-armed wave.

Bear Foot had a puzzled frown when he came into the house. "Was she crying?"

Mark shrugged. "I don't know. Allergies, maybe—the urn!"

Bear Foot lifted and held out the blue urn. "Yeah, you left this in the truck this morning."

"Totally forgot. Thanks." But when Mark took it, he nearly dropped it. It was quite a bit heavier than it should have been. "Is there something in here?"

"Water from Indian Lake. Vivian's part of the lake now."

Mark nodded. "Of course."

There was a screech from the basement. Then a loud thud and "Oh my God!" repeated several times.

Bear Foot looked at Mark questioningly. Mark shrugged in return. "I have no idea—oh, I saw you earlier walking toward Diner 37, with a guitar."

"Me? No."

"I would have sworn it was you."

"Nope. I don't play the guitar."

"Well your doppelganger does."

"My what?"

"There's guy out there who looks like you."

"I've been told that before, but I've never seen him."

"I thought for sure it was you going for some pie."

"I wish," Bear Foot said.

"In that case, there's some in the fridge."

There were running steps up the stairs from the basement.

"Least I could do for helping me out today—" Mark said as Emily spewed out of the kitchen.

"You're back!" she cried, grabbing hold of George's shoulder and shaking him before rushing toward Mark. "You're not going to believe this!"

"You got the stain out?" Mark asked with perfect equanimity.

"Forget the dress," she said breathlessly. "Your aunt. Vivian Peregrine, right? She's a doctor, right? Right?"

Mark nodded. "Yes. Why?"

"The book, her story about her time in Sarajevo."

"What book?"

"The book I was telling you about earlier, about Doctors Without Borders."

"Yeah, she was in Sarajevo a long time ago."

Emily's phone rang.

"This is so incredible," she cried out. She reached into her pocket for her phone and answered immediately, bursting into jubilant exclamations.

Mark shook his head. "I don't know what this is all about," he said to Bear Foot. "Go help yourself to the pie."

Bear Foot made straight for the kitchen.

"Did you say pie?" George said.

"Yes. There's a whole apple pie. Go in the kitchen and ask Bear Foot."

"That's a nice vase," George remarked.

Emily's voice had simmered down, and she now spoke rapidly, explaining how she ended up in Manistique.

Mark set the urn on the mantel and started for the kitchen but only got a few steps before he was tugged from behind. He turned around and was about to say "What?" but Emily kept chatting. "Yes, pretty sure," she said. "Yes, yeah, yeah. Okay. Gotta go." She hung up.

"What's all the commotion about?"

Emily took a deep breath. "I can't believe this. You won't believe this. Why didn't you tell me Vivian was a doctor?"

"What?"

"When will Vivian be back? I have to see her."

"Vivian's back?" George asked.

Mark turned around and shook his head at George, who was standing in front of the kitchen door holding the apple pie and a pie server. "No."

"Don't worry, I'm not going to eat all of this," George explained. "We're doing an experiment."

"I have something important to tell her," Emily said excitedly.

Mark turned back to her. "You don't even know her," he replied evenly.

"But I do. I do. We have a connection," Emily said.

"You're both doctors, I know."

"No, it's more than that. Much more. It's fate, Mark. I was meant to get stuck in this town. I was meant to stay here and to meet Vivian. It's fate."

Mark shook his head. "No it's not."

"It is," she said adamantly. "And when you hear—"

"Then fate is cruel to deer."

"What?" She frowned. "That's not funny. I'm being serious."

He shrugged. "Me too."

"You'll flip out when I tell you. When will she be back?"

Mark had reached his breaking point. He walked over to the fireplace and grabbed the urn. He walked back to Emily and shoved the urn into her bosom. "There you are."

"What's this?" She took hold of it apprehensively. "Why are you giving this to me?"

"That's Vivian."

"Huh? What are you talking about?"

"Bear Foot can explain."

"Have you lost your flippin' mind?" she asked, her eyes wide.

"No, that would be this one"—he pointed to an oblivious George—"who somehow remembers that there's someone named Vivian who owns this place, but can't remember that she's dead. Or Bear Foot, who thinks her spirit, or essence, or whatever it is, is in the water. I'll be back in an hour, or maybe not at all. Just tell the last person to lock up—or not. It doesn't matter here."

"What are you ranting about? Is this some kind of joke? Is this another of your impersonations?"

"Nope, no joke. Vivian is dead."

"What do you mean she's dead?"

"I mean she died. Passed away. Demised. Deceased. Kaput. Ashes frolicking in the Great Lakes—well, maybe not all them, but at least Lake Michigan."

"What? Is this for real?"

"Yes! I'm telling you she's dead."

"When did she die?"

"Three days ago. I'm sorry."

Bear Foot came out of the kitchen. "Laundry's ready. It's beeping."

Mark headed for the front door.

"Wait! You owe me an explanation."

Mark pulled open the door, and without turning, he announced, "You're in charge now."

Emily stood between the stairs and the front door, perplexed, holding firmly to the vase that Mark had handed her. She gaped at the closed door, frozen. Waiting, hoping that the door would burst open, and Mark would reveal this as one of his antics. But the door didn't open, and after waiting several seconds, she listlessly stepped to the fireplace and set the vase on the mantel. She stared at it for a second before plunging onto the sofa.

Bear Foot set two plates and two spoons on the table. "Let's see if you're right," he said to George before cutting into the pie.

"Bear Foot," Emily called out.

"Yes?"

"Is Vivian really dead?"

"I can't believe Vivian is dead," George said, shaking his head.

Bear Foot's eyes fell, and he gently laid his spoon down. With a tender nod, he replied, "May she rest in peace."

"But . . ." Emily's voice trailed off. For a moment, her world had made perfect sense. Now only cruelty made sense.

"I thought this was Vivian's hotel?" George asked.

"It is," Bear Foot said. "It was," he corrected himself. "We scattered her ashes this morning."

Emily's emotions, knocked off a high a few minutes earlier, now bottomed out in confused disappointment. She leaned forward, resting her head on her hands. "I don't understand," she moaned.

"Her spirit came to me the day she died and said something to me," Bear Foot said.

"What did she say?" George asked.

He hung his head. "I can't remember. It's all so blurry. I thought it was all because I was sick." He shut his eyes.

"I just don't understand why Mark didn't say anything," Emily said to no one. None of it made sense. Why didn't Mark tell her? What were the odds of landing in this house? And then only to learn that Vivian had died—

There was a knock on the door.

Bear Foot's eyes were still closed. "I guess I'll get it," she said. She felt a sharp pang in her chest.

She opened the door. Mark.

"I'd like a room, please," he said. "I believe Breakwater Lighthouse is free."

"Why didn't you tell me Vivian was dead?" Emily fired. "I don't get it."

He stepped around her and into the house.

"Wait! You owe me an explanation."

Mark stopped and pivoted back around. "On second thought, I'm just going to get my stuff and go to the Cozy Inn. Or maybe I'll take Peter's car out for a spin and stay at the graybar hotel." He headed toward the kitchen.

"Are you having a breakdown or something?"

"No, not at all. I feel fine. I'll just get my things."

"Wait!" she demanded, but he didn't stop. She sighed in frustration. Frustration that he had lied to her, but even more than that—he seemed not to care about her connection to Vivian.

"What the heck is going on here?"

Emily looked over at the dining room and saw the peculiarity that had struck Mark. George's hands were over his ears and his eyes were shut. Bear Foot was spoonfeeding him pie.

"A test," Bear Foot said, shoving the spoon into his test subject.

"Taste test?"

"Mmm." George opened his eyes and set his hands back down. "Nope. Definitely not from the pie tin."

While Emily approached, Bear Foot explained: George claimed to know if a piece of pie had been scooped straight from the pie tin.

"I can," George nodded adamantly. "It causes a yucky metallicky taste." He closed his eyes and covered his ears. "Ready. Try again."

This time Bear Foot scooped the apple pie directly from the tin. Both Emily and Mark stood there watching this. When George took a bite, his face soured. "Yuck. Directly from the tin, right?" He opened his eyes and uncovered his ears.

"Yes, but how?" Bear Foot took another spoon and scooped a bite from the tin. He ate it and shook his head. "It tastes normal."

Mark patted George on the back. "Maybe you have a superpower," he said and started for the kitchen.

Emily trotted toward Mark, reaching him as he pushed the swinging door into the kitchen. She forcefully yanked on his arm.

Mark spun around with an annoyed expression. "What?"

"Why didn't you tell me that Vivian had died?—I'm sorry, by the way."

Mark sighed. "And I'm sorry I didn't tell you. I honestly didn't think it mattered. You were supposed to be on your way home in a day, remember?"

"I wouldn't have stayed here in the first place if you had told me."

"Exactly."

Emily stood there, mouth agape, wanting to say something. They held a stare.

"The lighthouse!" Bear Foot cried out.

"What?" Mark said.

Bear Foot stumbled, tripped up by the chair.

"I remember it now. Vivian told me to go to the lighthouse."

"To the lighthouse? Why?" Mark asked.

"I don't know. I have to go." He skidded past them and ran out.

George mumbled, "It's on my list."

"You'd think she would have told him something more important than that," Mark said.

"You believe in all that?"

He shook his head at her. "No, Ms. Fate. Of course not."

She glowered at him.

"I have to admit, some unusual things have happened," he said.

Emily clapped her hands. "Speaking of which, aren't you curious about my encounter with Vivian?"

"What encounter?"

"When I was two years old. She got me out of a bad orphanage."

"In Wisconsin?"

"No! Sarajevo. I've always known that it was a humanitarian doctor who brought me here, but I never knew who it was."

"And you think it was Vivian."

"No, I *know* it was her."

"How?"

"The book, her story."

"What book?"

"The one I told you about earlier, the book about doctors. Weren't you listening?"

"Oh right, when you were snooping downstairs."

She waved her hand dismissively. "Yes."

"Vivian is in that book?" His tone was more tender.

"More than in it. She wrote about her time in Sarajevo. Did she ever talk to you about it?"

He sighed and hung his head. "To be perfectly honest, I barely knew her. She was always out of the country. I'd get letters from her every year, and she'd promise to visit when she was back, but I never saw her except once when I was a kid."

"Oh."

His gaze panned around the house. "So all of this is new to me."

"You mean you've never been up here before?"

"Nope. Had no idea Vivian was running a bed and breakfast until you showed up."

Emily's hand covered her unrestrained laughter.

"Why are you laughing?"

"I don't know." And she kept on, uncontrollably. Her way of letting go of any resentment. Then she stopped, remembering that Vivian had died, and that the long-odds coincidence turned out in the end to be bitter indeed. "This is a lot to take in." She dabbed her eyes with the back of her hand.

"Where did this pie come from?" George asked.

"It's from Diner 37."

"Did that girl bring it?"

"Who? Yvonne? No. Em and I brought it back. We had dinner there—well sort of." He looked at Emily. "Yvonne ran off, by the way."

"Ran off? You didn't try kissing her, did you?"

"No," he huffed. "Some kind of argument with Peter—"

George slammed his empty glass of milk onto the table. "This pie is almost as good as Trudy's."

Emily and Mark looked at each other. Emily said, "Trudy makes good pies?"

"Used to make the best pies."

"Used to? She doesn't anymore?" Mark asked.

His brow furrowed. "Of course not. She died years ago."

Emily and Mark shared a glance.

Mark asked, "So who are you traveling with on the casino tour?"

"No one. Why do you ask?"

"Well we thought you said you got into an argument with your wife," Emily said.

"My wife? No, I got into an argument with Trina, the tour director."

Mark and Emily swapped brief glances. "What was your argument about?" Mark asked.

George blew out an irritated *pfffffft*. "We ended up sharing a room at the Cozy Inn because I'm the only one traveling by myself and they ran out of rooms. Let's just say things got a little too . . . cozy. Yes, too cozy at the Cozy Inn."

Chapter Twenty-Two

Mark and Emily stood together in the basement. Mark held *Doctors on the Borderline*, reading a passage, pleasant chills pricking his neck. It was like a last, long letter from Vivian. "This is so crazy," he said finally, looking up.

A muffled wail came from somewhere in the house. Mark and Emily stared at each other momentarily. It could having been a laugh or a cry.

A resounding thud reverberated through the house. Mark dropped the book on the coffee table and ran for the stairs. Emily followed. "What's going on?" he asked George. But before George could say anything, a pleading scream came from upstairs. Mark sprinted toward the stairs. Emily chased behind.

A wailing noise echoed from one of the rooms. Mark and Emily ran through the hallway toward the commotion, halting when they reached the Lake Michigan room.

At first sight, it looked like a kids' game of dogpile. "What the heck!" Mark cried.

Bear Foot grunted. "Help me with him."

Yvonne was lying on the floor beneath Peter. Bear Foot was bent over trying to pull Peter off of Yvonne.

Mark bent down to help Bear Foot. "Get off of her!" Mark yelled.

"He's dead!" Yvonne screamed.

Yvonne slipped out from underneath.

Bear Foot closed his eyes and started whispering something.

"Turn him over," Emily commanded, falling to her knees. She checked Peter's pulse and his breathing. "He's not dead. What happened?"

Yvonne breathlessly explained that Peter had passed out while she was talking to him. She had caught him and then gotten stuck beneath him as they fell to the ground.

"Is he taking any medications?"

"I don't know," Yvonne answered. "Maybe."

"Go check his things," Emily said firmly.

Yvonne moved as slowly as if she were wading through a few feet of water.

Mark pulled out his phone. "I'm calling 911," he said.

Bear Foot got out of the way as Emily attended to Peter.

She looked around his body. "No bleeding."

"Here!" Yvonne pulled out a bottle, handing it to Emily.

"Never mind, Mark. Tell them not to come."

"Why?"

"He's narcoleptic, is all."

"He's what?" Yvonne asked.

Emily explained to Yvonne while Mark tried to convince the dispatcher that the man was narcoleptic. "No, we don't need an ambulance after all. He's only sleeping."

"Did he hit his head when he fell?" Emily asked.

"No. But I almost did! So he fell asleep standing?"

"Yes," Emily replied and turned to Bear Foot. "Can you hand me a pillow, please?" She turned back to Yvonne, who had her hands clasped over her mouth and was staring down at Peter. "It can happen at any time. There are certain triggers, like exhaustion or strong emotions."

Bear Foot handed Emily a pillow. "Mark, can you lift him up for second, please?" she asked.

Yvonne started to cry. "I thought he was dead."

"Bear Foot, why don't you take Yvonne downstairs to get a glass of water."

"Come on, Yvonne," Bear Foot said, a certain tenderness in his deep voice. He put his hand on her arm, guiding her out of the room.

"What's with those two?" Mark whispered, crouching down next to Emily, who was kneeling on the floor.

"What two?"

"Bear Foot and Yvonne."

"Didn't notice. Jealous much?"

"Ha!"

She smirked at him.

"When did Bear Foot come back to the house, anyway?" he asked.

"Beats me. I was with you."

Mark stood up. "I wonder if he'll still give me a good review."

"Who?"

"This guy." He tapped his foot on Peter's shoulder. "He can't hear me, can he?"

"No, he's asleep. You'll get an interesting review from me."

Mark laughed. "I'm sure glad this guy isn't dead. It'd make selling the house that much harder."

Emily stood up. "You can't sell this house," she demanded.

"Why not?"

"Because it's Vivian's house."

Mark shrugged. "What am I supposed to do with it? I live in Chicago."

Emily shook her head. "Just don't be hasty about it. There's something—I don't know. Magical or something about this place."

"Yeah, it causes people to fall asleep."

She shoved Mark in the shoulder, hard.

"Hey! What was that for?"

"That's for not telling me that Vivian had died."

"I told you I was sorry."

"I know. I forgive you. Now."

There was a knock on the door downstairs. Mark sighed. "I better go see who that is."

By the time Mark got far enough down the stairs that he could see the door, Bear Foot was opening it. He caught sight of law enforcement standing in front of Bear Foot. The 911 call . . .

"I told them over the phone that everything's okay," Mark hollered, hurrying down the remaining steps and toward the door as if it were a football drill. Bear Foot stepped out of the way.

Mark smiled, recognizing the man, but the uniform was different. "You sure put in a lot of hours."

"Do I know you?"

"Um . . ." He got close enough to read the name tag. *Bryst.* "You don't remember me from this morning?"

He shook his head. "No. I'm Officer Bryst with Manistique Public Safety. You're probably thinking of my brother. He's a state trooper."

"Oh, sorry."

"No problem. Happens all the time. Is there a man named Peter Hinton staying here?"

"Yes, I'm sorry you came out here for nothing. He's all right."

"What are you talking about?" the officer asked.

"I told the 911 dispatcher that he's all right. We have a doctor here."

"I got a call from Mr. Hinton about a stolen vehicle."

"What?!" It was Yvonne, who leaped off the sofa. "Peter really did call. I can't believe him!"

The officer stepped inside and raised an open hand. "Calm down, miss." He turned back to Mark. "Now, where's the man who made the call?"

Mark pointed up. "He's upstairs, sleeping."

"Could you wake him for me?"

Mark shook his head. "Nope."

"Why not?"

"Because he's narcoleptic."

Mark heard steps. A man in a plaid shirt and thin tie, carrying a brown valise, stood at the front door. Mark approached. "Sorry, we don't have vacancy. The Cozy—"

"I'm a doctor. Dr. Currant from the hospital."

"Hi, Jimbo," Officer Bryst said. "Do you know anything about this?"

"I just got a call about someone here needing medical attention," the doctor said.

"Sorry to have wasted your time," Mark said. "We already have a doctor here, and the man is fine. Turns out he's narcoleptic."

Dr. Currant's eyebrows lifted. "What doctor?"

"Dr. . . ." Mark suddenly realized he didn't remember Emily's last name. "She's a guest here."

"I know her," Dr. Currant said excitedly. "Dr. Davis. Emily, right? She helped with an accident this afternoon."

"Yes, that's right." Mark eyed him a bit suspiciously. "It was hardly an accident. It was more like stupidity."

"Sure," Dr. Currant replied dismissively. "Do you mind if I come in and see the patient?"

"Knock yourself out, doc. Upstairs, last room."

"Thank you."

After the doctor walked off, Officer Bryst said, "So there's no stolen vehicle?"

"No," erupted Yvonne. "It's in the garage charging!"

"Mind if I have a look?" he asked.

"Please do," she answered.

"No, I don't mind," Mark said deliberately. "The side door to the garage is unlocked."

"I locked it," Yvonne said.

"You did?"

She nodded.

"Give me a second. I need to find the key," Mark said to the officer.

The trooper nodded. Mark went into the parlor and grabbed the set of keys from the console drawer. He hoped one opened the garage side door.

When he came back out, he absorbed the scene for a second. Yvonne on the sofa, leaning forward with her head down, Bear Foot leaning down next to her, elbows on knees. Officer Bryst, who looked exactly like his brother, was standing in the entryway waiting.

"All right," Mark announced, holding up the keys, and he and the officer headed out the front door. The day was settling away, the sky a deep purple with pink highlights.

"Where's Vivian?" Bryst asked as he followed Mark.

Mark stopped and turned around. "She died a few days ago."

Bryst frowned. "I'm very sorry to hear that."

Mark nodded and continued on toward the garage.

"And Vivian was your . . ."

"My aunt."

"So does Bear Foot know that woman, what's her name?"

"Yvonne. No, he only met her today."

"And she's staying here with Mr. Hinton?"

"Yes, that's right."

"And now he's incapacitated?"

They reached the garage and Mark turned around. "Asleep," he replied pointedly. *Incapacitated* sounded a tad nefarious to him.

"And you have a guest who's a doctor?"

"Yes, she was in a deer-car and is waiting for her car to get fixed . . ."

His face lit up. "My brother told me about her—the one where the deer actually ran into her."

Mark put his finger to his lips. "Yes, but don't mention it. She's a bit touchy about it."

He kept smiling "No, I won't."

"I hope one of these keys works. I don't know why she locked it."

"City folk," the officer said, and snorted out a laugh.

"Right," Mark replied agreeably. "Darn city folk."

The third key worked, and they went inside and turned on the light.

"That's some fancy car."

"It's all electric. Get this, they're trying to be the first people to circle Lake Michigan in an electric car."

"Really? How far can it go before it needs to be charged again?"

"Over two hundred miles."

He whistled. After walking around the whole car he said, "Obviously no stolen vehicle here, so I'll be on my way."

Heading back toward the front of the house, Mark asked, "So are you and your brother twins?"

"No. He's two years older. Where did you meet him?"

"This morning at a stop sign. He brought back a guest who had gotten lost."

"I heard about him, too. He was part of that casino tour?"

"Yes, that's right."

"And they left this morning."

"*They* left. George is still here."

"What? Why?"

"He missed the bus." Mark considered telling Officer Bryst about the trip to St. Ignace. But they were on the walkway, and he spotted a car parked out front, the same car Emily had been in earlier.

"So how's he getting back?"

"Emily. The doctor, the deer-car girl. She's dropping him off on her way back home."

"That's generous of her," Bryst said. Now Mark really wanted to tell him about the St. Ignace trip. "Hopefully no other deer try to stop her."

The both laughed.

"Have a pleasant evening," Mark said. He hopped the steps and went inside where he found George talking a a man—the man Emily knew? His brown hair was streaked with gray, and he wore a soft brown blazer and jeans, the bottom of which pooled at his topsiders.

"Hello, can I help you?" Mark asked, approaching.

The man turned, and Mark's image of Emily's uncle vanished, replaced by a younger-looking man in his mid-forties. Behind the rectangular frameless glasses, his eyes scanned Mark briefly, disapprovingly.

"Are you the proprietor here?"

Mark shrugged. "More like ringmaster."

"Sorry?"

"Yes, I am the proprietor of this establishment. What can I do for you?"

"I heard there was a medical emergency, and I was worried about my friend staying here."

"Word sure does travel fast," he muttered. "What friend are you referring to?"

"Dr. Davis."

"She's fine. It was another guest who had an issue." Mark gestured with a wide arm toward the door.

"Do you need my help?"

"Are you a doctor or something?" Mark replied sarcastically.

"Yes, as a matter of fact. Dr. Bulcher." He stuck out his hand.

Butcher? Mark nearly fell back, punch-drunk, and it seemed for a moment the only thing holding him upright was the hand he thoughtlessly grabbed in return. "I'm Mark," he barely got out. This didn't make any sense.

Dr. Butcher asked a question. Mark blinked a few times and gathered himself. "What?"

"I'd like to see Dr. Davis," he said firmly.

"She's upstairs with another doctor."

"Another doctor?"

"A local." Mark laughed, derisively. "Three doctors for one narcoleptic patient who's sound asleep. Now that's what I call medical care."

"Would you mind if I went up to see the patient?"

Mark shook his head. "Be my guest. Upstairs. Last room down the hall."

"Thank you, Pastor."

"Huh?"

Butcher started for the stairs.

"Did the police officer leave?" Yvonne asked.

It took Mark a second to answer, his mind still trying to comprehend it all. "Yes. He saw the car in the garage and then left."

"Good," she said softly. Nodding, she dropped her head down again. "What do I do now? How will I get back to Green Bay?"

"Hitchhike," Mark threw out.

"No, no," Bear Foot jumped in his seat in an obsequious way. "No, definitely not. Too far." His voice drifted, "Maybe to Escanaba would be fine." He shook his head. "Green Bay is too far."

Mark winced, but Bear Foot didn't seem to notice. Smitten, he seemed.

George got up. "I'm going to bed. It's late."

Mark looked at his watch. Nine o'clock. "Have a good night."

"Good night, sir," Yvonne said somberly. "I'm sorry about the disturbance."

"What disturbance?" George asked.

"You're so sweet," she said and blew him a small kiss.

George hobbled away with a grin plastered on his face.

Mark felt giddily spent, suddenly more at ease, more in command, less inhibited, as if he'd had a few beers. He walked over to Yvonne. "So how long have you known Peter?" he asked.

"Peter? Let's see. It's been three days."

"Three days!"

"Yeah, I met him at a gas station in Green Bay."

"What?" Mark chuckled. "That's funny."

"What's so funny about that? He was coming from Minneapolis."

"No, not that you met him in Green Bay. The gas station. He drives an electric car."

Yvonne laughed. "I guess that is kinda funny. He was using the restroom."

"And you were getting gas?"

"No, I work there."

"I worked at a gas station once too," Bear Foot said.

"Oh yeah?"

Bear Foot nodded enthusiastically.

"We have a lot in common," she said.

"Wait." Mark sat down across from her and Bear Foot. "Let me get this straight. You met Peter at a gas station and you jumped into a car with him, on a trip around the lake?"

Yvonne shook her head. "No, of course not!"

"So you knew him from before?"

"No. I had a sign."

"A sign? What do you mean?" Mark asked.

A slight commotion erupted upstairs. Either the doctors were arguing over Emily or Peter had woken up. Mark walked to the edge of the stairs.

"What's going on?" Yvonne asked.

"I don't know."

Emily appeared at the steps a few seconds later and came down. "I need a glass of water."

"Aren't there any nurses up there to help with that?" Mark joked.

She responded with a steely glare. "I'll get it myself."

"Is he awake?" Yvonne asked.

"Yes, he's fine."

Emily blew by Mark.

"I sure hope so, seeing as three doctors are attending to him," he said.

She didn't bother reacting and continued into the kitchen.

Mark slid over and stood behind the dining room chair, staring at the kitchen door, waiting with crossed arms.

"So do you want to know the sign?" Yvonne said.

"Yes," Bear Foot answered eagerly.

"Mark?"

He turned his head slightly toward Yvonne. "Yes, of course. Do tell us."

"So the night before I met Peter at the gas station, I had a dream."

Emily came out of the kitchen. "Why are you glaring at me like that?" she protested.

"I'm not," Mark returned, shaking his head in an overdramatic denial. As she walked by, he added, "Just curious about your visitor."

Her shoe scraped the floor, but she progressed without turning back to look.

Mark returned his attention to Yvonne. "Sorry. You were saying—something about a dream."

"Yes. I had a dream that my father took me on a trip where we saw several lighthouses. So when I met Peter and found out he was going around the lake, I knew it wasn't a coincidence."

Mark didn't see that as much of a sign, but he didn't question that part. "So you asked him if you could come along, and he agreed?"

Yvonne shook her head. "No, he asked me."

"Just out of the blue? Did he have a dream of taking a trip with your father?"

"No, not like that. When he returned the restroom key, he told me that I reminded him of his sister. He even showed me a picture." She slapped her knee. "Sure enough, we looked a lot alike."

"And then he asked you to come along?"

"No, not quite. I asked him if he was on vacation—I had seen his Minnesota license plate. He told me about his trip around the lake in an electric car, and I told him about my dream. *Then* he asked me if I wanted to come along."

"I see," Mark said.

"And then Bear Foot told me about his vision with your aunt and the lighthouse."

"You were at the lighthouse?" Mark asked Yvonne.

Yvonne nodded and smiled at Bear Foot.

Mark found the entire episode absurd. Bear Foot and visions, and Yvonne getting in a car with a stranger on a days-long journey, and Vivian, in death, becoming some kind of matchmaker. But he was certainly glad to no longer be the target of frisky Yvonne.

Yvonne turned back to Mark with a slight scowl. "Why didn't you tell us Vivian had died?"

Mark put his hand to his forehead. Embarrassed, he looked away, shrugged, and then said, "Sorry." The day before flashed in his mind, when Emily had first arrived. She wouldn't have stayed had he told her, he thought. And so what? She would have left and found somewhere else, maybe, and all these people would not have been in the house now. "I should have said something, but things got a bit . . ." He muttered something about misunderstandings and extenuating circumstances.

The amount of movement upstairs increased, and soon Dr. Butcher came down the steps. "I'll be going now. Good night."

Yvonne and Bear Foot said goodnight, but Mark did not. He followed the doctor out, glaring steadily at the back of his head.

"Have a nice trip back," Mark shouted out.

"Thank you, Pastor," rang out before the door slammed shut.

What? Why did . . . Then it all rushed to him. Emily and Dr. Butcher. He was the mystery man on the other end of the phone. She had meant to meet up with *him*. That night when Dr. Butcher asked her to watch the other doctor, she was doing it as his girlfriend, not as an intern. That's why she felt so responsible for the death of that boy.

Chapter Twenty-Three

After Peter had been settled in bed and Dr. Currant had said goodbye, Emily stopped in her bathroom to rinse her face with cold water. She was certain Mark had made the whole connection between her and John. The night Nicholas died would be cast in a new light now. Then she thought angrily, *Why do I need to explain myself to him?*

Only Bear Foot and Yvonne were downstairs, sitting together on the sofa, when Emily came down. Yvonne stood up. "The other doctor said Peter is fine," she said, her voice shaking slightly.

"Yes, he is," Emily answered. She looked around, afraid Mark would pounce on her from some corner or closet. "It looks like he stopped taking his medication for some reason. Do you know why?"

Yvonne shook her head. "No. I didn't even know he was taking any."

"He shouldn't be driving, at least not until he gets back into the right sleep rhythm with his medication."

Yvonne crossed her arms. "I'm not driving back with him."

Emily shot a quick glance toward Bear Foot who grimaced in return. "Oh?"

"He accused me of stealing his car."

"Peter did?"

"Yes! Can you believe that?"

Emily grunted something noncommittal then asked, "Have either one of you seen Mark?"

"I think he went down to the basement," Bear Foot said.

Emily nodded and headed through the kitchen. She took a deep breath as she reached the steps going down. "Mark?" she called out.

"Yes?"

"Can I come down?"

"Sure."

With a long sigh, she descended at a deliberate pace, trying to figure out how to explain it. She found Mark in the large room sitting on the couch reading Vivian's story.

"Hey," she said.

"Hi," he returned flatly. He set the book down on his lap.

"You look different with glasses."

"Clark Kent." He flung his glasses off. "Superman."

"Not exactly what I was thinking, but I'm glad you have a healthy view of yourself."

Mark grinned.

She sat down next to him. "Wow, it's been a crazy day," she said patting her thighs.

"Yeah, crazy."

"Yeah."

He twirled his glasses. "Everything okay with Peter now?"

"I think so, yes."

"You and that other doctor were with him for quite a while, even after Dr. Bulcher left."

Hearing him saying John's name properly jarred her. "Oh," she said, turning away. "Yes, well, we were trying to figure out what happened. Seems he stopped taking his meds for some reason."

"I see."

"About Dr. Bulcher . . ."

Mark let out a low snort. He folded his glasses. "I have to admit, I did not see that coming. But now I understand."

"Understand what?"

"All of it, between you and him."

Emily felt her face burn. She took in a long breath. "Well that's private, and it surely has nothing to do with you."

"Of course not."

"Are you mad at me? Because I can't see why. If anyone has a right to be mad—"

"Who said I was mad? Do I sound mad?" Mark asked.

"No. But you seem, I don't know, distant or put off, like I've insulted you in some way."

"Nope. I only said things make more sense now. That's all."

"Like what?"

"Like why you feel the way you do about what happened that night at the hospital."

She bristled. "You don't know." She turned and started walking away. "Maybe I should find another place to stay."

"Why don't you just go and stay with Butcher?"

She stopped and spun around. "Maybe I will! This isn't a real B&B anyway."

"You're right," he yelled back. "And I should never have let anyone stay."

Emily ran up the stairs, and as she reached the top, he shouted, "And now I'm running an infirmary too."

In the kitchen she wiped her face with her hand and then, after composing herself, she came out, expecting to see Bear Foot and Yvonne in the living room. But they were gone.

As she reached the top of the stairs she heard a noise. She continued down the hall, worried that Peter had gotten up and was disoriented. Rather it was Bear Foot standing in the hall next to Peter's room as if he were keeping watch. Then Yvonne came out dragging a suitcase. Emily slipped into her room.

Falling on her bed, she stuffed her head in the pillow and cried softly for a minute, overwhelmed by her day. Mark. Vivian. Sarajevo. Vivian was dead. How could that be? *Fate cruel to deer. Really, jerk? I could have met my hero, and instead I got her screwball nephew.*

She thought about Peter and Yvonne driving around the lake. He could have gone cataplectic at any time and crashed into a tree or another car. Or hit a bus full of seniors touring the UP!

She thought about George. *How could they leave without him? Poor George. Traveling by himself, a widower with Alzheimer's who sometimes thinks his wife is still alive. What will happen to him once he's back on the tour?*

She couldn't believe that John had come all this way to find her. It wasn't just a silly fling with an intern. He obviously felt something strong for her, following her to Manistique, getting on the board of Lincoln Presbyterian. She was flattered, but she was also terrified. If she broke it off with him, could he make life miserable for her during residency?

And then Dr. Currant. Kind. Patient. Juxtaposed with John, Currant was easier, more comfortable with himself. She liked him. *We're always looking for talented, young doctors* played on a continuous loop as she drifted into sleep.

Chapter Twenty-Four

Despite my rant with Marie, I couldn't stay long after the two new doctors arrived. And they'd land in Sarajevo in less than a week. Getting Emela out of the orphanage was my mission now. But how? And to where? I didn't exactly know.

It turned out that Emela was not a common name, so I felt fairly certain the girl in the orphanage was the right one. But I needed to confirm that she was in fact the same Emela. Thank God for Eva. She found out the dead woman's name and even drove to her house and canvassed the neighborhood for information. She learned that her only relative, a cousin of the woman, had left with his family for Croatia at the start of the siege.

With no new word from Phil's State Department contact, I grew impatient and hatched a plan of my own: Getting a car ride out of Sarajevo and taking Emela with me to her relatives in Croatia. Who knew if it would really work, but I followed the contact instructions given to me by Ratko, the driver.

Two days later, in the evening, I got word that Ratko would be at the back door at exactly seven o'clock the following morning. I was prepared for this quick exit. I had told the hospital staff that new doctors were arriving, and that I would be leaving soon. In the dining hall, I said goodbye to my friends. They all thought I was taking a UN flight in the morning. Except Eva. I told her the truth, just in case something happened, so at least one person would know. Of course she tried convincing me not to do it.

When I opened the back door at seven o'clock, Ratko was pulling up. He got out of the car with a smile. "Time to leave beautiful Sarajevo, heh?"

I nodded. "Sort of." He helped me with my bags.

I sat up front with him and explained that we needed to detour to the orphanage.

His eyes narrowed on me for a brief second, then he pushed hard on the accelerator. I looked back at the hotel, pock-marked and dreary. I missed it already.

At the orphanage, Ratko translated for me. "I'm going to take Emela to her relatives in Croatia."

The women shook their heads. "Ne. Ne!"

"Didn't you arrange this with them?" Ratko asked me.

I shook my head. "Just tell them that it's what her mother would have wanted."

Ratko translated.

They said no again and started rambling angrily and gesturing for us to leave.

We started for the door. "How important is this to you?" Ratko asked me.

"Very."

Ratko stopped, said something sternly. His tone obviously threatening. The women immediately fell silent and retreated a few shuffled steps. One of them said, "Samo Emela?"

"Samo Emela," Ratko replied.

She left, went up the stairs, and came back down with the precious girl.

I placed my hand on Ratko's arm. "Thank you. Do I want to know what you said to them?"

Ratko shook his head.

"Why this girl?" he asked as we drove off. I was sitting in back now with Emela, holding her hand. He deserved to know.

We arrived in Split without incident. Before we parted, Ratko told me to try a refugee camp in Markaska if I couldn't find them in Split.

"Thanks for getting us out," I said to him. Then, very gravely, he thanked me for coming and invited me to return to "beautiful Sarajevo" in a decade or so.

Marie was happy to hear that I was safely out of Sarajevo when I phoned her. I didn't mention Emela, a serious violation of MSF rules. Marie told me the new doctors were arriving that day. I was both glad and scared for them.

The little girl accompanied me without protest to the various camps in and around the city. She had sad, roving eyes, conscious of the misery and hope-lessness all around. The camps were overcrowded, and more refugees came in each day, though the Croatian soldier at the border had told us that refugees were going to be turned back soon. With no luck finding Emela's relatives in Split, we headed south for Markaska the next day.

Markaska proved more organized. When I asked about Emela's family, an aid worker pulled out a list. Very fortunately, her relatives were on the list. The large camp had endless rows of blue and white tents. Men gathered in small groups, smoking, a sort of pleading despair on their faces, and women worked around their temporary homes, washing clothes and tamping down dirt; kids played soccer between rows of tents. A refugee there who knew some English assisted me with locating the family and translating.

Outside a low tent, I spoke to Emela's relative, her mother's cousin. I told him how Emela's mother had died in the shell attack waiting for water. His head fell, and he shook it slowly, and then he mumbled something.

"Emela means a lot to me." I didn't explain that I felt responsible for her mother's death, only that I had found her in an orphanage near the edge of Sarajevo. "I'm glad to have found you."

He explained that he had four young children of his own. He shook his head again, his eyes avoiding Emela, who was playing with her cousins, running around in the dirt. There was a smile on her face.

"Are you going back to Sarajevo?"

I shook my head. "No, to the United States for a little while."

"You take her. Nothing good here."

"No, I can't."

"Yes, to America."

I shook my head. "I'm not allowed to."

"Please."

I turned to Emela, still playing in the dirt. The camp was abysmal, but it wasn't any worse than other refugee camps I had been in. She'd certainly be cared for here. I could have left and that would have been that. But my conscience was not at ease. Her mother's desperate face kept appealing to me in my head. Would I leave my own child here? So I foolishly promised to get her to the United States.

Chapter Twenty-Five

When Emily woke up, disoriented, it was dark and quiet. She sorted slumber's fiction from yesterday's drama, certain only of the gloom that surrounded her. She sat up, realizing she had fallen asleep on top of the covers, and as she rubbed her face, it all came back quickly. She checked the time on her phone. It was 2:53. Thirsty, she clutched the glass on the nightstand, but it was empty. She headed downstairs to the kitchen.

She saw the light filtering up from the basement, and for a second considered turning back. She stepped softly to the water dispenser in the refrigerator door, and as she filled her glass, she listened for any sounds of movement, wondering why Mark was up so late. She deliberately re-ran their last encounter. A combination of sorrow, shame, and anger depressed her. The two of them had something there between them, even if she couldn't definitively pinpoint it. *Ruined now, whatever it was,* she concluded as the water brimmed. She carefully moved the glass to her lips and took a sip.

As she started the climb back to her room, she considered sneaking out in the morning without ever seeing him again.

The front door creaked open. Surprised, she jerked and nearly spilled her water. The moonlight barely entered the room through the front window, and she could make out only a silhouette—Mark's silhouette.

She briefly considered staying still against the wall of the dark stairs, but decided to speak instead. "What are you doing?"

"Aaah!" Mark gasped. "I didn't see you there," he whispered.

"Sorry," she whispered back.

He approached the stairs, a dark figure with an obscure face. "What are you doing?"

"I asked you first."

He let out a burst of breath. "I went for a run."

"At two in the morning?" she asked sharply.

"Yeah, I needed to relieve some energy. I stayed up reading Vivian's story." He shook his head. "It's hard to fully digest—come downstairs for a minute."

Emily's distance melted. She couldn't help it. It was as if they'd both just gone to Sarajevo and come back together. After considering it for a few seconds, she followed him.

In the basement living room, Mark explained the letters he'd received from Vivian when he was a child. "The last one I ever got was from Sarajevo in 1992." They were standing near the couch. *Doctors on the Borderline* was closed on the coffee table.

"You never heard from her again?"

Mark shook his head. "Nope." He blinked rapidly several times. "I tried contacting her when my mom died a few years ago, but I wasn't able to reach her."

"Oh," she said.

"I'm glad I got to read that. I never would've seen it if you hadn't pointed it out. It would've been tossed away. Just another book to box up for an estate sale."

Emily smiled. "Well I'm glad you did."

"And the end was surreal," he added excitedly. "It's crazy that you're part of that story."

"I know! I told you."

"I know, I know. It just didn't hit me entirely until I read it. . . . I'm so sorry about your mother. I didn't realize it while I read it, but when I finally did get it, it hit me hard." His eyes glistened.

"Thank you."

"You must think I'm a jerk."

"No, of course not."

"Of course you do."

She pressed her lips together.

"I should have told you up front that Vivian had died."

"The truth is, you were right. I wouldn't have stayed here. And if I hadn't stayed here, I wouldn't have read that book."

He sighed. "I shouldn't have judged you. It was wrong of me."

He sounded sincere. "No, that was my fault," she countered. "I let you in when I told you about that night at the hospital." She shook her head. "I certainly didn't expect *him* to show up here."

"Neither did I," he said with wide eyes.

She let out an abbreviated laugh. "I obviously wouldn't have told you his real name."

"But then I couldn't have made fun of it."

Emily shook her head and plunked onto the couch. "You know, deep down, I've always felt responsible for Nicholas's death. But I've always gotten past it by blaming others."

"You mean Dr. Butcher."

"Yes, and even Dr. Olsen."

"What ever happened to him?"

Emily's head drooped. "He quit. He moved back home with his parents."

"He quit being a doctor?"

She nodded. "It's a shame. But I've had thoughts—" She stopped.

"Of what? Quitting?"

She shook her head. "Never mind."

Mark sat down next to her. "You're a good doctor, a great doctor. You helped two people today."

She stared off. "But none of that makes up for what happened that night."

"There's nothing that can be done about that now."

"Maybe not." She stood up. "It's late—or early. Whichever. I'm going back to bed."

Mark yawned and stood up, too. He stepped toward her, put his arm around her and pulled her into an embrace. It felt strange and uncomfortable at first, and she stood there with dangling arms. But the way he held her, it lacked sensuality. It reminded her of her brother. *When was the last time Kyle hugged me?* . . . She shut her eyes and hugged him back.

"I'm sorry for being an idiot this whole time," he said.

"I'm sorry, too."

When they let each other go, he said, "I don't give hugs to all the guests, you know."

Emily chuckled, then whisked a developing tear from her eye. "I bet Yvonne wouldn't mind."

Mark laughed. "Don't be so sure. She and Bear Foot . . ."

"Yeah. How did that happen?"

He shook his head. "Beats me. He's head over heels, it seems. God knows why."

"Where is she now?"

"Upstairs, in Breakwater Lighthouse. Bear Foot's driving her back to Green Bay tomorrow."

"Is he with her?"

"What kind of hotel do you think this is?"

Emily laughed.

"It's got nothing to do with me! Law of Michigan," he announced.

"What are you talking about?"

"*Fawlty Towers.* Never mind. By the way, do you know why Dr. Butcher keeps calling me Pastor? Does he think this is a church-run hostel or something?"

Emily shook her head and shrugged. "You call him Butcher, he calls you Pastor."

"Weird . . . anyway, Bear Foot will be back in the morning to get Yvonne."

"So how's Peter getting back?"

"Driving."

"He can't! At least not yet."

"How long?"

"It depends."

Mark scratched his head. "Well this place is shutting down tomorrow. I've got a flight to catch. He'll have to move to the Cozy Inn."

Emily nodded, said good night, and walked back up to her room. Slipping under the covers, she felt good and optimistic and calm, glad they had reconciled.

Feelings for Mark? No, she didn't think so, but she did wonder if he had any for her.

Chapter Twenty-Six

Mark awoke awash in war, amongst the besieged, running from a sniper's bullet, ducking exploding shells, carrying a little girl out of the Valley of Death. It took a minute for him to disentangle himself from the night, a night full of blurry, swirling dreams. The intertwining of it all—Emily and Vivian and Sarajevo— kept circling back as fantastically impossible. And at the brief point where dream and real life were yet unsorted, that improbable coincidence seemed to belong on the side of persistent dream.

Mark got up off the couch and stopped the alarm on his phone. He had set it for six thirty and purposely placed it far away. Standing in the drab light of morning, he groggily thought about Emily, the massive coincidence that brought her to this house. Or was it fate? Either way, he had an extraordinary connection with her. And they'd soon be living near each other in Chicago. Again, fate or another unlikely coincidence?

He stretched before heading up the stairs, breakfast to be made. He was a little eager, which he would have admitted to no one. Breakfast was his meal specialty. He had inherited a scrumptious French toast recipe from an ex-girlfriend who was obsessed with it, and he could make eggs ten different ways, a skill he'd learned from his mother.

Before embarking on breakfast for five—or six if Bear Foot joined ("See you tomorrow morning," he had said)—Mark entered the dining room expecting to find George reading his book under a flashlight. But he wasn't there, and a rush of worry struck him. He dashed to the front door. Locked. George was still sleeping, he thought, and he was glad the old man was getting some rest.

Back in the kitchen, Mark opened the oven, which he had left ajar for two nights with slices of bread spread over the racks inside. Antithetical to the original purpose of *pain perdu*, he knew. He poked the bread, satisfied with its staleness. He gathered the ingredients: cognac, orange juice, a lemon, vanilla extract, eggs, butter, milk, nutmeg, cinnamon, sugar, and salt.

After a quick shower and shave, Mark returned upstairs and repeated the routine: checking for George, checking that the door was still locked. *Good, no chasing the streets for the old man.*

He removed the bread from the oven and set the temperature to four hundred. He lined a cookie sheet with foil, laid strips of bacon on it, and set it in the oven. He placed a pan on the stove and started cooking the sausages. As he quietly whisked the eggs and added the other items, he heard faint steps creak from the second floor. He hoped it was George or Emily. He didn't want to see to Yvonne this early—or alone. And certainly not Peter.

A few minutes later, the footsteps upstairs quieted. The muffled noise of a shower began. Then a knock sounded on the front door. Dr. Butcher eagerly coming for Emily, he wondered. But it wasn't even eight o'clock.

As he approached the door, he made out Bear Foot through the window and opened the door wide. "Good morning," he said softly. "There are still people sleeping."

Bear Foot nodded and stepped gingerly into the house. He removed his shoes and followed Mark into the kitchen. "You're still planning on driving Yvonne back to Green Bay?" Mark asked.

Bear Foot nodded. "Yep. Washed my truck and cleaned the inside and everything."

Mark nodded deliberately. "You seem, I don't know, struck by—"

"How did you know? Is my face still pale? I barely slept last night."

Mark shook his head. "No, you look fine. I only thought that after watching you with her last night."

"Who? What are you talking about?"

"Yvonne. Who else?"

"Oh, I thought you meant struck by another vision. Because I was."

"Another one? Did Vivian not like where we set her on the lake?" Mark chuckled.

"No, no it wasn't her," he answered seriously. "It was a man. Just a voice, strangely familiar though."

"A man? What did he say?"

"He said, 'Stay in Manistique.' He said it twice."

"Just a voice?"

"Yes."

"That's not much of a vision," Mark said, amused.

"I was lying in bed in the dark," he replied gravely.

"And you're still planning on taking Yvonne to Green Bay . . ."

Bear Foot sighed. "Yes."

Mark played along. "You think it's wise, given your vision?"

"It might not have been meant for me. I might only be a messenger."

"Messenger?"

"It's meant for someone else."

"Who?"

He shook his head, his eyebrows knitted. His voice drifted lower, "I don't know." Then he snapped his thick fingers. "It sounded like that old guy."

"What old guy?"

"The one who won't eat pie out of the tin."

"George?"

"Yeah, George. It sounded a lot like him, only different."

Mark grabbed a slice of bread and dunked it in the egg mixture. "He's upstairs. You can ask him about it when he comes down."

"French toast?"

"Yes. Would you like some?"

Bear Foot nodded eagerly. "Yes!"

Mark turned the gas stove on and set it to medium low. He got out a pan and cut a piece of butter, sliding it into the pan.

"Go have a seat in the dining room, and I'll bring it out in a few minutes. Care for some orange juice or coffee?"

Bear Foot nodded. "Coffee, yes." He grabbed a mug and set it under the machine.

"You know how to use that?"

Bear Foot nodded. He grabbed a pod out of the drawer and swiftly set it. "Vivian bought this machine only a month ago. She showed me how it works. It's fancy."

Mark nodded. The machine poured out Bear Foot's coffee. He took a sip before heading to the dining room.

The floor above creaked again. Mark didn't care if Yvonne came down now that Bear Foot was there, but he thought it was probably George.

Several minutes later, Emily emerged.

"This looks good," Bear Foot said as Mark served him the toast. "Thank you."

"Bacon will be out in a couple minutes," he said. "Good morning," he added to Emily. She was dressed. Her hair was wet, flat, combed down.

"Good morning." She smiled.

"French toast, or would you like eggs?"

"Coffee."

"Right, of course," Mark said and retreated into the kitchen. He was hit with a twinge of nervousness. There was an intimacy between them, though he couldn't quite pinpoint what it was.

Mark returned with Emily's coffee. "What are your plans for today?"

She took a sip. "I need to get my car this morning and then deal with my little problem at the Cozy Inn."

He resisted a smile, heartened that she'd referred to Dr. Butcher as a "problem."

"How about you?" she asked.

"Let's see, make breakfast, make sure no one else is coming, and make sure everyone is on their way. I have to leave tomorrow morning."

"So, last day running a B&B, huh?"

"Yep. Finally retiring."

"Where's George?"

"Still asleep."

"You sure?"

Mark chuckled. "I know what you're thinking because I thought the same thing." He pointed at the front door. "The door was locked this morning. Unless he took a key with him . . ."

"This is the best French toast I've ever had," Bear Foot said. "— Though don't tell that to Betty."

Mark didn't know who that was, and he wasn't curious enough to ask. "Thanks."

"I'll have to try it," Emily said, "but after I go for a walk. I need to clear my head."

"Sure."

Yvonne came down the stairs, and when Bear Foot saw her, he stood up, nearly tipping the chair over in his haste. His posture was comically erect. They all exchanged good mornings. Bear Foot glanced down at his half-finished plate. "Sorry, I should have waited," he said. He licked the bit of syrup at the corner of his mouth.

"No, it's fine. Sit down. Finish. I'll catch up."

"Coffee?" Mark said.

Yvonne nodded.

Emily followed Mark into the kitchen. He got a mug out of the cupboard. She was staring at him.

"What?" he asked.

She shook her head.

"You're worried about George, aren't you?"

Emily shrugged and nodded. "A little."

"You want me to go up and check?"

She shook her head immediately. "No." Then she closed her eyes momentarily and sighed lightly.

"All right, all right. Let me give Yvonne her coffee and get the bacon out, and we can go check."

She smiled, resting her hand on his upper arm.

Bear Foot was sharing his French toast with Yvonne when Mark set the bacon on the table. Bear Foot immediately reached for a piece. When he saw Emily's earnest stare, Mark said, "I'll make more French toast in a few minutes."

When they reached the top of the stairs, Emily asked if he had seen Peter yet.

Mark shook his head. "Do you want me to knock on his door, too?"

"No. I'd be worried about disrupting his sleep."

He glanced at her over his shoulder.

Stopping in front of the Indian Lake room, Mark reluctantly pressed an ear to the door. He didn't hear anything, so after looking over at Emily, who looked back with expectant arched eyebrows, he knocked lightly. No answer. He knocked again, a little harder. Still, no answer.

Shaking his head, Mark put his hand on the knob and turned it slightly. It was unlocked. Holding a breath, Mark twisted it the rest of the way and cracked open the door. "George?" he said in a hard whisper.

No answer. Concerned that George had somehow slipped out, he opened the door further. Relieved to see George in bed, Mark immediately retreated, backing up into Emily. She pushed him out of the way.

"What are you doing?" Mark whispered.

Emily rushed up next to George and placed the back of her hand against his face.

"What are you doing?" he repeated. "You're going to scare him to death!"

Emily shook her head. Her eyes drooped. "He's cold," she said.

"Then put another blanket on him."

"No, Mark . . . he's dead."

Mark felt his body sink through the floor before landing back in place, feeling wobbly. "He can't be." He trudged toward the bed, his legs heavy. He yelled out, "George!"

"He's dead, Mark."

"Come on, George," he pleaded. He stood in front of him but didn't touch him. He stared at George's peaceful face for any sign of breathing. None. He looked at Emily. "What happened?"

"I don't know. He's been dead for hours. My guess is heart attack. They'll have to do an autopsy." She pulled the sheet over his head.

"No, Emily," he murmured. He backed into the wall and then slid down.

"Did you hear me? You have to call the police."

Mark thought for a second. "Right."

"Right, what? Do you want me to call?"

"No. Can't it wait?"

"Calling the police?"

"Yes."

"Why would you want to wait?"

"I don't want to alarm the other guests."

"Guests? You mean Yvonne and Peter, who you didn't want here in the first place?"

Mark leaped up. "I have an idea. I'll be right back."

"I'm not waiting in here."

Mark rushed downstairs and forced a smile as he landed in front of Bear Foot and Yvonne. "Bear Foot, why don't you take Yvonne for a morning stroll to the boardwalk while I make more French toast?"

Bear Foot looked at Yvonne. She said, "That sounds nice."

Emily came down the stairs as Bear Foot and Yvonne headed toward the front door.

"What are you doing?" Emily asked Mark.

"Calling the police," he mouthed.

"Huh?"

Bear Foot opened the front door.

"Did you tell them?" she asked, gesturing toward the two walking out.

Mark shook his head. "They're going for a walk," he said, pulling out his cell phone.

While they waited for the police to arrive, Emily sat in the kitchen while Mark made more French toast. It seemed ridiculous to continue with a dead body upstairs, but it gave him something to do.

"Are you okay?" she asked.

"Who, me? Yeah, sure. I'm fine. Why?"

"Did you wash your hands?"

"Yes. But I didn't touch him."

She nodded. Then as Mark drowned the bread in the batter, she let out a little snort.

"What?"

"Nothing. Sorry. It's not funny."

"What?" he demanded.

"Nothing. It's just . . ."

"Just what?"

"You were going to leave him there."

"Leave who where?"

"You were going to leave George in bed because you thought he was still sleeping."

"How was I supposed to know he was dead? If a guest isn't singing 'Oh What a Beautiful Mornin',' I don't immediately think they're dead. This isn't the Burma railway!"

"The Burma railway? What on earth are you talking about?"

He laughed, a release. "Never mind. It's way too soon for joking around—though George would have certainly gotten that."

She shook her head at him. "Did he mention to you if he had any kids?"

"No. I'm not sure who to contact."

There was a knock on the door.

"Can you get that?" Mark asked. "I'll be right out."

"Yes," Emily said and headed for the door as he finished browning the piece of toast. There was a hushed discussion in the entryway that he could not make out. He placed the toast on a stack of three, turned off the stove and walked out.

It was Officer Bryst again. "What? Don't they give you any time off?" Mark said.

He shook his head. "Usually it's pretty quiet on Saturday morning, but with this place . . ."

"Sorry," Mark said.

"So this is not the guy with the electric car who has trouble sleeping?" the officer said to Emily.

"No," she said.

"Really his problem is staying awake," Mark said. The officer's stoic face slightly unnerved him. Mark cleared his throat. "It's George who died, the person your brother picked up yesterday."

"Oh, your brother is a state trooper. No wondered you look so familiar. He helped me the other day."

Officer Bryst nodded and turned to Mark. "So who found the deceased?"

Mark and Emily glanced at each other before they answered. Mark said, "We did." Emily said, "I did."

"It was *both* of you?"

"I opened the door and Emily went and found him. She's a doctor."

"Why did you go in? What made you think something was wrong?"

"He didn't answer when we knocked," Mark said.

"But why did you come up to his room in the first place?"

"He normally gets up early, so we were worried," Emily said.

"Normally? I thought he was only here for a couple nights."

"Yeah, that's right," Mark said. "But because of his issues, we thought he might have wandered off again."

"What issues?"

"Alzheimer's," Emily said.

"Okay," Officer Bryst said, nodding his head. "Why don't you take me to him?"

The officer followed Mark, and Emily followed the officer.

When they got to the room, Mark reached for the knob, but the trooper said, "Wait."

Mark abruptly turned. "Yes."

"Was it locked or unlocked before you decided to go in?"

"It was unlocked," Mark answered.

Officer Bryst gave a single nod and Mark opened the door and stepped aside.

Emily stayed outside the room with Mark, and the two watched as the officer pulled the sheet down. He checked only briefly before replacing the sheet.

"All right. I'll call the coroner, but it's Saturday."

"Yes."

"—Which means he probably won't be here for a couple hours."

Mark nodded. "Okay." He glanced at Emily before following the officer down the stairs.

Standing in the entry, Bryst said, "I'll need some information from you before I go."

"Sure."

"What's his full name?"

Mark shot a look at Emily, then grimaced and said, "Actually, we don't know."

"Didn't he fill anything out when he checked in?"

"No," Mark replied.

"Do you know where he lived?"

"Somewhere in the Milwaukee area."

"Maybe you can get some information from his wallet," Emily suggested.

"Should I go look for his wallet?" Mark asked.

"I'd prefer you not touch anything up there until the coroner comes. I'll come back after that."

"Will you take his things, then?"

"Only if you can't keep them until his next of kin arrives."

"I'm heading back to Chicago tomorrow."

"How about you? When are you leaving?" he asked Emily. "The coroner might want to talk to you."

"Today, after they install a new windshield on my car"

"Good luck with that," he said.

"Why do you say that?" Emily asked irritably.

He shook his head. "Nothing. What smells so good?"

"Oh, that would be either the bacon or the French toast," Mark replied.

"Mmm. Both sound good."

Mark simply nodded, feeling a bit guilty about not offering any, but he needed the officer gone before Bear Foot and Yvonne returned.

"How about that other fella? Is he still here?"

Mark nodded. "He's leaving once he gets up and has breakfast."

"And the woman?"

"Bear Foot's driving her back to Green Bay."

Bryst nodded, slowly starting for the door. "All right. I'll be back later."

Mark stared out the window as the officer got in his car and left.

"Why are you acting so funny?" Emily asked.

"I don't want Bear Foot and Yvonne to see him and ask questions."

"You're really not going to tell them?"

"Not if I can help it."

"Haven't you learned your lesson?"

"What lesson?"

"Being up front is better than hiding the truth."

"Oh really?" Mark replied bitingly.

Emily sighed. "Why are you so worried about them knowing, anyway? They're not children."

"Come on. Bear Foot will want to build a fire or read poetry or who knows what. As for Yvonne, she's a little wacko, so . . ."

"How are you going to explain the coroner?"

"He won't be here for a while. I just need to get them all out of here before then."

"If you say so. I'm going to call the dealership. The officer made me a little nervous."

"Why?"

"Because when I told him that they were fixing my car, he said, 'Good luck with that' a little sarcastically."

"He was probably just kidding, knowing the pace of things around here."

She sighed, "Hopefully."

"I'm going to finish making breakfast."

Emily left. When she returned several minutes later, she fell into the dining room chair with an abject look on her face.

"Uh-oh. W`hat's wrong?"

She grabbed a piece of bacon. "They can't find him."

"Can't find who?"

"The installer."

"What?"

"Yeah, I don't get it either. Apparently he doesn't live in town."

"He has to turn up, don't you think?"

"With my luck lately . . ."

Peter came down as Mark finished laying out breakfast. French toast, bacon, scrambled eggs, sausages, orange juice, fruit.

"Good morning, sir," Mark said to Peter as he approached.

"Good morning," he replied in an enervated tone. He avoided eye contact.

"How are you feeling?" Emily asked.

He cleared his throat, said "Fine, fine," and proceeded to deliver a mumbled apology that ended with, "Anyway, I'm sorry for whatever disturbance I caused."

Emily answered, "No reason to apologize. I'm just glad you're feeling better. It was a little scary there for a second because nobody knew about your condition until we found your medication."

"Are you a doctor?"

"Yes. I was with you last night after you had an episode."

"Thank you for helping me. It hasn't happened in a very long time. At least three months. I was sort of starting to think it might not ever happen again."

Mark asked him if he wanted something else besides what was on the table.

Peter looked, then asked, "Do you have any cereal?"

"Cereal?"

"Yeah, almost any kind will do. I'm not picky."

"Cereal. Okay, let me see. I'll be right back." Annoyed, Mark trudged back into the kitchen.

He heard Emily say, "I suggest you wait until you're on a good sleep cycle again before you get back behind the wheel."

Mark brought out a box of cereal, Ben's O's. It seemed to be a generic, store brand. "Will this do?"

"Sure. Perfect," he said and proceeded to pour the cereal into a bowl and add some milk from a pitcher on the table.

Mark asked Emily for help in the kitchen.

"What is it?" she asked when they were inside, the kitchen door closed.

"He can't stay here, and Yvonne's not driving him," he whispered.

"Fine. Why are you telling me?"

"He has to go to the Cozy Inn. He can hang with your boyfriend."

"He's not my boyfriend."

"Whatever. Bear Foot and Yvonne are bound to show up soon," he said softly. "One of us has to run interference."

"Interference?"

"Yeah. For an hour, forty-five minutes at least."

She shook her head. "Who knows when the coroner is coming."

"You heard. A couple hours. That should give us enough time to get rid of Peter and Yvonne and Bear Foot."

"Us?"

"Yeah, you and me. You're part of this plan." He grabbed her by the shoulders. "We're a team here."

Emily shook her head. "No, this is your thing. I'm fine with them knowing."

He released her. "So you're not going to help me?"

She hesitated a second. Sighed. "Fine, but how am I supposed to distract them?"

Mark shrugged. "I don't know. Be creative—oh, tell Bear Foot to take you and Yvonne to Indian Lake to see the Indian cemetery."

"How far is it?"

"It's like two, three miles."

"Wait, Indian Lake?"

"Yeah."

She thought for a second. "I think my friends live there." She pulled out her phone.

"What friends?"

She shook her head. "The people who helped me after my accident. They drove me to the dealership." She tapped her phone a couple times. "Here it is. I think they said it was on Indian Lake."

"Perfect. Go visit them."

"But I don't have anything to give them."

He remembered the white wine in the fridge. "I got it," he said and took out the bottle.

"Isn't a bit early to be giving someone wine?"

"If it's past nine, it's fine. Now that's poetry."

"You're an idiot." She reached for the bottle.

"Please go. I only need a short time to get rid of Peter."

Shaking her head, she tucked the bottle into the crook of her elbow. "All right, I'll play along." She turned and grumbled over her shoulder, "But I don't think this little plan of yours is going to work."

"We shall see," Mark muttered, and followed Emily out of the kitchen. She continued out the front door.

Mark clasped his hands together. "Anything else I can get you for breakfast?" he asked Peter.

"No, I'm fine. Thank you. This is perfect."

Mark smiled, then said, "So we have a ten o'clock check out, normally. But if you need a little more time . . ."

"I didn't know, sorry." He hectically glanced at his watch. "But sure, sure, we should be ready to go by then. I need to check with Yvonne. Have you seen her this morning?"

"She's not here, but you don't need to worry about her. She found a ride back to Green Bay."

"What do you mean? With who?"

Mark stumbled for a second before getting out, "A local."

"I don't understand."

"Well, after last night . . ."

"She's upset about what happened to me, isn't she?" He glanced away. "I should have told her about my condition. But it's been under control for so long," he explained.

"Do you remember *everything* that happened last night?"

Peter looked away and nodded uncertainly. "Most of it, I think. I know I passed out, Yvonne and I were talking . . ."

"Do you remember calling the police?"

"Police? No, of course I didn't. Why would I call the police?"

"And then you had an argument with Yvonne."

The stern lines on his face deteriorated. Looking away, he slowly shook his head. "I'm sure I don't remember any of that. What was the argument about?"

Not wanting to explain the little he knew, he replied, "I don't know much about it."

"So she's upset with me?"

Mark tilted his head back and forth. "A bit, I guess, though she was really worried when you passed out."

"I'd like to apologize to her," he said.

Mark heard the thud of Bear Foot's truck door. He slid over to get a view and watched as Bear Foot got into his truck with the two women as passengers. They drove off. It had worked. "The doctor said you shouldn't be driving until you're . . ." He couldn't think of a word other than *normal*. "Stable," he said, snapping his fingers. "Stable with your medications and sleep."

"I feel pretty good now."

"I recommend the Cozy Inn."

"Can't I stay here?"

"No, unfortunately, no," he said, sounding as melancholy as he could. "The Cozy Inn is a fine hotel, though."

"The Cozy Inn?"

"Yeah, just a mile or so east on the highway."

"Can I wait for Yvonne?"

Peter pouted slightly, which irritated Mark.

"I'll let Yvonne know you're there. That way, she can see you if she wants to. Okay?"

Peter nodded and grabbed the box of cereal. He poured a little more into his bowl, which had a little milk left. Then he poured a little more milk.

Mark started for the parlor. "If you need anything, just holler."

"Did George leave?" he asked.

Mark couldn't believe he remembered George. "He's . . . umm . . ." He groped with the truth, as Emily had suggested, but saying, *He's dead, and his body is upstairs* risked upsetting the man even more. He seemed emotionally on edge as it was. "He's gone."

A couple of minutes later, Mark heard the chair slide back. "Thanks for breakfast," Peter called out.

Mark stepped out of the parlor and gave him a single nod. "Sure."

"That was excellent cereal. I'll have to find that brand when I get back to Minneapolis." He told Mark that he would be back down quickly to check out.

Ten minutes later, Peter returned. He handed the key to Mark, who slipped it into his pocket and pointed at the suitcase. "Let me take that."

"Don't I need to pay first?"

Mark shook his head. "I'll send you a bill in the mail, if that's all right."

Peter shrugged. "Sure, okay."

Mark grabbed the suitcase and started for the front door. He halted when he heard a car door slam. He immediately turned around and nearly bumped into Peter. "Sorry, let's go this way! It's a shorter way to the car."

"Okey-dokey."

Another door slammed. Thinking it was likely the coroner, Mark charged toward the kitchen, Peter following at a distance. "This way, this way," he insisted pushing through the kitchen door. A bit embarrassed, he explained, "There's a back door over here that leads straight to the garage. Much easier than going all the way around."

"All right, thanks."

The doorbell rang. Mark ignored it and opened the back door.

"The doorbell just rang," Peter said and pointed back with his thumb.

"It's all right. They can wait a minute."

"No, I'm fine. I can see my way to the garage. Is it unlocked?"

"Yes." He set the suitcase just outside the door and stepped out of the way, practically pushing Peter out the door. "Thanks for staying."

"Tell Vivian thank you."

The remark caught Mark by off-guard. *That's right, he was asleep during all that.* "Right. Goodbye." He shut the door and ran to the front.

Mark stopped when he got close enough to see through the thin curtain. But he had made such a ruckus trampling toward the door that he couldn't tiptoe his way out now.

Mark opened the door. "Dr. Butch—Bulcher. Bulcher. Sorry."

"Good morning. Is Dr. Davis in?"

"Unfortunately, *Emily* isn't here right now. I'll let her know you stopped by." He started shutting the door.

"Wait!" the doctor protested.

Instead of opening the door again, Mark tilted his head to look through the crack. "Yes?"

"Can I wait for her to come back?"

"No, sorry, we don't allow visitors inside," Mark replied. "Unless it's a medical emergency, of course." He started closing the door.

"I waited inside yesterday," he protested.

It struck Mark as ridiculous to continue the conversation this way, so he begrudgingly opened the door wider. "Guests are allowed to have visitors, of course."

"Is he here?"

"Who?"

"The older gentleman who let me wait. I think, George."

"George? No, unfortunately, he passed away last night. Anyone else you want to check with?"

"Hello," came out behind Mark.

Mark finched. He turned around "Why are you back?" he asked Peter tersely.

"What do you mean he passed away?" Butcher asked.

Mark ignored the doctor.

"I forgot my guitar," Peter said. "You don't mind if I go up and get it, do you?"

"No, no, go right ahead," Mark replied nervously.

Peter started up the stairs.

"Are you serious?" the doctor asked.

Mark turned back. He looked at Butcher intently. "About George? Yes." *Dead serious*, he wanted to say.

"What happened?"

Mark shrugged. "We don't know. Emily and I found him this morning."

"You don't know the cause of death?"

"No. Emily thinks he had a heart attack, but we won't know until they do an autopsy."

Dr. Butcher shook his head. "This place has some bad karma."

Mark looked at him sardonically. "An elderly man passed away and a narcoleptic man fell asleep. I'd hardly call that bad karma. it's not like a ten-year-old boy died."

Butcher's eyes widened before he raised his hands slightly. "Didn't mean anything by it, Pastor."

"Why—" Mark heard Peter's footsteps coming back down the stairs behind him. Butcher's eyes focused behind Mark. He started shutting the door again. "Never mind. Good bye."

Butcher made a move, leaning his head inside the house. "How are you feeling, sir?" the doctor called out.

Mark scowled at Butcher. Peter squinted.

"Fine, fine. Thank you." He approached the door. "Do I know you?"

"No," Mark cut in. "This is the third doctor who came to help you yesterday."

"Three doctors?"

"I'm visiting from out of town, and I was in the area, so . . ."

"Thank you for helping me," Peter said in a gracious tone.

"Yes, of course. I'm John Bulcher."

"Peter Hinton." He extended his hand.

Mark got out of the way, and the doctor immediately stepped inside. "Are you feeling back to normal?" Butcher asked.

"I think so. Yes. But I'm staying one more day."

Butcher nodded. "I think that's a really good idea."

"Okay," Mark said, clasping his hands. "You got everything?"

"Yes, thank you for you hospitality."

"I thought you were staying," Butcher said.

Peter's eyes shifted briefly to Mark and then back to the doctor. "Unfortunately, there are no extra rooms tonight."

Behind the doctor, a white van slowed, the brakes squeaking. It stopped on the opposite side of the street. This was the coroner, Mark was sure. He pushed the door toward Butcher, who was standing in the way, then pressed firmly on Butcher's shoulder, shoving him inside so he could shut the door.

"Sorry. I don't want the mosquitoes to come in."

"Where are you going, then?" the doctor asked Peter. "You shouldn't be driving yet."

"Yes, Emily said the same thing," Mark answered, trying to speed up the conversation. "He's going to the Cozy Inn." He patted Peter's shoulder. "You'll still get the record even if it's an extra day."

Peter nodded.

"What record is that?" the doctor asked.

Peter's chest puffed slightly. "First electric car to do the Lake Michigan Circle Tour," he replied.

"Oh really? Interesting."

Mark peeked through the curtain. Someone was getting out of the van.

"Why don't you show him your car?" Mark said.

"Sure," Peter said excitedly. "Would you like to see it?"

The doctor nodded unenthusiastically.

Mark led the way with an outstretched arm, trying to rush them. "Go ahead and go out through the back."

Peter started for the kitchen, and the doctor followed, leaving Mark a distrustful look.

"Good luck," Mark said.

From the porch, Mark watched a man open the back of the plain white van, no markings indicating that it was from the coroner's office. For all he knew, the man was a painter or a handyman. After a minute he pulled out a stretcher that popped down on wheels as it left the van. He stood next to it for a moment, arms akimbo, then closed the van doors and crossed the street.

Mark pulled out his phone and texted Emily: *your boyfriend is here. the coroner showed up too.*

Mark expected a second person to emerge from somewhere, but no one did. The man, who was tall and lanky, had thin, brown hair parted down the middle. Late forties. He traveled up the path and removed his sunglasses.

Ding. Mark glanced down at his phone: *He's not my boyfriend!*

"I'm from the coroner's office," the man said as he walked up the path.

"Yes, been expecting you. Don't you need a second person?"

He sighed. His eyes were bloodshot. "Yes, but he hurt his hand yesterday."

"Not Conrad?" Mark blurted out.

"Yeah, you know him?"

"Not really," he said, whiffing a laugh. "We helped him yesterday when he got injured—well, my friend helped him. I only drove."

"Is your friend Dr. Davis?"

"How did you know?"

"Jimbo—uh, Dr. Currant. He told me all about her. I'm going to leave that there," he indicated to the stretcher behind the van, "until I see what the situation is."

Another car pulled up, an old Ford. The real estate agent, Ron.

"Excuse me one second," Mark said to the coroner and approached Ron. "Sorry, I meant to call you. It's actually a really bad time, again. I mean really bad."

"No, no. I'm here to help out Mike."

"Huh? I don't get it."

He pointed behind Mark. "The coroner. Mike."

"Ohhhh." They started up the walkway. "So obviously you heard we had a death."

He nodded. "A guest?"

"Yeah. It was the older gentleman from the casino tour."

"I'm very sorry to hear that."

Mark heard quick pounding steps and huffing. He turned to look. Running down the sidewalk came Dr. Currant.

"No need to rush, doc. The man is dead!" Mark called out.

Currant was winded. He appeared distraught. He stopped at the corner catching his breath, his shoulders slumped.

Mark texted: *your other boyfriend is here now too...jimbo*

"Are you related to the deceased?" the coroner asked.

"No, George was—is—was a guest here. He was traveling alone with that casino tour group that left yesterday."

"You run this place?"

Mark began with an explanation, then paused. "Sort of," he finally answered.

"Has anyone notified his next of kin?"

"No," Mark answered, hoping Mike the coroner wasn't expecting him, the hapless host, to do it. He watched Dr. Currant lumbering down the sidewalk toward the path.

"What happened?" Currant asked, throwing up his hands and dropping them exasperatedly. His face was ashen.

Mark shrugged. "We don't know yet."

Ding. *Who?* Emily had texted.

Mark texted *doc curant* quickly and shoved his phone in his pocket.

"I don't understand."

"Don't understand what?" Mark asked. He didn't think Dr. Currant knew George. "He was old."

A car turned out onto the adjacent street and honked. It was Peter in his quiet electric car.

Currant turned around.

Peter rolled down the window and waved, smiling like a kid off to college.

After a couple seconds, Dr. Currant lifted his hand as if he were holding a ten-pound weight, awkwardly waving back.

He turned back around. Color had returned to his face.

Mark figured it out. "It's George who passed away last night. Not Peter."

Currant exhaled loudly, then blew out a laugh.

Mark laughed too, then Ron and the coroner joined in.

"What's so funny?" Ron asked.

"Yeah, why are we laughing?" Mike asked.

Currant said, "I thought the narcoleptic man died. I didn't realize . . ."

Now the coroner laughed harder, then stopped himself. "I suppose we shouldn't be laughing."

"He shouldn't be driving yet," Currant said, frowning, pointing in the direction in which Peter had driven off.

"Don't worry. He's only driving to the Cozy Inn."

The front door opened, and Butcher appeared. "Hello, Dr. Currant," Butcher said, coldly professional, and stepped down onto the porch.

"Dr. Bulcher. It's good to see you again. Are you here for the deceased?"

"No." He shook his head.

Mark cut the slight awkwardness, "Why don't we get going? There is a guest returning soon, and I'd like to avoid all this if possible."

"Okay," the coroner replied. "Where's the deceased?"

"Upstairs, I'll show you."

They all followed Mark, including Dr. Butcher, up the stairs and to George's room. There, they stood around the bed, all five of them, silent for a second before Dr. Currant asked, "Did he complain of anything yesterday?"

Mark shook his head. "No, but he was talking strangely, and Emily—uh, Dr. Davis—said that he was likely suffering from the early stages of Alzheimer's."

Dr. Currant nodded and approached George.

A pit of sadness ached in Mark's chest, and he cleared his throat. "I'll be downstairs."

On his way down, the phone dinged. He stopped on a step and read his phone: *On our way back.*

He typed feverishly: *everybody still here!!!* but he didn't send it. He walked down the remaining steps and out the front door. *So what?* he thought. He stood there, on the front porch, looking out at the van with the stretcher behind it, thinking Emily had been right all along and he should have just been upfront about George's death. What could be the worst reaction from Bear Foot or crazy Yvonne? Mark laughed to himself. He deleted the text and instead thumbed, *it's fine... it doesn't matter*, and sent it.

When Mark looked back up, a car had pulled up in the street. Peter was back.

Mark ran down the steps, down the path, desperate again. At a minimum, he wanted to avoid Peter crossing paths with Yvonne. The passenger window rolled down.

"Hello," Peter said.

"Did you forget something else? A harmonica, maybe?"

"No, no," he replied with a slight laugh. "I don't play the harmonica." He pulled out a necklace and held it up, so that the two rings on it dangled.

"What's that?"

"It's Yvonne's necklace. She left it in my car. Can you make sure she gets it back?" He held it out for Mark. "The rings belonged to her parents, so it's obviously very precious. In fact, she got a little sad yesterday because George reminded her of her father. I can't imagine how upset she'd be if she thought she had lost this."

"George?" Mark muttered. "Here! You give it to her," he exclaimed, thrusting the necklace back toward Peter. "I'll tell her you're safeguarding it."

A glint surfaced in Peter's eye, "Yes, that's a good idea."

Mark quickly stood up straight and backed away. Bear Foot, Yvonne, and Emily would be back any minute.

Peter set the necklace down gently in the car's console. "Oh! Tell her I'll be in the restaurant next to the Cozy Inn until after lunch. They won't let me check in before noon."

"Got it." Mark felt a little guilty about kicking Peter out before the Cozy Inn would take him in. But only a little. He just wanted him gone now. "Bye."

Peter drove away.

About a minute passed, and then Mark heard a sputtering roar. He stepped into Lake Street and watched as the white truck rolled toward him—Bear Foot driving, Yvonne in the middle, and Emily leaning against the door.

Chapter Twenty-Seven

When Emily saw Mark standing in the street with his hand raised as if hailing a cab, she shook her head. *What plot or ploy now?*

"Is that Mark?" Yvonne asked. "Why is he out in the street?"

A white van was parked across from the house, and Emily knew it belonged to the coroner. "This should be interesting," she mumbled.

Yvonne nudged her lightly with her elbow. "He's such a goof, isn't he?"

"A goof, yeah," Emily replied absentmindedly as Bear Foot slowed and rolled up next to Mark. She cranked down the window.

"Hey," Mark said. Bear Foot threw the car into Park. "Peter left but he wanted me to tell you that he has your necklace."

Yvonne grabbed at her chest and gasped, "He stole my necklace!"

"No, no," Mark insisted. "You left it in the car."

"No I didn't!"

Mark pressed his lips together. Then a rigid smile appeared. "He's at the Cozy Inn. Just go see him, and you'll get it back—or actually the restaurant next door."

"Big Joe's?" Bear Foot said.

"I don't know. Whatever's next to the Cozy Inn."

"Yeah, Big Joe's. Great coffee."

"Do you recommend the fish?" Emily asked. Mark flicked her in the arm.

"It's not bad, but—"

"Why didn't he just leave it with you?" Yvonne asked, an irritated look on her face.

Mark's eyes darted down the street. "He said how important it is to you and wants to make sure you get it back personally."

Yvonne nodded and turned to Bear Foot. "Can you take me there?"

"Of course," Bear Foot answered. He shifted the truck into Drive.

"Wait!" Emily exclaimed. "I'm getting out." She fumbled with her seatbelt.

Mark pulled open the door, and she jumped out.

"Who's that at the house?" Bear Foot said with a head jab.

A man standing on the front porch was smoking a cigarette. She figured it was the coroner.

"Uhhh . . ." Mark shut the door. "Cleaning crew."

"Was I supposed to have checked out already?" Yvonne asked.

"No, no. Don't worry about it. Please take your time. Go get your necklace. Have a cup of the great coffee. Don't rush." Mark pulled Emily back away from the truck. "We'll see you later."

The truck sputtered, turned around, and then roared away.

"He's going to take her to Green Bay in that?" Emily asked. "I don't think they'll make it."

Mark headed quickly back to the house.

"I suppose that's the coroner?" Emily called out, hastening to catch up. The man on the porch had walked down the steps.

Mark nodded. "Yeah."

"Cleaners," she scoffed.

Reaching the front path, Mark called out, "Anything wrong?"

The coroner shook his head. "Nothing. Just having a cigarette."

"Sorry, I hate to rush you but I've got people coming back in about ten minutes, and I was hoping you'd be done before they got back."

"Ten minutes?"

"Yeah, can you do it?"

The coroner shrugged. "We can try."

Dr. Currant popped out of the house. "Hi, Dr. Davis," he said.

"Hello."

"Very sad . . ."

"Yes."

The coroner tossed the cigarette on the ground and hurried up the steps. "Hey, Ronnie, we got ten minutes to do this!" he yelled.

A voice came from inside the house. "Ten minutes? . . . Okay."

Mark, Emily, and Dr. Currant stood on the porch watching Ronnie and the coroner head to the van.

Emily glanced at the doctor, eyeing him. Shorter than Mark by a few inches, he was cute, with his slightly mussed hair and crooked glasses—a younger John without the arrogant slant.

"Em, guess who usually helps the coroner," Mark said with an impish grin.

"I don't know. Who?"

"The kid."

She made a quizzical expression. "What kid?"

"The kid who cut his hand yesterday."

"Conrad?"

Letting out a slight laugh, Dr. Currant said, "Yeah, that's right. He works at the mortuary. That's one of his jobs."

Behind the van the coroner took hold of one end of the stretcher.

"I didn't realize my real estate agent was the backup assistant," Mark said.

"Your real estate agent?" Emily muttered.

"His uncle used to own the mortuary," Currant explained. "Maybe his family still owns it, I don't know. Anyway he worked there at some point."

"Maybe it's good for business," Mark said. "You find out who dies, get a leg up on a potential sale."

"Maybe," Dr. Currant replied with a slight smile.

The coroner pushed the stretcher, with Ronnie helping to steer and jump the curb.

The three of them parted as the stretcher was lifted onto the porch and brought inside the house. Dr. Currant followed.

"What's the true story behind the necklace?" she asked Mark.

"What do you mean? There is no story. Peter has it."

"I thought it might be one of your schemes. It had that kind of ring to it."

"Scheme? No, of course not. The only *scheme*, if you want to call it that, is that I told Peter to give it back to Yvonne himself."

"I knew there was something more."

He shook his head at her. "Peter told me that George reminded Yvonne of her father. Can you imagine her reaction if she found out he was dead, watching the coroner bring down her lookalike dad in a bag?"

Emily shook her head and sighed. "No, probably not a good idea. She is a bit . . ."

"Loopy?"

"Don't be mean," she said, but then she nodded.

Emily and Mark walked inside the house and stood in the entry as the coroner and Ronnie talked, with the stretcher at the base of the stairs. The coroner said, "Yeah, we'll have to carry him down."

The two men plus Dr. Currant headed up. As the three neared the landing, John appeared. He stood at the top and pronounced: "I think you'll find ARF as a result of acute MI."

Emily cringed, embarrassed at the imperious way John shouted out the cause of death.

"Huh?" Mark said.

After pausing momentarily, the three continued toward the second floor. John's eyes lit up when he saw Emily. "There you are," he said and scurried down the remaining steps.

"Hi," Emily said blandly.

"You seem upset or something."

She shrugged. "Sad about George."

"He died quickly. He probably didn't suffer."

"Well I feel better," Mark exclaimed. He bumped Emily's shoulder with the back of his hand. "Don't you?"

She shook her head reproachfully.

After a heavy sigh, he said, "Time to clean up the kitchen and eat five servings of French toast."

"Sorry about that." Her eyes flitted to John and then back to Mark. "I'll have some later," she insisted.

"Sure," he sighed, and disappeared into the kitchen.

"So what are you doing here?" she asked John.

"You said you'd call me in the morning, and you didn't."

"Yeah, about that—"

"I can stay another day." His eyes had that intense beady look she hated.

"What?"

"I worked it out. One more day. Stay with me at the Cozy Hotel."

"No . . . no."

"Why not?"

"Because—" she stopped herself. "Come outside."

They moved to the porch and Emily shut the front door. "We can't do this anymore. I told you that yesterday."

"I thought I solved your issues."

She shook her head gently. "No."

"What, then?" he asked in an exasperated tone. Deep lines appeared on his long forehead, making him look his age. Older. "What else do you want from me?"

Emily took a deep breath. She knew how upset he could get. "This is difficult for me—"

"Only because you're making it difficult." His cell phone rang. He dug it out of his pocket. "I need to take this." He turned around and cleared his throat before answering, "Yes," in that haughty voice. "When I get back . . . Yes, I need to see him first thing on Tuesday . . ."

Emily stopped listening and stared out at the balsam fir. She imagined what fun it would be to string lights on that tree for Christmas. What a job! Maybe Bear Foot would do it. It'd look beautiful.

A commotion erupted inside. Emily walked to the door and peered through the glass but couldn't make out what was happening. She figured they were maneuvering George's bagged body down the stairs.

"—I asked for some big favors."

Emily wasn't sure if John was still on the phone or speaking to her. When she looked his way, the phone was by his side. "What?" she said.

"I asked for some pretty big favors so we could be at the same hospital."

Horrified, she shot John a confused look. It was John who had encouraged her to interview with Lincoln Presbyterian Hospital and to put LPH at the top of her list. But now she wondered—had they picked her because John intervened?

Emily flinched when the door opened. She stepped out of the way, and Ronnie came walking backwards through the door, rolling the stretcher.

"We should carry it now," the coroner insisted.

"Yep," Ronnie heaved. He hit a lever and lowered the stretcher.

The men bent down, picked up the stretcher, and carried it out the door and across the porch, between Emily and John. She touched the corners of her eyes as George's body, wrapped in a black bag, floated by. John maintained a delicate frown.

When they came to the pathway, the men stopped and raised the stretcher. They continued rolling it toward the van, wheels squeaking loudly.

Emily reached inside and pulled the front door shut. "Did you interfere in the match?" she asked firmly.

John turned away with a sideways smirk. He gently shook his head. "No, I wouldn't call it interfering," he said with little conviction. "They really liked you," he added.

"You mean, I wasn't at the top of their rankings?" She crossed her arms.

"I was a reference. I told them nothing I wouldn't have told them if—"

She grunted. "I can't believe this. You put your thumb on the scale." Getting matched with LPH had been momentous for her—a boost she needed after Nicholas's death. But now she knew the truth. John had meddled.

"Don't worry about the details. Just be glad it all worked out."

The men pushed the stretcher into the white van. The black bag vanished away. The doors slammed shut.

An anger that had been tamped down for a long while now burst. "It *didn't* work out!"

"Calm down, Emily," he said with clenched teeth.

"I'm done with being calm," she fired back.

"What are you talking about?"

Dr. Currant opened the door and stepped onto the porch. "Sorry. Excuse me," he muttered.

Emily's eyes fell, and her anger melted into a deep embarrassment.

"I have to get back to the hospital," he said, his head down. He scurried down the porch stairs.

"Goodbye," was all she could manage to say.

He raised his hand without turning around. The van started and drove off.

"Well I'm not going," Emily said.

"Going where?"

"To Lincoln Presbyterian." Her eyes moved away from John, and she watched as Dr. Currant in his white coat disappeared down Lake Street. She envied him.

John sighed deeply. When she looked back at him, he was shaking his head. An incredulous grimace creased his mouth. "You are completely overreacting."

"No. I don't think I am at all."

The door opened again. Mark popped out. "Are they gone?" he asked. He stood between Emily and John.

Neither one answered. Emily finally said, "Just left."

John grumbled, "Is there somewhere we can go?"

After briefly looking at Emily, Mark pointed back to the house. "I'll just pop back inside."

He started, but Emily hooked the crook of Mark's arm before he could turn away. "No, we're done here."

John's eyes focused intently on her. "You know what? I don't need this drama from you. Especially you."

Mark leaned toward him slightly. All she could think about at that moment was that Mark could take him. And for a small moment, she wished he would.

Instead John stomped down the porch steps. At the bottom, he turned abruptly. "You're going to regret this." Pointing his finger at her, he added, "You should be grateful for what I did."

"Ha!"

Mark took a step toward him. John turned and left.

"What a jerk," Mark said.

Emily, arms crossed, clenched her anger tightly, damming up the tears that yearned to spill. When Mark twisted back toward her, she darted inside.

She shut the door behind her and stood near the entry. Breathing as slowly as she could manage, she regained a bit of control.

Mark came inside after a minute. "You all right?"

Emily kept her back toward him. She nodded at first but then shook her head. "I just threw away the best opportunity of my life."

"What? That guy? No way!" He came around and stood in front of her.

"No, I mean—" She stopped. "I didn't deserve it anyway."

"Come on. You can do way better than him."

Then it sank in. All of it. The affair. The boy who wouldn't have died if she hadn't been involved with John. She buried her face in her hands and cried. She didn't flinch when Mark put his arm around her, pulling her toward him.

Emily sobbed.

Chapter Twenty-Eight

Emily lay in the living room reading *Doctors on the Borderline*, her legs fully stretched out on the couch. Mark liked seeing her like that, at ease in the house. He stared at her only briefly, long enough to realize that while he had no romantic inclinations toward her, he certainly had a strong concern for her well-being. For the first time, she seemed fragile to him.

Judging by the crack in the book, she was reading a different story. A new place, not Sarajevo. A new person, not Vivian. He approached, and he smiled a little, glad that she had dumped Dr. Butcher, and glad that Peter and Yvonne were gone. Though George's death still lingered. His belongings were upstairs, and his family was still unaware.

He plopped down across from Emily. She didn't look up. "Hi," he said.

Emily dropped the book on her lap. She turned toward him and managed a crooked smile. "Hi. What's up?"

He shook his head. "Nothing. Just seeing what you're doing."

She lifted the book and held it.

"I know you're reading. I meant—never mind. What do you want to do about lunch?"

She shrugged. "Not really that hungry."

"It's almost noon. Let me know when you do get hungry."

"You don't have to wait for me."

"No, I'm fine waiting."

She smiled before returning her attention to the book.

"Did the dealership get back to you yet?"

She shook her head. "No, not yet."

"Really?" he questioned, then cowered a bit under her glare.

She sat up, planting her feet on the floor, and pulled out her phone. After dialing the number, she sat up straighter.

"Hi Barbara, this is Emily again," she said pleasantly. The longer she listened the wider her mouth gaped. "So what now?" A tinge of tension cut her voice. She repeated "Okay" several times, then a sudden "Huh?" Her eyes grew wide. "What about tomorrow? . . . You're not open on Sundays?" She sighed. She listened for a few seconds before she said, "Please let me know as soon as you can. I've been here since Thursday." After a hollow thank-you, she ended the call and flung her phone on the cushion.

"What happened?"

"No one's in a hurry around here," she said with an exasperated sigh. "They can't reach the installer."

"Have they checked the jail?"

She rolled her eyes at him.

"Isn't there anybody else who can do it?"

"Yes, but they can't get ahold of him, either. Apparently he's not normally available on Saturdays. So if they can't find the first guy in the next couple of hours, it won't be ready until Monday, because the dealership is closed on Sundays."

"Look at the bright side."

She glowered at him. "Which is what?"

"You're getting the deer-car rate."

Emily sighed and hung her head.

"Well you're welcome to stay here as long as it takes."

"Thanks. At this pace, it might be a while."

"Fine by me. The house won't be sold for a while."

"So you're going to sell it? I thought you were thinking about keeping it."

"I am, sort of. I don't know. Regardless you have plenty of time to get your car fixed. Average selling time here is a long time—172 days."

"Why?"

Mark exaggerated a shrug. "Because not a lot of people want to live here."

"No, I mean, why don't you keep it?"

Her phone rang. She leaned over and looked at it. "It's the dealership," she said and then answered.

"What? You're kidding," she sighed into the phone.

Mark started thinking about changing his flight, going back on Monday evening instead of Sunday—

"Unbelievable," Emily said after hanging up.

"What? What happened?"

"The installer. He's off turkey hunting until the middle of next week."

It was around one o'clock when the doorbell rang. Mark was in the library reading *History of the Ottawa and Chippewa Indians of Michigan.* He headed for the front door and saw Emily, her neck craning. "Look, I didn't budge an inch."

"Your hotel training is complete."

"I'm starting to get hungry, by the way."

"Good. After I get this, we'll go get something."

When he got closer, he said, "It's Officer Bryst."

He opened the door and did a double take, mostly because of the uniform. "I was expecting your brother."

"Yeah, he isn't feeling well and asked if I would take care of this since I had encountered the decedent yesterday."

"Did he eat the fish at Diner 37?" Emily yelled out.

The trooper poked his head inside. "Who was that?"

"Emily. Remember? Deer-car. Come on in." Mark stepped aside.

"Oh, you're still here," he said, walking in.

"Yep. Know anyone who can install a windshield?"

Bryst shook his head. "We need to find and notify the decedent's next of kin. Do you mind if I go through his things?" He carried a folded bag.

Mark shook his head. "Do you need any help?"

"Actually, I'd prefer it if you were there while I look around."

As they headed up the stairs, Emily, who hadn't moved, said, "Maybe the bus tour has some information."

"That's a good idea, Em."

"I'll call the hotels in Harris and see if I can reach the person in charge."

Upstairs in "the decedent's" room, Mark watched as Trooper Bryst went through drawers. Bryst set a wallet and a box of antihistamine tablets on top of a book on the nightstand. Then he brought out several items from the bathroom: two pill bottles, a toothbrush and toothpaste, and a small pouch. He set those on the nightstand, too. He went through George's wallet. "Three hundred thirty-seven dollars in cash here." He fished out an identification card. "Brookfield, Wisconsin."

"A suburb of Milwaukee," Mark said. "He had mentioned he was from the Milwaukee area."

Bryst continued examining the contents of his wallet. "No other contact information here. Do you know if he had a phone?"

Mark nodded. "He did."

The trooper got down on the floor and looked under the bed. "Nothing down here." He got up and checked the armoire. Shirts and a jacket were hung in place. He rifled through the jacket pocket and pulled out casino chips. "Looks like he did well."

"He won those yesterday playing blackjack."

"Nineteen," Bryst said, and stacked the chips on the crowded nightstand. The other jacket pocket produced a flip phone. He started pressing buttons. "There's nothing under contacts. Worst case, we can try the last person he called."

Mark wasn't sure that would work. *Trudy's number,* he thought. Unless she was going to answer from the beyond. He tried to suppress a laugh, but it came out as a grunt.

"What's that?"

He cleared his throat. "Nothing."

Bryst closed the phone and set it on the nightstand. Next he lifted the suitcase and put it on the bed. He took a deep breath. "Everything seems in order here. My brother said you were leaving today?"

"Actually, Monday."

"Okay, fine. I'll take his suitcase and his personal effects with me. Hopefully I can locate his next of kin."

As the trooper finished saying this, Mark heard Emily running up the stairs. "I have some information!" she yelled out.

Mark stepped into the hallway. "What is it?"

"The tour director gave me George's emergency contact." She was slightly out of breath.

"Who is it?" Mark asked.

"His niece who lives in Chicago. Her name is Laura."

"Laura who?" he blurted. His mind raced to his ex-girlfriend. He had the panicked thought that she would turn out to be George's niece. *No way*, he told himself. *Impossible!* Yet Emily ending up in Vivian's house was just as impossible.

Emily shrugged. "I don't know. All I got was her first name and phone number."

"What's the number?" he fired.

With a quizzical look, she handed him the paper. "Why? What's the matter?"

Mark looked at the number; it was unfamiliar to him. "Okay," he sighed.

"Are you going to call her?" Emily asked.

"Me? Uh, I don't know. How about the doctor who declared him dead?"

"You found him first, right?"

Mark glowered at her.

"I'll make the call," the trooper said.

"No, I should do it." Mark said. "I at least knew him a little bit. What do I tell her about his things?"

The trooper gave him instructions, and with the slip in his hand, Mark stepped down to the library and took a deep breath before exhaling and doing it again. He was nervous about telling someone that their loved one was dead. He placed the call.

A woman answered. When Mark asked her if she had an uncle named George, she immediately asked, "Did something happen to him?"

"Yes. I'm so sorry to have to tell you this. He passed away last night in his sleep."

There was a stuttered whimper and then crying.

"I'm sorry," was all Mark could think of saying, and then he waited.

She sniffed. "Sorry. I just need a second."

"No problem. Take your time."

"Are you with the tour company?"

"No. He was a guest staying at my aunt's bed and breakfast."

"Bed and breakfast? Where?"

"In Manistique. Michigan. In the Upper Peninsula."

"He told me he was going on a bus tour of Indian casinos."

"He was, but something happened between him and—I don't really know what happened, but he ended up here."

"How did he die? Did he suffer?"

"No, he passed away while sleeping."

"Oh good," she whimpered. "He was starting to have issues. They thought maybe he had Alzheimer's, but he didn't believe it."

After a short pause he said, "So the state police here have his belongings. You can call them later and arrange to get his things."

"Okay. What town did you say?"

"Manistique." He spelled it for her, then asked her where she lived.

"Naperville, a suburb of Chicago."

"I don't live too far away from you. I live in Oak Park."

"Really? And how did you say you were connected to my uncle?"

He gave a short laugh. "It's sort of a long story. I'm actually temporarily managing a B&B that my aunt was running—she herself died this last week."

"Oh, I'm so sorry."

"Thank you. So you should call the police to arrange things. You can ask for Trooper Bryst. B-r-y-s-t."

"Bryst. Okay."

"Yes. He's here at the house now, but he should be done shortly."

"Okay. Can I have your number?"

"Sure," he said and gave her his cell number. Something nudged in Mark. She had a kind and gentle voice. "And you can call the mortuary tomorrow. You might want to talk to Trooper Bryst about that."

"I'm afraid I don't really know what Uncle George wanted. His wife was cremated."

"Can I ask you a question?"

"Yes, of course."

"When did she pass away?"

"About ten years ago. Did Uncle George talk about her?"

"Yeah, a bit. Maybe we can meet up when I'm back in Chicago. I got to spend a little time with him."

"Yes, I'd like that. Thank you for all your help."

"Of course."

He hung up, and momentarily lost himself in afterthought. Another Laura? But he put that out of his mind and admonished himself for even considering it.

Mark returned upstairs. He told the trooper about his conversation with Laura and that he should expect a call from her. A few minutes later, Mark helped the trooper out to the car with George's things.

The suitcase and a bag were placed in the trunk of the cruiser.

"We forgot one thing," Mark said suddenly. He went back to the house, grabbed Vivian's urn, dumped the water in a pitcher in the kitchen, left the lid on the counter, and ran back out.

"He was carrying a vase with him on the trip?" Bryst asked.

Mark simply shrugged. "Maybe he won it."

Back in the house after lunch, Emily clopped down the stairs, carrying bedsheets.

"What are you doing?" Mark asked.

"George's sheets need to be washed."

"Shouldn't they be thrown away?"

"No. They just need to be run through the sanitize cycle."

"I don't know." Mark thought for a second. "No, just throw them outside. I don't want to keep them."

"Really? Okay."

He nodded. "Thanks for doing that. You didn't have to, you know."

"I need to earn my keep."

As she walked out, the house phone rang. It took Mark a second before he moved to answer it.

"Hi, is this the Manistique Victorian?"

Mark hesitated. "Yes."

"My name is Ellen Terrence. You left me a voicemail about your inn being closed."

He remembered. Three nights. Arriving Saturday, leaving Tuesday. By herself. "Yes. I apologize for the inconvenience."

"Well I'm at the Cozy Inn, and they don't have any vacancy."

"I'm really sorry."

"I reserved a room here after you called, but they gave it away."

"Why?"

"Some kind of medical emergency, someone needed a room."

"Medical emergency?" His first thought was that Dr. Butcher was using his status to keep a room. That rat. But then he remembered Peter. "Oh."

"So now I don't have anywhere to stay."

"I'm very sorry."

"And when I asked them about another place, they suggested yours."

"Mine?"

"Yes."

"I'll call and correct them. Thanks."

"Wait. You didn't give an explanation in your message for why I couldn't stay there." She sounded a bit irritated.

"The owner died," he replied flatly.

"Oh," she said. "I'm sorry to hear that."

Emily walked into the room asking a question but immediately stopped.

Mark suddenly felt badly for the woman—Ellen. "Thank you. Do you know anyone in town you can stay with?"

"No. I'm actually here for the lighthouse."

"The lighthouse? For three days?"

She snickered. "It's a bit more complicated. You see, I own it."

"Own what?"

"The lighthouse."

"I'm confused. What lighthouse?"

"The red one on Lake Michigan. Is there another one?"

"No, but what do you mean you own it? You can't own the lighthouse," he said adamantly. "It's part of Manistique or the state or . . ."

Emily looked at him with her brow furrowed in concern.

"My husband bought it at an auction last year."

"Really, they sold it?" he asked. Whoever *they* were. Coast Guard?

"Yes, and I'm in town to look at it. My husband died a few months ago, and now I'm trying to figure out what to do with it."

"I'm sorry about your loss."

"Thank you."

"I'll tell you what," he said, already regretting what he was about to say. "If you can't find a place to stay tonight, stop by here, and I'll set up a room for you. But please come after six, and definitely lower your expectations."

Emily gave him a crooked smile.

"That's awfully good of you. I promise only to go there as a last resort."

"Okay, thanks. Good luck with the lighthouse."

He hung up and walked into the living room.

"What was that about?" Emily asked.

"Did your doctor friend check out of the Cozy Inn?"

She shrugged. "I don't know. Why?"

"Because there's no room."

"There's no reason for him to stick around."

"I'm going to call the hotel and find out."

"What was all that about the lighthouse?"

"Apparently, this woman owns it."

"What do you mean?"

"That's all I know. I don't get how a person can own a lighthouse."

"Maybe she's a lunatic," Emily said.

He twisted a grin. "Let's hope not. I told her to come here if she couldn't find a place. And I don't think there's another place available." He pulled out his cell phone, looked up the number for the Cozy Inn, and called.

The person on the other end answered in a tired voice.

"Hello, my name is Mark. I'm the—" He hesitated. "My aunt owns the Manistique Victorian."

"Oh, yes."

"I wanted to let you know that we're no longer taking guests."

"Are you full, too?"

"No. My aunt passed away last week, so it's no longer open."

"Vivian died?"

"Yes."

"Gosh, I'm so sorry to hear that. I didn't know—But I dropped someone off there the other day!"

"Oh, yes. George. He stayed here since he had nowhere else to go."

"That was nice of you."

He's dead too. But Mark didn't mention it. Too many deaths in one call. "I have a question for you."

"Yes?"

"Do you still have a Dr. Butch—Dr. Bul-cher staying there?"

"No, he checked out."

"Okay, thanks."

"The girl staying with you is still there, right? The deer-car girl."

"Yeah, Emily." His eyes moved over to her. "I think she might be a permanent resident."

Emily glared at him.

"I hope she's having a nice stay, anyway."

"Yes, I'm pretty sure she is."

He thanked her and hung up.

"Butcher checked out of the Cozy," he told Emily.

"Good riddance," she said.

Mark sighed. "Guess I'll go clean the room for the lighthouse lady."

"Which room?"

"Breakwater Lighthouse, right? Yvonne stayed in there last night."

"I already stripped the sheets. They're in the dryer. The sheets from Peter's room are in the wash, and I have a load of towels waiting to go."

"You did all that? Where was I?"

Mark spent the next couple of hours cleaning and going through mail and some papers he found in a desk in the library. Emily took care of the wash and read her book between loads. It was four o'clock when he asked her about dinner.

"Are you always hungry or something?" she asked. "Or do you like to push food on people?"

He chuckled. "No, just trying to make plans. We need to be back here by six, in case—check that—*when* Lighthouse Lady shows up."

As they waited for their pizza at Ace's, Emily announced, "I should be like Vivian and join Doctors Without Borders."

Mark's grin faded when he saw her determined expression. "Seriously?"

She nodded. "Yeah, why not?"

"Because it's bad out there. Aren't the other stories in that book similar to Vivian's?"

Her head wobbled. "Yes and no."

The waiter brought out their food. Mark immediately pulled out a slice of Three Pigs on Figs, a thin-crust pizza with bacon, pancetta, prosciutto, and a fig spread. He took a bite. "Hot . . . Mmm. It's good. You need to try it."

"I told you I can't. I'm allergic to figs."

"I thought you were kidding. Who's allergic to figs?"

"I am! My tongue tingles every time."

He shook his head. "So tell me about the other stories in the book."

"I think I told you—one of them was the wife of a doctor working in Africa. She felt out of place. There were some dangers too. But it was mostly about the strains on their marriage. She caught her husband having an affair with a Swedish doctor. And then she had her own affair."

Mark blew on his pizza. "Sounds like a soap opera."

She shrugged. "It sort of is, but it ended all right. They got back together once she and her husband returned to the US."

"And you weren't related to this woman, her second cousin thrice removed, or . . .?"

She waved him off. "Funny," she said, without laughing.

The pizzeria was cozy, four tables with white cloths under plastic covers. He had been here the day before, picking up George's dinner. It struck him that this had been the old man's last meal, a pizza from Ace's.

"Any other stories with a less salacious bent?"

"The one I'm reading now. It's about a doctor's first trip into the field in Africa."

"And why is he—he or she?"

"He. Kevin."

"Why is Kevin . . .'on the borderline'?" he said, gesturing quotes.

She looked away for a second, clearing her throat. "A woman he was attending to died during childbirth."

"So? No, I don't mean it like that, I mean it must happen so often that, you know—"

"I know what you mean." She stared blankly out the window for several seconds. "Kevin partied a lot with other aid workers—heavy drinking, some drugs. At first he resisted it, but after a while he joined in. So one night, after hanging out with the gang, he was called in to help with a woman who was having problems delivering."

"And he was messed up?"

She nodded. "And the woman died, and her baby."

"Oh."

Emily nodded slowly. "He naturally felt a tremendous amount of guilt."

"So what happened to him?"

She shrugged. "I don't know. I haven't finished it yet."

Mark could see that this topic was weighing on her. She was probably thinking of parallels to her own situation, the death of that boy.

Emily's pizza, the Pesto Presto!, sat on her plate. Mark blurted out, "Aren't you hungry?"

She shrugged. "I suppose I should eat." She took a bite. "Mmm." She nodded her head. "I love pesto."

"Yeah, their specialty pizzas are good." He regretted letting George order a plain pepperoni. "I hate to admit it, but I'm kind of curious about the Lighthouse Lady."

"Yeah?"

"I mean, I don't want her to stay, but I'm curious how someone could buy that lighthouse."

She nodded. "Yeah, or, like I said, she's crazy."

"Maybe. But if it is true, I wonder if she can do whatever she wants with it?"

"What do you mean, like paint it hot pink with purple stripes?"

He laughed. "Now that would cause a stir."

"What if she placed an advertisement on it? Stay at the Manistique Victorian!" She slowly flared her hands for effect.

He laughed. "That's all I need."

Mark's phone rang. Although it was Chicagoland area code, the number was unfamiliar to him. "Who could this be?" he mumbled before answering it. It was George's niece Laura, calling to tell him that she was planning to drive up tomorrow and should be there in the afternoon.

"Who was that?" Emily asked after he put down the phone.

Mark lifted the phone back to his ear. "And bring extra clothes because you're likely to get stuck here."

Emily spewed soda all over the table, and on Mark.

He smiled and grabbed a napkin to wipe his face.

"I'm so sorry! I haven't done that in a very long time. I'm so sorry."

"You used to do this regularly?"

"Ha! No, but—" She stopped and shook her head. "So who was that on the phone? Who's coming?"

"It was George's niece. She'll be here tomorrow."

She shook her head at him. "You're too funny."

He smirked. "Seriously though, name one person who's left this town?"

"Yvonne."

"True." He thought about Bear Foot driving her to Green Bay and wondered how that was going. "Maybe you need a local to escort you out."

She shook her head. "Let's hope not, because that means we're both stuck here."

They finished their pizzas, and after debating for a minute whether they wanted to stand in line at Nifty Treats for ice cream, they headed back to the house. It was a quarter to six when they arrived.

"Lighthouse Lady should be here any minute," Mark said.

"Maybe she let herself in."

"That does seem to happen a lot at the Manistique Victorian."

"Will George's niece be staying here too?" she asked as they entered the kitchen through the back door.

"Only if she's a one-eyed doctor," he quipped.

She shook her head. "You're not funny."

"Hopefully the Cozy Inn has some rooms available tomorrow."

Mark halted as he stepped into the dining room, déjà vu reverberating, until Emily bumped into him.

She exclaimed something, but none of it registered. "Wha—?" was all he could manage to get out. Yvonne was sitting on the couch, just like she had been the day before, when he'd first met her and Peter, except now Bear Foot was in Peter's place.

"Hello," Yvonne said.

Emily sidestepped around Mark. "What are you doing back here?" she asked.

"We came back," Yvonne replied simply.

"Obviously," Mark said.

"We got to Menominee, and we turned around," Bear Foot explained in a tired voice.

"Yes, but why?" Mark asked.

Yvonne's big eyes, glistening, stared at him. "I felt bad about abandoning Peter here."

Mark scratched the back of his head. He wanted to ask, *Why are you sitting here?* but instead asked, "What's your plan now?"

"Wait for Peter to leave."

"Wait?" Mark turned to Emily as Yvonne nodded. "But that could be a few days, right?"

"It could be. Could be tomorrow, though not likely. Really depends when he's back on a normal cycle—and obviously, no episodes."

He turned back to Yvonne, who looked at him with those manipulative eyes. And though he knew she was playing him, he felt bad anyway. She had come back for Peter. Finally he relented. "Do you want to stay here tonight?"

"Only if that's okay," she said.

"Tonight, yes, and tomorrow night, but I'm leaving Monday morning, so you'll have to figure out something else."

She nodded agreeably. "Thank you so much."

The doorbell rang.

"I thought you were leaving tomorrow," Emily said.

"I changed it to Monday."

"You did?"

He nodded, then pointed to the door. "You said I'm supposed to answer the door when it rings."

She smiled, shaking her head gently.

"Must be the Lighthouse Lady," he said evenly. He turned to Bear Foot. "Is it true that the lighthouse is privately owned?"

"Yes. Sold last year for fourteen thousand dollars."

Mark reached for the door and opened it.

"Hello, I'm Ellen," the woman said. She carried a box in her hands.

"Hi, Ellen. I'm Mark. Please come on in."

The woman, who was perhaps sixty years old, stayed put. With her steel-gray hair and her rimless glasses, she came across as no-nonsense. "No, I don't need a room after all. I just came by to thank you." She handed over the box. "A pie. I hope you like apple."

"Wow, yes, I love it. That's so nice of you. This was definitely not necessary, but thank you." He took the box. "Diner 37?"

"Yes. Someone told me they had the best pies."

"It's true. Please, come inside."

She smiled and nodded. "Just for a moment."

"So where did you find a room?" Mark asked, closing the door.

"Actually, a room opened up at the Cozy Inn. Apparently one of the guests left abruptly. They're cleaning the room now."

"What?" Yvonne jumped off the sofa, a concerned expression on her face. "Sorry, did you say that a room opened up at the Cozy Inn?"

Ellen looked over at Yvonne quizzically before replying, "Yes. That's what I was told."

Yvonne turned to Bear Foot. "I wonder if it was Peter."

Bear Foot's shoulders briefly inched upwards.

"I'll call the hotel and find out," Yvonne said, desperation in her voice. She darted for the door, muttering an apology as she whisked by.

Bear Foot had gotten up, his eyes chasing Yvonne as if deciding what to do. He appeared lost.

"I won't keep you," Ellen said. "Looks like you have guests."

"Yes—well, no, it's just . . ." The notion of explaining his "guests" in a simple manner left him tongue-tied. "No reason you have to leave," he bumbled out.

Emily approached and Mark introduced her to Ellen.

"Look," he said to Emily. "Ellen brought us pie from Diner 37."

"That's awfully kind of you."

"Have a seat, please," he said, extending an open hand toward the couch.

While Ellen made her way to the living room, Mark headed to the dining room. "Oh, and that's Bear Foot." He set the pie on the table. "Ellen here is the one who owns the lighthouse."

Bear Foot bowed slightly as he shook her hand. He sat down.

"Technically, yes, I own the lighthouse."

Yvonne burst back into the house. "No one's answering," she said to Bear Foot. "Take me to the Cozy Inn. Please."

Bear Foot hopped up and then sidled past Mark.

Emily said to Yvonne, "Can you please call me if Peter really did leave?"

Yvonne nodded. "What's your number?"

"It's—"

"Wait, do you have a pen? My phone just died."

Mark stood up to find a pen, but Ellen said, "I have one," and quickly produced one out of her purse.

"Do you need a piece of paper?" Mark asked.

Yvonne shook her head, then proceeded to write Emily's number on the palm of her hand. "Thank you," she said, returning the pen. She waved and left with Bear Foot.

"Do you think he took off?" Mark asked Emily.

"I don't know. He definitely had a cavalier attitude about his condition."

Mark turned to Ellen. "Sorry. Long story. Pie?"

The three sat in the living room enjoying apple pie. They talked about the lighthouse. Ellen hadn't known anything about it until after her whimsical husband had died. No, she really couldn't paint it hot pink with purple stripes or do anything else except maintain it in its current state. And she wasn't sure what she was going to do with it— half of her wanted to rid herself of the responsibility, but the other half felt guilty about it because of her husband. She had a few days to figure it out.

Chapter Twenty-Nine

Emily woke early feeling an aura of vague anxiety. It took her a moment to remember whether it was justified or merely the remains of a bad dream. Had Peter Hinton left the Cozy Inn after all? She didn't know because Yvonne had never returned to the house. Nor had she called. There was nothing to do about it, so she tried letting it go. She turned and lay on her left side, then a minute later on her right, but it was no use. She had exerted her mind too much and couldn't ease herself back to sleep. She stepped gently downstairs, and reclining on the sofa under a low light from a side table lamp, she flipped the pages of *Doctors on the Borderline* to find where she had left off.

She hadn't read any more the night before. Ellen didn't leave until after nine o'clock. Then she and Mark had stayed up talking for another hour before they went to their separate floors for the night. The more time she spent with Mark, the less capable she was of separating him from her brother, Kyle. This bothered her, not because she resisted seeing Mark that way, but because her brother was not as acutely defined to her anymore. His image was increasingly blurring around the edge. And then an unsettling fear came over her—that Kyle might disappear behind Mark.

As she searched for her place in the book, she felt a little chill and shivered. The living room window had remained open all night. Instead of getting up and closing it, she leaned over and pulled down the crocheted throw blanket draped over the top of the sofa. The blanket fell softly onto her legs and then she unfolded it and pulled it up around her shoulders. A cozy morning snuggle. She blinked heavily. She would not stay awake for long, not without coffee and maybe a shower. As she raised the book from under the blanket, she heard a noise in the house. She waited, holding her breath, listening. A scuffling sound from the basement. Mark was awake. Her ecstatic morning moment was lost when she heard his steps. She straightened a bit, checked her pajama blouse, and smoothed her hair with her hand.

"What are you doing up?" he asked, his tone much too lively for her pre-coffee condition.

"Couldn't sleep. You?"

"I slept fine. Going for a run. Do you want to join?"

"I don't run," she answered flatly.

"Okay."

"I'm just going to sit here and read."

"Sure. Did Yvonne ever call or text?"

She shook her head. "No, she forgot."

"Maybe she'll remember when she goes to wash her hands."

It was way too early to exert a laugh, though she did manage to muster a smile.

"All right, see you in a bit." He waved and left.

After a little while, once he had stopped stretching on the porch and when the sound of his footfalls had dissipated, the morning bliss returned to her. Her eyelids fell again, and before she could find her place in the book, she let it plummet onto her lap. Tilting her head against the soft cushions, she shut her eyes.

Slam!

Emily shot up dizzily. "Huh? What?"

"Oh sorry," Mark said softly. "I thought you were reading." He began tiptoeing past her, but it was far too late.

"What time is it?" she asked.

"I don't know. Guess who I ran into at the lighthouse?"

"At the lighthouse?" She didn't care. She wanted to go back to sleep. "Who?"

"Bear Foot."

"What did he say happened yesterday?"

"You're not going to believe this. So Peter was still at the Cozy Inn."

"Oh, good."

"But then he and Yvonne reconciled, and they left last night."

"Really? Yvonne drove, right?"

"I'm assuming."

"I sure hope so. How about Bear Foot? How's he doing?"

Mark shook his head. "I don't think he was so into Yvonne after their long car ride yesterday." He chuckled to himself. "Maybe that should be a thing. Before you decide to get serious with someone, you have to do a two-hundred-mile road trip together."

"So what was Bear Foot doing at the lighthouse so early?"

"He was trying to figure out why Vivian told him to go there."

"When did she tell him to do that?"

"She didn't. It was that vision he had, remember?"

"Oh, right. So he's not sad about Yvonne?"

"I don't think so. Anyway, she's Peter's problem again."

"She wasn't that bad."

He puffed out a derisive laugh. "I'm going to take a shower. Sorry for waking you. Go back to sleep. I promise to be quiet."

Too awake now, Emily found her place in the book. Dr. Kevin Sykes, unable to shake his guilt, continued to numb himself with drugs, especially after he heard about the husband. The husband believed his wife had died because she had been unfaithful. Suddenly he eyed his other children with suspicion. Sykes eventually looked for the man to tell him the truth, but he and his children had gone to another refugee camp.

Emily pushed herself to read on, to learn how Dr. Sykes came to terms with his actions. Guilt-ridden, he returned to his job at a Cedar Rapids hospital. But he couldn't shake the drug habit, and he feared committing malpractice once again, so he contemplated quitting medicine. But he didn't know what else he could do. All he knew was being a doctor. He wrote a long letter to his family, hoping they would understand. Then he took a few pills and went to sleep.

She turned the page expecting to finally read about Dr. Sykes's road to treatment and redemption. Instead she found this:

This story wasn't written by Kevin Sykes. it was written by me, Cynthia, his sister. When I heard Kevin had died from an overdose, I couldn't believe it. The thought of an overdose was absurd. Three days later a letter from Kevin arrived, and it was clear that he had killed himself. After a month of crying every day, I decided to trace his footsteps in Uganda and talk to the people he had told me about in his emails. Based on my interviews with locals, the emails he had sent, and his final letter, I wrote this story. I'm sorry if you feel betrayed, but everything in here is true as far as I know. —Cynthia.

"No!" Emily cried out, tossing the book away. She flung the heavy blanket off her and sat up, nauseated.

"Em? You okay?" She hadn't heard Mark enter the room. "You look pale."

"Yes, fine." She up from the sofa, barely holding herself together. "I need air."

She stumbled to the front door.

"What is it?" Mark asked in pursuit. "What happened?"

She waved him off. "I need a few."

"Okay, sure."

Outside, Emily landed on the porch steps and bent down, her face to her knees. It was several minutes later before she stood up, all at once concerned with decency; she was outside in her pajamas in front of the Manistique Victorian for the whole world to see. No one was outside, but she hurried back in anyway. Mark wasn't in sight—she'd half expected him to be waiting at the door. She'd gotten as far as the base of the stairs when he popped up out of the library.

She sighed, then grimaced.

He gave a wry smile of understanding and turned back around.

Feeling momentary relief, she rushed up to her room, went to the bathroom and started a shower, leaving the knob to the far right. Without taking off her pajamas, she got in. The chill reached her bones and numbed her skin, but it wasn't enough. Finally, she plunged her head under the stream. That always worked. A million needles stabbed her scalp at once. Anesthetizing pain.

Mark couldn't figure out what had disturbed Emily. A phone call from Butcher? Maybe. But she had looked suddenly ill. Pregnant? He hoped not. No. Regardless, he made sure to leave her alone.

He spent the rest of the morning going through more of Vivian's papers. Emily stayed upstairs. Something inside kept nagging him to go up and console her, be with her, whatever her problem. But that wasn't where they were, so he stayed put.

Past midday, Mark's concern grew. Not a sound from upstairs, not a single creak from the floorboards in two hours. He stood at the first step, worried about Emily, yet bated by fear of meddling. He went to the living room and was clumsily folding the blanket when he spotted *Doctors on the Borderline*, splayed on the floor. He threw the rumpled blanket on the back of the sofa and picked up the book. He flipped to Vivian's story, skimming through the part about Emily—Emela— when she was taken to her new family.

We were meeting Emela's new family at the baggage claim at O'Hare. She was mesmerized by the dazzling colored lights and the moving walkway in the tunnel that went under the airport. I couldn't help but think about the tunnel dug by hand that went under the Sarajevo airport where food and guns were passed through.

Emela's new family was a lovely couple with a friendly-looking twelve-year-old son. She took her new brother's hand without protest. All was well, and I felt a special peace.

He experienced that connection to Emily again, that tight feeling in his chest. Then he searched for the story she had been talking about over pizza. Dr. Kevin something. He found it: Kevin Sykes, page 99. He sat down and read.

Chapter Thirty

Mark gently knocked on the door. After a short time without any response or any noise whatsoever, he rested his ear on the door and
listened. He heard nothing. Deciding he was fine with waking Emily
up if she was napping, he knocked harder. Still nothing. Thinking she
might simply be in the bathroom, he tried the knob. Locked.

Tamping down a growing panic, Mark went downstairs. The keys
weren't inside the console drawer in the parlor. Hastily he checked
around the house and finally found them in the kitchen. Back in front
of Emily's room, he knocked once more, and called out her name. No
response. His hand shook as he carefully inserted the key. He slowly
opened the door.

Emily lay on the bed, wearing a robe, sprawled sideways as if she
had stumbled and landed randomly. "Emily?" Fearing the worst, he
scrambled onto the bed and shook her. She jolted, flailing, then kicking. She screamed, "Get away from me!" She sat up, her eyes wild, her
arms up defensively.

Mark backed away as the heat of embarrassment poured over him.
"Sorry, sorry, I-I-I thought . . ."

Emily twisted off the bed and pulled the robe tightly around her
and tied it. "What are you doing in here?!"

"Sorry, it's just—"

She raised her hand firmly to stop him, then pulled earplugs out of
her ears. "What are you doing in here?" she demanded again.

"You're wearing earplugs?"

"Yes! I barely slept last night. Why are you in here?"

"I was worried. It's one o'clock, I knocked, you didn't answer."

"It's one?"

He nodded. He whimpered nervously, "And I just finished reading that story."

"Huh? What story?"

"About that doctor, Kevin Sykes, and the pills, and you've been acting strangely, and it was awful."

As he spoke Emily's face shed its startled look and took on a sallow appearance.

"—And it got my imagination running," he finished.

Her face shot to red, and she clasped the robe tightly at her neck. "What?"

"Nothing. Sorry. Just worried."

"You thought I might hurt myself?"

"Well, no, not—" He stumbled. "No. I—"

"Get out!"

His head tongue felt thick. "But I only—"

"Out!"

"Okay, okay. Sorry." He walked out, shutting the door slowly. The latch closed with an all-too final-sounding snap.

As he trudged down the stairs, Mark wished he could redo the last five minutes. Collapsing onto the living room sofa, he lifted his trembling hand, the adrenaline only slowly receding.

Unable to shake his nerves, he got up and paced to the sitting room and back and then to the kitchen and back before walking outside. He drifted down Lake Street, all the while blaming his mother for putting all those stupid ideas about doctors and suicides into his head. He eventually ended up downtown, and having decided that a sandwich and a cold beer—especially the beer— might help ease his self-loathing mood, he landed at Jake's Bar. He chatted with Mikey, trying to forget the whole embarrassing episode with Emily, except Mikey brought her up.

"The girl must be gone. What was her name?"

"Emily. No," he answered. "Tomorrow."

"Tomorrow?"

"Yeah, the guy who installs windshields is out hunting."

"You must be talking about Carl. Yeah, he's out turkey hunting."

"Apparently there's someone else who will do it tomorrow."

Mikey shook his head. "I don't think so—not if it's the guy who helps out Carl."

"Why not? Is he hunting too?"

"No. He broke his finger a couple days ago."

"You serious?"

"Yeah."

"Not Conrad?" Mark blurted.

Mikey's eyes lit up. "You know him?"

Mark exhaled a laugh. Conrad hadn't broken his finger, but it was a technicality he didn't bother correcting. "Only because I drove him to the hospital. Emily's the one who attended to him."

"She a doctor?"

"Yeah."

"I heard about a commotion in here a couple nights ago between Conrad and some woman doctor. That was her?"

"Yep, that would have been Emily. She's going to flip when she finds out Conrad is the other installer. I think I'll let her find out for herself. She's already mad at me."

"Why?"

Mark laughed, then went ahead and partially admitted, "I accidentally barged into her room."

"Accidentally?"

Mark didn't care to recite the entire recipe: Emily's struggle with Nicholas's death. Reading about the suicide of Dr. Sykes. Her strange reaction earlier that morning when she ran out of the house. And staying in her room quietly for a long time, not responding to his loud knocking. All of that mixed with his mother's stories about doctors committing suicide. He briefly—only briefly—once again felt justified in doing what he did.

"She didn't look well earlier, so I just thought something might be wrong."

"So you barged in?"

"It wasn't like that," Mark replied defensively. "I knocked several times, loudly. It was one o'clock in the afternoon."

"Why didn't she answer?"

"She was napping and had earplugs in."

"She was just napping?"

Mark nodded. "I scared her awake." The scene flew through his head again, and he suddenly felt clammy.

"Oops."

"I should have just said I was checking the walls." He cupped one hand on the bar and tapped it with the other.

Mikey gave him a bemused smile and shook his head. "The walls? What's wrong with the walls?"

"Never mind. It's from a show, *Fawlty Towers*." He drank some beer. "The hospitality industry just doesn't suit me."

Mark walked back to the house in better spirits, optimistic that Emily would be forgiving. He understood now the gravity of what he'd done, as well-intentioned as it had been—he'd abruptly awoken her from a dead sleep and accused her of trying to kill herself. All right, not great, but now he hoped she'd see it differently, realize he cared about her well-being, and that with another apology, awkward as it'd be, all would be forgiven and all would end well.

A familiar-sounding truck came down the street. Mark turned around to see Bear Foot driving in his direction. He stepped out into the street and raised his hand. He held it stiffly, as if taking an oath, and upon realizing that it could be taken another way, he immediately dropped his arm.

Bear Foot stopped, leaned over and rolled down the window, smiling. "I thought I'd drop by and tell you I got my answer."

"Answer to what?"

"I was at the lighthouse this morning. Remember?"

"Oh right. What did you figure out?"

"I was about to leave when that lady who owns the lighthouse walked up."

"Ellen?"

Bear Foot nodded. "Yeah. Ellen told me her husband bought it. She didn't even know about it until after he died."

"Yeah, she told us the story last night."

"So we spoke for a while, and I explained to her why I was there." He slapped the seat. "She decided to give it to me!"

"For how much?"

"That's the best part. Free!" A big grin lifted his face.

"What?"

"Yeah. Can you believe it? Just like that, for nothing. I'm going to own Manistique's lighthouse."

"But how about the maintenance?" Mark asked.

Bear Foot blinked several times and looked back at Mark. "I can do most of the work myself. People will help pay for parts and paint and stuff. I know it."

Mark put up a smile. "Well I'm happy for you."

Bear Foot grinned. "Since you're leaving tomorrow, I wanted to make sure I said goodbye." He stuck out his hand.

They shook. "And thank you for all your help," Mark said. "And thanks for fixing the electrical problem. That reminds me—I never paid you. How much do I owe you?"

He shook his head. "Nothing. My last job for Vivian."

"Thanks."

"Have you decided to keep the house?" Bear Foot asked.

Mark shrugged. "Not sure yet. But do you mind if I call you if something comes up?"

"Please do." They shook hands again, and Bear Foot drove off.

The house was quiet when Mark walked inside. He figured Emily was still in her room. He was about to head to the basement when his eye caught an envelope on the fireplace mantel, where Vivian's urn had been. He walked over to it. His name was written on the front. He immediately guessed what it was.

Mark ripped it open and found a letter and cash inside. He fanned out the money, five twenty dollar bills. He shook his head as he unfolded the letter: "Mark, I thought I should just go now. Since my car will be ready tomorrow and you have to head out anyway, I thought it would work out best this way. I apologize for my reaction earlier. I'm not upset with you, really I'm not. I'll just leave it at that. It was great to meet you. Take care of yourself and thanks for taking me in for so many days. Good luck to you, Emily."

He sighed, tossing the letter and cash on the mantel. He suddenly felt exhaustion, a deep emptiness. He plopped down on the sofa, thinking about how upset she was going to be when she found out she wasn't leaving tomorrow. An idea popped into his head. Good or bad? He mulled it over for a couple minutes before getting up and going into the library. He sat at the desk, grabbed a pen and a piece of paper and started writing.

Emily dragged the gold, diamond-patterned bed cover—unwashed, she was certain—off the bed and let it slump on the dark red carpet that concealed things she had to force herself not to imagine. She sat on the queen bed, slipped off her shoes and fell back onto the stiff white sheets, laying her head apprehensively on the pillow, slightly comforted by the bleachy odor the pillowcase gave off.

She lay on her back, rigidly, thinking how much more at ease she'd felt at the Manistique Victorian—well, until Mark broke into her room and accused her of attempting to kill herself.

Staring at the popcorn ceiling, Emily tried to switch off. But it wasn't easy. That hectic scene kept replaying in her mind. Her reaction. His belief that she was capable of that. *How could he think that of me? How? How could he know?*

The thought infected her from time to time. In a perverted way, it comforted her. Not that she'd ever do it, but the distraction provided a relief. At the very least, Mark was right to think that her burdens might overcome her. That she would succumb to the voice tucked in the back of her mind saying, *You are a fraud!* She could no longer blame

John or Dr. Olsen for Nicholas's death. No matter how many people she had helped or would ever help, she'd never be able to put it behind her. *You are a fraud!* A better intern would have intervened; a better intern would not have gotten involved with the attending; a better intern would have been brave enough to page him. *You are a fraud!* Especially now that her selection to a great residency program had been rigged. *You are a fraud!*

The dismal feeling she'd felt in the pit of her stomach after leaving the Manistique Victorian returned. Did she blow it by leaving? She put her hands over her face. They had something, she and Mark, a connection. The odds of their meeting the way they had bordered on impossible. And she had thrown it away. . . . *Fate is cruel to deer.* Maybe not. Maybe fate had only intended for them to meet.

Emily heard a tap on her door. Listlessly, she sat up and slipped into her shoes. She moved toward the door, mostly convinced that no one was there. Maybe it was one of those pesky, pranking neighborhood kids, she thought, and laughed to herself. Stupid Mark.

When she found and flipped the light switch to the dark entryway, she saw an envelope on the ground that had been slipped under the door. She picked it up and saw it was addressed to Room 137. She looked through the peephole, saw that no one was there, then opened the door. The heavy door pushed against her back as she looked up and down the hallway. No one. She ripped open the envelope, suspicious but curious. Inside she found twenty-five dollars cash and a small note written in print: "Em, you only stayed three nights, so I'm refunding one night's worth ☺ I postponed my flight, so I hope you'll come back. Don't you miss the fantastic hospitality of the Manistique Victorian? Call me, and I'll come and get you. Mark."

Emily let out an unrestrained laugh that echoed down the hall. An energetic hope spread within her, and though she couldn't say why, she knew everything would be all right. She went back into the room, grabbing back the door as it rushed to slam, letting it close softly.

Chapter Thirty-One

Mark flinched when the doorbell rang. He tripped running up the basement stairs, barely catching himself by the rail. Running through the kitchen, he brushed off the emergent thought that it might be another guest—after all, he had left a message for everyone in the calendar through June. Instead he wondered how Emily had gotten there. He had expected a call.

When he was close enough to the front door, he saw her profile, the shoulder-length brown hair through the sheer curtain. He yanked open the door, ready to further whatever—

It wasn't Emily. It was a woman with similar hair and about the same height. "Hello," she said. "I'm looking for Mark."

"Um, I'm Mark."

She placed her fingertips on her breastbone. "I'm Laura, George's niece."

"Oh, right!"

"I'm so sorry for showing up like this. I should have called first."

"No, it's all right. I was just expecting someone," he said, imagining that his startled, apprehensive reaction had fazed her.

She smiled gently. "I won't stay long."

"No, no. It's totally fine." He stepped aside. "Please come on in."

"Thank you."

"Have a seat," Mark said, gesturing to the living room sofa. As he sat down across from her, he asked, "Did you drive all the way up or fly part-way?"

"I drove the whole way."

Laura had a more mature face, compared to Emily. He figured she was fairly close to his age. Dark brown hair, slightly darker than Emily's. Laura had softer features—her eyes, her cheeks. He suddenly realized what he was doing, measuring her against Emily. He didn't know why, and he stopped.

His eyes darted to her ring finger and then back. No ring.

"Let's see, I left at eleven this morning. I stopped for about an hour in Green Bay. What time is it now?"

"It's a little after five."

"So six hours, about five hours of driving I guess."

Mark explained how he had flown to Traverse City and then driven north to Petoskey and stopped for the night before heading north and west to Manistique.

"When are you heading back home?" she asked.

"Wednesday," he said, summarily pushing away the anxiety of having to cross the bridge again.

"And you said you lived in Oak Park, right?"

"Yes, that's right."

She nodded, smiled a little. "We're practically neighbors. It's a crazy coincidence."

"Yeah, crazy," he said agreeably, thinking that out of all the long-odds occurrences over the last few days, the fact that he and Laura lived twenty miles apart was the least crazy. Emily popped into his head, and he had a real longing for her to call. Realizing that he hadn't yet offered condolences, he said, "I'm very sorry about your uncle George."

"Thank you."

"I really liked him. I got to know him a little bit over the couple days he was here."

"Thank you for taking him in."

"Of course." He felt guilty, thinking how he had tried to throw the old man out when he first arrived.

She frowned. "I'm really upset with that tour company."

Mark nodded. "I don't blame you. They left for the next town without him."

"I'm going to file a formal complaint when I get back."

Mark nodded. "You should. So what are your plans? How long are you staying?"

"A day or two, just to collect Uncle George's things and then visit the funeral home." She shrugged. "Haven't thought it all the way through yet."

"He lived in a Milwaukee suburb, right?"

"Yeah, Brookfield. So I'll stop by there on my way back and go through all his things."

"Sounds familiar."

"That's right, you said your aunt died. I'm so sorry."

"Thank you."

"And this is her house?"

"Yes. It's a bed and breakfast."

"It's nice. Are you going to take it over?"

"As a bed and breakfast? No. I'm the worst innkeeper imaginable. Have you ever seen *Fawlty Towers*?"

She nodded and laughed. "Yes, Uncle George introduced me."

"Well over the last four days, I've re-enacted about half the episodes."

Her bright smile created soft wrinkles near her eyes. "You have to tell me about it." There was a certain twinkle in her eye that gave Mark the impression she might be interested in him.

"Do you have dinner plans?"

She shook her head. "No, I was just going to find a quick bite to eat."

"Any interest in going out to Diner 37? It's nothing fancy."

There was a knock on the door.

"Sure. Sounds great."

He stood up. "Great. Excuse me one second." He went to the door, and through the sheer he saw who it was—for certain this time. He opened the door.

Emily stood there with sad eyes and even a sadder frown. Her suitcase was next to her. She was holding her medical bag with her left hand.

"Welcome back," he said buoyantly.

She pointed back toward the street. "Whose car is that?"

"Laura, George's niece. Remember? She was coming today."

She nodded, picking up her suitcase. She walked inside.

"Here, let me take that."

She let him, and handed him her medical bag as well.

"Laura, this is Emily, Dr. Davis. Emily, this is George's niece, Laura."

Laura got up.

"I'm so sorry about your loss," Emily said.

"Thank you. You knew my uncle?"

Mark jumped in. "Emily is a guest here. Actually, she's the one who found George yesterday morning."

Emily turned to Mark. "I thought you found him," she mumbled.

He gave her a sidelong glance. "I'll just run this up to your room."

Emily said, "Is George from your father's side or you mother's side?"

"He's my mother's brother. They were actually very close for a long time." Mark reached the top of the stairs and set the suitcase on the bed in Emily's room. As he headed out of the room, he heard a thunderous, "No way!" from Emily.

Mark rushed to the staircase wondering what had prompted her to shriek. "Mark, we were wrong," she called out as he headed down.

As he reached the bottom of the stairs, he asked, "Wrong about what?"

"Trudy is Laura's mother."

It took Mark a second to digest this. "George's sister?"

"Yes," Laura said. "Who did you think she was?"

Mark and Emily locked eyes. He answered diffidently, "His wife."

"His wife? Where did you get that idea?"

Again, Emily and Mark stared at each other. "It's sort of a long story," Mark said. "I'll tell you over dinner." He looked at Emily. "Do you want to join us? We're going to Diner 37."

She shook her head unhesitatingly. "No, but you can bring me back a piece of pie."

Laura smiled. "Do they have good pies there?"

Emily nodded. "Excellent. But don't have the fish," she said.

"The fish? Why not?"

Mark narrowed his eyes at her and shook his head. "Never mind her. I'll be right back." He ran down to the basement to get his wallet. When he returned, Laura was laughing at something Emily had said.

"What?" he asked.

"Nothing," Emily said.

He frowned at Emily. Then he said to Laura, "If you're ready, I'll drive."

Laura got up and they headed out the front door. "What kind of pie do you want, Em?"

She thought for a second. "You pick."

"You trust me?"

She nodded. "Totally."

As Mark started to close the door, Emily called his name.

He stopped and stuck his head back inside. "Yeah?"

A little smile played at the corners of her mouth. She whispered hard, "Is she single?"

He waved her off, then smiled and nodded. "I think so." He walked outside, grinning.

Emily was surprised how at ease she and Mark were with each other now. There were no romantic notions between them. They had passed that awkward stage and survived. And she felt good about it, though she did feel a pang of jealousy. But even that passed quickly.

She went upstairs and lay comfortably on her bed. Soon her thoughts drifted to Dr. Currant. She liked him. And maybe he liked her. She invented a wild tale in her mind about staying in Manistique, staying in this house, and doing her residency at the hospital . . . and possibilities with Dr. James Currant.

Suddenly hungry, she went downstairs and found enough ingredients to make a decent sandwich. She ate it standing up at the kitchen counter. When she finished she poured herself a glass of wine and sat lazily on the couch anticipating the arrival of her pie, except now she had a specific kind of pie in mind. She thought of calling Mark but decided not to disturb him on his *date*.

As she sat there, slowly twirling her hair, that daydream returned. But this time she went beyond speculation and considered the idea of as a real possibility. Why not? She needed to find a new residency. Several reasons why not popped in her head immediately, mostly around the vastness of the UP, the smallness of the town and lack of exposure to diverse patients and medical conditions. But after another glass of wine, she felt more confident and determined to do something about it. Without ruminating any longer, she started the jaunt toward the hospital, hoping to catch Dr. Currant on duty.

When Emily returned to the house, the car out front was gone. On the dining room table, she found a to-go box with a fork lying on top. More sober now, and unable to see Dr. Currant at the hospital, she felt unsettled. She walked over to the box, picked up the fork, and slowly lifted the lid. It was exactly what she'd wanted.

Heavy thuds sounded up the basement stairs, and soon Mark appeared. "How did I do?" he asked.

"I almost called you."

"Why didn't you?"

"Apparently, I didn't need to. So how did it go?"

"Good. Really good." He pulled up a chair and sat down.

"She seems really nice. Did you find out if she's single?"

Mark nodded. "Divorced, no kids."

"So where is Laura staying tonight?"

"The Cozy Inn. By the way, how did you get here? I told you to call me."

"Marilou had a break, so she brought me. Why didn't you ask Laura to stay here? You know, this is a bed and breakfast. She's going to think you don't like her."

He grimaced. "That would have been too forward, no?"

She shrugged. "Maybe. So you're not going to believe this," she said. She hesitated, then said, "I'm not leaving for Appleton tomorrow."

"I thought you'd be more upset."

"Upset about what?"

"About Conrad. What are you talking about?"

"What happened to Conrad? Is he okay?"

"Didn't they explain it to you? He's the second installer."

Emily grinned and wagged her finger at him. "You had me there for a second."

"What?" He was completely straight-faced.

"Conrad is the other installer! Why didn't you tell me earlier?"

"Because when I got back this afternoon, you were gone."

She stood up. "But Barbara said—"

"She must not have known about his accident."

She stomped her foot. "I should have let that kid bleed to death."

Mark blew out a laugh. "But you just said you weren't leaving. What were you talking about?"

"I meant I was going to drive downstate."

"Downstate? Why?"

Emily looked away. "To make amends."

"With Butcher?"

She turned back to him. "No, of course not. I mean with Greg Olsen."

"Who's that?"

"Dr. Olsen, the resident on the floor when Nicholas died."

"Oh, right." Mark scratched his chin. "Why are going to see him?"

"I feel like I owe him some kind of explanation. He quit his residency because of it."

He nodded. "So when's your birthday?"

"Thursday. You buying me a present?"

Mark laughed. "Maybe. You still can't rent a car."

"No, not until Thursday, but I hope to have my car back before then. But who knows, right?"

Mark pulled out his phone. "Where does he live?"

She didn't say immediately. "Gaylord. Why?"

His thumb glided swiftly over the phone. He mumbled, "Two and a half hours," then something incomprehensible.

"What?"

"I'll take you."

"What? No. I can't let you do that. You have a flight to catch."

"I already postponed it until Wednesday."

"You did?"

"Yeah, when I found out you were going to be here another day."

"You sure you want to do this?"

He nodded. "I just need to back before six. So if we leave at nine or so, we can easily be back in time."

Emily sat down again, feeling warm inside. She grabbed Mark's hand and held it tightly for a second. "Thank you. Honestly, it'd be good to have someone with me. I'm not entirely sure I can do this alone."

Chapter Thirty-Two

Mark lay on his makeshift bed, the basement couch, hoping to fall asleep and forget what he had done. But his heart thumped defiantly, and it only got worse the harder he tried not to think about it. In the moment, he had felt invincible. His fear of the bridge had vanished behind his zeal to *be there* for Emily. But now, thinking it through, he hated himself for his recklessness, certain he couldn't master the Mighty Mac. He toyed with a familiar way out: fake a minor illness or claim exhaustion when they got close. Emily could drive across the bridge even though she wasn't supposed to drive the rental car. He didn't see any other way. He wasn't going to drive over.

When he finally reconciled himself to this idea, his thoughts drifted to Laura. New Laura. There was something there, an easiness between them. And they both lived in the Chicago area. *Fate*, Emily might say. They had agreed to meet for dinner again the next day, and he felt excited about it. What he knew of her so far he really liked. His mind dabbled with possibilities.

What about Em? There was something there, too, but it was completely different. A slight physical attraction—he couldn't deny it. But it was much broader than a romantic feeling. Maybe it was that unlikely relationship that some said was impossible between a man and a woman who weren't related. . . . Or maybe they were related somehow. Cousins. Yes, cousins. After all, Aunt Vivian had been her temporary guardian.

As he drifted to sleep, he jolted suddenly when he heard a creaking noise on the main floor. He lifted his head. Now that he was familiar with the house's reverberations, he knew someone was walking around. Emily? He identified a slight squeak as the sound of the front door opening, and then a couple seconds later, he heard it close. He got up, wondering if Em had gone outside.

At the foot of the stairs, he stopped. He heard voices. He tiptoed his way up, keeping to the far edge of each step to avoid making a sound. He slunk through the kitchen, which was dark save a dim light that spilled from somewhere in the front room. He listened intently.

"Don't get me wrong," a man said in a hard whisper, "I'm very glad you're considering it." It was silent for a second, then, "But what happened to your residency in Chicago? It's one of the best hospitals in the country."

"It's a long story. Suffice it to say I've changed my mind," Emily whispered.

"Are you sure?"

"Yes."

"All right. I think the board would be very interested in you. It's hard to get young doctors up here. And with the new hospital opening up . . ."

"When can I interview?"

"Let me talk to the director tomorrow, but we should be able to set something up soon."

"Okay, thank you. Thank you."

"I just hope you've thought it all the way through—believe me, no one wants you to stay more than me. I just want you to be sure."

There was silence for a moment. "I have thought it through, Jim, and I'm sure." Her voice had taken on a more tender tone. Mark stepped slowly back down to the basement and sat on the couch. He wondered why Em hadn't told him about staying in Manistique. He was struck with grief that she wouldn't be in Chicago. He was a little envious of Dr. Jimbo, too. He wanted to be the one to be there for Emily.

At six thirty in the morning, Mark got up, the taint of a repetitive dream lingering. Emily had fallen into a large crater, and Mark kept chasing her to the edge over and over. Each time he arrived, running through molasses, it seemed, he saw nothing. Pitch blackness. Silence. There was nothing he could except jump in, and he couldn't force himself to do it. Then he'd stir, flop around, and have the same nebulous dream all over again.

He dressed for a jog. The dream receded, and sadness crept in. For a moment, everything had seemed perfect: Em would have been near him in Chicago. But no more. Did she really like Dr. Jimbo that much, that she'd commit to staying?

"Fate," he scoffed in a scratchy voice. What was the point of all this?

When he stepped out of the kitchen, Emily startled him. She was standing next to the stairs, stretching in the low light of the morning. "It's about time you got up." She smirked. "I'm very limber now."

"It's a little too early for that, isn't it?"

"Stop it." She held her arms out to her sides. "Aren't you impressed?" Her hair was pulled back, and she was dressed in shorts, a tight tank top, and running shoes. "I'm going running with you, if it's all right."

"Yeah? Okay."

"Do you mind keeping a slightly slower pace? By which I mean, *a lot* slower?"

"Yeah, sure. But I thought you hated to run."

"I do." She rested her hand on her stomach. "But I swear I've gained five pounds since I got here." She pointed at him. "And it's your fault."

Mark blew out a laugh. "Me?"

"Yeah, all the food and pies."

He shrugged. "Let's go."

The morning air was cool but still. The two started a quick-paced walk south down the dim street, toward the lake. As they approached the end of the block, Mark poked: "That doctor really likes you."

"What doctor?"

"Jimbo. Doc Currant."

"Come on. No," she protested weakly. "I don't know."

He turned to Emily for a second and said, "It's totally obvious."

She didn't say anything, but her mouth quivered like she was suppressing a smile. Mark bolted, making a left on Porter Street.

"Well, Laura likes you," she shot out awkwardly. "Hey, wait up. You said!"

He slowed, waiting for her to catch up. "Laura and I just met."

"Same with me and Dr. Currant," she heaved. "We just met."

"It's not the same. You've spent quality time together with your patients."

"We haven't been on a date like you."

"That wasn't a date. That was a courtesy dinner."

"Whatever."

After a few seconds, he added, "Though tonight might be considered a date."

"You're going out again?" she said. "Oh, that's why you changed your flight."

Mark turned his head toward her. "No, I changed that for you, before I met Laura. Before I even knew for sure that you'd come back." He eyed her briefly, her arms pumping violently and her legs bouncing awkwardly. *Definitely not a runner*, he thought.

"How did you know I'd come back?"

"You can't fight fate, right?"

She made an ambiguous grunt.

They stayed quiet, making a turn on a street where the sidewalk and driveways ended and the houses became more dispersed. The street eventually ran into the highway.

"There's the Cozy Inn and Big Joe's," Mark said as they passed a dense row of evergreens.

"Doesn't seem so far," she replied, panting.

They crossed the quiet highway, then followed the pathway that led to the start of the lakeshore trail. Soon the trail transitioned from blacktop to boardwalk, their footsteps thudding pleasantly. With their backs to the sunrise, they watched gray gulls resting on the calm purple water and ripples drifting to and from the sandy shore. Between the boardwalk and the beach, tall grasses stood perfectly still. Yet the beach was scattered with reposing driftwood, a reminder of the lake's latent fierceness.

"How did you sleep last night?" he asked.

"Not well . . . nervous about today."

"Running helps."

She nodded, letting out a long exhale.

"We'll go to the lighthouse and take a break there." The red lighthouse stood about a quarter mile from shore, at the tip of the east-side breakwater.

They soon deviated from the boardwalk and onto the sand, running by the boulders on the beach that formed part of the breakwater. They approached two signs, one red and one yellow.

Danger: Waves Flood Surface, Keep Off During Storms.

Warning: Structure Is Not Designed for Public Access. Proceed at Your Own Risk.

Mark glanced over at Emily to see if the sign had gotten her attention, but her shoulders were slumped and her eyes were down. He ran ahead slightly, leaping onto a boulder and stepping up to the flat pathway on top of the concrete barrier that separated Lake Michigan from the harbor.

He stopped and turned his head, expecting Emily to climb timidly. But she scaled the barrier effortlessly and landed next to him in a second.

The lighthouse stood at the end of the breakwater. The uneven concrete pathway to the lighthouse stretched ten feet wide. As they ran farther down, the path smoothed and widened to nearly twice the size, protected on both sides by large boulders. About two hundred yards from the lighthouse, the breakwater veered sharply right. When they got within a hundred feet of the lighthouse, Mark took off, racing up the six concrete steps, tagging the red cast iron tower as if he were racing against a childhood friend.

Emily did not follow. She bent down, planting her hands above her knees. "Whew!"

He pointed toward the large harbor. "That's where the Manistique River dumps into the lake."

She barely looked up and nodded, gasping.

He patted the lighthouse again. "Bear Foot's lighthouse," he announced.

After a few more seconds of catching her breath, she craned her neck to look up at Mark. "What do you mean by that?"

"I thought I told you."

"Told me what?"

"Ellen gave Bear Foot the lighthouse."

She straightened. "Seriously?"

"Yeah, that's why Vivian told him to go to the lighthouse, in that vision." He winked at her.

She managed to barely shake her head. She glanced across the harbor and seemed to be thinking.

"Ready to head back?"

She straightened. "Do we have to run?" she asked.

Mark smiled. "I'll tell you what. Let's walk back to the boardwalk and then we'll start running from there."

Emily trotted up the lighthouse stairs, placing her hand firmly on the lighthouse, and said softly, "Bear Foot's lighthouse." She looked over at Mark. "Can we climb up to the top?"

Mark rubbed his cheek. "No, I don't think so. We can ask Bear Foot for a tour once he gets official possession."

Emily jogged back down the cement stairs, and they started their walk back to the hotel.

"Exactly what day does your residency start?" Mark asked, prodding her to confess what he already knew—that she was not doing her residency in Chicago. That she was planning to stay in Manistique. He turned his head to look at her but she kept her eyes in front and slightly down.

"It's complicated."

"What do you mean? The hospital hasn't given you a start date yet?"

"Umm . . ." She paused. "It's hard for me to say it."

"It's hard for you to say what?" He was gentle, like the finishing motions when sawing through a board.

"I'm not doing my residency in Chicago anymore."

"What do you mean?" he said, feigning surprise. "Why not?"

"Because . . ." She cleared her throat. "John interfered with the process."

"Who's John? Dr. Butcher?"

"Yes," she sighed. "And not only did he interfere, he's going to be on the board there. So there's no way I'm going there now."

Mark took in a deep breath. He hadn't known her reasons. He had figured she was doing this because she was interested in Dr. Currant. "I'm so sorry."

"I'll be fine."

"So where will you do your residency now?"

She hesitated. "Here."

"Here in Manistique?"

"Well, hopefully. It's not decided yet."

"I think you might be suffering from Stockholm syndrome."

She smiled and laughed. "Maybe. They're building a brand new facility that opens up in the fall." She pointed west. "It's about a mile west of here, off Highway 2."

They reached the boardwalk. She bent down and tugged on her laces. "I spoke to Dr. Currant about it. He came over last night after you went to bed."

"He did? There are rules about having men at the house at night."

She laughed. "He didn't stay. It was purely professional," she replied evenly. "He said he was going to talk to the hospital's director and set me up with an interview."

"Sounds promising," he said, but only because she seemed truly interested in staying.

"We'll see," she said, and began running.

When Emily was in the shower, Mark made himself a cup of coffee and walked out the back door. He sauntered around the side of the house and across the lawn to the tree. There he drank his coffee, staring back at the house. Vivian's house. His grandfather's house before that. He couldn't sell it, though he didn't know exactly what else to do with it, either. Then as he surveyed the quiet neighborhood, his mind wandered a little further, and he considered briefly what it would be like to live in Manistique, before laughing out loud.

As he stepped inside through the front door, he heard Emily calling him from upstairs.

"Yeah?" he yelled back.

"Can you get me a cup of coffee? I haven't had any today."

"Sure."

After getting her coffee, he went upstairs and knocked on her door.

"Come in."

After a brief hesitation—he was unsure that he had heard right—and with a certain anxious tension in his heart, he walked in.

Emily was in the bathroom, brushing her hair. She was wearing a robe.

"Here you go," he said, walking toward her. He stopped and held out the mug, remaining on his side of the threshold.

She moved over and took it. "Thank you, thank you." She blew into the cup and took a sip. "After I got out of the shower, all I wanted to do was go back to bed."

Mark nodded. "After you're done getting ready, I have something to tell you."

"I have something to tell you too, but don't leave. Just tell me."

"It can wait," he answered, feeling uncomfortable.

"Sit down and tell me," she said, pointing to the bed.

He sat down where he still had an angled view of her. She brushed at something on her face. "I'm going to keep the house."

She turned toward him. "Yeah?"

"Yeah. I'll come and visit you once in a while."

"That'd be nice—assuming I get the job here."

"You'll get it," he said, slapping his knees and standing up. "That's it. That was my news."

"Where are you going?"

"I was going to let you finish getting ready."

"No, stay. Remember, I want to tell you something."

He sat down again. "Okay."

She was silent for a moment, putting on mascara. "I'm not sure I can do this today."

"You can," he said evenly.

"He's going to be angry with me. He quit being a doctor because of me."

"Maybe he'll reconsider after you talk to him."

"Maybe." Her answer came from far away. "I'm going to get dressed."

Mark got up again.

"No, no, sit down," she insisted.

"But—"

"Just shut your eyes."

Hesitantly he sat back down and shut his eyes. "My eyes are closed."

"Don't peek." He heard her step into the room near him.

"Completely shut. I promise."

He heard her robe fall to the ground. A nervous twirl played in his stomach. He pressed his eyes closed even tighter.

"You weren't totally wrong yesterday."

"About what?"

She didn't answer him immediately. "I totally related to that story and at the end when he, you know . . . I don't know, it struck me hard. Like I might be going down that same path."

"But you're n—"

"Not that I would ever do that exactly. But I thought about quitting. Like Dr. Olsen. Nicholas's death struck me really hard at first. I dealt with it by being angry. I was angry at John. Even at Dr. Olsen. I used my anger as a shield. But it had other effects. I stopped socializing with my friends and coworkers. I lost my appetite. I was unhappy. And then came Match Day."

"Match Day?"

"It's the day you learn which hospital you get matched with for residency."

"Oh right." He heard the gentle swish of clothes being put on.

"And I got matched with Lincoln Presbyterian, which was a huge confidence-booster. Of course I was still upset and sad about

Nicholas, but suddenly I was distracted by all the excitement. Moving to Chicago and all that. And now I feel really badly for Dr. Olsen."

"Everything will work out in the end," Mark said.

There was silence for a moment, and then she said, "You can open your eyes now."

He did, finding her barefoot, wearing jeans and a soft white ruffled top. He stood up. "Any interest in day-old French toast?"

She smiled. "Definitely. I'll be down in a few minutes."

When Emily came downstairs, Mark met her in the dining room with two plates of French toast, four pieces each, carrying the maple syrup under his arm.

"Smells great. Sometimes leftover food is better than fresh. Like stew."

Mark nodded. "And meatloaf."

"Yes! What about chili?"

"Definitely." He pulled out the chair. His heart immediately sank. *Speak, Memory* on the chair. He sighed.

"What?"

He picked up the book and showed her.

"Oh."

Setting it on the table, he said, "That reminds me."

"What?"

Mark sat down. "Bear Foot had another vision."

Emily took a bite. "Mmm. This is really good."

"Thanks."

"So what did Bear Foot see this time?"

"Actually he didn't see anything, only heard a voice."

"How's that a vision?"

"That's what I said! Anyway he said it sounded a bit like George."

"Really?"

"Yeah. And it was the night George died."

"Not that I believe in any of this, but what did George say?"

"He told him not to leave Manistique. And he was right. Bear Foot should never have driven Yvonne. He could have saved himself all that time."

Emily's mouth twisted skeptically. "That's ridiculous."

"I know, I know. It was just a dream he had."

"No. I mean the message is ridiculous. You're trying to tell me that George came to Bear Foot in a *vision* so that he would save himself a two-hour drive?"

Mark shrugged. "Yeah, it does seem trivial."

She laughed. "Yeah." She took another bite. "You definitely got the second B in the B&B covered. Now, if you only worked on your hospitality . . ."

He shook his head. "Bear Foot did say the message could have been for somebody else."

"Like who?"

He gazed out into the living room. "You, maybe."

Her eyebrows lifted. "But I've already decided to stay." She pointed at Mark. "Maybe it was meant for you." She winked at him.

Mark frowned. "No way. No way."

Chapter Thirty-Three

Waiting to turn east onto Highway 2, Emily gazed in the opposite direction, west, toward Appleton. She wished they could go to her parents' house and have a relaxed Memorial Day barbecue in the backyard. She missed her dad's beef brisket, smoked for eight hours—

"You thinking about your car?" Mark asked.

The dealership was in that direction, two blocks west around a small bend. "I would have been really upset if I had called them this morning without any idea."

"I know."

Several cars were lined up behind a slow truck. When the last car passed, they turned left, and a sharp pain shot through Emily's gut with a cold wash of anxiety.

"So did you talk to them?" Mark asked.

"Who?"

"The dealership."

Emily nodded. "Yeah, I called when you were in the shower. At first no one answered. It just rang and rang. I thought for a second it might be closed."

"Memorial Day."

"Yeah, but finally Barbara answered."

"What did she say?"

"She was shocked to find out about Conrad's finger. She had no idea."

"Look at us. We're insiders, we know more gossip than the locals."

She smiled. "Yeah, but is that good or bad?"

He chuckled.

Lake Michigan came in and out of view through a line of evergreens. When they drove by the hotel that was being renovated, Mark commented, "I heard that that hotel actually burnt down, and that's the reason for the renovation."

"Really?"

"I'm thinking it was one of Bear Foot's ritual fires gone wrong."

"To rid the hotel of evil spirits?" Emily laughed.

"Oh, I guess I never explained that to you."

"Explained what?"

"Bear Foot's fire that day. That was for Vivian. A gesture to keep her warm during her spirit's journey to heaven."

"And you put it out?"

"No," he replied defensively. Then, "First off, you don't believe in that stuff. Secondly, I started a fire inside the house for her, okay?"

"I'm not sure if that's the same, but okay."

"Don't worry, Bear Foot gave me his full blessing."

The view of the lake opened and Emily stared out there, trying to calm her nerves.

"What did he say when you called?" Mark asked.

"Who?"

"Dr. Olsen."

She hesitated a second. "I haven't called yet."

"You haven't?" He gave her a look of consternation. "So how do you know if he's actually there?"

She didn't answer immediately, not until he turned and looked at her again. "I don't know," she muttered.

"Seriously? We're going to drive all that way—"

"You don't have to go." She stretched her neck and stared out her window, partially expecting the car to swing around.

After a loud breath, Mark said, "Sorry, sorry. I know this is difficult for you, but . . ."

She was quiet for a moment and then explained, "I'm not sure he'd be willing to see me if I wasn't already there."

"Yeah. I sort of get that."

"Sorry, I should have said something."

The Indian casino came up. A few cars were parked in the lot.

"A little early for gambling, isn't it? Like drinking pop for breakfast."

"I interned with a doctor who drank Diet Coke for breakfast, put it in his corn flakes."

"Yuck."

"Hey!" Emily tapped on the window. "Doesn't that look like George's niece?"

Mark looked back toward the casino, but they were at a bad angle by the time he looked. "I don't know." He slowed down, then pulled over.

"What are you doing?"

"Turning around. I want to see if it was her."

"What, are you planning to confront her or something?"

He let a car pass and then made a U-turn. "No, I just want to see if it was her."

"Why?"

"Because I'd like to know before I get any more involved."

"Know what?"

"Whether she has a gambling problem."

Emily sighed. "Come on."

They pulled into the parking lot. She said, "Are you going inside? Maybe someone will see you and think *you* have a problem."

"Nope. I'm just going to look for her car."

Only a dozen or so cars were in the lot. He stopped behind a white Ford Explorer with an Illinois license plate. "Yep, that's her, all right," he said.

"So what?"

They drove off. "Nothing," he said. "Except that I'm not having dinner with her now."

"Come on. You're kidding, right?"

They got back on the highway. He shook his head. "No, I'm not kidding. She has some kind of gambling addiction."

"Addiction? You're totally jumping to conclusions."

"What other conclusion is there?"

"Maybe they have great breakfasts there. Have you thought of that?"

He answered her with a murky glare.

"You can at least ask her about it."

"I wouldn't believe her anyway—unless she admits she has a problem."

"But you said you liked her."

"I do—I did."

"So . . ."

"So this changes everything. I don't need this kind of complication in my life."

"Ha!" she said. "*My* life is complicated. Your life is a walk in the park."

"And I'd like to keep it that way."

She shook her head.

Mark recounted a story about his friend's girlfriend—a gorgeous woman who wrote award-winning children's books, was working on a graduate degree in child psychology, and was from a wealthy family in New York. "She turned out to be a complete fraud."

"What do you mean she was a fraud?"

"She wasn't a writer of children's book—she had the same name as the author. Just a coincidence and she ran with it. She wasn't studying in school. And she wasn't from a rich family in New York."

"I don't get it. You said she was attractive."

"She was. She must have felt inadequate or something."

Emily said, "Oh no," softly.

"What."

"This is where—" She shut her eyes.

"Huh?"

"The deer."

Mark spotted a red stain on the left side of the road. "Oh . . ." After a moment he said, "That was one determined deer."

"What do you mean by that?" She opened her eyes again.

"It made it to the other side."

"No it didn't."

"But . . ." He thought for a few seconds, running it through his mind, confirming the logic. "The damage to your car was on the left side—"

"Can we talk about something else?" she snapped.

But they didn't talk about anything at all. They rolled silently through long straight roads past trees and grassy clearings, isolated houses and dilapidated buildings that looked like they had never been new, and through the scarce township.

Emily stared out at the landscape, worried about her meeting. Mark thought about Laura. A bit of regret pushed on his chest, but he remained determined. When they stopped somewhere, he'd call her and cancel dinner.

Mark's cell phone rang. He smiled when he saw who it was. "Do you mind if I get this?"

"No, I don't mind."

"Bradley, what's going on?" he said, on speaker.

"Oh, thank God, you're alive."

"Reports of my death have been greatly exaggerated."

"I suppose so."

"Why would you think otherwise?"

"First off, you missed the party."

"That's right! I'm so sorry, Brad, I forgot to call—by the way, don't say anything obscene. You're on speaker."

"Yeah, who's there?"

"Emily."

"Emily who?"

"Hello, I'm Emily."

"Hi. Nice to meet you, Emily. You don't have any kids, do you?"

"Come on, Brad," Mark pleaded. He looked over at Emily and shook his head. "Ignore him."

"Sorry, sorry. Only kidding," Brad said. He asked, "So who are you?"

"It's a long story," Mark replied, looking over at her with a grin.

"Very long story," she said.

"I promise to tell you all about it when I get back."

"Back? Where are you?"

"Michigan. The UP."

"Seriously?"

"Not for long," Emily interjected.

"True," Mark confirmed. "We're heading to the Lower Peninsula."

"What are you doing way up there? You didn't mention anything about a trip."

"I should've called you. My aunt died last week. She lived up here."

"Oh. I'm very sorry to hear that, Mark."

"Thanks. I'll be back in a couple days. We can catch up then."

"Sure. Glad you're okay. I'll let Steve know. He was worried too. Thought you were stuck in jail without bail money."

Mark laughed. "Steve always thinks the best."

"He does."

"You guys know I'd call one of you to get me out."

"That's what I told him."

"All right, Brad, I'll call you later this week."

He ended the call.

"That was an old high school buddy," he said. "I totally forgot he had an invited a few of us over to his house for a barbecue yesterday."

Emily nodded.

They were quiet again. A few minutes later, as they neared Naubin-way, Lake Michigan appeared. Mark broke the silence. "You okay?"

"Huh? Yeah, I guess. Sorry."

"It's fine. You don't have to talk."

"I mean, I'm sorry about back there."

"Back where?"

"The deer."

"Forget about the deer," he insisted.

"No, you don't understand what I mean. I didn't want to tell you because I'm embarrassed."

"What are you talking about?"

She took a long second before revealing, "I was going east when the deer hit."

"East? You mean west."

"No, I was heading east."

"Weren't you heading toward Wisconsin?"

"I was, but I turned around near Manistique."

"Turned around? To go where?"

She held for a few seconds. "Mackinac Island."

"Why?"

"John was waiting for me there."

"Oh," he said softly.

"I'm really disappointed in myself."

They were silent for a second, then Mark said, "Why? You never made it there."

"Only because a deer stopped me."

"But you're also assuming you wouldn't have changed your mind again somewhere in between."

Her head swayed back and forth before she nodded gently. "I guess that's true. Thank you."

Mark felt good—he'd even have said proud if were forced to admit it. It was something his psychiatrist mother might have come up with.

Changing the subject, he asked, "How many siblings do you have? There was a brother when Vivian brought you to your parents."

She hung her head. "Yeah, Kyle. He died ten years ago."

"I'm so sorry. I didn't mean to . . ."

"No, no. It's okay."

He grimaced in apology.

She tugged on the ends of her hair. "I've been meaning to tell you about Kyle."

"Oh?"

"Yeah. You remind me a bit of him."

"In what way?" he said, a bit sullenly.

She hesitated, not sure whether she might overwhelm him if she got into it. "I don't know exactly how to explain it."

"What happened to him? If you don't mind me asking."

She winced slightly, before tucking her hair behind her ear. "I hardly ever talk about it. It's awful."

"I'm sorry. You don't have to—"

"No, I can tell you."

Mark remained silent, preparing himself for a rare form of cancer or suicide or . . .

She cleared her throat first, but her voice quavered anyway. "He fell off a bridge."

"What?!" Mark felt instantly unsteady. He grabbed the steering wheel firmly with both hands.

"I told you it was awful."

"B-b-but how did it happen?" he asked, not really certain he wanted the details.

She took a long, shaky breath. "Kyle was helping someone who had gotten into a car accident on a bridge. He tried pulling open the driver's door, but it wouldn't budge. So he tried the passenger side, which was near the railing of the bridge. He yanked hard on it, and it practically came off its hinges. He lost his balance and fell right over the short railing."

"Oh God, that's awful."

"Twenty feet to the road below."

Mark became lightheaded.

Emily sat up. "Mark, are you okay? You're completely pale."

"I'm fine," he said breathlessly.

"Pull over. Now!"

Mark assented with a trembling nod. The car shook as the tires crossed the roadside rumble strip, thunk-thunk-thunk-thunk-thunk-thunk-thunk-thunk, stopping half on the blacktop and half on the dirt-and-grass shoulder, some twenty feet from the tree line.

He gripped the wheel firmly to keep his hands from shaking.

"You okay?"

He shook his head. "I need air." He got out of the car and stumbled toward a row of bare evergreens. A weight pulled on him, and after a dozen steps he stopped and sat down on the hard ground.

"Mark! Are you okay? Mark!"

Mark came to, unsure how he'd ended up on his back. His vision unclouded slowly after several blinks. He sat up. Emily was down next to him.

"Yeah," he got out groggily. "What happened?"

"You passed out."

He tried nodding. When he sat up slightly, the dead trees in front of him spun around like a skipping record. He felt nauseated.

Emily held her hand gently on his wrist. "Your heart is beating fast." She put her ear to his chest.

"What are you doing?"

"Shhh."

"I feel funny. Like I can't catch my breath."

"Quiet."

After a few seconds, she said, "You're in a-fib."

"Is it a heart attack?"

"No. You'll be fine. Just relax and put your head to the ground," she told him, gently pushing his head down.

He complied. "What are you doing?"

"Tell me if you stop feeling that funny feeling."

After a dozen seconds, Mark felt normal again. "Okay," he said, sitting up. "I think I'm okay now."

She checked again. "Yes, back to normal. Has this ever happened before?"

He shook his head. "A few times but it always stops pretty quickly on its own."

"Can you get up?"

Mark stood up. Emily held her arms out ready to catch him.

"You'll have to drive," he said. There was no way he was going to psych himself up enough to get over the bridge now.

"All right. Do you want to go back home?"

He shook his head. "No, I'm fine if you drive."

They got back into the car, Emily in the driver's seat. "You sure you trust me? I haven't been driving for very long. I'm not even twenty-five."

He let out a breathless laugh. "Shut up." He felt exhausted.

She started driving. "When was the last time that happened?"

"What?"

"The arrhythmia."

Mark closed his eyes. He finally said, "You'd laugh if I told you."

"Laugh? I'm a doctor. I only laugh at patients when they're not around."

He smiled. "Last week before I tried crossing the bridge."

"The Mackinac Bridge?"

"Yeah . . . I can't cross bridges. I admit it. There."

"What do you mean, like you have a phobia?"

"A major one."

"I get it now," she said. "When I told you about Kyle . . ."

He nodded. "Do you know how much of my life is controlled by this stupid fear?"

"I can see how it could be, yes."

"If I go somewhere with other people in the car, I either have to make sure we don't cross a bridge or a long overpass or make sure someone else is driving."

"That must be hard."

Mark nodded. "I've never told anyone about this. I mean, *no one.*"

"So how did you get across the Mackinac Bridge?"

He huffed out a laugh. "So first I thought about taking a boat to Mackinac Island from the Lower Peninsula and then taking another boat to St. Ignace and renting a car in there, but I couldn't find a rental company in St. Ignace."

"So what did you do?"

"I found out the bridge workers provide a free service. They drive scared drivers across the bridge."

"That's nice of them."

"Yeah, and apparently I'm not the only one."

"But how were you planning to get us over now?"

He shrugged. "I was hoping my fear of embarrassment was greater than my fear of the bridge."

"And what if it wasn't?"

"I'd use my backup plan: invent an excuse as we got close to the bridge, and make you drive."

She patted him on the leg. "I'm sorry you have to deal with this."

He looked at her, smiling. "Actually, I'm kind of relieved, telling someone about it."

"You should see someone."

"You mean a psychiatrist?"

She nodded.

"No, my mother was a psychiatrist."

"You told me. So?"

"I've been sufficiently tortured by that profession." He let out a chuckle. "No way."

"Does your mother have a fear of bridges too?"

"No."

"Interesting that Vivian did."

"How do you know that?"

"It was in her story. When she crossed one of the bridges, she had to close her eyes. You don't remember reading that?"

Mark thought for a second and shook his head. "Maybe I closed my eyes during that part."

She laughed. "I suppose it runs only in part of the family."

"No, Vivian and I aren't blood-related. She was adopted."

The lake disappeared, and soon after, buildings popped up here and there, curio shops and a motel, before a stretch of several billboards, most of them advertising boats to Mackinac. And then a small explosion of restaurants, motels, and gas stations. Mark pointed. "Let's get gas here. I think we're only a couple miles from the bridge."

"Okay." She got out her purse. "Here, let me pay for gas."

He waved her off. "Don't worry about it."

He pumped gas while Emily headed for the convenience store. "Want anything?"

"Yeah, get me a coffee."

"Decaf, right?"

"No."

"You should really avoid caffeine with your arrhythmia."

"Fine, but only if it doesn't look too bad."

"How bad is bad?"

He shrugged. "I trust you."

She nodded and smiled. "Cream or sugar?"

"Cream, but only if it's in those single-serving containers."

They were off again within ten minutes, Emily driving and Mark with a cup of not-horrible decaf coffee, black, in his hand. Shortly ahead was the turnoff for Highway 75 South and the Mackinac Bridge.

"I should tell you," Emily said as they merged. "I actually love bridges."

"What? We can't be friends," he declared.

"My dad is a bridge engineer. Well was. He's retired. So he always had bridge drawings and photographs on his desk, and he spent a lot of time talking about bridges with us."

Mark kept his gaze straight ahead, the lake in view on the horizon. The bridge would show itself soon. He drank one more sip of coffee and set it in the cup holder. He kept his thoughts to himself. *How can you love a bridge when your brother died falling off one?*

A few seconds later, the Mighty Mac emerged from the distant haze. He exhaled sharply. He pulled out a jacket from the back. "I'm just going to take a nap for a while."

"Why don't you just use your hands as blinders and see if you can cross looking straight ahead?"

"That's a five-mile bridge."

They quickly approached the toll plaza. After Emily paid the four dollars, Mark said, "Good night," and ducked under his jacket.

As she steered into the merge, Emily yanked on the jacket and threw it to the back.

"Hey! What did you do that for?"

"Because you're going to confront this—at least a little bit."

"No. Not now," he said in a panicky tone. He took off his seatbelt and leaned back to grab his jacket.

"Mark, stop and look at me."

He gripped the jacket tightly as he put his seatbelt back on. "What?"

"You can do this if you put your mind to it. Just look straight ahead, nothing else, and talk to me about something." She moved her hand toward him, and he squirmed away from her.

"I can't," he said.

She placed her hand on his thigh, near his knee. "I think you can."

"Even if I look straight ahead and pretend I'm on some yellow-brick road, I'll still see the towers. And I know the towers are holding up cables that are holding up the road. So, no!"

She grabbed his hand and squeezed tightly. "I think you can do it."

They were already over the water, but low, before the bridge lifted up.

Mark glanced at her, sighed, and relented. "Fine. I'll try. But if I die from that heart thing . . ."

"Atrial fibrillation. No, it won't kill you, I promise."

"If I get real nervous, I'm pulling the jacket over me."

"Talk to me about something," she said, ignoring him. "Tell me about your friend who called. Brad, was it?"

Mark's gaze had contracted to the grooves in the road. "Yeah, Brad. High school friend."

"Yeah? Tell me a story about Brad."

"I can't think of one—oh, he just tried to set me up with his sister."

"Yeah, and what happened?"

"I said, 'No way.'"

"Why not? Looks? Personality?"

"No, she's fine. It's mostly because he loves his sister, and if it didn't work out, I'd lose a good friend too."

"I get it."

"I think it's pretty cool that Brad and his sister are so close. I sort of wish I had a sister like that."

She remained quiet.

"Oh sorry, I—" He grimaced. "I should just hide under the jacket."

"No, it's fine. It was a long time ago."

"It's never long enough."

"True," she agreed somberly. Then, "I want to tell you about Kyle."

"Sure."

"He's the reason I went to medical school. He was a doctor. He was doing his residency when he died."

"Where was he doing his residency?"

"At the University of South Carolina. I was sixteen at the time. He was that perfect big brother." She sniffed.

"Sounds like it."

She cleared her throat. "He went away to college when I was in fourth grade. I totally missed him, but he'd call me at least once a week.

He'd come home on weekends quite a bit too. He went to Madison for his undergrad, so not too far from Appleton. When he was home in the summer we did a lot of hiking. And cross-country skiing in the winter. He loved the outdoors, so I did too."

Mark stayed silent. He could no longer avoid seeing the first tower. "Sorry. I may have to shut my eyes."

"The tower?"

"Yep."

"Think of it as a tall building."

"That holds—"

"A tall building, a tall building."

"Right . . . sure."

He kept taking shallow breaths as they drove toward it. He wanted to jump out of his body.

They passed it.

"You did it. See?"

"Yes," he replied tensely. "Barely." He blew out and concentrated on the grooves again. "And there's still another one."

"So you're an only child?"

He cleared his throat. "Yes, and no other family. Though I just found out that I might have a cousin out there somewhere."

"What do you mean?"

"Apparently Vivian gave up a baby for adoption."

"Really?"

"Yeah, her lawyer told me the other day."

"Are you going to look for him? Or her?"

Mark shrugged. "I don't know. Half of me wants to and the other half doesn't. I mean, what if they want to be left alone?"

"And you don't have any other relatives?"

"Nope. My dad was an only child, and Vivian was my only aunt."

Emily placed her hand on top of his, holding it firmly for a second. "Well you've got me."

Mark stopped staring at the road and turned his head to her. A warm, broad smile met him before she turned her attention back to driving. Outside her window was Lake Huron—far below and beyond. But it didn't bother him. Joy and strength swelled in his heart.

"Corny, right? Sorry."

"No, no. I appreciate that. More than you know," he said. She turned briefly again to him, nodding and smiling. Her eyes were sincere and he knew she meant it. "In fact, I was thinking something like that yesterday," he said, continuing to gaze at her.

"What's that?"

"That you and I are sort of like cousins."

"Yeah?"

"Yeah. Vivian is my aunt. And she was also your guardian for a short while—albeit she kidnapped you."

"Thank God she did. I see the connection." She nodded slowly. "Yeah, we're like cousins."

"Yeah."

"Look," Emily said. "We just passed the second tower."

His head snapped back and the tower was gone, vanished as if it had been magically erased. The land on the other side was close. "Hey, look at that, we did."

"You're doing great."

He took in a deep breath and let it out. "Yeah." He turned his head to the right toward Lake Michigan, and his stomach did a twirl, but he kept it together. He tossed the jacket to the back and released his grip on the door handle. "Look at me, no hands!"

Emily laughed. "There you go!"

He let out a nervous laugh before setting his clammy hand back on the door handle. "Okay, I shouldn't get carried away."

A minute later they passed the end of the suspended road, and the causeway carried them toward the Lower Peninsula.

"See. I told you you could do it," she said.

"Terra firma," he declared. "That was exhilarating."

"We'll do it again later."

He groaned. "Don't remind me."

"Should I take the next exit so we can switch?"

"Sure—oh shoot."

"What?"

"I have to make that call."

"What call?"

"Cancel dinner with Laura."

Emily moaned, "Seriously?"

"I don't know."

"Just go, even if you decided not to continue with it."

He thought about it for a second. "I'll consider it." He pointed to his left. "That's the phone booth where you call to get picked up."

Emily glanced over and nodded. She took the off-ramp and immediately turned into a nearby gas station to switch places. They both exited the car at the same time and started clockwise around the car. Mark started a fast walk. Emily noticed and started running. Mark ran, too.

They jumped into their seats.

"I won!" they both exclaimed.

"I went around the long way," Mark protested.

Emily protested back: "I had to go around both doors."

"True. Fine, it's a tie."

Once they were back on the highway, Emily looked out her window, her bleary eyes catching only a smear of green, the passing trees.

"You okay?"

She shook her head. She had distracted herself with Mark's bridge phobia. Now they were on the last leg, an hour away from Gaylord. The dread poured over her, a spell of soggy heat. "I don't know if I can do this."

"What's the worst that can happen?"

She groaned. "I think I'm going to be sick. Can you pull over?"

He slowed the car and pulled to the shoulder.

Emily rolled down the window. The fresh air on her face relieved her. But she still felt anxious, and she opened the car door.

"Where are you going?"

She got out and leaned back against the car.

"Em?"

Her eyes rested on a single birch tree that stood out against a wall of evergreens. She stared at it. The leaves high up on the white tree quivered.

"Emily?"

She imagined herself walking over and putting her arms around the white bark and holding on tightly. When she shut her eyes, the trunk remained, etched for a few seconds in the darkness, a remnant of the bright sun on the white bark.

When she opened her eyes, Mark was in front of her. "Are you all right, Em?"

"Ever notice birch trees?"

"Huh? Birch trees? Sure."

"Seems like they don't belong or . . . or like they're ghosts of the forest."

"I suppose, yeah. Are you okay?"

Then she thought and unintentionally whispered aloud, "Immunity from contrived guilt."

"What do you mean?"

Emily blinked several times. "Sorry. Never mind."

"What did you say?" he insisted.

After a second, without looking at him, she answered, "Immunity from contrived guilt."

"What does that mean, exactly?"

"It's from John. He said that no one in geriatrics feels guilty when a patient dies. But pediatric oncologists and surgeons and specialists always contrive guilt when a child dies. Only a few make it unscathed—those who are immune to the guilt because they understand."

"Understand what?"

"That even more children would die if doctors didn't intervene."

"Hmm."

She burst out in coarse laughter. "He even said I should use Nicholas's death as a lesson, maybe my most important lesson as an intern."

"He said that?"

"Yes. Maybe I'm not cut out for peds."

"Don't listen to him. You have feelings. Good, I say."

She shook her head languidly. "I thought I could do this, but I don't know. I haven't seen Dr. Olsen since that morning. It's going to bring all that back. Not to mention how upset he's going to be when I tell him what happened that night."

"He'll be upset, of course. But he'll be upset with Dr. Butcher, not you."

"I can't tell him the whole story. John could get into serious trouble."

"Why do you care what happens to him?" he hissed. "You need some of that immunity from guilt, or whatever you call it, when it comes to him."

She turned to him with pursed lips. Tired, she pleaded, "Don't make me defend him."

Mark crossed his arms. He moved over and leaned against the car, the two side by side.

"Besides that," she said, "I still need a recommendation from the hospital. I don't think they'd be too happy with me if Dr. Olsen went back to the hospital with the full story."

"So what will you say to him?"

"I'm not sure. But I'm going to encourage him to go back and finish his residency."

Mark straightened up. "All right, let's go, then."

Back in the car, Emily said, "I wonder if Doris and Evelyn are on."

Mark's eyes lit up. "Yeah, I could use some of their homespun humor right now." He turned on the radio.

The station came on, but it wasn't the voice of Evelyn or Doris. It was the gruff voice of a man reading out the fishing report.

"Which station?"

"It's this one. The ladies probably don't come on until after nap time, and by then we'll be too far away."

She laughed. "You're awful."

"Wonder if they're back together."

"I hope so." She turned off the radio.

"Hey! I was listening to that. What part of that lake are the walleye biting in?"

"Shut up. I know more about wetting a line than you do."

Mark smirked. "I have no doubt you do."

"My dad used to take me fishing. I mean, I'd tag along to hang out with him and my brother."

"Sounds like fun."

"That reminds me. I need to call my parents. They're expecting me today." She pulled out her phone. "Obviously that's not going to happen." She called.

She explained to her father that the person who was going to replace the windshield had hurt his finger—she left out the part where she had saved the finger. "No, you don't need to come. I'll be all right. . . . Yes, I'm still staying at the Manistique Victorian." When Mark looked at her, she gave him a wink. She told her dad that she'd be in Appleton in a couple of days, and that she had some important news to share when she got home. "No, I'm not getting married." She glowered at Mark's stupid grin.

"I take it your parents don't know about Dr. Butcher," Mark said when she finished.

"No. God, no."

"Do they think you're dating someone?"

"No. Ever hopeful, though."

"Did you date anyone in medical school—besides Butcher, of course?"

"John and I weren't dating," she answered firmly. "Unless you consider hanging out in his office at the hospital or eating at the hospital cafeteria dating."

"You weren't afraid of being seen together at the hospital?"

"A little. But he was my mentor, so there was good reason."

"Okay, so anyone you actually dated during med school?"

"One guy. During my first year. He was a graduate student in public policy."

"Public policy? Sounds dull."

"It was. It got serious enough that I went with him to North Carolina to meet his parents."

"Why did you break up?"

Emily laughed. "A fly on scrambled eggs."

"Huh?" Mark looked at her with converging eyebrows. "You broke up over a Dr. Seuss book?"

She shook her head. "That's not a Dr. Seuss book."

"Sounds like a Dr. Seuss book."

"Anyway, it wasn't *only* about a fly on scrambled eggs. That was just the culmination of months of frustration that I kept bottled up inside."

"I'm confused."

She slapped her thigh. "Fine. Here's the story. One morning Buff and I—"

"Buff? Your fiancé's name was Buff? For real?"

"We were never engaged. His nickname was Buff. His real name was Ted."

"Buff," he repeated in a deep voice. He snickered. "All right, so what happened?"

"So one morning we decided to have breakfast at this place just outside of town. I asked for two eggs, fried, and other stuff—bacon and whatever. At some point I went to the restroom, and when I came back, there's scrambled eggs, not fried eggs. I said something to Buff about it."

"And what did *Buff* do about your scrambled eggs?"

"He didn't do anything! He just nodded his head. He didn't even pay attention to my order. But easygoing as I am—"

Mark burst out laughing.

"What? I'm easygoing," she demanded.

"Sorry. Of course. I was still laughing at the name. Buff. Go ahead. Go on."

She narrowed her eyes. "Anyway, I started eating the scrambled eggs, until I saw a dead fly. So I pointed it out to Buff."

"What did Buff say?"

Pinching her fingers together, reenacting the scene, she said, "He picked up the dead fly and tossed it on the floor."

"He did?"

"Yeah, can you believe that?"

"He should have waved the waitress over and gotten you new eggs, *fried* eggs."

"Yes! Thank you!"

"And you broke up right there?"

"Not only that, I got up and walked home. Five miles."

"Really?"

"Yes, and when I got home almost two hours later, I made myself two fried eggs."

"Good for you."

"How about you? What about your last girlfriend?"

"Would you believe we broke up over a cockroach on couscous?"

"Shut up." She waved him off. "Seriously, what happened?"

Mark shrugged. "Things were fine between us until Laura brought up marriage."

"You have a thing for Lauras, don't you?"

"You don't know the half of it. My first serious girlfriend in college was named Lora too. But L-o-r-a."

"Laura wanted to get married, but you didn't?"

"We were just on two different timelines. She was ready, and I wasn't."

"So that was it?"

"Yep, that was it," he sighed. Her son's anguished expression popped into his mind.

"How long were you together?"

"Um, over a year." He cleared his throat and muttered, "Almost two."

"Two years! What's a reasonable time for you before you start discussing marriage?"

He turned his head and stared at her with a wry expression. "At least one week."

She grinned. "Fine. I'll wait a few more days before I bring it up."

Mark laughed. "Okay. Sure."

"So how long ago was this?"

"That we broke up?"

"Yeah."

"A few weeks ago."

"That recent? That's not long ago at all."

He sighed. "No, but it feels longer. I haven't really thought about her much since I came up here."

"So you feel like you're over her?"

"Yes, definitely." He cleared his throat. "Her kid, Shane, well that's a bit tougher."

"She had a son?"

"Yes, and his father lives out of the country, so guess what?"

"You became a surrogate."

Grimacing, he nodded.

She laid her hand on his shoulder. "Must have been hard for you, too."

He laughed to himself. "So my two friends—Brad is one of them—have banned me from dating women with children."

"That's why he asked me if I had kids?"

Mark grinned coyly. "Yes."

"Maybe they're right."

He chuckled, "Coming from you . . ."

"What do you mean by that?"

"You're seeing married men."

"Hey! Not men. One man. And not anymore. And besides that, we barely saw each other."

He raised both hands off the steering wheel. "Sorry. So are we done with this phase of our relationship?"

"What phase?"

"Rehashing old exes."

"I don't know. How many other girlfriends have you had?"

"How far back?"

"Since high school."

Mark thought for a second. "Serious ones? Four."

"So what happened with the L-o-r-a Lora?"

"We got together at the end of our junior year in college and broke up after graduation. She wanted—"

"Wanted to get married, right?"

"Not exactly. She got a job in Indianapolis near her family. She wanted me to move there with her. Yes, there was talk of marriage. But I decided to move back to Chicago. I was twenty-two and needed some space."

"So you broke up?"

"Not immediately. We tried the long-distance thing, but it didn't work."

"I see. Who came after Lora?"

"Lorelei."

"Another Laura/Lora?"

"No. I thought so too until it was explained it to me by her father. Lorelei and Laura are two separate names. Lorelei is a German siren. In the Rhine, I think. Her father majored in German literature."

"All right, so what's the story with Lorelei?"

"We met at a friend of a friend's party, and we sort of hit it off. It lasted a while. Almost a year."

"Why did you break up? Wait! Let me guess. She started talking about marriage."

Mark grimaced. "It was a little more complicated than that."

"I'm sure it was."

He hesitated then, "In my defense, she started talking about marriage on our second date. Kid names and all of that. I was in my mid-twenties, and I had things to do before getting married."

"What things?"

Mark sighed. "Well, grad school, for one. And traveling. Buy a house. Things like that."

"Where did you travel to?"

He bit his bottom lip. "Nowhere," he conceded. He sighed, a deep sigh. "But I really wanted to. See all of Europe, Asia."

"Just because you get married doesn't mean you can't travel."

"It does. You get married. Have kids. Suddenly twenty years go by and you've been nowhere but the Dells."

Emily laughed. "Come on."

"I did get a master's degree in wealth management, and I did finally buy a house two years ago."

"Good for you. At least you didn't dump poor Lorelei for nothing."

"I didn't dump her. It was mutual. Plus she did all right for herself, married some kind of multi-millionaire from Minnesota."

"I'm sure she still thinks of you as *the one who got away.*"

He shook his head. "I doubt she's thought of me since."

"What's the deal with buying a house on your own anyway?"

He shrugged. "I don't know. Just something on my list to be checked off."

"So you're ready now?"

His head wobbled indecisively. "I guess."

"So what about the last Laura? If you're ready for marriage now . . ."

"I don't know. Sometimes I think it was a mistake breaking up with her. I just didn't feel quite ready for family life."

"Maybe you've gotten so used to not being ready, you don't know what being ready feels like."

"Maybe."

"How about the other girl? You said there were four. Who's the other one?"

"Yeah, Nora. She came after Lorelei."

"Come on. Lora, Lorelei, *Nora*, Laura. Really?"

"God's honest truth."

She shook her head in disbelief. "What's Nora's story? When did she start asking about marriage?"

He shot her a side glance. "You think you have me all figured out, don't you?"

"Let's see. Mark dates girl. Girl mentions marriage. Mark breaks up with girl. How's that?"

"It's much more complicated."

"I'm sure. So what happened with Nora?"

"She died."

"What?! I'm sorry. I didn't mean to—"

"I'm kidding. She didn't die."

She punched him in the arm. Hard. "Ouch. Geez. What happened to 'First do no harm,' doc?"

"That's only when you want to help someone. I felt really bad, I thought she had died."

"You sure turn quickly."

"I'm emotionally nimble."

"Right." He laughed. "So Nora. I met Nora when I worked at a financial planning firm, and then later she became my second client when I struck out on my own."

"So she's wealthy?"

"Not exactly wealthy, no. She had inherited a fair sum from her grandparents and she needed assistance with financial planning."

"Isn't there a code of conduct about dating your clients?"

"You serious?"

"No."

"Well there should be because she was my first client to leave—in fact, she's the only client who's ever left me."

"So what happened between you?"

"In a nutshell—case!"

"Case? Huh?" she asked, confused.

"Nutcase—she was a hypochondriac."

"Oh. So you dumped her instead of helping her get over it?"

He turned to her with pressed lips. "Please. There was no helping her. She'd exaggerate every little ailment. A dull headache was brain cancer, a sharp one was an aneurysm, a sneeze was pneumonia, a stomach ache was—I can't remember."

"Crohn's disease."

"Yes! The internet sucks when you're involved with a hypochondriac. They'll find any and every disease and convince themselves they have it."

"Ha! Try being a doctor. And it's not just hypochondriacs. Everyone's an expert because they read some obscure blogger who lives in his parents' basement."

"I can imagine it's bad. Anyway, Nora would often say, 'I'm going to die before I ever get married.' That was her passive-aggressive way."

"How long did it last with her?"

"Six months, though we got back together a few months later. I had forgotten how bad it was. But that only lasted a month. Not even. I couldn't take it."

"She must have had some redeeming qualities."

"She did, for sure. She was kind when she wasn't pretending to be sick."

"Pretty?"

"Yes. But that's not what attracted me to her, or at least, that's not what kept my interest."

"I knew it."

"Personality is much more important to me. How about you and Dr. Jimbo?"

She shook her head. "What? What about him?"

"Would you be considering staying in Manistique if he weren't there?"

"Honestly? No."

Mark was taken aback by the quick admission. "Really?"

"First off, it's nice to be wanted at a place where your help is truly needed. And second—never mind. It's none of your business."

"Em and Jimbo sitting in a tree . . ."

She sighed. "How old are you?"

"Twelve."

She shook her head. "Yes, I like him. And stop calling him Jimbo! You have a thing with nicknames, don't you?"

"That's what his friends call him," he answered defensively.

"Are you his friend?"

He shrugged. "Maybe. Seems like a nice guy."

They rolled quietly through several miles of thin and thick forests and the occasional farm under a sky with puffy bright white clouds. A sign came up: 23 miles to Gaylord. "I'm nervous, Mark. Talk to me about something."

"Okay." Mark's back ached from the car ride, so he repositioned himself and straightened. "Let's see. I told you about my ex-girlfriends. I suppose I shouldn't talk about my mom next."

"Seeing that she was a psychiatrist, no. How about your dad?"

"He died when I was three years old."

"I'm sorry."

"It's okay." He smacked the steering wheel with his hand. "Ooh, got it! How about a history lesson to distract you?"

"Okay, sure," she replied, indifferent to his grin.

"I'm sort of a history buff. Have I told you?" Mark laughed. "Buff. Was Buff a public policy buff?"

"Shut up."

"Okay, how about a history lesson on the UP?"

She shrugged. "Sure. All I know is they don't have many Saabs, and they have a lot of deer."

He chuckled and began, "So the UP ended up being part of Michigan because of a dispute with Ohio. The two states—or rather, the territory of Michigan and the state of Ohio—nearly went to war over a small strip of land in Toledo."

"Holy Toledo!"

"Yes. Anyway, Michigan gave up the Toledo strip and got the UP in a compromise and then obtained statehood."

Emily listened as Mark explained the history of Native Americans in the area . . . fur trading . . . the French and British . . . the French and Indian War . . . the War of 1812. But as he went on she heard less and less. She dreaded the green signs irregularly counting down the miles.

Gaylord 6 mi. She stared off to the right.

"Hey, did you know that Manistique was originally Monistique with an 'o'?" Mark said.

"Isn't that the WiFi password at the house?"

"Yeah. Vivian was being clever."

"Nice."

"When they incorporated the city, someone in Lansing made a typo."

"A careless mistake," she muttered.

He finished a story about Manistique, the paper mill, but Emily wasn't listening much.

"You okay?"

She turned toward him. "No. I've got the deepest pit in my stomach."

He patted her leg. "In a short while, you'll be past this, and we'll be on our way back."

"Okay. But no history lectures on the way back."

"Lectures?"

"No, it's been great. It's distracted me for sure, but I think I know as much as I want to know about it right now."

"Sorry. It's in my nature to find out about a place and its history."

"Sure," she said absentmindedly as they came up to another sign: Gaylord 2 mi.

Soon, warehouses and pole barns, trailers, and a small industrial area emerged behind a thin stand of trees. They entered Gaylord township limits. Population 3,545.

"I'll get off at the next exit."

She nodded. "I need to call him, see where he wants to meet."

Mark made the turn off the highway onto Main Street. "I'll pull over at that gas station until we figure out where we need to go."

"You're not going to be mad at me, are you?"

"For what?"

"If he's not able to meet."

"Not really."

She grimaced.

"No, I won't be mad. I promise."

He made a left turn into the gas station and parked at the far end.

"I'll make that call." She pulled out her phone and got out of the car.

Mark watched in the rearview mirror as she scrolled through her phone. She drifted away and then paced back and forth, perpendicular to the car, while holding the phone.

Mark saw her in the mirror, coming over to his side. He rolled down the window.

Emily rested a hand on the door. "I got ahold of him. He's going to meet us in ten minutes."

"Where?"

"Crenshaw's Coffee Shop."

"Where is that?"

"He said it's on Main Street. Just down the street here." She stretched, rocking up on her toes. "I need to walk around. I'm anxious." She left, heading toward the gas pumps.

After a few minutes, Mark got out of the car and looked about, but he didn't see Emily. Figuring she was in the convenience store, he locked the car and walked over. After checking the five aisles, he thought maybe she was in the restroom.

"Where are the restrooms?" Mark asked the clerk, a lanky young man with black thick-rimmed glasses.

"Outside, on the side of the building." He held out a stick with a key dangling from it.

"No, I don't need it. I'm looking for my friend, a woman."

"Yeah, a woman is using the women's restroom right now."

Mark nodded. "Thanks," he said and started for the door. "Oh, where's Crenshaw's Coffee?"

"Our coffee here is just as good as theirs," he claimed, puffing out his chest.

"No, I don't want any coffee. Just meeting someone there."

"Oh." He gave Mark an embarrassed smile and pointed down the street. "About a mile down Main Street, to the left."

"Thanks," he said.

Mark waited outside next to the door. A minute later, a woman hobbled around the corner carrying a stick with a key.

He went back around the corner of the store, expecting to see Emily next to the car. But she wasn't there, either. She only had a few minutes before she was due to meet up with Dr. Olsen. He avoided thinking that Emily was backing out. He called her cell phone. No answer.

Chapter Thirty-Four

There were only two tables taken at Crenshaw's Coffee. Three women, all in their mid-fifties, sat at one table, and two older men at the other. Perhaps Olsen had come, seen no one, and left, though it seemed strange that he wouldn't have waited for a few extra minutes.

Mark approached the counter and asked the young woman if a man had come in a few minutes earlier.

She nodded. "Yes. He came in, looked around, and left."

Mark thanked her and then ordered a cup of coffee. "Decaf!" he added. As he paid, he said, "The gas station down the street claims their coffee is as good as yours."

She laughed. "Arnold said that?"

He shrugged. "I don't know his name. Dark-rimmed glasses . . ."

"Yeah, that's Arnold. He doesn't know anything. Their gasoline is better—how's that?"

Mark chuckled. When the girl returned with his coffee, she jerked her head. "He's back," she said.

Mark twisted around, and saw through the window a man who was walking toward the entrance. He was tall, with thinning blond hair and a sturdy build. He was wearing a pale blue sweater and had a slightly bulging belly.

"Is that who you're looking for?"

"Not sure. Maybe. Thanks." He grabbed his coffee and approached the door.

The man wore a sullen frown as he entered.

"Hey," Mark said, stopping him near the door. "Are you Dr. Olsen?"

He leaned back, glaring at Mark in suspicion. "Who are you?"

The man smelled strongly of mint. "I'm Mark, a friend of Emily's." Behind the mint he smelled alcohol. He stuck out his hand.

He took it, barely. He looked around the coffee shop. "Don't call me doctor. I'm not a doctor. Call me Greg. Are you Emily's boyfriend?"

Mark puffed out a laugh. "No. Just a friend. I drove her here."

"From where?"

"Manistique."

"In the UP?"

Mark nodded. "Yes."

"So where's Emily?"

"Nearby. Stretching her legs. You know, two and a half hours in the car." He didn't know how to explain Emily's disappearance. His mouth was dry, so he took a sip of his coffee. Lifting his cup, he said, "Can I buy you a coffee? A danish?"

Greg shook his head immediately, and said, "I'll get myself something." His words were slow with no inflection. He left for the front counter.

Mark tried calling Emily again.

She picked up. "Where did you go?"

"I'm at Crenshaw's." Mark stepped outside.

"Why did you leave without me?"

"You disappeared, and I couldn't find you. I'll come get you now."

"No, I'm close. I see the sign. So you just left without me?"

He spotted her a block away. "I tried calling. Anyway, he's here. And don't call him doctor. He's touchy about it. And I think he's been drinking."

"Well, I'll see you in a couple minutes."

Back inside, Mark waited near the front door. Olsen stood at the counter waiting for his order.

The door creaked open. Mark turned, expecting to see Emily, but it was a Gaylord police officer. The officer stepped inside, swapping a firm nod with Mark.

Outside, Emily was crossing the parking lot. He went out to meet her. Mark quickly apologized, but Emily dismissed it with a slight wave of her hand.

"Is he drunk?" she asked.

"He's not acting drunk, not that I could tell, at least."

"It is Memorial Day after all."

The two locked eyes for second, and Mark could see her nervousness. "Sure," he said.

"All right, let's go," she said.

Inside, Olsen stood near a table holding a cup.

"Hi, Greg."

"Hi," he said flatly. His face showed no expression.

"Do you want me to get you something, Em?"

"Sure. Just a cup of black coffee. Thanks."

Olsen and Emily sat down at the table. Mark couldn't hear every word as he got in line, but the staccato start to the conversation was noticeable.

Mark and the police officer exchanged another firm nod as he turned to leave. Mark became worried for Olsen, imagining the police officer pulling him over for driving under the influence.

"Was that him?" the girl behind the counter asked.

"Huh?" he replied, approaching the counter. It took him a second to realize what she was asking. "Oh, yes. Thanks."

"Sounds like there's a story there."

He nodded. "There is. A long one."

Mark ordered Emily's coffee. As it was being made, he heard Emily say something about Mark not being her boyfriend. Greg said something about Lincoln Presbyterian and Emily circled around with *wells* and *buts*.

With Emily's coffee in hand, Mark approached the table. When he set it in front of her, she looked up at him with a strained smile. "Thank you."

Mark slipped away, taking a seat near the window, unable to really listen in but with a clear view of Emily's face. He pulled out his phone and started searching.

Gaylord. Was there anything of significance to this town? He found his answer in its most famous resident: Claude Shannon. A mathematician, an electrical engineer, a cryptographer. The *father of the information age*, as he was called, was born in Petoskey and grew up in Gaylord.

Mark glanced up. Emily's face had blanched. Greg's head was hanging, and Emily was saying sorry multiple times. After a couple of minutes, things seemed to have settled in the aftermath of whatever revelation had been made. Mark buried himself with his phone again. This time he searched for Emily's brother Kyle. But he found nothing about an accident involving a bridge and a medical resident in South Carolina.

They spoke for about thirty minutes. There was a quick, awkward hug before Greg bolted out the door.

Emily was like a zombie as they headed to the car. Mark didn't ask about their meeting, waiting for her to volunteer the information.

It was in the car when she said, "He admitted drinking a little bit before coming over. He was nervous. He doesn't have a drinking problem."

Mark didn't exactly believe it, but he wasn't going to argue the point. "That's good."

"It turns out that Nicholas was buried nearby, apparently near their summer home. He gave me directions. It's about ten miles south of here. Do you mind if we go?"

"No." Mark started the car.

As they drove away, Emily said, "By the way, you were wrong."

"About what?"

"About doctors."

"What did I say about doctors?"

"Turn right up here," she said.

"What did I say about doctors?" Mark repeated.

"Greg attempted to commit suicide."

"He did?"

"Yes."

"When did I ever say anything about him attempting suicide?"

"You didn't. You said doctors don't fail at it."

Mark sighed. "Maybe he's not a good doctor."

She punched his shoulder.

"Ouch!"

"Mark, you can be awful."

"Too soon?"

"Yes! Way too soon."

"Sorry."

They traveled south, quickly leaving the heart of the town, toward wide-spaced lots with spotted commercial and retail stores, and then to the semi-industrial warehouses and to the brief forests of tall evergreens and clearings of spindly grass.

They made one more turn. Down the road about a quarter mile, headstones became visible behind trees and scraggly bushes.

"Stop here," Emily said.

Mark pulled over. "Let's go through the front entrance," he said, but Emily had already opened the door. She headed between two oak trees toward the nearest headstones.

"Wait up," Mark said. She didn't.

After a long walk toward the other side of the cemetery that led them across the graves of long-ago generations, they eventually found the more recently deceased.

"He's around here somewhere."

They split up.

Mark couldn't help but wonder what each life had been like as he scanned the gravestones. He stopped in front of Susan Anne Farch. 1964-1999. Then Margaret "Meg" Louise Meeks, two years old.

"Over here!" Emily cried. "He's over here." Her voice wobbled.

She was about fifty feet away. Mark headed toward her, trampling over the meager, wispy grass. She was on her knees in front of a torn patch of earth that had almost fully healed, with only a faint outline revealing that it had been opened. She buried her head in her hands and crumpled to the ground. She sobbed in torrents, shaking.

The inscription on the headstone read: *Our Beloved Son, Nicholas Jeffery Stipe. November 20, 2003-January 1, 2014.*

Emily bellowed something unintelligible.

Mark got down next to her. He placed his hand on her back.

She cried a little more, before lifting her head and sitting up. She dabbed her face with her sleeve. Catching her breath, she said, "You must think I'm a crazy mess."

"No, not at all," he answered softly.

She inhaled deeply and let out an unsteady breath.

They walked over to a nearby bench and sat down. Without saying much, they detoxed together on the bench, shoulder to shoulder. At one point, one grabbed the other's hand. There was a new bond between them.

In the distance, where birch woods bordered the cemetery, Mark spotted three wild turkeys. He was going to point them out and say something humorous about the windshield installer and turkey hunting, but he kept it to himself.

Mark's phone rang. He clumsily extracted it out of his pocket. "Vivian's attorney. I should get this."

He stood up but stayed nearby.

"Are you still in the area?" Frank Walters asked. "I'd like to give you something in person, if at all possible." His voice was flat and sober.

"Actually, I'm near Gaylord right now. I'm about to head back to Manistique."

"Gaylord?"

"Yeah, long story. Is this urgent?"

"Urgent? No, I wouldn't put it in that category. I can always mail it to you. But if you're able to stop by . . ."

"Is Petoskey on the way?"

"Sort of. An hour—maybe less—northwest of you. It'd be only a slight detour on your way back."

"Okay. Hold on a second. I'm with someone." Mark muted the phone.

"Do you mind if we swing through Petoskey on our way back?" he asked Emily.

She shrugged and shook her head. "No. But you still have your date tonight."

"Oh, right! I've got to call and cancel."

He unmuted the phone. "Okay, we're leaving here in a few minutes. I'll see you in about an hour—at the office, right?"

"Yes. I'll be here."

Mark ended the call, thinking Walters had some information about the adoption.

"What was that about?" Emily asked.

He shrugged. "He didn't say—said he had something for me and wanted to give it to me in person."

"Do you think it's about Vivian's child?"

"That's what I was thinking."

Emily stood up. "Let's find out." She pointed. "Look! Turkeys."

He turned to them nonchalantly, as if he hadn't seen them and said, "Oh, yeah."

"Maybe my installer is lurking around here somewhere."

Mark laughed. He put his arm around her shoulder, pulled her toward him.

Her eyes twinkled. "What was that for?"

He shook his head. "Just because."

"Okay," she said, amused.

Mark scrolled his phone for Laura's number. "Here it is," he said to himself.

"Are you calling Laura?"

"Yes."

"What are you going to tell her?"

"That I can't make it tonight."

"What time is your date?"

"We were supposed to meet at the house at six."

"We have enough time, don't we?"

Mark sighed. "I don't know. It's two o'clock now. Not sure how long this thing in Petoskey's going to take. And it's about two hours from there back to Manistique. *And* it's been a long day."

She rested her hand on his arm. "Why not wait and call her from Petoskey?"

"I don't know . . ."

"The casino?"

"Yes!" Though he didn't feel as strongly about it now as he had earlier. With some distance, his judgement of her felt more petty than accurate. "I guess."

"You should wait."

"You think so?"

She nodded. "Definitely. No harm in waiting."

They got back into the car, leaving the cemetery and Gaylord behind, heading northwest toward some revelation in Petoskey.

Seeing Nicholas's grave had left a hole in Emily's chest. She felt it every time she took a breath. "Where are you having dinner with Laura?" she asked, trying to distract herself.

"I never decided. And since it's probably not going to happen, I haven't given it much more thought."

"Suppose you were going, where would you take her? Not Diner 37 again?"

"No, no. I wouldn't want to come across as boring."

"No, you have such an exciting personality."

"Hey! Anyway, the only other place that comes to mind is Jake's or Ace's."

"A bar? No. And definitely not pizza."

Mark snapped his fingers and pointed at her. "But I could add a sentimental twist to the pizza."

"How?"

"That was George's last meal. Pepperoni pizza from Ace's."

"No!" She looked at him askance. "Bad idea."

"Really? Okay. Well, there's that restaurant next to the Cozy Inn."

"Big Joe's. Yeah, you could go there. I went in there for coffee."

"Is it a nice place?"

Emily shrugged. "It's not fancy, but it's nice enough. The coffee's good. It's all I had there."

"Who told me that? About their coffee? Anyway, sounds like a good place for breakfast."

"There's always the restaurant at the casino."

He shook his head. "You're not funny."

She laughed. It felt good to laugh. That hole in her chest closed a little. "I can call Dr. Currant and ask him about a good place."

"Great idea. Double date."

"Ha, ha."

"I'm serious. Give him a call and ask him."

She waved him off.

"Oh sure, when the shoe's on the other foot . . ."

"Laura doesn't want extra people on your date."

"She'd be fine with it. Call him and ask where we should all go."

"No," she said. "He might be working. Speaking of which, what about your job? You said you work for yourself?"

"You're changing the subject."

She shrugged. "I'm just curious."

"Yes, I work for myself. Technically, I'm an independent contractor with a financial firm. I have my own clients. I set my own schedule."

"So you can do your job from anywhere?"

"Yes and no. I mean, I do have to meet with clients every once in a while, but mostly everything I do is over the phone. I try to meet each client face-to-face at least twice a year."

"So you could come out to Manistique whenever you wanted. You have a place."

"I suppose so. Better yet, why don't you stay at the house?"

"Really?"

"Why not? Live there until you move in with Dr. Currant."

"Shut up." She couldn't help but smile. "I barely know him."

"That's exactly why you should invite him to dinner."

Emily didn't answer.

They arrived on the outskirts of Petoskey thirty minutes after leaving Gaylord. Mark wasn't sure how to get to the lawyer's warehouse coming from this direction.

"Look up 'Frank Walters, attorney-at-law' on your phone, would you?"

She looked it up and gave directions. As they arrived she said, "This is where his law office is?"

"Yeah, next to Arnot's Body Shop. It's kind of convenient, actually. If you're in an accident, you can drop off your car at the body shop and walk next door and get some legal advice."

She laughed. "Just seems like an odd place."

"It suits this guy. Really down-to-earth."

Mark pulled up in front of the attorney's office, parking next to an old Chevy Suburban that was backed in. Emily asked, "Do you want me wait to here?"

He shook his head. "No, no, come inside."

Frank Walters carried a file storage box into the reception room as Mark and Emily entered. Walters, in worn jeans, sneakers, and a blue Hope College T-shirt, greeted them and apologized for the mess, setting the box along the wall next to three columns of boxes four feet high.

"You've been busy," Mark said.

Walters sighed. "I forgot how tiring moving can be."

Mark introduced Emily and Walters to each other. Walters waved them into his office.

"Where are you moving to?" Emily asked.

"Just down the street here, the space closest to the road."

"Better location," Mark added, winking at her.

Once all were situated at his desk, Walters said to Mark, "I'm sorry for not giving you this when you were here last week. With all this moving . . ." The attorney's eyes dropped to an envelope, where his curved fingers sat at attention as if ready to type. "It's a letter from Vivian." With both fingers, he slid the envelope across the desk to Mark. "I found it this afternoon. It's unopened."

Mark took the envelope. *Mark* was written on the front in Vivian's hand. He turned to Emily, whose careful smile and near-imperceptible nod encouraged him to open it now.

Walters stood up. "Well I need to move some boxes into the truck, but feel free to stay as long as you'd like. And if I can answer any questions, let me know."

"Thanks." There was a letter opener on the desk. Mark reached over and grabbed it. He slit open the envelope and pulled out the letter.

Dear Mark,

Greetings from Manistique, Michigan. Have you ever heard of Manistique? It's where I grew up. I don't suppose your mother talked too much about living here, but to me it's home. This letter was never my best-laid plan for telling you all of this. So let me explain a bit in hope that you'll understand and perhaps forgive me.

My biological father left before I was born, and my birth mother died in a car accident when I was a baby. The man who became my father, your grandfather, worked as a doctor in the community and decided to take care of me. He eventually adopted me (he himself was a small part Indian). Margaret became my big sister. Mother was not exactly thrilled with the new addition, and when I was eight, my parents separated (Dad always said it wasn't my fault, but I knew better). I stayed with Dad in Manistique, and Margaret left with Mother to live in Milwaukee. When I was a freshman in high school, Dad died. With nowhere else to go, I moved to Milwaukee.

I went to college and then medical school. While I was an intern, I carried on with a doctor at the teaching hospital and became pregnant. I told Margaret about it, and she encouraged me to consider adoption because I was thinking of the alternative. After all, I had been adopted, so it should have been an easy decision, right? But I always felt that I was the wedge that broke up my parents, and I didn't want that to happen to anyone else.

I don't know if it was Margaret's idea or mine, but I placed my beautiful baby boy completely in Margaret's care. Mark, you are that boy.

This resolved my turbulent feelings (at least at that moment). I thought I'd visit you often as your aunt Vivian and be at least a small part of your life. I wasn't expecting the guilt and hurt that came afterward. I ran away—far as you know—and worked in places where others' pain distracted me from my own. I'm sorry if I've caused you any pain. When you were in high school, your mother contacted me, saying that you had romanticized my life in the field. I couldn't think of you going out there somewhere danger-ous. So I stopped with the letters altogether. That wasn't the answer either, but it was all I could think of.

When Margaret died, I thought about contacting you. But I had promised her to never tell you the truth. She was to raise you completely as her own. That was our agreement. I was, and still am, wracked with guilt. Since you're reading this, I never sorted out these feelings, and I'm too late to tell you in person. I am very sorry you're learning about this this way. You de-served to know the truth long ago.

I love you, and I hope you can find it in your heart to forgive me.

Your mother and aunt,
Vivian

Mark blindly handed the pages to Emily. His head felt as if it had swelled, and his feet felt numb as if not fully touching the ground. "That's not possible," he mumbled as Emily took hold of the letter. As he pulled the string of what he thought he knew, his own history un-raveled. He scooted the chair back and leaned over, forearms resting on his thighs.

All the years flew past him. He had never been as adventurous as she was. "But I'm not like her," he sputtered.

"Huh?" Emily exclaimed. She tugged at Mark's arm. "Vivian's your mother?"

As Emily said this, Walters walked back into the room. "Everything okay?" he asked.

"No need to keep looking for Vivian's son," Mark replied casually. "You're looking at him."

"What?"

"But I don't know how. I've seen my birth certificate and my mother—rather, Margaret is listed as my birth mother."

"Your birth certificate was probably reissued," Walters said. "After the adoption was signed by the judge."

As Mark and Emily headed out of the lawyer's office, Walters invited them to the The Tell-Tale to watch the hockey game that night. "That's a fun crowd," Mark said. "But we have to get back."

Mark still seemed anxious to her, so Emily asked if he wanted her to drive.

He shook his head. "I'm . . . I'm fine." He walked to the driver's side of the car. "That's just a lot to take in."

When they were inside the car, Mark said in a tired voice, "I should call Laura before we leave."

"To tell her tonight is off?"

"Of course."

"Come on. We'll be back in time. I'll even call Jim."

Mark looked at her with a suspicious grin. "Really? After our day today?"

"Especially because of our day today. We need a distraction. But check with Laura first, before I call."

"This isn't some kind of trick, is it?"

"No. I'll call him. I promise." She held up her hand in an oath.

Laura sounded happy to hear from Mark. "I've had the craziest day!" she said. "Guess where I've been all day."

"I don't know." With an impish grin, he turned to Emily and said, "Where have you been all day?"

"The casino."

"The casino? No kidding." At least she wasn't hiding it, he thought. He couldn't decide whether that better or worse. "So how did you do?"

"Great. But it was all Uncle George."

"What do you mean by that?"

"He left some chips in his jacket pocket. I went to the casino to cash it in, but they wouldn't let me because the chips were from their casino in St. Ignace."

"So what did you do?"

"Well we finally compromised. I don't really gamble, but they gave me tickets for the slot machines. So I played slots and lost most of it. Until the end when I won the jackpot."

"Wow. How much?"

"Ten thousand dollars."

"What?! Ten grand? Are you serious?"

Emily looked at Mark with wide eyes.

"Yes. Are we still on for dinner?" she asked. "My treat."

"Actually, yes, but do you mind if another couple joins us, Emily and her doctor boyfriend?"

Emily shoved his shoulder.

"No, not at all," she answered quickly. "Tell them dinner's on me!"

"Great. Meet us at the house, around six."

"Okay. See you then!"

He ended the call.

"What? She didn't lose a bunch of money, did she?"

"No. She won ten thousand dollars. I feel like a complete idiot now."

"Why," she scoffed, "because she won?"

He explained.

Emily laughed. "Let me not say I told you so. But didn't I tell you so?"

"Yes, you did. Now call your boyfriend."

"Stop calling him that!" She dialed the number. There was no answer, so she left a message. "We'll see if he calls back."

"He'll call. He likes you."

"And how do you know?"

He didn't answer immediately. He started the car.

"On Saturday, when he heard you were coming to the house, he got all anxious, like some high schooler."

Emily shook her head at him. "Please."

"Oh, sorry."

"For what?"

"Didn't mean to insult you—you just finished high school, didn't you?"

"Funny. At least I'm not going to my twentieth reunion."

"It's not my twentieth reunion!"

"Next year?"

"No!" He glanced at her sheepishly. "A couple years."

Jim Currant called back before they made it out of town. He said he'd love to have dinner with the three of them. He suggested the country club restaurant at the Indian Lake Golf Course.

"Is it fancy?" Emily asked him.

"No. Come as you are."

"Hold on," she said, and muted the phone.

"There's a restaurant at the golf course at Indian Lake. Is that okay?" she asked Mark.

"Why yes, Lovey," he answered in a haughty tone.

"Huh?"

"My golf game is a little rusty."

"Shut up. Do you want to go there or not?"

"A country club?"

"It's not fancy."

"I can't imagine."

"Don't be pretentious."

"Pretentious, *moi?*"

She held out the phone in frustration. "Yes or no?"

"Yeah, sure."

As she unmuted the phone, Mark said, "Maybe afterwards we can all take the paddleboat out."

She waved him off. "Hi Jim. Yes, the country club sounds good. Can you meet us at the house—at the Manistique Victorian— at six?"

"Yes! I'll definitely be there! And, Emily, thanks for asking me."

"Of course. See you then. Bye."

"Wow, he sounded excited," Mark said.

"You could hear that?"

"Yes."

He could see Emily barely contain her grin. And it was nice to see.

A few minutes later, she rested her head against the window and stared down at the edge of the road. "Let's make a pact," she said.

"What? Not one of those stupid, 'If neither of us is married in a hundred years we'll marry each other' things?"

"No! I'm talking about what happened in Gaylord. Let's not bring it up tonight. I don't want to think about it for the rest of the day."

"Or about Vivian being my mother," he added.

"Deal."

As Crooked Lake came in and out of view, Emily said: "I just had a thought."

"What's that?"

"Remember you said that we were like cousins?"

"Yeah. You backing out, cuz?"

"No, I was just thinking, since Vivian is actually your birth mother..."

He nodded, turned to her and beamed. "That makes us siblings. Yes."

They stared at each other for a long second. And it all felt good and right.

"Were you serious about letting me live in the house?" Emily asked a short time later.

He nodded. "Of course. But you have to let me stay whenever I come out."

"Sure, but you should really stay the whole summer."

"And run it as a bed and breakfast too," he added sarcastically.

"You should!" Emily exclaimed. "We should. I'd help."

"No way."

"It'd be fun."

"First off, you'll be working at the hospital, and I'll be doing all the *fun* stuff. Second, you said I was an awful host."

"I never said you were awful—or did I? Did I?"

"Yes."

"But you've gotten so much better, don't you think? And your breakfasts are awesome."

"I do like making breakfast ..."

The idea sat deep for a while, and by the time they were a mile from the bridge, he couldn't believe he was seriously considering it, even fantasizing about it. He could do it. And having Emily there only added to the appeal of the idea. An overwhelming optimism suffused him.

"Jamet Street. Last exit before the bridge, half a mile," Emily announced.

Mark shook his head defiantly. "I'm going to cross."

"What? Really? No."

He turned to her. "You sound nervous."

"Nervous, *moi?*"

He shook his head. "You don't get it. We have some shows to get you caught up on."

She shrugged, grinning, and set her attention on the radio.

Doris and Evelyn came on, having a fierce but friendly squabble over the best way to thicken canned soup. Emily and Mark looked at each other and shook their heads and laughed.

And so without hesitation Mark pushed passed the Jamet Street exit toward the bridge and its three-paned tower, and they forged ahead together toward Manistique.

Acknowledgements

And now for something completely different. . . As I look back on writing and rewriting *Stuck in Manistique*, I think about the many good editors, friends, and family members who helped shape the book along the way. Those who listened to plot lines, those who braved early versions of the manuscript, those who offered encouragement during this story's long journey to completion. I'd like to name a few of those people here.

I'm very grateful for the editors who worked on this book during various stages. I would not have been able to complete it without their guidance. Andi Cumbo-Floyd, Ronit Wagman, Ashley Strosnider, and Cindy Marsch. Their critiques and suggestions helped me improve the novel during each revision. And their thoughtful and kind words meant a great deal to me as I moved forward.

I'd also like to thank family and friends who read and gave their opinions and support. That includes Jennifer, Joan, and Loree, who dared to read the earliest—and longest—versions. Special thanks to *The Real Book Club of Almaden* (Jessica, Kerry, Laurie, Stephanie, Tina, and Jamie), who graciously read the novel as one of their monthly reads and allowed me to invade their reading group for one evening. Their feedback led to some important changes.

Finally, I'd like to thank my wife, Jamie. After we hit that deer in Manistique nearly twenty-five years ago—or did the deer hit us?—and we were stranded in town for those few days, I wistfully thought that I'd like to write a novel about it someday. Like most things I do, it took much longer than I had expected, so your patience, encouragement, and love will always be cherished. Thank you for indulging me a few years ago, agreeing to go back to Manistique as our summer vacation trip—we did have fun, though!

STUCK *in* MANISTIQUE

——— A READING GROUP GUIDE ———

Topics and Questions for Discussion

1. Later in the novel, Emily admits that she probably wouldn't have stayed at the B&B if Mark had been upfront about his aunt's death. Was Mark wrong for not being completely truthful? For her part, was Emily justified in snooping around the house because she was suspicious of Mark?

2. Emily found medication in George's room when she went searching for clues the morning he couldn't be found. Should she have told Mark that George had cognitive issues or do doctors have an obligation to maintain medical confidentiality with non-patients?

3. Consider Mark's reaction to Dr. Bulcher showing up at the house, and how Mark handled the full revelation when he spoke to Emily about it. What do you think motivated his response to her?

4. Discuss Emily's internal conflict with Nicholas's death. Does she deflect or accept too much blame?

5. Consider Emily's flirtation with suicidal thoughts. She tells Mark, "Not that I would ever do that exactly." Analyze her thoughts and actions and discuss whether you think her statement is completely credible.

6. Mark was influenced by his mother Margaret's stories about doctor-suicide. Given all his information, should he have barged into Emily's room the way he did? What about Emily's decision to leave the Manistique Victorian? In particular, consider her reaction as it relates to Question #5.

7. Why did Emily decide to go downstate to meet with Dr. Greg Olsen? Discuss her decision not to tell Greg the entire truth about that night. Compare this to Mark's tendency to withhold information.

8. Emily confesses to Mark that she had turned around and was heading east toward Mackinac when she got into her accident. Would Emily have turned around again, as Mark suggested, or do you think she would have made it to Mackinac if not for the accident?

9. Was fate really cruel to deer, as Mark said to Emily? Point out instances in the novel where fate appears to intervene.

10. Discuss any parallels between Emily and Vivian. What does the text not reveal but might be inferred from their similar (and intertwined) stories?

11. At the end of the book, it is revealed that Mark's Aunt Vivian was his biological mother. Discuss points in the book where Mark is pulled between nature and nurture, between the predispositions inherited from his biological mother and the acquired behaviors from the mother who raised him?

12. In the end Mark and Emily don't end up together romantically, but they end up as friends—a kinship, as it were. What do you think of this conclusion and how do you feel about it?

13. For those familiar with *Fawlty Towers*, name the corresponding characters that show up in the novel. Which scenes/episodes appear similarly in the book?

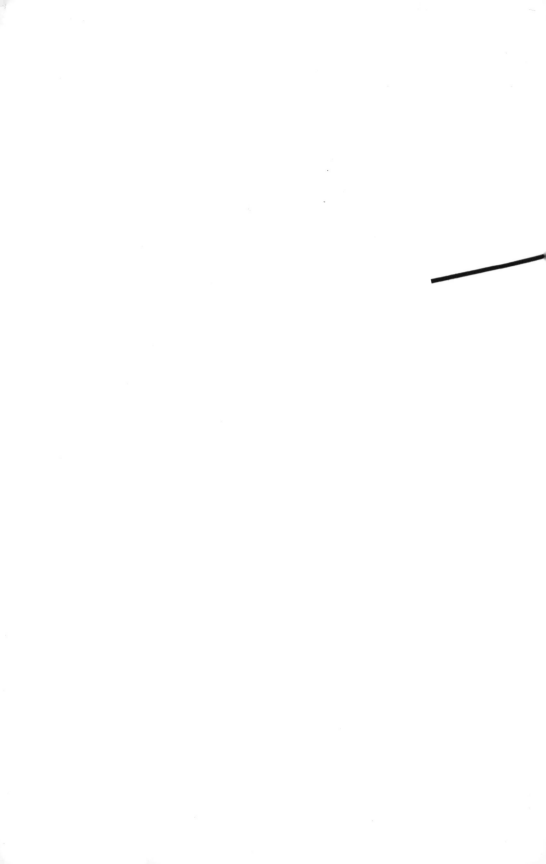